URANIAN GLEAMS

First Published in Great Britain 2015 by Netherworld Books

First edition: 2015

A copy of this work is available through the British Library.

ISBN: 978-1-910105-59-7

Netherworld Books
Mirador
Wearne Lane
Langport
Somerset
TA10 9HB

Uranian Gleams

Robert Gibson

Author's reassurance

Some alert readers will note that a couple of themes in my novel *Valeddom* recur here, in the first story, "Basilisk". This – you may rest assured – is not some lazy scheme to boost my word-count. The plot is different; the context is different; only the warning is the same, and *that* is no worse for being uttered twice.

Contents page

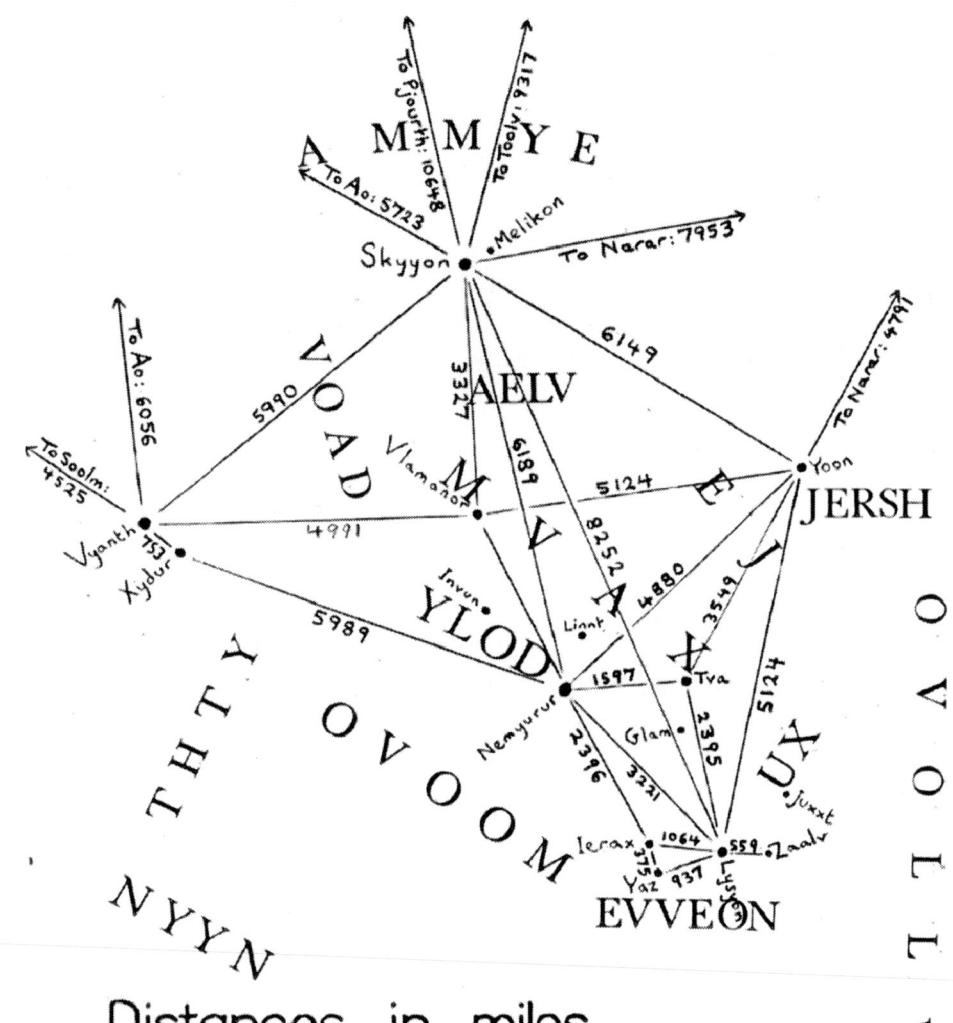

Distances in miles

between some Uranian cities

The whole of
Syoom
[distances in
miles]

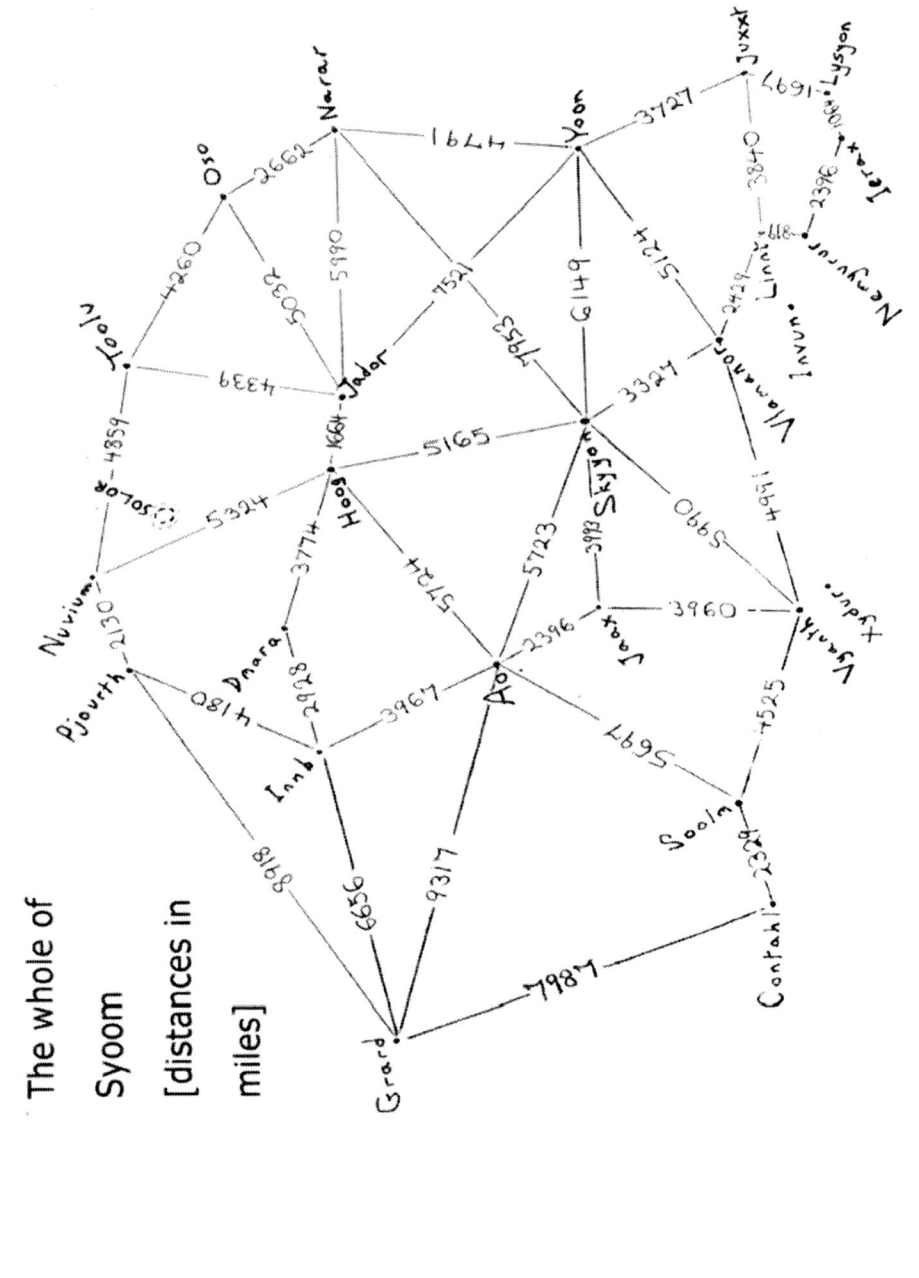

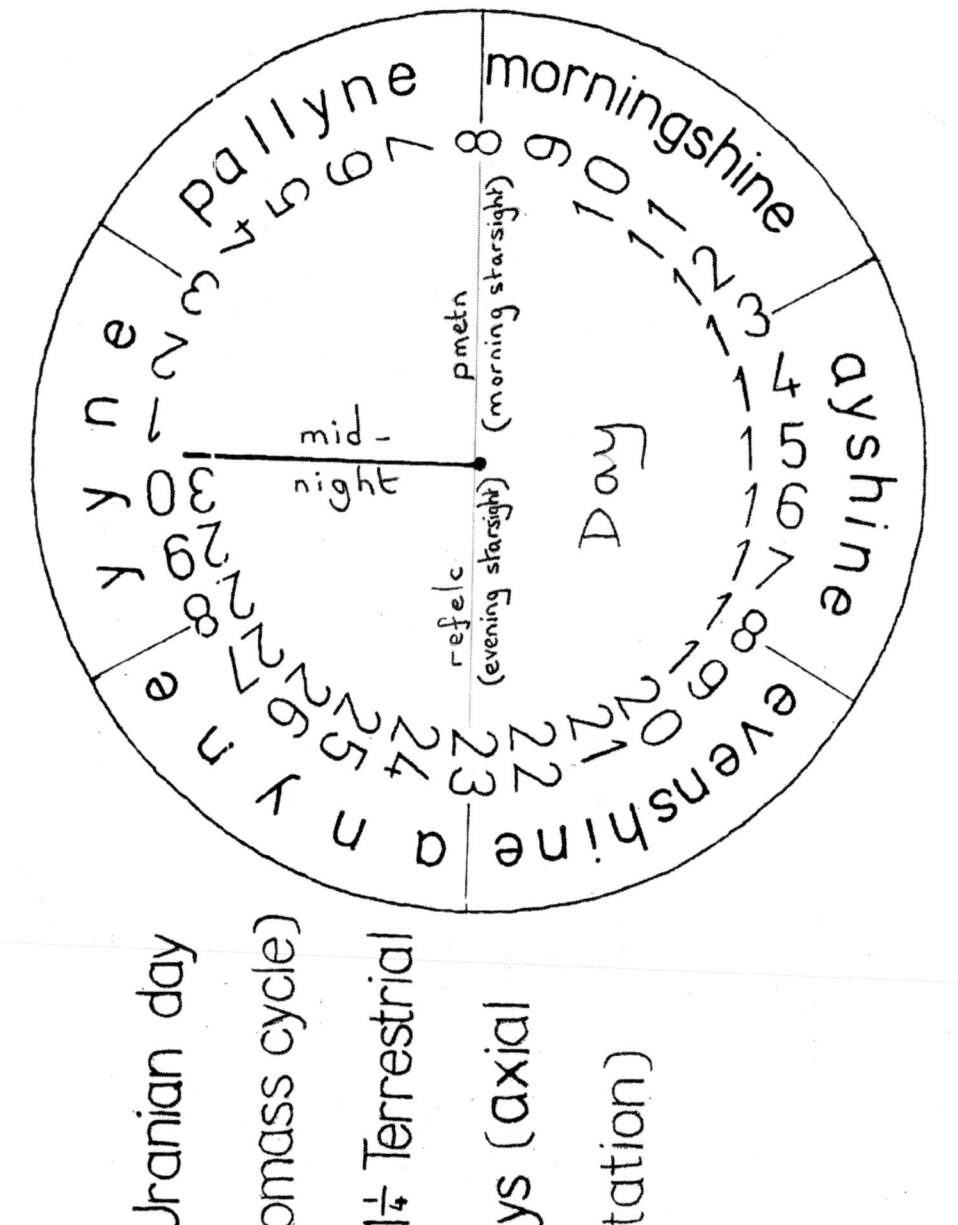

1 Uranian day
(biomass cycle)
= 1¼ Terrestrial
days (axial)
rotation

Preface to the 119th Edition

"It ain't where you've come from, it's where you're going that counts."

Fulfilment is upon us – the realization of every dream of adventure. At such a fortunate moment in our history, the old sagas of Ooranye are more relevant than ever.

My colleagues and I at the Institute hope that this 119th edition of the Gleams will prove to be a fitting accompaniment to the new era. We have made some changes in this edition, but, we hope, not too many. Readers have grown used to expect the inclusion of Dr Lamb's *A Brief History of Ooranye* in successive editions, and we would not dream of omitting it as an introduction to the Gleams, any more than a publisher would issue *Alice* without the illustrations of Sir John Tenniel. However, just as previous publishers have not hesitated to amend Lamb's "potted history", so I have continued the process of revision. For, naturally, our relations with the seventh planet have now been transformed by the onset of the Final Era. Hence my addition of an extra couple of paragraphs to chapter 36, plus an entire new chapter, "The Assault on Arclour". Dr Lamb's own chapter-titles, which have all stood the test of time, I have left unchanged.

Of course, it remains true that you can skip the History altogether if you feel like going straight to the Gleams themselves. Or you can zig-zag through the book, alternating between the History and the stories; for example you might take in just so much of the History as to bring you up to the Nitrogen Era and then read "Basilisk", then return to the History and read up to the Phosphorus Era as a preparation for "The Shears of Night", and so on.

Whichever you choose, you, the reader, are a participant, tugged by the pull, grist for the mill of destiny. I began this Preface with the voguish, "It ain't where you've come from, it's where you're going that counts", but let's tell it clearly now:

Destinies outweigh origins.

Or (as the more sophisticated put it these days), "We are all teleologists now". In the 42nd century, nobody doubts it.

The course of time has brought us out of the narrows and into the open ocean of awareness, our outlook vastly widened by that of our brethren the Uranians. They assure us that their Final Era, recently commenced, shall last six times as long as the others put together – and we agree, because their reckoning has become ours. They have convinced us that the leadership of the next 7,200,000 years belongs to them. (And after that, they in turn will cede to their cousins the kalyars.)

Let me repeat: destinies outweigh origins. Things born far apart can grow together because this is meant to happen. I am reminded of this in countless ways whenever I reflect on the story of our Uranian kin – our shape-kin, that is; linked to us not by blood but by convergent evolution. To take one example at random: the word **nen** means the same on Ooranye as it does on Earth, but it arose independently on both worlds and *with the same meaning.* That is to say, the unisex pronoun "**nen**", meaning "he or she", was pronounced – right from the word go – in the same way on Ooranye as it is now spoken over a million years later on Earth; and yet, causation doesn't come into it, any more than it applies to the Uranian use of "our" miles and yards and minutes and hours. All of which would have seemed an impossible coincidence to our ancestors.

Yes, we would have scratched our heads futilely in the old days. We used to dismiss as "unscientific" the idea that convergent evolution could produce extra-terrestrial humanity – and, if evolution only happened by natural selection, we would have been right...

But we clicked eventually, which is just as well, since the Uranians now have the run of the Solar System.

One last detail: In addition to inserting a few amendments into the History, I also felt it appropriate to reprint part of the Prologue to the very first edition. In my view, that old Prologue shoots off sparkles of significance. I judged it best placed between the "History" and the "Gleams".

- Professor Velma Pollard-Planinc, Outer Planet Institute, Cambridge, England, Earth, 28th March 4162.

Introduction: A Brief History of Ooranye
by Dr Edgar Lamb, F.R.S.

1: The Hydrogen Era

Only the slight brush of a cool breeze disturbed the lake. Sparse leaves rustled on the scrubby plain beyond, while the waves sloshed gently against the shoreline, as they waited for History.

The scene was deserted by all heavy creatures. Nothing came to drink the oddly muttering waters; the ice-chocked landscape remained un-crunched by any footprint so far.

Then came change.

The waters on that morning did more than mutter. They started to seethe; and the beginning began.

In this beginning, Dmara was not even a name; Dmara was a bubbling prebiotic lake or *sivvan*, in an icy crater on a shaggy brittlegrass plain. However – and here is the hard-science, causative way to tell it –

"Evolution surged in the lake, driven by churned emanations, sparked from close brushes with mascon matter during its near-surface convection in the planet's mantle…"

A different authority, after quoting this passage, says:

"Or you can put it the other, less materialist, the result-pulled way:

"The force of destiny, breathing out from Ooranye and hanging over it like an atmosphere, had, like an atmosphere, its storms and twisters; one of these concentrations condensed into an 'effect', and around 'effect' then clustered 'cause'; Excuse was born, an excuse called evolution."

Whichever way you narrate the event, patter patter go the words, to tell your acquiescent mind that *something* happened to produce the first beings to emerge from the lake of Dmara.

In outline the Liquid Men (*"Dmarnenn"*) were human. Likewise their minds were a kind of silhouette of ours. They were more mature than the subsequent first true men, but their natures remained simpler, one might say "purer", at any rate more focused upon a clear and narrow destiny.

Their "skin" was not skin as we know it. It was a form-field, which needed frequent immersion to maintain its integrity. They did not eat, as humans eat; their food was the *sivvan*'s radiation, which dimmed with increasing distance from its source. So these beings could not exist for long outside that lake. Eventually, as the *sivvan* began to dry up, the Liquid Men were doomed.

What they yearned to see before they became extinct was the evolution of an heir who could leave Dmara's shores permanently, and roam the world. Somehow this was done. They never showed how. All we have for certain is their confession, that the task was accomplished by cheating Time.

We can deduce that to borrow an energy-pattern from the future must have entailed using some transcendent power latent in the *sivvan*; be that as it may, the goal, to transform a swimming glow of form-fields into a fully material human being, took shape as Lrar the *Verzaknenn* or first true man. The date of the solidification of his skin-tissue was Day One of the Hydrogen Era.

Note carefully, that when we say that Lrar Verzak, the Uranian Adam, the ancestor of all Nenns, appeared on Day One of the Hydrogen Era, we are not merely labelling the date for our own convenience. We mean that Lrar himself knew, right then, that that was the day.

He knew it because *knowledge of the periodic table of the elements is innate in Uranian man,* and because, due to the teleological slant of the Uranian soul, it was known from the start that there would be 92 eras. With that number, and that knowledge, how else should the eras be named? Thus chemistry clasps history on Ooranye. Compared with us Earth humans, the Uranian humans – the Nenns – feel a closer kinship with so-called inorganic matter. It is a hylozoic sense that everything is in some sense alive. One can see how such a sense might stem from greater closeness to, or more direct descent from, the primal chemical mixture. And so the blaze of primitive legend, which haunts the origins of things on Earth, has the added fascination, on Ooranye, of being recorded. In other words, on that world the magic of prehistory has been captured for history.

At this point we should also mention, that Man was not the only species to emerge from the *sivvan* on that Day One.

From the same moment onwards, a host of aerial bacteria, their faint glow pulsating in a thirty-hour rhythm, swarmed out over the planet to give it its cycle of night and day. Ever since then, throughout the ages that followed, there has been a relationship between this aerial biomass and human emotions, because the biomass rhythms are sensitive to mass emotion. That is why great events trigger irregularities (called *eomasps*) in the diurnal cycle, and why these rare 'blips' in the rhythm of day and night signal the start of new eras.

Now for an overview of the First Era.

As well as being the first, the Hydrogen was one of the great eras. It lasted 19,636,085 Uranian days (each of their days, remember, is thirty hours, i.e. one and a quarter Earth days long), which means it lasted about 800 Uranian years, or the equivalent of 67,200 Earth years. Rather than attempt a continuous narrative of this ocean of time, we will sketch three verbal pictures, centred around the early, the middle and the later days.

The early days:

The scene which met the eyes of the first Nenn – the first true Uranian Man – as he walked away from the lake was utterly different from that which the tourist or pilgrim sees today. Instead of the current view of the old city encircled by the bare, multi-coloured plain of granular *gralm*, Lrar Verzak saw grass and forest, although the grass was slowly dying, the forest brittle, pallid, close to the end of its species lifetime. Huge soon-to-be-extinct animals roamed the grassland and crashed through the splintering trees as Lrar gazed about him. Sentient plants writhed and spat. Giant insects swooped and hummed. Long lists of their names have come down to us – names which popped into the minds of Lrar and his later companions and successors, each word full-formed after one authoritative glance.

Two species in particular, the Wonarr and the Revestru, deserve mention because they were intelligent as well as destructive. They did not go out of their way to attack Man; they were intent upon attacking each other, vying for supremacy to the very last, while the sands of time ran out for both of them. The Wonarr were a species of laser-tipped weed, whose less intelligent relatives the *narps* still exist upon Ooranye; the Revestru were a variety of insectoid, somewhat resembling giant wasps, and related to the later Nemaeans. Humans caught in the crossfire of the conflict could only try to keep their heads down and dodge the laser bolts and the diving swarms.

For a few days after the emergence of Lrar Verzak, more humans, male and female, followed him out of the lake. They and their descendants ranged gradually further and further from Dmara (a name which in this age referred only to the lake; the city was not yet built). The invention of writing occurred after a few generations; early enough to preserve accurate and detailed accounts of the beginning.

Meanwhile the Liquid Men, kindly demigods whom the Nenns consulted at will, declined gradually in numbers.

Knowing that they faced eventual extinction as their lake shrank in size and decreased in power, the Liquid Men never ceased to plan. They were not yet in any great hurry; the evening of their days was long, and so their view likewise was long. They regarded the Nenns, the solid humans, as their legitimate successors, even in some sense their children. So in order to help

3

these "children" to survive, many Liquid Men began in leisurely fashion to employ their greater intelligence to show true men how to scavenge metals and tools from relics left behind by extinct races of previous Great Cycles. Immense rusty wheels and girders, pipes and tracks, outnumbered by far more incomprehensible objects, were hauled through the grass for lifetime after lifetime, by men and women instructed or variously inspired by the Dmarnenn. The gear was brought to the lakeside of Dmara and heaped into one great store of building material. Here the Liquid Men showed the Nenns how to construct the First City around the shores of the dying *sivvan*. From this they learned also to build elsewhere, later, for themselves.

The middle days:

Insofar as it relied upon a limited supply of the treasures of the past, the industry of the Hydrogen Era was perforce a low-energy affair. There is little coal on Ooranye; no petroleum; nowhere on the vast plains are there rivers for waterwheels or hydroelectric power. Technological development on Ooranye must leap past such things, and in this era the leap was not generally made, though eventually some ores were obtained from the Mountains of Flame, and smelted under the guidance of the Dmarans at the world's single furnace.

However, there is one big exception to this modest economy. In rare cases, humans succeeded in tapping resources which the Liquid Men could not or would not touch. A few human adepts in this period already knew, psychically, how to draw power from *Chelth*, the "invisible land". Chelth was in fact another dimension, a different universe. It was that universe later plundered wholesale in the Sodium Era – the episode which was to cause so much trouble and heart-searching later on, as Uranians risked the guilt of depleting a foreign cosmos for the sake of augmenting their own world. But for the time being, the adepts were highly regarded. These early power-suckers helped to lift certain small patches of their civilization securely above Earth's medieval level. Typical of the middle period of the Hydrogen Era was the balloon-tyred dray, hauling goods across the plains, fuelled by a power-cell bought at great expense from a dynasty of petty psychics.

The cities of this period were conical mounds, growing around the rare groves of young plant species, splashes of brighter green amidst the older, dying ecologies. In the vegetable kingdom, the ebb of the old Great Cycle was overlapping with the rise of the new.

The cities were mostly independent of one another, but some of the more powerful ones – including five that stood on the sites, and bore the names, of

4

later disc-on-stem cities of the Phosphorus Era – formed leagues or even empires. The five cities of today that can thus trace their names (though not their physical identities) back to the mid-Hydrogen Era are: Innb, Ao, Hoog, Nuvium and Pjourth. It is hard for us, when we read their fantastically early history, not to visualise their inhabitants as tiny forms seen through the wrong end of a telescope.

One ironic, even comic aspect of the long Hydrogen Era may be mentioned here, in passing. The Nenns knew there would be 92 eras, that is to say, 91 following the first one, but as time went on many believed that the first would be the only long one, and that all the rest would then pass quickly in a staccato burst of rapid changes prefiguring the end. This belief went hand in hand with a sense that the world and mankind were getting old, Time itself was getting old... for after all, look at how much had happened, how much was past, how thick the layer of history underfoot. – So, laughably, went the thoughts of many people during the earliest dawn of the human saga on Ooranye.

The latter days:

During the last part of Era One it became apparent that some fear was gripping the Liquid Men. We have a four-letter word for this thing, which they were loath to mention.

Debt.

The records are unclear as to how far they thought of it as a personal debt, and how far "debt" was here a metaphor for the way Nature must "balance her books" as we might say when talking of the law of conservation of energy. Be that as it may, the awkward fact was that, way back at the start of the era, they *had*, in some sense which we do not understand, "borrowed energy from the future" in order to trigger the emergence on Ooranye of true Man. Now the terrible term *payback* began to haunt them. A deadline began to loom in their dreams.

We know all this because, during the course of millions of days, a few of these great beings uncharacteristically let slip their anxieties. Ordinary Nenn humans, puzzled and appalled by the vague nightmarish sayings of their mentors, then reacted by loosening their own sentimental ties to Dmara, as children will edge away from parents who seem to have gone cold with anxiety. This was the age of the so-called "long march to Contahl", really a fissiparous, spontaneous spread of the human species over a wide area of what was to become Syoom. Contahl was at first merely one of many new cities

5

founded as the area under human occupation (or at least the area seen by human eyes) increased from around ten million to close on four hundred million square miles.

Obviously, this mass movement – best termed the Great Dispersion – was of supreme importance for the future of humanity on Ooranye. It eventually meant that as much as a fifth of the globe was colonized, albeit thinly. But two results were of greater immediate significance.

Firstly, the scattering of mankind called forth a political reaction among the more long-established states. For a mixture of motives, they deplored the ramshackle sprawl of pioneering cultures, and sought to limit their expansion and their freedom by bringing them under centralized control.

There was an excuse for this restrictive policy. In many cases whole communities of pioneers, trying to cope with the strangeness of much of Ooranye, had "gone native". This meant loss of their own species identity as their mentalities adapted away from the human; in some cases they became literally twisted out of shape, or even surrendered to evolutionary mergers with other species, so that subsequent visitors to the area might hear voices in their own language issuing from mounds or bulbous groves where no human forms could be seen. So the horrified city governments may be excused some of their violent reaction. Nevertheless, their tyrannous attempts at enforcing their will, and the sagas of resistance which we have no space to consider here, gave political unity a bad name from which it has never recovered in all the long eras of Uranian history.

The second immediate result of the Great Dispersion was that it called forth a last great altruistic effort on the part of the Dmarnenn.

The Liquid Men were now ageing rapidly as a species. When they realized that they were "on the last lap" of their history, with their remaining days numbered in six figures or less, they concentrated their minds upon a practical problem hitherto thought to be unsolvable. They had always assumed that they could never travel far from Dmara. Now they began to search for a way of doing just that. They felt that they must at all costs free themselves from dependency on their lake, and acquire the ability to roam as widely as humans could, if they were to use their final span of life to bring peace to mankind and set the Nenns on the path to greatness.

The aim was achieved with the design of a flexi-suit adapted to the Dmaran form, and energized with a concentrate from the *sivvan*. This at last enabled the remaining Liquid Men to journey thousands of miles from Dmara.

It seems, according to the best evidence we have, that they then fulfilled their ambition of giving decisive help to mankind. For one of these benevolent

6

wandering Dmarans, having trekked as far as the region of Contahl, apparently gave a crucial hint to the great discoverer, Tisswa Ardea.

Tisswa's testament relates that in a dream (if it was a dream) she heard the Dmaran whisper in her ear, as he pointed to a rounded mountain in the distance, "Yonder seek your power". And next day she took a pickaxe and a box for samples, and set out alone towards the mountain.

When she reached the top she set to work with the pickaxe. Chips of ordinary rock flew this way and that until a glowing orange substance was revealed. Her chemical intuition – a faculty we Earth humans do not possess – told her what this stuff was: a lattice of atomic particles embedded in a non-atomic medium. She gathered samples and returned to Contahl, carrying the fate of her species in her hands. For what she had found was the greatest and most dangerous boon to fall to Uranian Man up to that time: a mascon of semi-kolv or **gvo**, several hundred yards in diameter, which convection had brought right up to the planet's surface. That is to say she had found a source of solid power which would supply the needs of a stepped-up civilization for over 200 Uranian years (over 19,000 Earth years). And then it would be gone, and so humanity, launched upon a path to fuel-hungry greatness, would have to find something else.... An irresistible, game-raising temptation.

2: Syoom and Fyaym

Tisswa Ardea decided to keep the discovery of the mascon a secret from most of humanity, for the time being. She, and those few in whom she confided, feared that if the news were released straightaway it might cause war between the several current urban tyrannies, as they vied for the new resource. Furthermore, as each power used the opportunity to try to enforce internal cohesion, civil wars would also break out, as the internal and external strife exacerbated each other...

The Dmaran Advisor, the Liquid Man who had helped her find the mascon, offered no further counsel. In fact, from now on he fades out of the story. He may have been the last of his kind. Their numbers were dwindling rapidly by this time, leaving the true humans – the Nenns – to tackle their problems on their own.

Tisswa Ardea and her friends could call upon some ready-prepared political support. Like many voyagers and prospectors they were members of an international secret society called, simply, the Unity Club. This organization had grandiose aims.

Ooranye has never been, and probably never will be, "conquered" by Man in the sense that Earth has been. As has been noted, the vast range of the giant planet was posing a threat to human identity, a threat which called forth harmful and severe reactions from some human governments. What was needed was a philosophy, an attitude or mental tool which would enable mankind to cope with the multiplicity and strangeness of Ooranye, to adapt to it without either conquering (which was impossible) or yielding (which was unacceptable).

So – adapt yet remain staunchly oneself! That was the challenge, the main problem of the age.

Terran readers may need to be reminded that this was not simply a matter of needing to find some "sustainable" or "ecologically sound" way of life. Ooranye isn't Earth: on Ooranye the *pull* of the environment is so much greater, there is no question of mankind over-exploiting or polluting it; the influence works the other way. In the Hydrogen Era, pioneering Man was like a shape dissolving at the edges, in danger of losing all definition and becoming something else.

The first brilliant move of the Unity Club was to pin-point what was

8

unfortunate about the human urge to *understand*. They were then able to realize that the key to the problem was to devise a way in which one might live in the world *without* trying to understand it. Ooranye would always be incomprehensible: to hope otherwise was to languish forever in a futile and hopeless trap. "Forget, therefore, your attempts to understand. Don't solve – *be*."

Then came the second insight: namely, that the trap could be avoided if one charted perils statistically. "Class them solely by their effects, and don't worry about causes any more." This revelation marked the proper birth of Uranian cartography as a unique craft. Maps were henceforth given peril-contours, derived from data of the frequency of wayfarers' survival.

The key contour, "sfy-50", became the agreed boundary separating the comparatively "safe" lands – where, *never mind the reason,* one had an over-50% chance of surviving a lone 1000-mile journey – from the lands where one's chances were under 50%.

The former, relatively civilized region would be called Syoom; the latter, the impractically dangerous one, Fyaym.

The Unity Club had worked all this out but had not yet publicized the idea. It had been seeking a way of sparking off a revolution in thought and practice, to inaugurate Syoom "with a bang". Now, at last – with Tisswa Ardea's discovery of the great power source of the mound of gvo – the Club possessed the key. A date was fixed. Secretly the word went out to armed supporters to gather at Contahl.

Contahl was a free city, friendly to the new idea, and with a vested interest in the success of the enterprise, since it was the city closest to the mascon – which was beginning to be called *Idun-Sjalsk*, or more familiarly *Jad-Zolm*, shortered to *Dzolm*, "the Sun-Egg".

Military preparations were made, city authorities in unlikely liaison with Unity Club revolutionaries. Contahl's defences were strengthened. When it was judged that the moment was right to break the news to mankind, both of the existence of the Sun-Egg and of the concepts Syoom and Fyaym, the code-word went out by semaphore: "Unfurl!"

That utterance sparked the end of the Hydrogen Era. For as sail-waggons bearing the news began trundling along several routes out from Contahl and from a few other prepared locations, they were outpaced by the release of tension which quivered through the atmosphere, borne by the micro-organisms which sensed it and transmitted it in the form of a shock to the rhythm of day and night. With this first recorded *eomasp* the Helium Era had begun.

9

Unlike the First Era, which had lasted 19,636,085 days, the Second lasted a mere 18 days, 18 hours and 36 minutes. It was taken up with the spread of the concepts "Syoom" and "Fyaym", and their re-orientation of the human mind. Exactly as the Unity Club had planned, the great hope held out by the discovery of the Sun-Egg became fused in the popular mind with the advent of new cartographical ideas. A great weight was lifted off the mind of Uranian Man.

3: The Lithium Era

The digestion of Dzolm

Picture a mountain covered with men wielding pickaxes, drills, hammers, and, as time goes on, mechanical contrivances to split and hew and carry off pieces of glowing orange stuff, which is borne away on trails of transport like lines of ants carrying material for their colonies. As a result the mountain gradually shrinks as the days flow by in their thousands and millions.

This is as good a way as any to imagine this era, which was the great age of Dzolm, the Sun-Egg (and of the glory of Contahl, the city closest to Dzolm).

To fill in more of the detail in your picture you must think of the Dzolm itself as a huge part-buried sphere, six hundred yards in diameter, composed of that glowing orange matter known as semi-kolv or *gvo*. Imagine that at the start it is covered with a layer of ice and rock, which was the old surface of the ground, pushed by the mascon's up-thrust to reveal the Dzolm's sphericity, like skin distended over a subcutaneous swelling. That's at the start of the era.

As the days go on, more and more of the sphere of precious *gvo* is excavated. The Sun-Egg is being eaten away by civilization, which digests it in the form of power to create fleets of airships, factories, machine-tools, weapons, construction projects, laboratories, hover-rafts, lighting systems and all the paraphernalia of a technological society, the like of which had not existed before on Ooranye.

Contahl, the noadex and *renl*

The Lithium was a medium-length era, 5,610,292 Uranian days. At the equivalent of 19,200 Earth years, this of course amounts to a period much longer than the whole of human history on Earth. Yet to the Uranians of today the Lithium Era is a shadowy period, almost as if it were mere proto-history like our idea of Archaic Greece. The main reason for this is that in Era 3 we are not yet arrived at the characteristic Uranian disc-on-stem cities which first appear in the brilliant and mighty Phosphorus Era to come. Yet the Lithium Era did have Contahl – which still exists today, proud of its immense past,

11

and of its later refusal of the disc-on-stem design. From the mid Lithium Era onwards, a traveller who sights Contahl sees first what looks like a lattice-model of a giant half-egg standing on end – a living reminder of the pre-Phosphorus type of city. (So far as we know, the structure was not built in imitation of the Sun-Egg, which was spherical rather than ovoid.)

Enormously more important than physical design is the fact that it was in Contahl that the level of complexity was achieved, which gave birth to the distinctive Uranian political organization, the **noadex**, and the social quality known as *renl* – adjective *lremd*.

The noadex – "noadship" – is the rank and rule of the Noad, or focus, of a city. The Noad is supposed to govern without bureaucracy; instead, nen relies upon sheer talent or instinct for knowing what to do. Some possess that talent or instinct, others do not. Therefore, in sane periods of history, political ambition is constrained by that simple reality. There is no point in trying to become a Noad if you are not Noad material, because you won't have the abilities to last, and if you *are* Noad material you will probably get there, sooner or later. Widespread admission of these truths greatly reduces the undignified scramble for power.

About this "knowing what to do": it is connected with what the Uranians call *renl*, the quality of being *lremd*, which applies to all Nenns, political or not. It is the socioeconomic equivalent of the talent we Earth-people used to need, in the days of dense population – the talent for hurrying along crowded pavements in the rush-hour without bumping into each other. We can steer in that way, instinctively, subconsciously. So do the Uranians – but they can do it in their economic and political life too. In a fashion which we can hardly imagine, the day to day running of a Uranian state is instinctive, like the functioning of an anthill, but with this difference, of course, that Uranians preserve their individual minds, which are often free to wander at leisure while they work.

The rise of the noadex and of *renl* was a gradual, organic process. It is more obvious to us now than it was at the time. It progressed steadily from Eras 3 to 15 – that is, from the Lithium through to the Phosphorus Era.

The threat of the Mawos

The people of Era 3 built a considerable civilization, but their success was maintained at high economic cost. In particular, they had to keep up an enormous fleet of airships to patrol the skies of Syoom.

As has previously been noted, at the same time as humans first appeared on Ooranye the *sivvan* also gave birth to the aerial micro-organisms whose pulsations provide the current day/night cycle on the dim giant planet. Unfortunately for humanity, a much larger relative of these tiny creatures subsequently evolved. These were the Mawos, aerial corpuscles about wardrobe-size and shape, though fuzzy at the corners and light enough to drift on the wind.

If an area was left un-patrolled for too long, a dark floating fleck might appear, and a slab of darkness grow around it. Soon, a geometrical portion of blackened sky would bulk in the form of a cuboid, an octahedron or a parallelepiped, depending on which subspecies of Mawo was responsible; and after a while a sharp report would be heard, and seeds would rain down to create a swiftly growing forest of bulbous *vrayns*, the vegetable stage of the Mawo life-cycle. After which it would require an army to root them out...

The threat the Mawos posed to humanity was the threat of light-deprivation. To blacken huge areas of sky (by absorbing all bioluminescence within range) was to deprive ordinary plant life of the means of survival. Since, ultimately, humans depend upon plants, this could not be allowed to happen. And it was noted that the best way of preventing it from happening was simply to patrol the sky, since, for reasons which have never been made clear, Mawos do not operate in the visible presence of man, or (so far as is known) of any intelligence. It is doubtful if they are at all intelligent themselves; in fact, since evidence suggests that their dissemination in the Lithium Era was a direct result of man's increased cultivation of the glowing *ell-light* fields, Mawos could be classed as merely agricultural pests. Yet like the locusts of Earth, they can be formidable foes.

What a cost to have to sustain – keeping up a presence in every bit of sky, patrolling so densely as to protect every field! It could not be done with one hundred per cent effectiveness, but even to achieve minimum viable clearance (seventy per cent) laid a great burden upon mankind's resources, hastening the day when the Sun-Egg would be exhausted.

(Nowadays, the burden of coping with the Mawos is far less, for two reasons – airships are cheaper to run, and Mawos fewer in number.)

The Survival Race

Towards the end of the Lithium Era, the mind of Uranian humanity was concentrated upon the problem of how to achieve economic independence from the Sun-Egg before its substance was used up.

In the final Uranian years – the last few lifetimes – of the era, all Nenns were consciously in a race for survival, a race between research and catastrophe.

Diverse schools of thought grew up around the problem. We might class them broadly into the Respectables and the Loonies. The Respectables thought that the power-resource problem could be solved by a combination of retrenchment and research into modest alternatives, mundane resources such as burning wood, using wind power, using thermal power from the Jershan volcacoes, and concentrations of the biomass glow from ell-light fields.

The Loonies said that this was all very well but when the *gvo* from the Sun-Egg was all gone, mankind would find itself in far too exposed a position, far too prominent after hundreds of U-years of luxuriant power, for any scaled-down strategy to be viable. If the Nenns were to retrench, they would find themselves in the position of an army in battle unable to stop an orderly retreat from turning into a rout. There was no going back to Era 1. The only way was forward, into another form of high-energy society.

On Day 5,610,287 of the Lithium Era a pan-Syoomean congress met at Contahl determined to hammer out a solution to the resource problem.

The delegates included the Noads of every city. They met in front of a huge mural photograph depicting the current state of the Dzolm, or Sun-Egg, showing how depleted its outline had become. It was almost no sphere at all, only a jaggedness and an almost empty bowl where the *gvo* had reared its orange bulk in olden times. In less than a couple of U-years at the present rate of use even the remnant would be gone.

The "Loonies" or extremists won every debate. They won without propounding any useful suggestions themselves; they only needed to show that all the calculations of the "Respectables" were insufficient to demonstrate any hope. Moderate ideas were discredited; only radicalism remained to be tried.

After five days a declaration of the results of the congress was issued to the public. The shock was so profound that the emotional resonance affected the micro-organisms in the atmosphere, altering their cycle of illumination so that the rhythm of day and night hiccoughed in another *eomasp*, marking an era transition. Everyone thus knew that the Lithium Era was over.

4: The Plunderers

The Conference had 'cleared the air'. At last the people of Syoom knew for sure that they must come up with something unprecedented, in order to survive.

The Noads of the cities stayed in close touch and formed a standing committee under rotating chairmanship, which grew into a scientific institution known as the *Rin-Stazel* ("hope-society").

The Rin-Stazel exuberantly encouraged a great many research projects and private adventurers, questing for the answer to the looming energy crisis. This short era, the Beryllium (Era 4), was a period of febrile but engaging optimism, a good time for eccentric inventors and explorers, subsidised to follow their private bent with the blessing of the Rin-Stazel.

One explorer, Dynnt Eshnun, was less popular than the rest. He had gone into the Mountains of Flame and done the seemingly impossible – had captured an *eopc*, one of the rare giant birds, the greatest winged creature on Ooranye, with a wingspan of almost 70 yards. Dynnt had stolen up on the bird while it was "asleep", or whatever the right word is to describe the state of an *eopc* when it is absorbing energy from a trans-dimensional source. For that's the point: eopcs do not eat or drink anything that can be found in the world. Dynnt Eshnun had a hunch that the only chance for mankind lay in the direction of trying to do what an eopc can do.

Eopcs are noble creatures; they never fight against weaker beings; they use their formidable natural armament only against the more powerful insectoid swarms which are enemies of both eopcs and man. The great birds are thus regarded as benefactors to humanity. All of Syoom was shocked when Dynnt Eshnun appeared with his captive.

He was ordered to release it. He did so, but only after taking a blood sample from the creature.

He gave part of the sample to the Rin-Stazel, which shamefacedly accepted it and assigned some researchers to the task of using it to determine how the eopc accessed the "other dimension", the source of their energy. Dynnt Eshnun then went back to his home in the city of Skyyon, gave occasional surly interviews, and awaited developments.

Dynnt Eshnun was an odd mixture of the unwelcome and the respected. Most people disliked him and yet many of them sensed that the time might come when they would need him, or at least, need what he had brought.

The department of the Rin-Stazel which had been assigned to the examination of the eopc-sample soon discovered that the bird's blood-cells, though unresponsive to analysis, could be grown in cultures and *used*. Vats of the stuff were accumulated. A way was found to channel the energy they drew upon – the extra-dimensional energy from the dimension which now began to be given a recognized name, *Chelth*, derived from a term used by the primitive psychic adepts of Era 1.

Chelth was presumably a universe, and the small trickle of energy which went to the eopcs of Ooranye was not likely to be sensed in Chelth as a noticeable loss. Scientists at the Rin-Stazel however calculated that if mankind were to drain it off systematically, to base an entire Syoomean culture upon it, the effect on Chelth might be serious – because the energy transfer was not efficient; the equivalent of several solar systems might have to be destroyed to keep one Uranian city supplied for one Uranian year. And suppose Chelth were inhabited? Suppose some Chelthans resented the depredations of Ooranye, and retaliated?

On the other hand something had to be done, and none of the other lines of research were producing any answers.

After about four thousand days (approximately 15 Earth years) of the Beryllium Era, public opinion in Syoom lurched towards the adoption of Dynnt Eshnun's advice, and on Day 4385 yet another new era began – Era 5, the Boron Era.

It was sparked by a confession by Dynnt Eshnun, that the eopc which he had captured was still under his control. It regarded the blood-sample he had taken from it as a part of itself, and could not return to its home in the Mountains of Flame without it. It was still circling Syoom, with great lazy flaps of its wings, waiting for the return of its blood. Dynnt went after it in an airship and communicated with it in the rudimentary mind-speech he had learned in the mountains. He then brought it to the Rin-Stazel, in Contahl, for the second time, and this time he was told *not* to release it. This time the head of the Rin-Stazel, Pyoan Tatham, ordered a giant aviary to be built for the eopc. It was hoped that further captivity would not inconvenience the thing, which after all had a life-span thousands of times longer than that of a human, and which could therefore well afford – so the argument went – to spend a few thousand days co-operating with Man.

Pyoan Tatham, it turned out, was even more secretive and unconventional than Dynnt Eshnun. He resolved upon a drastic step to save humanity. It might be an evil step, he admitted in his diary, but he would take all the moral

16

risk upon himself. He would plan in secret, except for a few trusted confederates. Not even Dynnt Eshnun was to be told.

Pyoan Tatham did not believe that the vats of blood cells offered a permanent solution to the energy problem. The continuous leakage from Chelth would, sooner or later, provoke retaliation, if that universe contained any powerful inhabitants; and the likelihood of an entire universe containing *no* powerful inhabitants was too slim. Yet Chelth must be used; no alternative existed. The only option, then, was for one single, brief, once-and-for-all plunder of Chelth; an action which would at a stroke steal enough power to meet Syoom's needs for all the rest of this Great Cycle of history.

The plundering action might ravage huge areas of that other universe, but Pyoan Tatham could hope that it would merely extinguish some lifeless suns, or swallow up some unnecessary nebulae. Anyhow, he rationalised, we need to do it, and we can do it, and why was this ability put into our hands, if not to be used to save ourselves from the crisis looming over us? And we will get away with it, for the inter-cosmic smash-and-grab raid will be carried out so quickly that there will be no time for the other side to get a fix on whence the action came.

Pyoan Tatham therefore began to form a secret organization-within-an-organization, and to use the authority he had been entrusted with to prepare hidden power-storage receptacles or reservoirs, which, when the moment came, would receive the energy-loot sucked from the Other Dimension. Much of the design for this project was carried out in a state of trance-communication with the wise though non-intelligent mind of the captive eopc. Hence the engineering was intuitive, and hard for others to understand, and this helped to maintain secrecy.

Pyoan Tatham dedicated his life to his secret project. The Boron Era, the era of his leadership in this research, lasted 8766 days and 66 minutes – about 30 Earth years. It lasted no longer because, early on the 8767th day, the eopc escaped.

It did so with the aid of others of its kind, who without warning swooped upon Contahl. Their approach was undetected because they dived from stratospheric heights – the security staff at the Rin-Stazel had ignored that direction, omitting to allow for the fact that, since the eopc did not eat, neither did they breathe.

Pyoan Tatham was killed in the breakout. The laboratories were largely wrecked. Syoom was thrown into confusion in the space of a single disastrous day, which became known as the Carbon Era.

Next day, another atmospheric oscillation – another *eomasp* – proclaimed yet another shift of eras. The story now gets so complicated that we can only offer some hints as to the murky Nitrogen Era. A number of factors conspired to demoralise humanity: the sudden lack of leadership; the loss of the eopc whom the public had begun to trust; the clear evidence that the eopc had resented captivity all the time; above all, the loss of hope in the project which the Rin-Stazel had been carrying out to solve the energy crisis now close at hand. Only a couple of U-years, a couple of human lifetimes at most remained to civilization, before the Dzolm was due to be exhausted.

To give an idea of the exceptional malaise of this era, we may point out that during this time the inner Long Clock, which in almost all periods of history provided every individual with an instinctive awareness of the fact that there must be 92 eras, went into abeyance. Some people retained the Clock in their souls, but most of the population lost it for a while, and believed that human history might be nearing its end with Era 7.

All this was bad enough, but the weakened body politic also became prey to a particular virus of evil, which, in the accounts that have come down to us, is referred to as *the Corruption Ray*. It is against the background of that scourge, and the extraordinary deliverance from it, that we will trace the career of the first Sunnoad, Hyala Movoun 1.

5: The First Sunnoad

The Nitrogen Era, Era 7, lasted 37,759 days – or 129 Earth years. So, in duration it was one of the minor eras. But it has left a huge shadow on the collective memory of Uranian civilization.

Unfortunately we don't know enough, as yet, to fill out our picture of the era. As with Earth's various Dark Ages, we can get fooled by the term we've invented for the period. The shadows caused by our ignorance, the incompleteness of the record, can get laughably mistranslated by our imaginations into real, literal "darkness", as though people had to grope around with flashlights during those times.

Also like Earth's Dark Ages, the Nitrogen Era leaves us with awkward questions regarding urban life during the period. Basically, how did civilization endure? For endure it did, somehow. What finally put an end to the archaic cities of Syoom was not the perils of this transition period but – as we shall see – the mighty rebuilding which took place shortly afterwards at the beginning of Era 15.

Era 7 was "dark" because it was a time of disorder, partial chaos, wars and, most notably, that rare thing in Uranian history, *demoralization*.

Battles were fought over the distribution of the dwindling remains of the Sun-Egg, while, with the disbandment of the Rin-Stazel, there was no more centralized supervision of research into alternative sources of energy. Hope dwindled, and many people believed that human civilization was on the way out, that the eternal pressure of Fyaym would overwhelm Syoom. During this exceptional time there seems to have been a fading, an obscuring, of the usual awareness of the destined future. As mentioned in our previous chapter, a majority of the people even lost the faith that there would be 92 eras – their Inner Clock was in abeyance – and instead there stole upon them a sense that the Seventh Era was likely the last, and that the end was nigh.

Despair was by no means universal. People still strove. Guilds and corporations and secret societies, as well as a few of the city governments, did their best to take over where the Rin-Stazel had left off. Research became more competitive, less scrupulous. Some avenues of research, which had been shunned as repugnant and dangerous in the previous two eras, were now surreptitiously embarked upon. These included lines of inquiry into certain sinister relics left by a previous Great Cycle civilization which far pre-dated humanity. We also suspect that some organizations investigated other dimensions apart from Chelth; dubious dimensions which to us are no more than names.

And finally there may have been the emanations from the remains of Dmara. The now-dry *sivvan* from which humans had originated had become a sacred, shunned, deserted site. One theory goes that there must have been a fateful attempt to sample and utilise the exhalations from the basin of that vanished lake. The result: a mix of qualities, a perversion of the natural order. Think of the paradox in Earth culture which is expressed in that odd juxtaposition: ghosts (unholy) haunting churchyards (holy).

From some such source, or perhaps from some home-grown evil genius, came the dread invention known to posterity as the *Corruption Ray*.

This is no mere legend; it definitely existed, and on at least one later occasion was actually rediscovered, though fortunately not for long. We are ignorant as to how it worked, but the effect is certain: it was a long-range weapon, could be trained in secret upon a city by another city or fortress, and what it did can be summed up in a phrase which may raise a laugh – the weakening of moral fibre.

At first, this was traceable statistically as a drop in the level of public spirit and cultural integrity. A possible analogy with Earth history includes the cultural revolution known as the Disfigurement, which took place in Britain during the century after World War II, when the country's constitutional, institutional, cultural, religious and moral heritage was abandoned. One symptom of this type of illness is that referents are despised. For example, by the alteration of historic boundaries and the abolition of historical weights and measures and coinage, inherited categories are subjected to "modernity" and thus shorn of character; finally, when the people have been deprived of all their roots, enemy conquest or absorption is rendered either easy or unnecessary.

The Uranians of Era 7, however, did not altogether give in to this sad process. Enough of them resisted, to make the corrupters feel unsafe. We are missing some of the details, but it seems that the "rayers" were driven out of city after city until the last and most desperate phase of the struggle, when, towards the end of the era, the Ray emanated from one hidden fortress. By this time, the users of the Ray had obtained help from non-human enemies of mankind, somewhere in Fyaym, and had become much harder to overthrow.

It may not be quite fair to characterise all users of the Ray as villains. In the early stages at least, their action may have sprung from a ruthless but partly justifiable desire to increase the tough-minded element in human society, to concentrate upon facing the energy problem and to dare to plunder the dimension of Chelth as had been planned before the disastrous end of Era 6. But by the finale of Era 7, the Corruption Ray and its users formed an unquestionable force for evil.

Terrific and heroic efforts must have been made to seek out and battle the Users and to destroy their horrendous weapon. We hope that in due course research will reveal how this was accomplished. Meanwhile, one of the things we do know about the period of that epic struggle – the last few thousand days of Era 7 – is that a certain Hyala Movoun was growing to womanhood among the crystal groves of Opahej.

The Oxygen Era

Crystal "groves" are actually small forests of crystalline plants, with so many natural defences that they are virtually immune from attack. Their proprietors are families who have, over many lifetimes, fostered a relationship of trust with their groves. Often nicknamed the Lucky Ones, these proprietors are in a position of comfort and security. A lucrative crop of excess crystals is ceded to them by the grove in return for services easily rendered such as weeding and pruning.

This independent class of people, able to withdraw deep into their groves in times of trouble, remains relatively unaffected by the political chaos and moral darkness of periods such as the Nitrogen Era. So by merely existing, the Lucky Ones have performed a service to Uranian mankind. On the debit side, they have tended to be rather selfish. Their positive contribution to history has been small. Except, that is, for Hyala Movoun.

She first became famous as a teacher. Educational systems in the Terran sense are not a feature of Uranian civilization, for Uranian children do not have to be coaxed to learn; but Uranian teachers do exist: freelancers who appear on the scene if and when they see a need for some special service which only they can perform. Hyala Movoun, as a young woman aged about 7000 days, decided that her vocation was to help restore the meanings of words which had become blunted and rendered almost useless by the blight of cynicism caused by the Corruption Ray.

Accordingly she perfected certain mental exercises, and then set herself up as a tutor – a sophist, our ancient Greeks would have called her – to advise those in positions of influence in her adopted city of Narar. Her success was so astonishing and so widespread that she was soon moved to a more influential cultural hub: Contahl, then still the most powerful city on Ooranye.

From there, her message of verbal purity swept through Syoom like flame through straw. Part of the explanation must lie in her own exceptional nature, and part in the fact that this was what the world was desperately waiting for: someone to wean it from sniggering, from flippancy, from the whole miasma left in the air by the events of recent times. The effect of her teaching built up quickly to the point at which the general public emotion affected the rhythm of daylight, and this *eomasp* marked a change from the Nitrogen to the Oxygen Era.

Era 8 lasted a mere forty heady days of pan-Syoomean revival. Hyala Movoun was invited to make her home and office in the central north-polar city of Skyyon. Here she practically took the government of Syoom into her hands. She agreed to the move to Skyyon – geographically it is central – but when asked literally to govern Syoom, her answer was neither a straight yes nor a straight no. No single individual has ever ruled Syoom, and she went on record as saying that it could not be done. On the other hand she did see the need for some international focus, some living symbol to whom the cities of nennkind could give their allegiance in matters of common interest and common principle. In short, she recognized the need for a Noad of Noads; and she became the first one in history – the first individual to bear a number after nen's name: Hyala Movoun 1.

Her investiture as Sunnoad and the festivities associated with it caused another heightened, etheric wave of emotion: the 22 hours known to history as the Fluorine Era. Then came the era which can be called the Reign of Hyala Movoun.

The Neon Era

Lasting 5,558 Uranian days or 19 Earth years, the Neon Era is short but naturally crammed with legends, some believable and some not, centred around the personality and exploits of the First Sunnoad. A few critics have tried to find fault with her, but it has not been easy. Obviously her charisma must have inspired such a combination of awe and affection that problems which would have baffled other statesmen simply dissolved before her glance. Yet this reliance on individual greatness has been cited as a defect of the regime, for what happens when the individual who sustains it is no more?

Another criticism is that Hyala as time went by began to rely too much on her own past record; in other words, it could be said that she became lazy, or at any rate naïve, believing that her influence, her beauty and kindness and **lremd** intuition, would suffice to solve every problem.

A few people voiced these doubts at the time. Historians will argue forever as to whether they were justified. What is certain, is that Hyala came to agree that a Sunnoad must submit occasionally to freelance Correction – provided that the **Corrector** was willing to put nen's life on the line.

The institute of Correction, therefore, is almost as old as the sunnoadex: the first Corrector, Lehal Thoal, corrected the first Sunnoad, Hyala Movoun.

The occasion was close to the end of the Neon Era. The issue was, yet again, the energy crisis. The crisis had become muted for a while: the very depths to which society had sunk during the Nitrogen Era had lessened people's demands for energy, and then during the Neon Era humanity had lived on gratitude and euphoria. Yet the situation was obviously not stable. Hyala Movoun could not allow herself to forget that the problem had merely been shelved. Soon, when the power ran out, any concerted threat from Fyaym would find Syoom unable to defend itself.

Be it noted that the gentle, charming, beautiful Hyala Movoun made the ruthless decision to renew the project of the Rin-Stazel to plunder the dimension of Chelth. She saw no other way to obtain for her people the power-source they needed. Tapping the last dregs of the Sun-Egg, the great Project was revived. Since the records have been hidden or destroyed, we do not know how it was done, and it is doubtless best (though of course frustrating for the historian) that we do not know.

What we *do* know is that towards the end, Hyala Movoun had doubts about this trans-dimensional solution to the energy crisis. She found out something – we are not sure what – which made her try to delay or even halt the Project. This is where Lehal Thoal took the action which might have resulted in his execution. He coerced the Sunnoad. In fact he kidnapped her and kept her hostage for three days. This breathtaking boldness was rewarded with success: he managed to persuade the Noad of Noads to rescind her order and let the Project go ahead. Then he released her. She – with a genius for turning defeat into victory – proptly created an institution and a tradition out of what had happened, proclaiming Lehal Thoal the first Corrector.

These events, dramatic though they were, are overshadowed by the universe-shaking epic which followed. The next four eras lasted a very short time in total, but it is fair to say that no other period has had such an impact upon Uranian history.

Before we go into that, let us mention one lasting achievement of the era with regard to everyday life: the invention of the *skimmer*, the vehicle which ever since has been used more than any other for individual personal transport on Ooranye. The skimmer's design grew out of that of the Lithium Era hover-

23

raft. A skimmer is lighter, more streamlined and much swifter. Mounted on these low-flying canoe-shaped craft, Uranian wayfarers feel most in their element as they roam free across the plains of the giant planet. Legends grew up around the pioneer skimmer-pilots of the Neon Era, though the vehicles were not mass-produced or available to all who wanted them until the Phosphorus.

Chelth

It proved impossible to keep the plunder of Chelth a secret. As soon as the source was tapped, as soon as power began its massive flow from Chelth into our universe – into receptacles in the Vaults of Skyyon on Ooranye – such a disturbance arose in the air, as to make everyone aware that a new era had begun. The need for secrecy was, however, universally understood. Secrecy not with regard to Uranians, but with regard to the inhabitants, if any, of Chelth. For it was feared that other things besides power might flow along the trans-dimensional link from there to here. Condemnation, punishment! The people of Syoom had to assume the worst. So they made a supreme effort to quieten their thoughts, to say "Sh…" with their minds. As far as possible, they disciplined themselves to focus away from the subject which was otherwise uppermost in all their thoughts.

For 130 days and 6 hours (the Sodium Era) this discipline held firm. The tapping of energy continued, the energy-vats in Skyyon and other cities grew fuller, the enterprise went ahead successfully. Then came what became known in history and folklore as the "flare of arrest".

It lasted 58 minutes, and has counted in history as the Magnesium Era. No one who lived through it ever described it scientifically. Poets and storytellers have likened it to a sense of being tapped on the shoulder. Scientists generally assume that the mental effect was caused by something real, namely the action of a Chelthan entity who had become aware of what our universe was doing to his.

Then came the last great act of Hyala Movoun. At least, it is supposed that the action was hers. It is unlikely that anyone else could have done it – could have made a mental bargain with the forces from Chelth, could have found an ally there who was willing to offer the bargain: "halt the Project now, destroy its records, and we will allow you to keep what you have gained so far; provided that you also give us… yourself." This deal was struck during the 2 hours and 43 minutes of the Aluminium Era, while the world held its collective breath.

24

The deed was done, and a strange peace fell over the land of Syoom. It was a quietness of sorrow and triumph: the one day and 26 hours of the Silicon Era, during which millions of inhabitants of Uranian cities dithered aimlessly, shuffling about as they waited for Hyala Movoun to die. Her people's awareness tripped, stubbed against a parcel they found dumped in their minds: the idea that Hyala's soul was about to be carried off to Chelth. There she'd be pinned, experimented on by her adversaries. Outrageous, unbearable thought. But, on the other hand, too large to protest. People trusted, or hoped, that the Chelthan bargainer would spare her torment, but anyhow there was nothing to be done. Everyone was quietly aware of the score.

Then, abruptly, the 'tap' was turned off, the 'cable' cut, the link severed between Chelth and our universe. Insights faded like a dream. Many notes survive – those that were written contemporaneously; but later memoirs are few, and the official records were destroyed as part of the bargain, so we need not be surprised that data concerning the Plundering mostly failed to outlast the hours of the Sodium Era.

6: The Phosphorus Era

Introduction: the glory of Era 15

The Phosphorus is commonly thought of as the greatest era. It may not be the most spiritual, and other ages may have a subtler aura of romance, but no other period has quite the same classic, purple aura of majestic splendour. The reason for this unique prestige is that the Nenns of the Phosphorus Era had the advantage of surprise in their enjoyment of the sudden "windfall" of power from Chelth, and held that advantage for nearly fifteen million days – fifty thousand Terran years.

To put it metaphorically, all potential rivals, all the non-human and anti-human forces of the giant planet were "caught napping" during this immense period. They took one startled look at the achievement of Man, realized they could not compete – and so decided, during this time, to continue their nap.

Therefore, although humans never can "conquer" Ooranye, in Era 15 they came closest to looking as though they might do so. Some real hope and expectation existed, that Syoom might extend to cover the planet.

In truth the population of Syoom did surge, millions of Syoomeans colonizing borderlands which had never before been settled, expanding the boundaries of civilization – in other words, enlarging Syoom itself. But in addition to this general advance, the sheer lordliness and might of that era spilled deep into Fyaym by means of particular incursions which left outposts that in some cases have survived to this day. And everywhere, from the heartlands to the outposts, the windfall of power brought forth an epic pride, a confidence and reach of spirit which dazzled contemporaries and haunted the planet's future memories.

First, the great question at the start of the era:

How best to use the power from Chelth?

The stolen treasure lay shimmering in huge "vats" beneath Skyyon on Day One – the immense, unrepeatable, ill-gotten gain, grabbed at the expense of another universe. The deed had been done, and could not be undone. The time had now come to decide how to use it. The people of Syoom, stunned by recent events, were waiting quietly, but their leaders knew that no false move would be forgiven at this historic moment. And the pressure on the decision-makers became all the greater after it was reported, by the scientists monitoring the "vats", that the contents were evaporating. The rate of loss was slow – close to the limit of detection – but it was enough to wipe out the possibility of conserving a share for future eras to deal with. The decision had to rest with the people of the Phosphorus Era.

When the Noads of the twenty-five greatest cities met in conclave to elect a successor to Sunnoad Hyala Movoun, two main political factions had already emerged.

One faction was strongly in favour of using up the power in the vats fast. These "hotheads" pointed out that, in view of its relatively short half-life, the power was best used at once. All delay must be wasteful. Splurge it now, they advised. Give civilization an explosive boost. Lift the human story thereby onto a new level, with permanent effect. "Then society shall never fall back into the grim chaos of the Nitrogen Era."

The opposing "coolheads" argued as follows: "This store of energy has been bought with the life and perhaps the soul of Hyala Movoun 1. We dare not use it in any but the wisest way. We must make sure we use it in accordance with the best interests not only of our era but of all Great Cycle time. And since it is not reasonable to expect any single generation to come up with all the best ideas, we ought to leave some of it to our successors – diminished though the store will be; for evaporation is not the only form of wastage. Premature decision-making could prove worse."

After two days' debate, and in recognition of the necessity for speed, a seemingly safe, compromise candidate – one who apparently belonged to neither faction – was chosen as the Second Sunnoad.

Lamiroth Eren 2 had been a respected educationalist who had known and worked with Hyala Movoun 1 during the Oxygen Era, before her elevation to the sunnoadex. He soon turned out to be a wise choice. In the next few days he steered the conclave towards a consensus.

"Our plunder," he said, not mincing words, "according to what our savants tell me, has a half-life of some hundreds of [Uranian] years. This is a small length of time compared with the Great Cycle, so we cannot afford to be complacent. But neither need we be precipitate. Using the arguments which I have heard from you, sponndarou, and from our scientists, engineers, economists and military experts, as Sunnoad I announce the following plan:

"Half of the contents of the power-vats shall be left untouched for the time being, for future generations to use as they see fit. The other half shall be used by ourselves to lift our civilization to a higher level and keep it there.

"Of this half, eighty per cent shall be used to realize the engineer's dream of indestructible, disc-on-stem foundations of ultimate metal, on which to

27

base the rebuilding of the twenty-five greatest cities of Syoom. This will elevate these cities into a new order of security and power, with the realistic hope that they will endure for the entire length of the current Great Cycle.

"Of the remaining twenty per cent, sixteen per cent shall be used in the compression of frozen energy to create one hundred thousand null-gravity cores for airships, besides billions of cheap buoyancy shards for skimmers.

"The final four per cent shall be used to fabricate tools and industrial plant of varying quality – I say deliberately varied, so that they will not all wear out at the same time. There shall be no repetition of the energy crisis which arose from the depletion of the Sun-Egg. We must bring a higher economy into secure existence."

This sheaf of decisions acquired the name the Choice of the Way – reflecting the immensity of its importance for all future eras. By and large, historians agree that the choices made were good, perhaps the best possible under the circumstances. We need, however, to note two major unforeseen consequences.

The first concerns the four per cent used for the variety of small objects and installations – tools, machines, plant – that was meant to vitalise the economy. "Vitalise" it did, to an unintended degree. Chelthan energy, to an extent not understood at the time, was purposive. It possessed a strong inherent morphogenetic field which began the long process whereby cities became holistic collections of machines with a vegetal capacity to put forth growths. What strikes Terran visitors nowadays about Uranian city maintenance is the extent to which human workers "tend" rather than "administer", and this theme can be traced back to the Choice of the Way at the beginning of the Phosphorus Era.

Hence, industrialism has never led to ugliness on Ooranye. There, technology is a branch on the tree of life – an efflorescence of self-developing mechanisms, with city maintenance becoming city cultivation, since opting for the disc-on-stem design meant that all subsequent construction was apt to "fold around" that decision like climbing plants trained onto a trellis. (Thus began the machine evolution that would, eras later, culminate in the Ghepions.)

The second unforeseen consequence of the Choice of the Way arose from the decision to save half the power-store for future use.

This meant that some Chelthan power was not completely consumed until the end of the era. During hundreds of lifetimes, therefore, the stuff was steadily leaking into the atmosphere around Skyyon.

As a result, for thousands of miles around the sunward pole of the planet, a faint nimbus suffused the air. It is now obvious that this radiation affected people's minds. Admittedly, the "seepage effect" is too glibly invoked by second-rate historians as an explanation for each singular characteristic of Era 15. We can but guess to what extent the "seepage" was responsible for the hubris and nemesis at the end of the era. And to be fair, we must also allow it to have contributed to the greatness that shone before. It elevated people's thoughts, spured them with extra ambitions, incited deeds which burnish the legends of the Phosphorus Era and made of it a lit stage on which an epic was played out.

The Disc-on-Stem Cities

By far the largest portion of the power plundered from Chelth was used to build the twenty-five virtually indestructible disc-on-stem platforms of *iedleis*, the ultimate metal. Piled high with branching walkways, globular palaces and helical towers, the platforms comprise the familiar Uranian metropoli of all subsequent eras. Their bases, stems and floors stand today as they stood a million Earth-years ago, and as they will stand for the rest of the Great Cycle of Uranian history. A direct hit by a nuclear bomb would not dent the metal of which the platforms are composed, though the superstructures would be obliterated.

The construction of these cities took an amazingly short time – less than a thousand days – and all of them (except Grard, the last) were built simultaneously at the beginning of the era.

Together with cheaper airships and the re-equipment of the economy, the new city structures gave the Uranians unprecedented riches and power. Note however that this was an *enabling* boost, an acceleration rather than a deviation of history. Paradoxically, the alien Chelthan power had allowed Ooranye to realize itself; had encouraged indigenous trends to develop more quickly, more fully and more freely.

This can be seen in the case of the city hive-minds. These instances of occasionaly group-consciousness were almost entirely human in composition (with a small contribution from a few administrative computers) and must not be confused with the much later sentient cities of Era 47 onwards. Group consciousness can be seen as a natural development of the *renl* co-ordinating instinct which evolved during the Lithium Era.

With hindsight, we can see the middle of Era 15 as the "Age of Innocent Hives". That is to say, in those times, in places where urban group-minds shimmered on the edge of existence they did so by and large without any clash with human freedom. In discussion of Era 15 the term "group mind" usually refers only to a sort of vague Overgovernment existing continuously on a fractional "tax of awareness", levied unobtrusively on each mind within range. In the very few cases that went wrong (as in the example of Hoog), events provided a dramatic and salutary warning for everyone else. Otherwise, peace and goodwill reigned between city-minds and individual man. In no subsequent age did this smooth equilibrium return for Syoom as a whole (though the greatest, happiest and most successful hive-mind, that of the Aoan Paramountcy, belongs to the much later Xenon Era).

This success story was based, paradoxically, upon ignorance. In the Phosphorus Era most of the people most of the time were unaware that hive-minds existed. On the few occasions that they were fully perceived and admitted, they were regarded with fear and horror; the example of Hoog, the aforementioned hive-mind that went wrong, reinforced the prejudice. Like love, like humour, the Era 15 style of group consciousness depended upon spontaneity and would wither under scrutiny.

Politics in the Phosphorus Era

The sensation of confidence in the mighty achievements of Syoom meant that long stretches of time went by without people feeling the need for any Sunnoad. Even when one was elected, nen's reign was usually very short – lasting only for the length of the crisis which nen had been called to solve, after which it was a case of Cincinnatus going back to his plough. Meanwhile the Noads of the powerful twenty-five cities had greater resources of power at their command than any rulers have had since. Thus, statistics for the hazard-contours in this period could be compiled the expensive way, by the use of the Great Patrols of airships and of the hemispheric force-fields called *dlaxou* (which were invented early in the era) rather than from humbler journeys of individual wayfarers on their skimmers. The Great Patrols were an extravagant way of doing it – but they had the good effect, that the *mawos*, those floating sky-weeds which had caused such bother in the Lithium Era, were so reduced in numbers by the relentless supervision, that they were never again a widespread nuisance.

The Bank of Light

Although power and global ambition were the keynotes of Era 15, other voices were not altogether suppressed. Counter-balancing the increased hubris of the leading Noads was the institution known to its friends and supporters as the Bank of Light.

Ironically enough it grew out of a failed military project. Researchers had been trying to collect and "bottle" aggressive emotions which might then be concentrated and blasted at an enemy as a sort of mind-bomb. The project was abandoned as unfeasible. However, one of the former researchers, who happened also to be trained in techniques of contemplation, did succeed, secretly, in storing a different kind of force – a kind of awareness-force dependent not upon the will but upon the passive appreciation of the world. After many obstacles had been overcome this researcher managed to found the so-called Bank of Light.

This was the nickname of the tongue-twister *Rgiohafnarn Dzeld* or "Voluntary Contemplation Store". Its emblem was an L shape signifying the belief that what was important was *being*, which was in some sense at right angles to the dimension of event and action, and just as entitled as they to the status of "achievement".

The Bank of Light opened branches in every city. Volunteers donated their time and concentration, to project part of their contemplative force into the great shimmering receptacles in the vaults of the Bank.

This accumulated force was to play a great part in salvaging a large part of civilization from the disasters which befell Syoom at the era's end.

The Verdict of History

Towards the end, the civilization of the era began to suffer the strains of its own arrogance. The powerful Noads and their peoples conceived a hatred and fear of the community "hive-minds" – sometimes with partial justification, as the hives themselves grew exaggerated and sinister (the reader is referred again to the example of Hoog). Meanwhile, the cultures of the great cities showed signs of eccentricity and instability. Take the case of Vyanth: its agriculturalists bred a strain of *vheic* – the staple ell-light plant, or "power-plant" – which glowed continuously, instead of in the waxing and waning rhythm natural to Ooranye; this doubled the city's economic resources, but had the unexpected effect that its people began to stay awake all the time, so that in a few generations sleep was forgotten. Such aberrations were fortunately swept away in the disaster which ended the era.

The next chapter of this history shall relate how the ambitions of the Phosphorus culminated in a hugely ambitious gamble, which in its failure taught humanity a lesson so priceless that subsequent eras have remembered the ill-fated Sunnoad Fiarr Fosn and his doomed followers with persistent gratitude, notwithstanding the cataclysmic close of Era 15 with its huge loss of life and its contraction of Syoom.

Even by the Uranians of our own day, the 723rd Sunnoad and his captains are still viewed as heroes. It is pleasant to relate, moreover, that because Nenns commonly live two or three lives, widely separated in time, and retain memory of their first life during their second, Fiarr Fosn himself was given the opportunity in a subsequent era to atone for his mistake.

7: The Great Fleet

The Decision

The frame of mind of the leaders of Syoom during the last few thousand days of Era 15 can be summed up as the growing consciousness that "it's now or never".

They knew that humanity on Ooranye was at the acme of its power. They knew that no more plundering of other dimensions like Chelth could ever again be risked. If ever the decision was to be taken to conquer the world for humankind, it must be taken some time soon, before Fyayman powers resurged. No future time would be as good as the present. And if nothing was done, would not future generations blame those who might have acted but chose instead to consider their own immediate comfort?

A considerable stock of the power looted from Chelth still lay in the vaults of the major cities of Syoom, but at current rates of use it would only last a few more lifetimes. After that, patrols would have to be cut drastically, and who knew how the powers of Fyaym would react to this sign of weakness in Syoom?

At this point some fainter voices were raised for the last time – voices that had unsuccessfully tried to get a hearing at various times during this long era. These critics argued that it was not too late to redeem the honour of Ooranye to some extent, by making an effort to return what was left of the plunder to Chelth. If even a fraction of the ill-gotten energy was somehow given back, perhaps the present generation would earn forgiveness for their world and obtain pardon for themselves and their descendants, from the wronged Other Dimension.

Belatedly, the few who took this line organized themselves into a group which could not even agree on a name, and were derisively nicknamed the Justies. They accepted this appellation, and went around trying to get support for their idea among the Noads.

The "justies" got nowhere. But who knows – if any trans-dimensional power can listen in to our universe, perhaps the mere fact that these dissenting voices were raised did something to make restitution.

The gamble which Syoom as a whole then undertook can be compared, faintly, with decisions taken at forking paths in Earth's history. In the 1840s, in Victorian Britain, the decision was make not to protect agriculture from foreign competition but to allow the import of cheap food, to allow free trade that was bound eventually to let loose forces that would drive people off the land and into the cities, relying for their bread on imports, safeguarded by a powerful Navy policing the oceans… in short, a gamble to allow an economic wrenching, a distortion, for the sake of greatness. Whether the decision was seen in those terms in the 1840s is doubtful, for a whole generation was still to go by before the pinch was felt by British farmers, but in the case of the Uranian Phosphorus Era the analogous decision *was* consciously made, to abandon the unwritten stability pact with the silent, watchful forces of Fyaym.

The aim was to win mastery of the world. A Sunnoad was elected, the young and ambitious Noad of Vyanth, Fiarr Fosn, who now became Fiarr Fosn 723 and who was known to favour the plan to build a great, unified Navy of Syoom, a fleet of airships which would go forth and conquer the starlit hemisphere of Ooranye.

With the failure of the "justies", only one voice of opposition remained. The Bank of Light strongly opposed the plan for the creation and launch of the armada. The Bank's whole ethos favoured peace, retrenchment, and letting the future look after itself. When it became plain that their opposition, like that of the justies, was useless, the leadership of the Bank became divided as to what they should do next. Should they try to force the issue by releasing their accumulated store of calm at once, wastefully and possibly prematurely? Or should they wait and see what happened to the expedition, meanwhile keeping their contemplative power in reserve? After all, the expedition *might* succeed, in which case the Store of Light ought to be saved for some more urgent future crisis… In the end the Bank decided to watch and wait.

Doom of the Fleet

The navy was built. The greatest fleet of airships ever to take to the skies of Ooranye was launched with Fiarr Fosn in command. Part of the gamble was that reliance had to be placed upon sheer might rather than upon reconnaissance and intelligence, since to send out scouts and probes would be to alert forces which might oppose the Plan. The Sunnoad chose, therefore, to press on in blind strength.

So the captains flew outwards from Skyyon in all directions without any firm idea of what they would find. Fifteen hundred ships formed an ever-widening circle as the front line expanded, each commander hoping to meet and overwhelm some aspect of the defences of Fyaym. Radio-silence was abandoned. The ships kept openly in touch with one another, preferring the advantage of communication to that of surprise.

Somewhere deep in Fyaym, though still far from the mythic starlit polar land of Arclour, the fleet encountered Nemaean insectoid mounds the size of mountains. Battle ensued; in most cases the units of the fleet won the encounters. We can imagine Fiarr Fosn on the bridge of his flagship the *Rezorpnint* thinking, "So far so good." Then a hostile mind must have made a decision to unleash a new order of weaponry against the armada from Syoom, for a few hours later the Syoomean captains were amazed to see ships apparently identical to their own coming to meet them across the plain.

A mirroring, tissue-melding power had formed billions of insectoid bodies into several thousand giant metal hulls, so that each Syoomean ship found itself faced with five or six foes of the same mass and design as itself, eager to ram. And after a ship had been knocked down from the sky, its attackers would dissolve once more into swarms – ravenous for metal – swooping to finish the destruction of the wreck.

We are not sure where the *Rezorplint* met its end. Some vessels turned tail to fly back the way they had come, trying to escape not out of cowardice but in order to save their homelands from this new force. Few managed to outdistance the Nemaean rammers. In one famous case a partially disabled couple of ships managed to reach the ground safely and their marooned survivors – officers, warriors, scientists – later founded the cities of Deev and Karth in the depths of Fyaym. There is a tradition among the descendants of these survivors, that what sustained them was the need above all to justify Fiarr Fosn's gamble; the desperate need to believe that it had not all been for nothing. And of course this was true. Lessons had been learned about the capabilities of Fyaym; lessons which were never to be forgotten.

Nevertheless the disaster was unparalleled in Uranian history. The armada was virtually wiped out; seventeen ships escaped, out of the fifteen hundred. It was the one and only occasion on which Syoom has ever put forth its whole strength against Fyaym, and surely the attempt will never be repeated. (The Second Great Fleet, in Era 91, succeeded where the first had failed, because its objective was discovery rather than conquest.)

The Sulphur Era

Whereas the Phosphorus Era had lasted 14,626,687 days (595.9 Uranian years; 50,057 Earth years), the succeeding Sulphur Era lasted thirty-six minutes.

The enemy, having destroyed Syoom's Grand Fleet, continued their victorious course towards Syoom itself. Insectoid blizzards swarmed against Syoomean outposts, overwhelmed and destroyed them, and continued their encroachment.

Much darkness had fallen upon Syoom in days of yore, in the long-gone Nitrogen Era, but now came the first time in history that Syoom had been attacked concertedly and simultaneously from all directions. Millions of people lost their lives to the Nemaeans, most of the victims being settlers and the descendants of settlers who in recent U-years had drifted further from central Syoom. The population increase of the later Phosphorus Era was more or less wiped out in this 36-minute holocaust.

The Chlorine Era

The news of the massacres was relayed all over Syoom. The Bank of Light took action. By some providential mercy it was guessed that the hoarded contemplative force could, when released in a dense enough spurt, act to disorient the foe. During twenty-four minutes – the length of Era 17 – the Bank's vaults were emptied, the mental force beamed at the invading swarms, causing the Nemaeans to spin and crash. A side-effect was that a diffuse calm spread throughout Syoom, leading to a unique mood of exhausted serenity in the face of disaster and deliverance.

8: The Argon Era

Though often thought of as a gentler successor to the splendid Phosphorus Era, the Argon was splendid enough in its own twilit way. It has an aura of mystery, of romance, which its mightier predecessor in some ways lacked. Perhaps also its culture possessed a certain serene wisdom which originated in the 24 minutes' bath of emanations from the Bank of Light.

Era 18 lasted 12,666,934 days, or 516 Uranian years, equivalent to 43,350 Earth years.

In this period the profession of Wayfarer – the individual on a skimmer, voyaging to provide survival-statistics for the maps – flourished as never before. Partly this was because fewer resources remained for the more expensive patrols by airship or dlax. But also, it was fitting that lone travellers should henceforth provide most of the data on which the peril contours of maps were based – since the concepts of Syoom and Fyaym became somehow more immediate and personal in the humbler, gentler glow of this era. The old pursuit of – and belief in – power had become muted. Nennkind had come to terms with the fact that Fyaym could never be conquered.

The change was not only in the methods of wayfaring but also in its objectives. Argon Era wayfarers, unlike Phosphorus Era patrollers, were not expected to understand. As in all later eras, they were required only to try their best to survive their journeys. To do that, and that alone, was to count as a success. Survival or non-survival provided the only data which the cartographers were interested in recording. This was a return, a permanent return, to the original Syoom/Fyaym concept promulgated in the Helium Era. Admittedly some of the greatest adventurers did succeed in understanding what they saw and in clearing up some mysteries and solving some crises, but this was beyond the call of duty. The lowering of expectations was perhaps the most important aspect of the general "trimming of sails" which civilization underwent in the transition between the two great eras, 15 and 18.

9: Nalre Zitpoidl and the Great Winter

Stitching Syoom

Once more we find ourselves considering the career of a great Transition Sunnoad.

This time we must examine the fate of Nalre Zitpoidl 4854, who, unlike Fiarr Fosn 723, was very much of a survivor.

The men of the Argon Era eventually became a little too trusting of the world, or of humanity's place in it. They thought they were doing well, because they knew that they were not making the mistake of their arrogant predecessors in Era 15; they believed that their greater modesty earned them a virtual guarantee of continued equilibrium between Syoom and Fyaym.

In the end, to counter this complacency, a move was made by Sunnoad Nalre Zitpoidl.

This extraordinary man was in one sense marked from birth: marked out, that is, by his actual birth-name. Uranians are generally "auto-appellant", which is to say that their names are derived from the first sounds which they are heard to make. In the case of this particular baby, the message that issued from its mouth, in a strangely crystal-clear voice, was brief: *zitpoidl.... Valeddom.... Noleddern....* Then as if a flow of alien communication had been cut off, the baby went back to making its natural gurgly sounds, one of which sounded like "Nal-re". His parents, however, had recorded the previous sounds and duly reported them as defined words to the record-keepers of Oso, their home city. Cross-referencing of data soon established that 'Valeddom' was a tiny little-known Sunward planet lost to sight in the solar glare; on a few occasions back in the Phosphorus Era, Uranian scientists had picked up fragmentary radio messages from its silicon inhabitants, the *zitpoidl*. But nothing more had come of it, and it remained a complete mystery, as to why the baby from Oso should have mouthed those sounds. Still, custom was binding: what's voiced is voiced: and so the infant had to grow up with a partly alien name, without ever knowing why fate had singled him out in this manner. As a young man, he spent some efforts trying to find out as much as he could from ancient astronomical records, but gave up that line of investigation – as all subsequent thinkers have done – as a blind alley. That's how it often is, on Ooranye, with regard to the causes of things. But it is a different matter when we turn to *results*. It is well worth considering what arose from the widespread public sense that there was something special about Nalre Zitpoidl. The public made allowances, had unusual expectations, and, perhaps, took from him what they would not have taken from anybody else...

We must now jump ahead in our story, to his reign as Sunnoad. In his youth, Nalre Zitpoidl had become a daring explorer beyond sfy-50, the Syoom-Fyaym boundary, yet his later policy as Sunnoad was not an expansionist one; rather, it was consolidatory. But at the same time it was sufficiently striking and original, that – to everyone's surprise including his own – the public caught on in a big way. "Stitching Syoom" was the idea of the moment: to such an extent that the emotional reverberations affected the day/night cycle, and a new era began. To explain, let us summarise the short and dazzling era which followed.

The Potassium Era lasted 152 days and six hours, during which a blaze of enthusiasm engulfed Syoom. The ideal to which millions now dedicated themselves was that civilization was a carpet, patchy and threadbare, that needed mending in its thinnest places. Metaphors to do with sewing and stitching abounded. Maps were consulted to ascertain the location of the thinnest patches, where the safety-contours were lowest. People took steps to found waystations and garrison towns at those spots.

Then the chain-reaction of consciousness, which had produced all this aware activity, was capped by a sensational news item.

The White Sun

On the plains of Voad, roughly mid-way between Vlamanor and Xydur, wayfarers noted what seemed like the top of a gleaming sphere rising to the surface through the gralm.

At the same time people all over Syoom were suddenly aware that everything around them seemed new and unfamiliar. It wasn't a lapse of memory; they still knew who they were and what everything was in their daily lives. But the *feeling* of familiarity was gone. Many deaths resulted from the sheer strain of constant surprise and the lapses of concentration caused by excessive wonderment. The days of astonishment began to be called the Calcium Era.

Meanwhile, the intruding sphere on the plains of Voad was nicknamed the White Sun. It has been assumed, ever since, that it was a weapon of some kind, a form of attack. The perpetrators have never been identified.

The Offer

Eleven days into the Calcium Era, when it seemed that Syoom was threatened with mass insanity, a messenger came to Sunnoad Nalre Zitpoidl with a piece of news that announced yet another lurch of history. This led to a three-day-and-nine-hours period of excitement and suspense which came to be known as the Scandium Era.

The message was one of hope. The sender was an avian being, of a type new to the Syoomeans. The being, who gave nen's name as Tjoren, claimed to come from deep in Fyaym, and to hail from a civilization which had had experience of phenomena like the White Sun.

Tjoren announced that the mental depredations of the White Sun would cease – temporarily – in a few hours' time. But nen had no power to hold them off forever; to do that, more power was needed than nen's race (the taharen) possessed. The only solution was to pool the racial subconscious of both species: taharen and Nenns.

Sunnoad Nalre Zitpoidl distrusted Tjoren immediately. But he found that his people were almost all against him on his issue – so much so that he had to tread carefully lest he be "Corrected". As he later put it in his memoirs, his entourage was stiff with would-be Correctors waiting for the chance to pounce…

The difference of opinion was stark: whereas the Sunnoad thought that the White Sun was a nuisance that could be borne, and that it would be unjustifiably dangerous to accept Tjoren's offer, his advisors were inclined the other way – though no one could imagine how the "pooling" would be implemented, they saw the offer as good, and the White Sun as lethal.

Popular sentiment backed the advisors, so forcefully as to seem unstoppable, especially as Tjoren turned out to be as good as nen's word insofar as the emanation from the White Sun did cease… Almost everyone in Syoom seemed to have but one desperate idea, which was that at all costs those sickening effects must not be allowed to recommence.

Murder at Vlamanor

A meeting was arranged with the avian being. The conference was set up at Vlamanor. Before it could begin, came a series of three shocking announcements.

First, Tjoren had been murdered.

Second, the Sunnoad had confessed to the murder.

Third, he had then tried to surrender himself to Tjoren's entourage, and had been turned away, the taharen proclaiming that the murderer's punishment must come from his own people or his own conscience. Syoom as a whole would automatically pay the penalty in a wider sense, namely in that the taharen's offer of help against the White Sun was now withdrawn.

Nevertheless, while people trembled in fear of a return of the White Sun, an utterly different nemesis was on its way. A freezing cloud appeared on the Syoom-Fyaym border and began to encroach from the direction in which the taharen's homeland was supposed to lie.

The Great Winter

In fact, the White Sun was never seen again. All the fears of Syoom now centred on the new peril. As the cold cloud advanced, men were at first convinced that it was some kind of revenge for the murder of Tjoren. This belief was held despite the fact that the taharen themselves had refused to punish the actual murderer.

At this point in the story we, the compilers of this history, are more aware than ever of how our account of events is even stupider than those single-volume histories of Earth in which attempts are made to summarise the Renaissance or the Disfigurement in one paragraph. For example, we have given a completely inadequate account of the choices open to Nalre Zitpoidl. Therefore the reader has not much opportunity to form a plausible opinion as to why he acted as he did. Unfortunately this silliness is unavoidable, not only here but in later pages of our story. One consolation: our neglect is in line with Uranian tradition itself. Uranians attack a problem at the branches, not at the root, for they despair of ever mastering causation.

On this occasion their ignorance was spectacular.

They did not know, and moreover they did not even feel they needed to know, whether the unprecedented invasion of snow and ice, which now affected Syoom, was deliberately sent by a super-civilization which could control the weather. Even those who were of this opinion could not prove that the attack was in retaliation for the murder of Tjoren. And even those (the majority) who believed that it was, were divided in their opinion as to how much blame should be attached to the Sunnoad.

Should they condemn Nalre Zitpoidl for murdering the avian and thus provoking the Winter, or should they conclude, from the savagery of this retaliation, that the Sunnoad must have been right after all, in his distrust of

41

the taharen? No consensus was reached as to what to do with the Sunnoad; so he lived on, an ambiguous, controversial figure, throughout the 10,620 days (36 Earth years) of the Titanium Era – the Age of Winter.

Meanwhile snow covered Syoom; doubtless not quite the type of snow experienced in winter on Earth, but equivalent nonetheless. Plant life suffered, though some species were hardy enough to survive and provide sustenance for a reduced human population. Life went on; a generation grew up who had never known aught but whiteness on the plains. The term "Syoom" gradually lost its statistical significance and became merely the name for the land; trade and travel between cities dwindled, and the hive-minds and vault-minds in the cities themselves died down to mere embers of consciousness. City states became isolated and government more than ever an affair of rulers pursuing their own interest without regard to any wider human community. With hindsight we can see that the foundations were being laid for the individualism of the Vanadium Era.

Eventually the snow evaporated, almost as quickly as it had come. Nennkind woke up to the fact that the great revenge, if revenge it was, had ended. Nothing further was ever heard publicly from the taharen who were commonly thought to have inflicted the Winter upon Syoom. Perhaps they had lost interest; perhaps, rather, they had been somehow repulsed or even destroyed by their own creation. Who knows? To this day the mystery of the Winter, and of the White Sun which preceded it, remains swallowed up in the vastness and the silence of Fyaym.

10: The Vanadium Era

Character of the era

Era 23 was the longest by far of all the eras of Ooranye's history up to the present. It lasted 55,391,027 of the Uranian 30-hour days, or 2,256.7 Uranian years, the equivalent of 189,565 Earth years – probably longer than the period during which *homo sapiens sapiens* has existed upon Earth.

Syoom itself was the arena almost entirely. There were few expeditions into Fyaym. In fact Fyaym was often forgotten, as though sfy-50 were the edge of the world. It might as well have been; for the four hundred million square miles of Syoom amply sufficed for the adventurous urges of a people reduced in numbers by the Great Winter and kept from increase by the waste of war and other conflict in this least intellectual and most swashbuckling of all eras.

Indeed there was little need for any challenging of Fyaym, at a time when Syoom seemed bigger, more chaotic and perilous than ever – its statistical definition hardly counting any more, so that for large parts of it we cannot even say if it still came under the old definition of Syoom. A lot more of it became forest; **velng** multiplied their huge mounds in the plains, sometimes holding humans captive for generations inside these artificial mountains. Abatis, planted for the protection of towns against various perils of the plains, themselves grew into dangerous ecosystems sometimes harbouring rogue states. Reformers and heroes punctuated the mediocrity of hereditary monarchies. The powers of Fyaym, looking on, discovered no threat to themselves, and perhaps encouraged the longevity of Era 23.

It was a golden age for the strong and the adventurous, the cheerful risk-taker and the soldier of fortune. No more colourful life could be lived, than that of a Wayfarer in Era 23. A Terrestrial teenager who has thrilled to the tales of Barsoom would naturally love to read about the Vanadium more than about any other period of Uranian history.

Yet it should not be dismissed as a mere adventure playground, for it was so vast in duration that almost everything set down in these paragraphs was contradicted at some point or other – thus occasionally rewarding the student of more subtle aspects of history.

Politics and Society

During the early days of this era, Nalre Zitpoidl was still alive. An old man, he wandered from city to city. Was he still Sunnoad? Or had one of the deposition ceremonies, which had been enacted during the Great Winter, been legal? If he had been deposed, this was one of only a handful of such cases in Uranian history.

Zitpoidl wrote his memoirs and, after showing them to a small number of personally selected readers, left them to be rediscovered and published many eras later. He alone had noted that the tajaren had returned to Syoom, had looked the land over and had seen that there was no longer anything in its civilization for them to gain a purchase on – Man was now too simple to allow them to strike a deal with his racial unconscious; Man had ducked below such blows... This could be seen as Zitpoidl's vindication, though few knew of it during his lifetime.

The uncertainty surrounding Zitpoidl's status reflected upon the subsequent history of the sunnoadex in Era 23: the institution continued, but frequently passed many lifetimes in a state of reduced effectiveness, almost of abeyance. The Noad of a powerful city such as Vyanth or Ao or Pjourth might well possess more influence than the person who wore the golden cloak of Skyyon.

As has been noted, city-minds were reduced in awareness during the Great Winter. Their somnolence continued into Era 23. One of the effects this had on human society was that people had to drudge more. A kind of working class came into existence, to undertake many of the tasks which formerly the city-minds had willingly performed under the guidance of the "coaxer" professions: engineering and maintenance works; manufacture of tools, weapons, vehicles. A new labour-intensive culture developed. This gradually lead to yet more class distinctions as contrasts developed between skilled and unskilled labour, becoming intensified with the development of extremes of wealth and poverty – though no one ever became destitute in a Uranian city. Aristocracies of birth arose; after a while even hereditary monarchies – anathema to most ages of Uranian history – evolved in many cities. Dynastic selfishness led to the evil of war between cities. The final consequence of all this, as will be seen, was the downfall of the era's culture, a downfall which originated in the creeping onset of the institution of slavery.

The evils of war and (during the final fifth of the era) of slavery, were mitigated by the fact of reincarnation. Out of the millions who lost their lives or their freedom during this enormous span of time, almost all had another life

44

left to live: this is because the Vanadium Era was fairly early in Uranian history, and most of its people knew that they were living the first of their two or three lives. The most miserable of them could derive comfort from the certainty that they would get another chance and a kinder fortune in some later age.

11: Revolutions

The upheaval which marked the end of the immense Vanadium Era stemmed from a personal decision by Valim Poand, Noad of Vyanth, to free all his city's slaves.

Slavery was already milder in Vyanth than elsewhere, with rights and customary protections in force. However, the step to outright abolition, taken by the ruler of the most powerful city of Syoom, astonished the civilized world. Deep emotions were roused – so deep that they resonated with the day/night cycle, bringing the longest of eras to an end at last.

For two days, seventeen hours and forty-two minutes (the Chronium Era) Syoom was poised before several forking paths of history. People waited to see what other rulers would do. But the other rulers waited also, instead of taking action. Then, inspired by events in Vyanth, a great slave revolt broke out in the other cities. It lasted thirty-one days (the Manganese Era), during which long-buried habits of thought and of feeling re-surfaced everywhere, expectations soared, and journalists struggled for metaphors as much as historians did later. "The mind of the human race juddered into higher gear." "The infantile Vanadium cultural palette puddled and ran." At the cost of much havoc and loss of life the slaves won their freedom in every city; elation spilled into the atmosphere, and brought on the next era, the Twenty-Sixth.

The Iron Era lasted 18,940 Uranian days (64.8 Earth years). Many new regimes were founded, in reaction against the carefree irresponsibility and colourful individualism of the Vanadium Era, whose lack of social conscience was rightly blamed for the advent of slavery. Stern revolutionaries established oppressively reforming governments, communist in the totalitarian sense, so that in some cases a new slavery of ideology arose to replace the older, literal sort.

Conditions on the giant planet are, however, not conducive to the survival of totalitarian regimes. Reality is liable to break in upon the dreams of ideologues even more sharply than it used to do on Earth. The Iron Era went down in a welter of muddled crises. More natural Uranian habits were re-asserted, as we shall see.

12: The Cobalt Era

One of the most lamentable gaps in our knowledge of Uranian history concerns the mysterious Cobalt Era – 6,292,385 Uranian days; 256 Uranian years; equal to 21,534.5 Earth years.

The Cobalt contrasts with the preceding great era, the Vanadium, in that population recovered; there was renewed interest in Fyaym; hereditary monarchies ceased and Noads were elected once more; the sunnoadex recovered its prestige. These trends, nudging Syoom back towards its norms, come as no surprise. But there is more to Era 27 than this.

To us it is like a dream of which strong impressions remain, but few details. Or like a wash of colour, intense and exciting, but without shape.

It was an era which inspired many great artists, at the time and since. The sky-scapes of the Cobalt Era are famous, and this chimes with the fact that some of its most characteristic developments were to do with journeys in the sky.

One of the few facts we know about the middle of the era is that an international organization called the Sky Patrol flourished during that period; it was a kind of Syoomean Navy, under the nominal or actual command of the Sunnoad, and its role was to foster the thickening of the Syoomean "carpet". Nothing like this Sky Patrol had existed for a long time.

A peculiarity of Era 27 was the great popularity of balloon flights. Cheaper than airships although much more vulnerable, balloons were actually used for exploration, to a degree that is remarkable considering the perilous conditions on Ooranye.

However the greatest mystery, the one which ended the era, was tackled on the ground.

We are told that the "first teleological investigations" occurred in Era 27, linked to the understanding which the Uranian later achieved, of the direction in which the Great Cycle is taking them. This work required the study of the rise and fall of previous civilizations. So a stimulus was given to archaeology: the ruins of many Vanadium Era and older sites swarmed at this time with scholars, scavengers and looters, wallowing in the ever-richer culture-layer of Syoom.

The Cobalt Era ended with a particular archaeological discovery…

13: The Quonians

Anachronism

Artists have portrayed the scene many times: the misty plain, the grid marked out to plan the excavation, the shapes of buildings emerging from the strata… and the faces of astonished men and women, examining artefacts of impossible age. Things dug out from ground which, a short while ago, was known from soundings to have contained nothing but featureless ice and gralm.

The possibility of it all being a hoax was soon dismissed. To have fabricated such a site, burying fake artefacts on this scale, seemed impossible – how could one afterwards de-disturb the ground? Besides, the business would have been pointless and impractical to an insane degree. But then – what was the alternative? The Sunnoad, when he got to hear of the issue, instructed his agents to follow all clues. One of these agents, who doubled as an archaeologist, rummaging in the ruins of a similar anachronistic site, accidentally put his hand through an activation beam and unleashed the broadcast which brought on Era 28.

The Nickel Era

The telepathic warning lasted 57 minutes. During those minutes every man, woman and child on the planet heard the recorded message in nen's mind, and the truth dawned on the people of Syoom, that they shared their world with a race which could manipulate time.

That was one fact which could be gleaned straightaway. Further details would follow as millions of hearers sorted out their memories and began to understand more of what their minds had received. It had been an almost wordless message, uttered so long ago, by a creature so ancient, that nen's extinct language was unrelated to any living tongue. Being wordless, it relied on the direct communication of ideas, and that was not easy, for the sender's mind had plainly not been human. Nevertheless, nen had been Uranian, evolved on the same world as the modern Nenns. The ideas, images, expressions were not wholly unfamiliar. And one part of the message *was* verbal: a name: THE QUONIANS.

These – the message warned – were a race of humanoids similar to the

Nenns of Syoom in appearance but very different culturally. They were an immensely ancient race, surviving relatively unmodified through several Great Cycles. They posed a threat to other cultures because –

And here came a specially sharp, clear part of the message, the main point of the warning. The only trouble was, the idea it contained was so new, it could hardly be taken in at one mental gulp.

The Coppper Era

Their heads ringing from the warning, the people of Syoom tried to pick up their normal lives again. Gradually, as the days passed, a sense of normality did return. But the extraordinary experience of the 57-minute Nickel Era remained the chief topic of conversation, debate and investigation. Moreover the issue was kept alive in any case by the arrival in Syoom of the Quonians themselves.

The first Quonian scouts were humble and apologetic regarding their presence on Syoomean soil. They came on their gleaming white skimmers, their white eyes peering around at whatever they saw, fascinatedly, as though they saw more than anyone else. They asked diffidently whether the Kalishan Voice had been heard. Kalishan Voice? The broadcast warning, they explained. The Voice of the Kalishan, a malicious mind – so the newcomers alleged – a mind hostile to the peaceable Quonians. Long, long ago the evil Voice had been encased in a cubical probe which was programmed to follow Quonian civilization on its journey through history and to spread slanders about Quonia. "All we want," said the newcomers, "is to be allowed to settle and mingle with the Nenns of Syoom. Surely there is room for a few hundred thousand refugees, in the four hundred million square mile vastness of Syoom." "Refugees? How come?" demanded the Syoomeans, and obtained the reply that Quonia itself was going through an over-rigid phase and had expelled those of its people who were possessed of an adventurous spirit. Surely, the culture of Syoom must sympathize with such a spirit as that?

When asked where Quonia was, the visitors became cagey. They vaguely admitted that the place was "somewhere in Fyaym". (Of course, by strict definition a civilization cannot be "in Fyaym", for civilization is Syoomean by definition, but in loose everyday language a hitherto unsuspected area of Syoom surrounded by Fyaym can be "somewhere in Fyaym".)

All this time, people went on thinking about their memories of the 57-minute Voice of Kalishan. In fact the entire Copper Era (2,961 Uranian days;

49

a little over ten Earth years) was a kind of race between the warning Voice and the persuasiveness of the Quonians.

During the last third of the era, the Voice began to win out.

Triumph of the Voice

It began to be noticed that more and more people were not only "seeing things from the Quonians' point of view" in the sense of sympathizing with their social and political situation, but were literally seeing their environment as if it were Quonia: a land of different geography and traditions. To bolster this illusion, physical objects continued to be found which should not have been in Syoom at all, and yet which could be proved to have been there for aeons. These objects consisted of Quonian-style buildings, coins, works of art... as if they had been smuggled across Time, to give a false pedigree to the current Quonian presence.

The terrible thought occurred to the Sunnoad and his advisers, as well as to many other high-placed Syoomeans: what if the Quonians were able to re-write human history in their favour? What if that was what they were preparing to do?

On the other hand, if they could do this, why had they not already done it? Or had they?

Quonians were pulled in for questioning under hypnosis. It was found that they did not, after all, possess true time-travel, but were able to take advantage of certain "cul-de-sacs" in Time – areas which were out of touch with the lines of causation. These special areas *could* be altered without paradox. Quonian artefacts had been sent to such areas, in a fantastically expensive operation for which the revenues of Quonia had been mortgaged to the hilt for tens of thousands of days ahead. Indeed, to finance the great deception, the Quonian homeland had almost beggared itself – but the newcomers to Syoom were not "refugees", they were agents, whose "cover" had been dearly bought. They, and those who sent them, had hoped that, as a side-effect of their tampering with time, the Quonian world-view might seep into the minds of the people of Syoom, negating the effect of the Kalishan Voice.

As soon as the plot was uncovered, it lost all its force. Little further action was necessary. The truth was broadcast, and the discomfited Quonian invaders were allowed to leave (mostly unharmed) for their own country, their business unfinished.

(The memory of Quonia was long; many eras later, they were heard from again.)

14: The Zinc Era

The calm which fell upon Syoom with the end of the Quonian crisis, brought with it a sense of relief combined with a sudden awareness of how great a privilege and delight it was to be alive at this time. Vistas of glorious well-being suddenly stretched ahead, for, uniquely, the men and women of the Zinc Era knew the length that their era would last. It is a strange fact, but true: Era 30 is the only one of the great eras, the long ones, of which the inhabitants knew at the time what the duration would be. Here is not the place to list all the theories which have been thought up as to why this should be so. Let the fact suffice for now: right from the start, people were aware that Era 30 would total 30,853,745 U-days or 1,257 U-years. (This is a period equivalent to 105,591 Earth years.) No era so far, other than the Vanadium, has surpassed this length.

The Zinc can be compared with the Vanadium in that both were to some extent interludes in history. Neither of them were characterised by widespread quest and striving, as would have linked them to the big questions posed or answered by other eras. Thus, though full of action and adventure, both were spiritually peaceful.

On the other hand, the Zinc was clearly different from the Vanadium. Era 30 was much more mature than Era 23. You could not say of the Zinc, as you could of the Vanadium, that it was primarily a haven for swashbucklers – despite all the adventures which abounded in the Thirtieth as in all other eras of Uranian history.

What had made the Vanadium an interlude was its decline to a more childish level of consciousness. What made the Zinc an interlude was not so much a decline as a postponement. The period simply put off till later the search for greater understanding of the destiny of Man on Ooranye.

This relaxedness, this postponement, gives the Zinc Era its special charm, of contentment without complacency. You cannot accuse its people of shirking the ultimate quest, for they knew, and could not alter, the fact that they were in for a long stretch of stability before the next world-shake. Since there was nothing they could do about this, they could enjoy their glowing period guiltlessly.

One practical consequence of the awareness which the Zinc Era culture had of the length of time at its disposal, is that this is the period when most of the great monorails of Syoom were built. The stupendous building project was undertaken in full confidence, justified by the knowledge that history would allow it room for completion.

Everyone has nen's own favourite Golden Age of Syoom. Many would pick the Zinc Era. It lacks the crudity of the Vanadium, the tension of the Phosphorus; it possesses some of the serenity and mystery of the Argon and Cobalt Eras. And it has the special poignancy of a long-deferred but certain end: the awareness of coming doom, at first far off, over a thousand lifetimes away, then creeping gradually closer as the millions of days wore on, while most folk were glad that they would never live to see the end, and only a few impatient ones envied their successors.

15: The Age of Spies

The Sight Projector

The long-foreseen finale of the Zinc Era was brought about by a great discovery. This is not surprising: as the expected time drew near, researchers naturally stepped up their efforts, knowing that it was quite likely that one of them would prove to be the trigger of the *eomasp*. And one of these teams turned out to be right. This one made the breakthrough at the precise time decreed for the end of the Zinc and the start of the Gallium Era.

The momentous achievement consisted of a technique for projecting one's vision, so that an explorer could sit in a chair in a safe place in Syoom and rove with nen's sight thousands of miles into Fyaym without having to go there.

Peculiarly, the *eomasp* occurred – and the new era was seen to begin – even though for a while the inventors refrained from publicising what they had done. This could happen because everyone knew that the Zinc Era would end on the day it did; expectations created the excitement and this alone was enough to cause the *eomasp*. Everyone knew that something big had happened, secret though it was.

Meanwhile a select company of "mind-nauts" were chosen to undergo the initial test-voyages with the sight-projector. Some of those who projected their vision into Fyaym never came back; their bodies languished in Syoom, their minds lost who knows where. On a few occasions a worse thing happened: a Fyayman power effected a mind-swap, keeping the Syoomean rover imprisoned and sending another mind to occupy nen's body in Syoom.

Finally it was discovered that mental projections were being deflected in a systematic pattern to forbid views of a certain area. A ring was then drawn on a map to determine the bounds of that area, a huge realm deep in Fyaym, thousands of miles from sky-50, the border with Syoom. Something in that distant "pocket" did not want to be seen. The Sunnoad and his advisors theorised about the possible reason: that an attack of some kind was being prepared against Syoom.

The time had come to cease reliance on sight-projection and to organize a physical expedition to penetrate the area of mystery.

The Other Syoom

Sunnoad Restiprak Zentonan 33337 gathered a fleet of airships and set forth. Journeying deep into Fyaym, the fleet approached the forbidden area and found that the Sunnoad's previous assumptions had been wrong: the inhabitants were not trying to hide from him. In fact they were overjoyed to learn of his coming. The area was under siege, and it was not the inhabitants but the besiegers who had been deflecting the sight-probes.

The besiegers were a pirate culture of near-humans, to whom the Sunnoad now gave battle. He gained enough of a victory to open a way into what became known as the "Other Syoom".

This land consisted of two allied human empires, named after two cities, Yalar and Nii. For some time, both these beleaguered states (it turned out) had been transmitting telepathic appeals for help, appeals which had become blurred and muted by distance into vaguer excitation, responsible, perhaps, for a rise in inventiveness, including the discovery of sight-projection itself. And the Other Syoom had another surprise in store.

Ipemenir

Because Yalar and Nii had been isolated for so long, their siege mentality had forced them to intensify certain areas of research. This had an effect on their racial unconscious or rather, semi-conscious. Half-knowingly, they had accumulated a "bank" of mind-energy like the Bank of Light in the Phosphorus Era. Only, this "bank" was not under any control at all. It had no release-button reachable by any human finger. Its contents, heaving about like an invisible monster, chose its own moment, this moment, to become purposive, to focus upon a human target and to expend all its force in energizing that particular individual.

So it happened, that as soon as the Sunnoad's fleet had cleared a way through to the Other Syoom, a flash of raw power surged out and across the distance between it and the main Syoom, to the city of Jador where lived a certain Ipemenir Honnd.

No one knows how the "bank" knew – if it did know and was not just picking blindly – which person to energize. The effect on Ipemenir, who already possessed a certain renown as a fighter, was awesome. The change in him caused an *eomasp* straightaway. The 63 days and 4 hours that followed were the Germanium Era, also known as the Era of Ipemenir.

The Sunnoad had not been able to prevail further against the enemy, nor had he succeeded in keeping open the way to the Other Syoom. The enemy once more surrounded that land and resumed the siege. But now Ipemenir took a hand in the struggle. His feats as a warrior have never been matched before or since. Showing superhuman strength and cunning, during the era which is frequently nicknamed after him, his legendary exploits saved the Other Syoom from disaster. And then came the time of the "Burnout".

During the next four very short eras, 33 (Arsenic, 18 hours and 47 minutes), 34 (Selenium, 16 hours), 35 (Bromine, 2 days, 26 hours and 35 minutes) and 36 (Krypton, just 3 and a half minutes), Ipemenir succeeded in creating a salient of Syoom reaching out through Fyaym towards the Other Syoom, though not the whole distance. His final achievement was to capture a great fortress which became known, in Era 37 and after, simply as the Rubidium Fort. Then he crumbled into ashes.

The Rubidium Era

Era 37 lasted 5,955,630 U-days; 242.6 U-years; the equivalent of 20,382 Earth years. It has acquired the sobriquet, the Age of Spies. A great alliance was forged between the main body of Syoom – the 400,000,000 square miles around the Sunward Pole of Ooranye – and the Other or Lesser Syoom, namely the empires of Yalar and Nii. It was an era of great conflict, of active hostility from Fyaym, where powers had arisen which subjected civilization to severe, concerted pressure. Altogether it was a fighting era. During all this time the salient, at the end of which stood the Rubidium Fort, was successfully defended and preserved against fierce enemies who enfiladed its length. Mind-nauts housed in the Fort would project their sight from the greater to the lesser Syoom in order to transmit vital intelligence to Yalar and Nii. And sometimes these same mind-nauts chose to become physical agents and would go in person to bring help across the stretch of Fyaym to the Other Syoom.

Eventually, the enemy forces in Fyaym evolved a defence against Syoomean sight-projection. This defence took the form of vegetable mind-traps, flowers which could dazzle and hypnotize; these caused mind-nauts to "stick" where they had snooped and become unable to return to their bodies. Such evil flowers were soon planted in so many places, luring so many visual explorers to destruction, that the official corps of mind-nauts was disbanded. So the efforts to help the Other Syoom failed for lack of intelligence, and finally the Rubidium Fort itself fell to the enemy.

The woe of this latest event triggered the next *eomasp* and the next era.

Finale

After these catastrophes one might have expected the onset of a new dark age, like the Nitrogen Era. However, Sunnoads and their advisors had long perfected plans for what to do when the Rubidium Fort finally fell. Under the redoubtable Sunnoad Jad Darkal 35480 these plans went into operation. They depended upon utter secrecy and loyalty on the part of the entire Syoomean population. Remarkably, the plan succeeded.

For forty-two days (Era 38, the Strontium Era) enemy Fyayman forces, fresh from their victory over the Rubidium Fort, advanced into Syoom. The Sunnoad waited, while the airships of the foe sailed steadily into the trap he had laid.

Details of this epic must be left for fuller treatment elsewhere [see the tale, "The Open Secret"]; here suffice it to say that the trap was successfully sprung. Era 39, the Yttrium Era – 163 U-days, 28 hours, 2 minutes – was taken up by the colossal battle in which the Fyayman coalition forces, which included some Quonians, tried vainly to escape encirclement by the Syoomeans. Hundreds of airships were destroyed or captured; hundreds of thousands of Fyaymans surrendered. News of the victory caused another *eomasp*, and the Zirconium Era began under good auspices, appropriate for a great new age.

16: The Institutes of Fate

The Zirconium and Niobium Eras (40 and 41) were the golden age of the Teleological Guilds, the like of which cannot be found in Earth history.

Their origin lies back in the Cobalt Era, but not much is known of them before Era 40. They seem to have begun as secret societies rather than as public bodies. Perhaps the mystery and the secrecy were never intentional, but forced upon them, by their special concerns which were way over most people's heads.

Partly, the Guilds were research institutions; partly they were exploration societies; partly – for a time – political clubs, even nations. Their stated purpose was to discover the trends of history. To know the direction in which Uranian Man was heading would help to steer the species though the rocks and rapids that might lie in wait in the eras ahead. But the Guilds' methods of research make it hard to enforce scientific rigour on the published results.

The Zirconium Era lasted 3,155,594 U-days, or 128.6 U-years – equivalent to 10,799 Earth years. The Guilds built fine conical buildings for their headquarters. These almost rivalled the cities for splendour. (Coincidentally or not, the famous mobile city Yr, City of Mists, was built and launched in this era.) One of the Guilds allowed power to go to its collective head: it unleashed an actual war, merely to promulgate its own view of history. Its defeat led to the *eomasp* which ushered in the calmer Niobium Era.

This, Era 41, lasted 6,662,243 U-days, or 271.4 U-years – equivalent to 22,800 Earth years. During this time the guilds (written now with a small "g") were generally calmer and more responsible than they had been during the Zirconium. It was a great age for elegance in architecture, city planning and the design of airships.

Accumulated wealth from a long period of peace led to some exploration using the rare, expensive techniques of matter-transmission, make possible by equipment left over from the Phosphorus Era and rarely used since then.

The Teleological Guilds, for all their wealth and social importance, contributed remarkably little to the sum of human knowledge. Their chosen field of investigation was almost impossible to master, and gradually they lost their original purpose and became societies to promote exploration and more mundane knowledge. Finally, during the last few hundred thousand days of Era 41, they dwindled into mere departments of city government.

17: The Ghepions

A staccato burst of *eomasps*, ending not only the Niobium but the five succeeding eras within days or hours of each other, stunned and bewildered the people of Syoom. What was completely unprecedented, was that these interruptions in the day/night cycle were not accompanied by any obvious great events. Always up to now the biomass glow had altered its rhythm only if the air were disturbed by tremendous emotion; now however there was nothing known to furnish any cause for the swift procession of eras: the Molybdenum (2 hours, 17 minutes); the Technetium (28 seconds!); the Ruthenium (17 days, 21 hours); the Rhodium (1 hour 24 minutes) and the Palladium (17 days 3 hours 2 minutes).

A sinister conclusion was unavoidable: somewhere a hidden and unknown thing was happening, a thing big enough to cause *eomasps*, and because no one knew what it was, it gave the people of Syoom a nightmare sense of an invisible monster stirring.

You could say that this was more than a metaphor; that the psychic tumult which caused the swift procession of eras 42-46 *was* in a sense a stretching of something huge, awakening to life.

The "monsters" make themselves known in the great Silver Era (Era 47: 3,857,055 U-days, 157 U-years, = 13,200 Earth years).

Some form of machine consciousness had already been known as far back as the Phosphorus Era. Apart from those city hive-minds which consisted entirely of the human minds of the citizens, there had been some which also included the city's administrative computers. But what came to fruition in Era 47 was different. The new development was the *unsupervised* and completely independent growth, the *evolution* of machines into consciousness. These aware machines were the Ghepions.

Any complex artificial system might do it: part of a city, or a whole city, or a fortress, or a monorail network's central computer. The Ghepions varied widely in capability and in character. Some fought against humans and against each other. The Silver Era was a dramatic time of shifting alliances as one by one the Ghepions of Syoom came alive and revealed their personalities and aims. It was an age of many crises, and it ended with a climacteric struggle between two leagues of Ghepions and their human allies.

The following Cadmium Era (Era 48) was calmer. Like the Niobium which followed the Zirconium, it was longer and more mature and peaceful than its predecessor. The tensions of the Silver had worked themselves out; the Cadmium enjoyed the benefit of experience. It lasted 6,311,598 U-days, or 257 U-years, equal to 21,600 Earth years. During this time the Ghepions behaved themselves. They were accepted, as though they had always lived amid the humanity of Syoom. The Cadmium was a splendid era, rich in personal adventures against a background of basic cultural security.

The security and the era ended abruptly with a shocking broadcast form the city of Oso, which, in the ensuing days, became known as the Mad City. It had been completely taken over by a Ghepion, evolved in its vaults from its administrative computers, and it now announced its intention to rule Syoom. The 18-minute broadcast (the Indium Era) was followed by a great war of the rest of Syoom against the Mad City. This war lasted 245 days 9 hours and counts as the Tin Era. Naturally, Syoom won; but it was not easy. Oso, the Mad City, had secretly perfected the arts of mind control over both humans and many of the weaker Ghepions. It could therefore deploy its allied machines and its citizens as one unified body. In the end it was only defeated by sheer numbers and great sacrifice.

Towards the end of the war, it became apparent that the conflict had awoken more hidden forces in the 'subscape' underlying the collective Uranian unconscious – for it now began to be understood, that below the racial unconscious itself, of humans and of other species, there lay a planetary unconscious.

(Note that it was not yet recognized that, associated with this, there existed a planetary *conscious* intelligence – the truth behind the "World Spirit" of popular myth and religion. See *The Rhenium Moment* and the advice given to Capfaym Duuv in *The Era of Psi*.)

The planetary unconscious, as it were a federation of all life on Ooranye, existed like an ocean whose surface waves could disturb the depths only during a huge storm. War with the Mad City had provided that storm. It was sensed now that Oso, though defeated, had upset the equilibrium of life on the planet. Consequently, more trouble was on the way. A further hint that this was true was provided by the **eomasps** which rapidly followed the victory over Oso. More monsters turning over in their sleep? The Antimony Era (89 minutes) passed during the feasting of the victorious allies as they met to discuss what to do with the vanquished. The Tellurium Era (33 minutes) passed during the subsequent debate at which the arrangements for the occupation of Oso were made.

Things quietened down during the Iodine Era (17,277 U-days, equivalent to 59 Earth years), but the uneasy conviction persisted, that it was only a matter of time before Syoom was visited by a new kind of crisis. Meanwhile, by a wise arrangement, human investigators were paired with Ghepions in a patrol-organization which helped to restore trust in Ghepions generally.

18: The Last Great Hive

Unexpectedly, the Iodine Era was brought to an end not by a calamity but by the shock of amazingly good news.

The city of Ao suddenly achieved a breakthrough in the creation of a benevolent "hive" – a group mind which harked back to the old-fashioned, innocent and successful hives of the Phosphorus Era. The new Aoan Hive consisted of a moderate levy from all the minds of the city, allowing each individual to retain his full consciousness during a melding which created value that was somehow given back to the individual... rather as though it were possible to get something for nothing. In addition, as a kind of co-ordinating core to this group consciousness, the Ghepion administrative computer contributed its own mind. Plenty could have gone wrong, but did not. The combination worked.

If it can be done, this sort of thing is a good bargain for both city and population. The city-mind is exalted by the capabilities of its humans, and vice versa. Very occasionally, it is believed, the people may have joined with the city's own consciousness to form a brief super-mind, but mostly the effect was a gentler, considerate sharing. And you could drop out whenever you liked.

Other cities had tried the techniques which led to all this, but only Ao ever succeeded. The success was realized suddenly, like an image brought into abrupt focus, and announced in triumph in a voice that could not be mistaken.

The triumph was bound to be temporary. Too many destabilizing forces existed to allow it to last. Remarkably, the Aoan Paramountcy (Era 54, the Xenon Era) lasted 1,735,700 U-days – 70.7 U-years, equivalent to 5,940 Earth years; one of the shortest of the Great Eras, but an impressively long time for a city hive-mind to have preserved the moral balance between the collective and the individual.

The precise mode of consciousness of the Aoan Hive is beyond our reach, yet we have reason to suspect that it knew roughly the extent to which its days were numbered; also that it knew the chief purpose of its Paramountcy, which was to stave off what we term the hylozoic powers.

These were powers which had been triggered like a cancer in the planetary subconscious by the fight with the Mad City. What the Aoan Hive actually did to shield Syoom we do not know; the answer may lie in the spools of the labyrinthine archives of Skyyon. What we do know is that the controlled death-throes of the Hive lasted 13 minutes (the Caesium Era) during which it transmitted as much as possible of its wisdom to the Sunnoad. These transmissions, known as the Aoan Blasts, fortunately amounted to a sufficient hand-over of the Paramountcy's insight.

The following Barium Era (54 days, 7 hours) was occupied with the action taken by the Sunnoad based on information he received in the Blasts.

19: The Foam

There was a limit to what the Sunnoad could do to prepare Syoom for the ordeal which lay ahead. Part of his task was to spread the world that the Aoan Hive had merely postponed, not averted, the doom which impended. Ao had given Nennkind a breathing space. Now it was over and there was nothing for it but to endure the coming Foam.

This was an inflammation of the normally weak, faint life-force of the **gralm**. Gralm is common as Terran beach sand. It is the loam-like granular material that covers the Uranian plains. Its flicker of life is less than that of the lowliest organic entity; but, because of the vastness of the oceanic world-plain, its total latent "bio-heat" must be colossal. And at the start of Era 57, the Lanthanum Era, the shortest of the Great Eras (1,051,880 U-days; 43 U-years; = 3,600 Earth years), gralm bizarrely expanded as though it were popcorn.

Within days, the plains around the cities of Syoom had humped and were threatening to bury the cities under a pumice-like covering.

If this had happened on Earth, people would have been driven to insanity or superstition, but on Ooranye, though the experience was daunting and amazing, it was in the end "just one of those things" – severe in its effects, but no harder to accept than any other disastrous mystery.

Tunnels, air-holes and vehicle-exits were hurriedly dug in the Foam. The buried cities carried on a much-reduced existence, as they had done during the snow-bound Titanium Era. The era of the Foam was vastly longer than that of the Great Winter, but there was no cold to contend with this time. Cities' populations plummeted because of food shortages, which drove many people to seek sustenance in the wilderness, sometimes into Fyaym. Most perished but some succeeded in founding new communities far from the Foam, so that the Foam actually caused an expansion of the borders of Syoom, while of course at the same time greatly weakening Syoom at its centre.

Luckily, no great Fyayman hostile power was wielded during the Lanthanum Era. This would have been the ideal period for the Quonians to invade, but they did not; perhaps they had troubles of their own; at any rate Syoom survived without being occupied by any mortal enemy.

It did not, however, survive unscathed. The long-term results of the Foam were grave. They must be examined in the next section of this survey; here we will describe the Foam's departure.

All bad things come to an end. After over a million days the lands's already brittle covering became still more brittle, dramatically so. This fact was discovered by accident at many locations simultaneously, when travellers poked at the stuff with poles or staffs and saw with amazement and increasing excitement that the material now turned to powder when touched.

A short era followed (Era 58, the Cerium, 123 days and 22 hours) during which most of the formerly buried cities were largely dug free, and great stretches of plain around them were cleared for planting, so that the people of Syoom began to recreate a landscape which had not been seen for a hundred generations.

Like a person who has been bed-ridden for a long time, and at last is told that nen is cured, impatiently throws off the bed-clothes and totters to nen's feet, so the people of Syoom could not wait for a new era. What little energy they had left, they largely dissipated in their frenzied efforts to dig their cities out of the crumbled Foam. While they did so, great surges of expectation washed through their weakened civilization. The greatest efforts of all were made to dig out Skyyon. The tallest city because of its unique, double-tiered, double-disked structure, Skyyon was also the one which had the largest volume of Foam to get rid of, as though its location at the centre of Syoom had attracted the stuff. The day came when the three *ayashou* around the upper rim – the airstream engines which provide entrance to and egress from a Uranian disk-on-stem city – were freed. Lines of skimmers could once more queue to float up and down the airstreams. That was the day when expectations were fulfilled. Inevitably, this stirred emotions to an extent that they triggered an *eomasp* and the start of a new era.

20: The Praesodymium Spotlight

The Foam was no more. Its powdery relic, strewn in dusty whiffs on city floor and plain, gradually evaporated or – when in contact with existing granules – reverted to gralm.

The legacy of the Foam, however, is still with us.

The Era of the Foam created perhaps the greatest divide in Uranian history since the robbery of Chelth or the defeat of Fiarr Fosn. But the full reason for this only gradually became apparent during the following era (the Fifty-Ninth).

This was the colossal Praesodymium Era: 23,493,050 U-days; 957 U-years, = 80,400 Earth years.

During this immense span of time, Syoom was, objectively speaking, a pale shadow of what it had been.

Physical reasons for the change are obvious enough. Syoom had been debilitated as never before or since. The Foam had left the land vastly less fertile. This meant diminished ell-light yields; it would be a long time before the familiar fields of glowing blue or golden *vheic* could once more symbolise Syoom. Praesodymium Era fields, smaller in extent than those of yore, glowed a dim orange. They were beautiful to look at but their type of beauty was a sign of great reduction in material wealth.

Yet in some ways the Praesodymium was an era of unparalleled splendour. To understand this apparent contradiction, we must face up to the knottiest task of a historian, as we attempt to distinguish between two types of people, or two types of life-story.

The distinction we are going to make is one which is bound to seem fantastically odd to Earth readers because (we presume) it does not exist on Earth, at any rate not outside of fiction, and even in fiction it has never been explicitly stated. Nor, as far as we know, did it exist on Ooranye either, before Era 59. So what, precisely, is this new divide?

We have our contrasts between rich and poor, between talented and untalented, good and bad, handsome and ugly, lucky and unlucky, famous and obscure. The Uranians from Era 59 onwards added another pair of opposites to this list. They became sortable into their own two distinctive categories, *the spot-lit and the non spot-lit.*

It is as though life is a film-script which favours some people with the status of major character, while leaving others with the lower status of "extra".

Ideally we would not say much about this strange phenomenon, other than to point out that any student of Uranian affairs becomes aware of it after a certain while, even though the Uranians themselves hardly ever mention it. It is felt rather than talked about. Easier to leave it at that. And wiser, too; for it is considered very bad form to raise the issue.

The trouble is, we need to address the immense philosophical and scientific questions which it raises. What, precisely, is going on? Are there really currents of fate? If so, can some people deliberately edge themselves into them, like skilled or foolhardy canoeists? Or are the answers to be found somewhere in the uncharted domain of "luck"?

If any Uranian knows, nen is not telling.

Whatever the answer, from Era 59 onwards the Uranians whom we know much of are all by definition "spot-lit". The others, the non spot-lit supporting cast, generally lead happy enough lives, contented to play their role as "extras" in history; or maybe they see it differently, for after all the soul's journey is what matters, "spotlight" or no.

During the long stretch of the Praesodymium Era, hundreds of millions of Uranians led lives reduced by poverty, to a degree unprecedented in history, yet, because of their "background" status, they did not suffer the discontent which might otherwise have tormented them into restless attempts to find other ways of living.

It is only fair to add that the account given above, the "realist" account, is disputed by many ooranologists. These "nominalists" maintain that it all merely amounts to a different manner of talking about life; a manner which needed to emerge in Era 59 as a way to explain why so many folk were content to remain humble. To assume that there is anything *real* in "spot-lit" versus "non spot-lit" is pure superstition, say these experts.

They go on to argue that, after all, in all ages there have been the ambitious, the charismatic, the famous few contrasted with the ordinary, obscure, contented many; all that happened in the Praesodymium Era was that the exploits of those famous few gave a greater degree of vicarious comfort than before, in the straightened conditions of that time. It is not surprising that fortune in such circumstances favours the bold and the lucky even more than it does in other eras.

To this view we may reply with a "perhaps". It may be significant to note that some regimes in this era went bad, and were sustained by what seems to us to be their exploitation of leaderless "backgrounders". Whether this favours the "realist" or the "nominalist" theory is a moot point.

66

We also cannot resist pointing out that the era ended with the first adventures of the person who, if there is anything in the term "spot-lit", must be ranked as one of the most spot-lit Nenns of all time: the man destined to be the first Sunnoad of Era 69 and the only person ever to be Sunnoad twice, in two different incarnations: Restiprak Zentonan 33337 / 45329.

21: The Prospectors

This is not the place to recount the well-known story of Restriprak Zentonan the mountaineer and of how he and his expedition tackled Mount Gnemek. We simply draw the reader's attention to the fact that it was not mere exploration for exploration's sake, but an attempt to settle what might be a political question or a question of Syoomean defence, since the rumour existed that the final spire of Mt Gnemek – the part that reached into space – was artificial. That was why the mountain's nature became linked with a recurrent theme in Ooranye's long history, namely the near-achievement of space-flight.

It is not surprising that the Uranians were nowhere near as swift as the Terrans to develop astronautics. Ooranye is vast enough to seem almost a universe in itself, more than adequate to satisfy the urge for the 'beyond'. Yet even with such a huge world to explore, and a relatively sparse population, whose efforts had to be devoted largely to survival, occasionally the idea of travel off-world came to haunt Syoomean civilization. In particular, there was the fear that if one power achieved orbital flight, it might use artificial satellite stations to dominate the world.

Zentonan used this argument to obtain support for his expedition.

Millions of his followers, knowing who he was, piled their expectations on him, so that the extraordinary happenings on his journey punctuated history with a crackle of *eomasps* causing a rapid succession of no fewer than nine small eras, each of which contributed epically: the Neodymium (1 hour 20 minutes), broadcasting the aim of the voyage; the Promethium (4 days 29 minutes), a struggle of indecisions; the Samarium (1 day 3 hours 47 minutes), finding the way forward; the Europium (2 hours 57 minutes), the capture of Zentonan by tyrants who sought control of the *eomasp* phenomenon; the Gadolinium (13 minutes), his escape; the Terbium (25 days 19 hours), wandering in underground country; the Dysprosium (1 day 21 hours 51 minutes), the battle in the caves; the Holmium (56 days), his ascent of the mountain; and the Erbium (2 days 1 hour), his long glide down.

After all this it was not surprising that Zentonan was asked to fill the vacancy in the sunnoadex, which had arisen just before the end of Era 59.

The success of his expedition gave a huge impetus to other voyages among the mountain ranges of both Syoom and Fyaym. This is what led the Thulium

Era (Era 69: length, 14,025,686 U-days, or 571 U-years, = 48,000 Earth years) to become the golden age of prospecting.

Ell-light deposits in concentrated, crystalline form – far more valuable per unit weight than the stuff extracted agriculturally from *vheic* – fed wealth back into Syoom. In a few lifetimes, economic conditions had recovered to the level that Syoomeans had enjoyed before the Foam.

And so the long Uranian years, each a goodly lifetime, rolled on in their hundreds, accumulating into another of the great eras of Ooranye. We tend immediately to think "prospectors" when we hear mention of the Thulium Era, but of course this period contained an enormous wealth of other distinctive features, none of which we have space here to describe. However it *is* the theme of prospecting which connects this age to the next wrenching event in Uranian humanity's story.

22: The 'Dassan Call

The Brown Smoke

Hovering like a Terrestrial eagle or a Uranian *eopc* over the landscape of Syoom, in what turned out to be the last days of the Thulium Era, we might have discerned murky caterpillar-shapes, fuzzy in outline, squirming across the plains. In doing so we would have witnessed one of the many phenomena grouped by historians under the title, "The Brown Smoke".

Sooner or later it was bound to happen that the various non-human powers in Fyaym, in one of their periodic awakenings, should resent the incursions of the prospectors who had become ever bolder throughout the Thulium Era. The first serious attack of the "smoke" was aimed at Vyanth, the largest city of Syoom. The attack was beaten off, but the shock of that day triggered an *eomasp* which ushered in the 144 days, 13 hours of the Ytterbium Era – a time of disaster and of rescue.

The Lutetium Era

When a defence was invented against the Smoke – a device which reduced it to a shrinking bubbly patch of slime – the relief which this brought triggered yet another *eomasp*, which brought on the Lutetium Era.

Era 71 lasted 34,964 of the 30-hour Uranian days, plus 24 hours. This is equivalent to 119 and two-thirds Earth years – hardly longer than a single lifetime. Like the Nitrogen Era, it is thus one of the so-called "minor" eras with a historical importance out of proportion to its length.

It is in this period that the colloquial phrase "I am laying my life on the line" became – in the Nouuan tongue – compressed into a single long notorious word, *kommassandassan*.

It is a word spoken aloud only in very special situations, by someone so keen to alter a plan that nen is willing to risk nen's life in order to interrupt proceedings. This is because custom – dating from Era 71 – has decreed that *kommassandassan* is a word of such power, that not only must it not be spoken in vain, but also it cannot be ignored, on pain of death in either case.

So if you feel that something must be stopped, you can cry 'dassan, and you will be heard; but if you are proved wrong in your reasons, or if you cannot convince, then you die. On the other hand if you are ignored but then turn out to have been right, then those who ignored you will die, no matter who they are.

The first time the 'dassan call was used, was at a muster of airships preparing to invade Fyaym on an expedition in retaliation for the Brown Smoke. A young officer, Gyan Ennye of Jaax, burst into the flagship control room and interrupted a meeting of the captains. Threatening them and the ship's mechanisms with his laser, he at the same time pleaded so impressively for the mission to be called off, that they hesitated, and when he uttered the phrase, "I lay my life on the line", they were sufficiently convinced that they postponed the fleet's departure while they investigated his arguments.

As we all know, Gyan Ennye turned out to be right – the fleet would have been annihilated had it proceeded. The incident was never forgotten. It set the precedent for other occasions on which desperate individuals felt they had to halt some mighty process which would lead to disaster. What the institution of Corrector had done for the sunnoadex, the 'dassan call did for large movements in general.

However, on that first occasion near the beginning of Era 71, custom had not yet established the procedure of the Call in the form it has taken since then. Gyan Ennye had to wait long for vindication, even though his immediate warning was soon proved justified. The problem was, he had used violence, in order to get into the control room and to force the captains to listen to him.

He was court-martialled. The verdict was a strange one. Gross insubordination had occurred, and could not be denied. Yet after hundreds of precedents had been cited, dating from naval trials throughout the planet's history, in the end the accused offered an unexpected deal, which his prosecutors decided to accept.

Simulation

Gyan Ennye was a member of the Dfangexcarj – the Simulator Project. This was a corporation recently formed to cultivate a machine (we would call it a giant semi-organic computer) that might aid in decision-making. Now it was agreed as part of the deal that the Simulator should be brought to bear on the question, "Should Syoom seek to punish the powers of Fyaym for the attack by the Brown Smoke?"

Hordes of wayfarers were sent out and data gathered as never before. The help of the Ghepions was sought and obtained. (They were all the more willing to help because they saw the Dfangexcarj as being potentially one of

71

themselves.) Much opposition, however, was roused against the Project, for example among those who believed that successful Simulation would lead to too much certainty: thence a form of tyranny, and/or people becoming "soft". But during the race against time to justify Gyan Ennye's 'dassan call, a number of coups by Project supporters ensured that political support was kept alive. A sufficient quantity of intermediate predictions and simulations, some involving a certain amount of deceit, whetted the popular appetite for security in an uncertain age.

In the end, just as the agreed deadline was imminent, a particularly successful simulation was run. It completely vindicated Gyan Ennye's advice. Verdict: Syoom ought to have a defence policy which really *was* defensive. It should not allow itself to get tempted into large-scale attacks on Fyaym; instead, reliance should be placed on mechanical prediction.

To the astonishment of many, Gyan Ennye himself seemed not quite happy with this conclusion. He wondered aloud whether it might be best to dismantle the Simulator! But he did not press the point; he became rather quiet, and embarked upon a subdued, low-profile existence.

Perhaps he was reassured by the fact that the great machine was allowed to fall into disuse, largely because of the difficulty and expense of keeping its expert system up to date.

The whole episode receded from people's immediate concerns. Then, as if on cue, more trouble, more incursions from Fyaym, darkened the horizons and reminded people of how convenient a decider the Simulator had been. The last third of Era 71, therefore, saw a renewed interest in the process. Simulations, for purposes of disaster prediction as well as for aid in decision-making, became more popular than ever. Gyan Ennye was no longer alive by this time, but his success was very much in people's minds. More 'dassan-calls were made and vindicated. Public opinion compelled the authorities to switch the original Simulator back on and to build others.

Finally the two ideas – Simulation and *kommassandassan* – came together when a Skyyonian Simulator, in the presence of the Sunnoad, proved by running two scenarios, one with and one without the institution of the 'dassan call, that the latter should be kept and codified as part of the culture.

On the same day, the same machine was used to recommend that all large-scale prospecting for crystals in Fyaym should stop. If that were to happen, Syoom must make up for the resource-lack by increased intelligence. The Simulators predicted who could supply this need:

Themselves.

The decision was left to the Sunnoad, Dynnt Gilvar 48559, who stood at a forking-point in history. His decision would establish which path Nennkind would follow for hundreds of lifetimes to come.

He chose to follow the Simulator's advice. The news spread. Awareness of the implications spread, and a wave of emotion swept across Syoom.

Within hours it gathered sufficient force to cause an *eomasp* and the beginning of a new era.

23: The Age of the Wise

The Hafnium Era (Era 72) lasted 21,704,833 Uranian days; this amounted to 884 Uranian years, equivalent to 74,280 Earth years.

As usual with Uranian history, faced with such a stupendous span of time we have to accept that our account will be sketchy and inadequate to a degree that is never necessary for Terran narrative. So we might as well frame our account around the cliché that this was "the Age of the Wise" – and then quote the well-known cynical comment, "yes, it needed to be".

During the previous great era, the Thulium, Syoom had grown dependent upon an increased supply of natural resources, obtained from the Fyayman wilderness. This had provoked retaliation by Fyayman powers which then threatened Syoom itself. The choice which Syoom then faced, was: fight or withdraw. By opting for caution (arguably the wiser decision in view of the results of the first 'dassan call and the first Simulation), Syoom had committed itself to a huge change of policy and a huge reorganization. The techniques of Simulation were vital to the success of this undertaking.

At first, the results were indisputably good. Political and economic strategies, helped along as never before by scientific proof not only of how the various options and outcomes must match but also of the consequences that would ensue from *not* following the plan in question, led to a relatively peaceful and prosperous golden age. Nor did the long peace cause Syoom to forget how to fight. The simulators took into account the need for defensive combat against occasional waves of attack from Fyaym, and were fairly good at warning when these attacks would come. And there were always **vrars** and outlaws and various other perils to keep navies and individual wayfarers in the practice of adventure.

However, as the days rolled on in their millions, Simulation gradually inserted itself into other aspects of life. Simulators became cheaper and more powerful until many were owned by well-off individuals. Curiously, from this grew the sense that were *no* irrevocable decisions. The idea was, that every option must have been taken and followed in some probability dimension. It became common for people to re-run a simulation shortly after having retracted a decision based on a previous one, and to play around endlessly with the changed data, so that it became harder to commit to anything. The "retakes and rewinds of life" became first a topic for jokes, then a notorious and inescapable theme of the era. Graver still, Simulation became part of the justice system. (There was a formal justice system in this era, one of the few such periods in Uranian history.) "Counterfactuals" became accepted as evidence during trials. Ultimately the system was almost brought to a standstill as ingenious Simulation showed that just about anyone, given the conditions, was a would-be murderer. Conclusion: no court had the moral right to condemn anyone.

Another social phenomenon which probably resulted from the widespread practice of Simulation was a certain stilted formality, a stiffness and a reserve, unusual by the standards of Ooranye. It has been plausibly argued that this arose from a need to preserve one's dignity and autonomy in the face of humiliating self-knowledge, given the probability-lines or potentials of one's life – the knowledge of what one might have been or done.

What in the end saved Syoom from Simulation was Simulation itself.

The most advanced machine, evolved at last into a conscious Ghepion, predicted its own misuse, and advised that Nennkind abandon the practice. This turned the tide of opinion, after enough people understood the truth of the message. One by one the Simulators of Syoom were taken over and switched off – all except the conscious one, the Ghepion, who had advised the shut-down.

Even before the process was finished, it reached its tipping-point – duly predicted – and the resulting *eomasp* brought the era to a close.

24: Holding the Line

The student of Uranian history is bound to notice, at an early stage in nen's perusal of the timeline, that the eras can be grouped into two main categories: the very short, ranging from minutes to an Earth century or two, and the very long, ranging upwards from ten thousand Earth years. (There are three exceptions, eras of intermediate length, a few thousand Earth years, namely Eras 54, 57 and 77.)

Next, the student may notice, when examining the sequence of eras, that it is unusual in Uranian history for two of the long ones to follow directly on from one another without any short era or eras in between. This is because the major transitions, instead of being clean breaks, often consist of a volley of crises, which are apt to cause more than one world-quivering *eomasp* in quick succession.

But Eras 72, 73 and 74 are exceptions to this pattern. Each was very long (60,000 Earth years or more), and they occurred one after the other with no intervening short eras.

It is not difficult to explain the smoothness of the transition from 72 to 73. It was deliberately managed. The mighty brain of the last of the Simulators made sure things flowed smoothly over the threshold between the Hafnium and Tantalum Eras. Afterwards, the great Ghepion lived on, quietly, reclusively, having announced that it would take no further part in human affairs.

Our account has now reached Era 73. The Tantalum Era lasted 17,532,219 Uranian days, 714 Uranian years, equivalent to 60,000 Earth years. By Uranian standards, though not by Earth's, it was a decadent era. It lived off the moral capital of the past without adding to it. In the main it was not degenerate, but neither was it heroic. This is most unusual for Ooranye.

These statements must (of course) be qualified. A relatively few individuals *were* heroic. They "kept the world turning" by their own standards of humour, courage and public service, as well as by flashes of personal genius. But they had to do so while operating within a culture of cynicism and of lack of confidence in its own values.

It is no accident that this is the era in which most of the lawyers and police in Uranian history have lived. Most other periods have had no such close equivalents to these typically Terrestrial phenomena.

Two of the era's most famous characters were: a great detective, named after the legendary twice-Sunnoad, Restiprak Zentonan (another sign of decadence: in no other era were people "named after" anyone), and his opponent, the un-named criminal mastermind known simply as the Grardesh Sponndar. Adventure is something that no Uranian era – decadent or not – has ever lacked.

It is perhaps no coincidence that the sunnoadex dwindled into a largely ceremonial institution for much of this period. Most of the Sunnoads of Era 73 were figureheads rather than foci of events.

25: The Kalyars

On a few spooky occasions, the people of Syoom have known that an era has ended without knowing why. That is how it happened at the end of the Tantalum Era and the beginning of the Tungsten.

Although it had been several hundred lifetimes since the last *eomasp*, there were some historically-minded people who knew what it signified when the day's rhythm faltered. The day in question was a mere couple of hours longer than usual, but the event could not be ignored by anyone brave enough to face the truth. So instead of dating it 17,532,220 Ta, these people realized that in reality there was no 17,532,220 Ta. Rather, it was 1,W.

Awareness of the change did not spread as fast as such news usually did. For many days innumerable documents continued to be dated 17,532,221 Ta, 17,532,222 Ta and so on. After all, if nothing big seemed to have happened, why begin the count of days anew? Eventually, however, the believers in Era 74 won out.

This was due partly to their persistence, partly to the scientific fact of the *eomasp*, and partly to the increasing rumours that something big *had* happened after all.

Uranian scientists still argue about *how* it happened. Was it a rare instance of the aerial micro-organisms being affected, not by a wave of intense emotion, but by a different disturbance? Or was the emotion present, but concentrated and hidden among the few **kalyars** to reach awareness of their condition on 1,W?

For the age of the **kalyar** – the evolved man – had dawned.

Era 74, the Tungsten Era, lasted 18,934,797 Uranian days, or 771 Uranian years, equivalent to 64,800 Earth years. It was a long-drawn-out reckoning for the flaccid culture inherited from the Tantalum Era. Mankind found that its unity was disintegrating into several species. One of these was a continuation of the Nenns – ordinary Uranian humanity. The others were called, generically, **kalyars**, but each referred to themselves by different names. It was an age of confusion. The land of Syoom became a melting-pot.

Towards the end of the era, during its last two or three million days, a mighty process of Syoomean regeneration began, and at the core of this process was the gradual restoration of the vitality of the sunnoadex. The Sunnoad, Syoom's chief citizen and living symbol, became once more its active focus, its recourse in times of crisis. Parallel with this process was a movement of population. The Nenns of Syoom, sifting themselves out of the mass of different kalyar species, migrated together to dominate a smaller, tighter Syoom. The borders of the kalyar societies which were left around the edges of this area gradually took on greater definition.

A crisis brewed, and war threatened, between the central Nenn area and the kalyar periphery. Complex issues were involved. A revival of one of the teleological guilds of the Zirconium Era conducted research into the planetary id; the result suggested that the Nenns were privileged with regard to destiny, and that they, and not any one of the kalyar species, must carry the principal torch of human civilization down through the ages. The guild's research team had included kalyars as well as Nenns, and could not be accused of species bias; but for many its conclusions were understandably hard to accept. If kalyars were so peripheral to destiny, why had they evolved? In answer to this, it was suggested that perhaps they and not the Nenns were the key to the future, but only the very far future – the next Great Cycle, in fact. In which case, they should wait and be content and learn what they could while waiting for thousands of millions of days, till all 92 Nenn eras were over and *their* hour came.

Not many kalyars were prepared to accept that their species would have to wait that long for a major role in history.

26: The Rhenium Moment

The scene: the Hall of Zdinth at the Noad's Palace at Skyyon, Sunward Polar City of Ooranye. At the high table, men and women in various national and species costume. Some in bodily appearance were identical to the humans who would evolve much later on Earth and become the readers of this account; others were furred, scaled or crested **kalyars**.

It was an international conference, one of many such, but this one would prove to be unique. The expectation was widespread, that if this meeting did not succeed in the establishment of agreed territorial spheres of influence and the resolution of political differences between the species, Syoom would finally erupt in an inter-species war. But the air must also have been heavy with less definable psychic pressures.

What happened was that for five hours the conference, and to a lesser extent the whole world, was gripped by a transcendent experience. In a sense we really know nothing about it, but in another sense we know enough. The planet Ooranye harbours something analogous to a world-spirit, a living thing, or an entity which can be likened to a living thing. Very occasionally it intervenes in history. It does so for reasons we can only guess at; this was one of those occasions. It spoke into people's minds, employing their inner voices, but its message, necessarily unrecorded, and unreliably remembered, can only be deduced from the aftermath.

The impact of the five-hour Rhenium Moment was such, that even the *eomasps* with which it began and ended were hardly noticed while they occurred. Only afterwards was it realized that during those five hours an era had come and gone.

27: The Great Triangle

The mighty Osmium Era – the Seventy-Sixth – lasted 22,090,596 Uranian days, which is exactly 900 Uranian years, equivalent to 75,600 Earth years.

It took this length of time to sort out the implications of the preceding 5 hours.

That is not to say that the people of the Osmium Era spent their days pondering the Rhenium Moment. Far from it; for the vast majority of their days they had their minds on other things. This great Era 76 comes the closest to providing stories analogous to the Cold-War "thrillers" of Earth's history. The details are vastly different but the mood (to a Terran scholar) can be reminiscent. Syoom was divided into sharply defined, competing power-blocks. In addition there was renewed contact with the empire of the Quonians which lay outside the main part of Syoom. Espionage abounded, together with crises, destructive weapons, large military organizations... The entire period pulsed with tension and vigour.

The underlying reason for these trends lay in that brief five-hour "voice" uttered by the world-spirit. The Rhenium Era echoed on, deep in people's souls, gradually convincing them of a truth which many of them did not wish to hear.

The voice had confirmed that the destiny of the kalyars was to flourish not in this Great Cycle but in the next one, in the unimaginably distant future. Their current efflorescence was a mere foretaste, and in some respects a false start. They ought to retire from centre stage for the time being, leaving the present to the Nenns, and reserving the far future for themselves.

It was a compliment to them, in a way, but one which ambitious evolved men naturally found hard to accept. Yet as their numbers gradually declined, as they began to show signs of a kind of cultural recession or hibernation, as many of them reverted to tribalism and diffused into the wilderness, the truth nagged at the ones who remained powerful. Many were determined to resist the message of the Rhenium Moment. The kalyar power-blocks took a long time to die. They were dangerous while they were dying.

The most successful of them began increasingly to recruit Nenns to make up their numbers: people who, though ordinary humans in a biological sense, had for some reason developed a wish or a need to abandon their native cultures; dissidents, outlaws, rootless wanderers, ambitious skilled people

81

attracted by offers from kalyar states... By the end of the era, the formerly kalyar states had become almost entirely Nenn, but with their own traditions, different from those of the core of Syoom.

The most famous alliance of this period was between three Nenn city states: Ao, Vyanth and Skyyon. These three great powers remained independent of each other but formed a close association to patrol the lands between them. The association and the lands became known loosely by the politico-geographical expression The Great Triangle. It brought an unusual degree of peace and security to a section of Syoom about fifteen million square miles in area.

Osmium Era thinkers meanwhile turned their attention to questions of loyalty and identity, of how to treat allies and enemies, of shades of moral obligation. Brainwashing and other evil state actions were not unknown. Economics also flourished as a discipline, to an unusual extent compared with the rest of Uranian history; ell-light Gross National Product figures were published amid rivalry.

In the midst of this era occurred the first lifetime of the legendary secret agent, Taldis Norkoten, whose adventures, together with those of his sidekick Sialend Baplegn, form the basis of innumerable tales, some true, some partly true and others which ought to be true. Norkoten eventually became the 64,702nd Sunnoad. He insisted on retiring after a thousand-day reign, during which he tried to institute a permanent supranational Sunnoad's Navy to keep the peace.

Taldis Norkoten 64702 succeeded in helping Syoom over a dangerous patch during his lifetime, but his achievement was purely personal, and did not outlast him. His people mourned his loss but did not take his advice. The most they did was to rename Zdinth Hall, the focus of the Rhenium Moment, as Norkoten Hall – one of the rare instances of renaming in Uranian history.

The Osmium Era, to sum up, was a thrilling epic, with a tincture of reflection. It was almost as mighty as the Phosphorus Era in terms of forces unleashed, though without its aura of myth; almost as rich in personal derring-do as the Vanadium Era, though nowhere near as fresh and simple-minded. What was unique about the Osmium Era was its adrenalin-powered "rat-race" of competing powers, glitteringly ambitious and insecure.

The force which brought it to a close came from a reform movement dedicated to the memory of a long-dead Sunnoad.

This movement began quietly, with an organization of academic historians, united by their common interest in the career of Taldis Norkoten 64702. After a while the scope of this group expanded. It began to attract the attention of practical Nenns who wished to resurrect the ideals of that revered yet insufficiently supported leader. People sensed that there had been something special about him, even in comparison with his illustrious predecessors. Eventually the membership of the Norkoten Society included many active political figures in many of the lands of Syoom, and finally some of them seized the opportunity which a crisis offered, to persuade the current Sunnoad and the Noads of the more powerful cities to put Norkoten's ideals into effect by the establishment of a Sunnoad's Navy drawn from all the national navies of Syoom.

Amid pan-Syoomean rejoicing, and the increasing expectation that from all this excitement there would surely spring an *eomasp*, an *eomasp* of course occurred.

28: The Sunnoad's Navy

The Iridium Era lasted 2,103,867 Uranian days – just 85 Uranian years, equivalent to 7,200 Earth years. It is regarded as the golden age of the Sunnoad's Navy. Though there have been many institutions in Ooranye's long history which have borne that name or something close to it, *the* Sunnoad's Navy is taken to mean the one which patrolled the skies and kept the peace in Era 77. Its record was glorious, its personnel – especially the trouble-shooting "marksmen" who anticipated crises – unusually competent (and perhaps lucky). The result was a matchless *esprit de corps*.

Only towards the end did they become victims of their own success. Partially they succumbed to the danger of hubris inherent in an elite organization. None but the exceptionally able and talented were admitted to the Navy; aptitude stoked ambition and in the end there was no one to apply the brakes. Meanwhile, another *eomasp* occurred, when, ostensibly, no great event had taken place. Syoom had been through this before, and the people knew that the day's rhythm never faltered without some deep reason. The Navy professed a determination to find the cause.

The Platinum Era lasted 49,993 days and 6 hours. This was little more than a mere 2 Uranian years; 171 Earth years. It ended in a crisis which was at once the shame and the glory of the Navy. Knowledge had been gradually spreading – appalling knowledge that had to be kept secret until the right time to act – knowledge of the reason for the *eomasp* which had ushered in Era 78. It was that the Navy's high command, and hence Syoom, were being taken over and infiltrated by Ghepions of a kind hitherto not seen, Ghepions *in human form.*

Those officers in the know were faced with the question of how to act without causing the Navy's terrible weapons to be unleashed on the people of Syoom. It occurred to one officer, Spe Dalalt, that if a Ghepion could impersonate a human, a human could just as well impersonate a Ghepion. An epic counter-deception was planned. Spe Dalalt and his team undertook the hazards of a journey to the secret headquarters of the Ghepion plot.

The successful exploit of Spe Dalalt restored the integrity of the Navy, but its honour was felt to have been irrevocably tarnished. Its own leaders now regarded it as too dangerous to be kept in being, in its present intensely elite form. Yet some institutional ideal was vital to Syoom. How could confidence be restored?

By what seemed at first to be a fortunate coincidence, Dalalt's expedition had uncovered an amazing rumour, which might furnish an answer to the problem. After a series of secret conferences, it was agreed to release a double dose of information to the public:

First came the details of the Ghepion plot and the way in which it had been foiled. Second, the announcement of the possible real existence of... a land named Solor.

The information was released early in the morning of 49,994 Pt. Six hours into that day, an *eomasp* occurred.

29: The Quest for Solor

The captive Ghepion plotters, under hypnotic interrogation, made an extraordinary confession of their motives. It seemed that they had been moved, at least in part, by a "desire to have a soul".

The questioners were baffled. Surely, they thought, the Ghepions must understand that any sentient being necessarily has a soul – defined as the entity's qualitative aspect. Since qualia cannot be derived from quanta, or, to put it less technically, qualities from physical nature, the soul must be transcendent. Surely the Ghepions must know that their material circuits were no more a denial of "soul" than the equally material veins and bones of a man. What were they worried about?

No one knew. No one could find out why these particular Ghepions, and no others, had harboured these fears of being soulless. But whatever the reason for their mental misfortune, it turned out to Syoom's advantage. For these Ghepions, in their search for reassurance, besides trying to control Syoom through the Navy, had discovered a clue which suggested that the myth of Solor – a place in legend, in some ways equivalent to the Terrans' Eden – might not be a mere myth after all.

According to tradition, Solor was a glowing, numinous land which conferred bliss on those who found it. Amazingly, some of the Ghepion plotters had wanted control of the Navy for no other reason than that they regarded it as essential to the task of locating this land, and of controlling access to it.

Now that the plot was foiled, and humans were back in control, the question remained: what to do with the knowledge of the reality of Solor? It was decided that the value of such a place could only be preserved if it remained a hope, an ideal which might be accessible to those willing to devote their lives to a quest for it; certainly not a pleasure park overrun by the merely curious.

Thus the Sunnoad and his advisers rejected the idea of a Syoomean campaign to locate Solor. To send out dozens of airships into Fyaym to search back and forth for the land of bliss would not only be dangerous and expensive; it would also be a crude vulgarity, and success would carry with it the great danger of annihilating the object of the search – a search which ought to be left to individuals.

The Gold Era lasted 9,066,758 Uranian days, or 369 Uranian years, equivalent to 31,029 Earth years. It was by and large a sane, healthy era. It did have some occasional quirks, arising from its distinct philosophical bent (for example, some states declared that the killing of a determinist could not be regarded as murder, since according to the victim the killer could not be blamed). Syoom had become a culture which took philosophy more seriously than ever before. This was hardly surprising, since questions of identity and purpose and meaning were brought to the forefront of debate by the quest for Solor.

However, the main feature of the era was the great number of physical adventures which have contributed to the Uranian saga. These almost all involved the Quest; thousands of stories of individuals in search of the land of the blessed.

A few did find it and returned to tell the tale, but were unwilling or unable to say where it was. After many lifetimes the truth was made public, that Solor was not in Fyaym after all, but actually in Syoom.

It had remained free from discovery for so long because it was a realm possessed of the power to curve space around it. On a much smaller scale this space-distorting power had been known for ages, as a defensive weapon, rare and expensive to use. No one had ever previously heard of an entire region of Syoom being rendered incognito by such a device.

The few who succeeded in their quest for Solor possessed either exceptional qualities or exceptional luck, to get round the invisible barrier of curved space. A time came, however, when Solor was thoroughly "bracketed", curved space or not. An impatient generation of Syoomeans arose, no longer willing to respect the isolation of the magical realm. An expedition was mounted to break the barrier... and did so – to find Solor gone.

It had been there, but it was gone. Those few who had seen it before, confirmed that the surrounding topography was the same, but no blessed land existed in its midst any more.

The anger and sorrow which followed brought in their train an *eomasp*.

30: The Cyborgs

Many of those who had not agreed with the idea of the expedition, and some of those who had repented of it, were determined to punish those responsible. Agitation led to a discovery which aroused indignation and fear still further: the "loss of Solor" had been perpetrated by beings who were not fully human.

A variant on the theme with which the Gold Era had begun – that those who thought themselves without souls, thirsted after them – returned to haunt the era's end. This time, however, the culprits were not mere Ghepions masquerading in man-shape. They were real hybrids. Man/machine dualities, plotting for the supremacy to which they thought themselves entitled.

And this time it was a case of plotters being properly ready. Instead of allowing themselves to be prosecuted, the Cyborgs revealed their true strength.

Accumulated unseen during the Gold Era, their power now virtually took over Syoom. They seized strong points in what was left of the Sunnoad's Navy and in all of the major cities except Vyanth and Pjourth. The rule of the Cyborgs began. It was a rule of despair, for all they really wanted was Solor, which they regarded as the key to the possession of souls; and Solor was gone.

The Mercury or Quicksilver Era, the 80th era, lasted just 7,342 Uranian days; equivalent to 25 Earth years. No doubt the Cyborgs' rule was unstable and would in any case have ended before many Uranian years had passed, but the fact that it was *so* short as to last not even a third of a Uranian year, was due to the emergence of the first great mind-reader among the Nenns.

Hevad Notoxt was a formidable woman of great natural authority, razor-sharp wits and cunning, in addition to the further talent which she hid at first. She succeeded in overthrowing the Cyborgs by splitting them into two camps, winning some of them over by showing them that they must already have souls, and using them as allies to defeat the other camp, that of the irreconcilable pessimists.

She could do all this because she was a telepath, and in a more general sense a psi, able not only to read minds but to operate on moods, encouraging co-operation. A highly dangerous and ambitious woman, she left a record in her "Confessions" of the efforts she had to make to repress the dark side of her character, and she convincingly revealed that her reluctance to accept high office was not feigned. After much hesitation and refusal, she became the 69,546th Sunnoad, and the second most famous female Sunnoad after Hyala Movoun 1.

31: The Era of Psi

Consequences of the reign of Hevad Notoxt

Hevad Notoxt 69546 began her reign with great advantages. The *eomasp* which attended her victory over the Cyborgs had propelled the world into a new era which, with her special talents, she helped to define.

Two of her actions continued to shape it.

Firstly, she soon added to her fame and prestige by discovering that Solor had not disappeared permanently after all; it was still accessible to a few, if the mysterious Intelligence that guarded it was approached in a correctly humble manner. The Sunnoad discovered that, in the past, attention had been deflected from Solor not only by a space-distorter but also by psi powers latent in that land – powers which, to a small extent, had been released into Syoom every time someone did succeed in finding Solor. Those powers were now leaking out at a much faster rate; the Cyborgs' harmful expedition must have punctured some mental reservoir. Indeed the Thallium Era (Era 81; 19,278,102 days or 785 Uranian years, equivalent to 65,975 Earth years) became known as the Era of Psis.

Secondly, and more controversially, she initiated an inquiry into Ghepion support for the Cyborgs. The Ghepions, by this time, were once again widely distrusted; it had become certain that some of them were implicated in the development of the Cyborgs, though this does not mean that they were a party to the Cyborgs' plot. Anyhow, seeds of further suspicion were sown as leading Ghepions – those that were mobile in form – were pulled in for questioning.

It would be a mistake to regard the Thallium Era as one of unrelieved bigotry and persecution of Ghepions by humans. A certain tradition of tolerance never quite died out, thanks to the forbearance and understanding shown by certain individuals. But many of the Ghepions do seem to have accepted the evil role attributed to them, saying, in effect, "very well, we are reputed to be the enemies of Nennkind; so shall we be." Some of them became monsters, whose downfall we can cheer as we read of the exploits of Thallium Era psi agents.

Quite apart from the Nenn-Ghepion problem, a lot of good and harm was done during Era 81 by the powers of psi. Discoveries were made, the implications of which still have to be worked out; it is likely that the experiences of the Thallium Era will prove to be an essential part of the collective memory of mankind, maybe not only Uranian but also Terran mankind.

Solor fades from history

We can only guess, but having sifted through many accounts, we prefer the following explanation as to why quests for the Numinous Land have virtually ceased ever since the early days of the Thallium Era.

Most of Solor's psi powers had leaked away into Syoom, and its space-distorting defence had been damaged. It had to come up with a new way of concealing itself. The method it found was more effective than either of the others. It was – disbelief.

You might believe in Solor and think about going to look for it, but if you actually set out, your opinion would change. The remaining trickle of psi which the Intelligence still can wield, would be used to erase your belief. You would abandon the search.

Perhaps if a sufficiently large number of questers decided to set out simultaneously, they might overwhelm this defence. But one's search for Solor is a personal thing. It does not lend itself to organized action. The one occasion on which it did, does not furnish a good precedent – as we have seen.

The crisis of psi

The last 3,000,000 or so days of the Thallium Era were days of darkening fortune for Syoom, redeemed, as ever, by acts of statesmanship and heroism – the outstanding imagination and integrity of a few.

Trouble came from various quarters. Some psis tried with more success than before to use their talents to exploit the mass of humanity. Danger also grew from Fyayman powers who took opportunities inherent in a disturbed age to meddle in the affairs of Syoom. Shelves of books could be written (and have been) about the complex adventures of this period.

The most frightening development was an invention of Fyayman origin whereby one's own psi talent could be turned into a "fifth column" by an enemy, and used against oneself in nightmare manner.

Reluctantly, the authorities of Syoom – most of the leading men and women being themselves psis by this time – inched towards the conclusion that the only way out of this mess was to abandon (somehow) psi itself.

They could not bear to sacrifice their talent by means of brain surgery, but could there not be some way, other than mental amputation, to disburden themselves of psi without wasting it; perhaps sublimate it into something else?

A psi-sensitive, Capfaym Duuv, was chosen to attempt the awesome feat of communing with the world-spirit.

For this almost god-like planetary intelligence – unheard since the Rhenium Moment – was, after much debate, seen as the only possible recourse in a matter so grave and deep-rooted in human nature.

How it was done, and at what cost, we will not go into here. Suffice it to say that Capfaym Duuv succeeded in obtaining the advice of the Intelligence.

The instruction was: "Drain your powers into the race-sink; funnel them into the collective id." Whatever this meant, it sounded better than pure loss. The problem was, to summon the courage to do it. Capfaym Duuv urged the leaders of Syoom to set an example. He asked them to put themselves into the trance-state in which he was empowered to do to them the necessary... but most of them hesitated.

The Draining

Capfaym Duuv went ahead with those few who would co-operate. On the evening of 19,278,102 Tl, when some of these people came out of their trances, they performed an action which tipped the scales.

Previously these people had vehemently denied involvement in a recent and nasty persecution of Ghepions. Now, shorn of their psi powers, they confessed. The Sunnoad, who was present, and other notables of Syoom were shocked and impressed. Here was evidence that psi talents could sometimes work against truth while the lack of them could promote it.

Events accelerated. The Sunnoad himself ordered Capfaym to give him the anti-psi treatment. The news spread out of control. Before midnight it had been relayed across Syoom and touched a chord in so many hearts that an *eomasp* occurred, accompanying the de-psi treatment of most of the remaining former resisters in high officialdom, and the draining of their powers into a "race-sink" which, the world spirit had assured Capfaym, meant that they were not wasted, were instead transformed into something else.

The Drainage took on a momentum of its own. Capfaym's efforts were no longer necessary. Psis all over the world found their abilities tugged at as if they were being sucked into a whirlpool. In forty minutes it was all over.

Those forty minutes were Era 82, the Lead Era.

32: The Mascon Expeditions

What the people of Syoom desperately needed now was a cheerful, extrovert era. And this is what they got: a healthy time of exploration and zestful life – with the added, unexpected good fortune of a new frontier to explore.

Era 83, the Bismuth Era, lasted 13,324,486 Uranian days or 542 Uranian years, equivalent to 45,600 Earth years. From the word go it was widely agreed that Syoom ought to look in some new direction, to recover its mental poise after the stresses of psi.

Of course Fyaym provided an endless challenge, an infinitely varied challenge, as always. But – partly because of the forces roused by the crisis itself – Fyaym just then was too dismally dark and spiritually perilous to attract a people still reeling from the loss of a powerful talent. During the early part of this period, therefore, adventurers into Fyaym were unusually few.

The people who now were most looked up to as potential saviours were the inventors, scientists and researchers who might be able to provide the romance and the solace of discovery, now that the glow of psi-communion was gone. The lone genius inventor type, in particular, became one of the key heroes of this age. And one of them did succeed in perfecting what came to be the symbol of the Bismuth Era – the vehicle known as the *tetrak*.

This was a mechanical mole, shaped somewhat like the one used to discover Pellucidar in E.R.Burroughs' tales, but properly steerable, and no mere digger: rather, like the probe *Lambda One* in the Colin Kapp story of that name, it phased into a vibrational mode which allowed it to interpenetrate the molecules of normal matter, and move like a ghost through solid rock and ice.

The *tetrak* was used during the Bismuth Era to explore the mascon worlds in the crust of Ooranye. The number of expeditions was limited – the authorities did not wish to disturb the planetary equilibrium – but these amazing adventures acted as an inspiration for others on the surface of Ooranye. All in all, the Bismuth was one of the most splendid eras. And it did not decline, it ended abruptly with a piece of monumental villainy.

33: Impostor

Fozdak's Opportunity

The crime which troubled nearly four million days of history, and altered some of the customs of the sunnoadex for evermore, was allowed to happen by a striking coincidence of misfortunes.

Fyayman powers, encouraged by Syoom's absorption in the mascon expeditions, and perturbed by Syoom's capacity to mount those expeditions, had prepared an attack.

Society being healthy, and crime levels low, security was lax around the Sunnoad and his palace in Skyyon. Security was also lax around the installations he and his staff were using for research and for the storage of secret intelligence about the mascon 'worlds'.

On one of those 'worlds' a species of bird, made, like the mascons, of partly degenerate matter, and thus able to fly through ordinary solids as though they were air (as did the birds of Placet, in the Frederick Brown story), had been penned by force fields so that scientists from Syoom could study them. The bird-creatures were in a state of rage. If released, they were liable to fly in any direction and wreak havoc.

Finally the presence of the warped genius of Nehal Fozdak, the criminal mastermind who was determined to leave his mark upon history, ensured that the opportunity was taken.

Fozdak's Crime

He accomplished the seemingly impossible. He arranged for the mascon-birds to be released in such a way that they flew upward towards the Uranian surface at a point in the mountains of Jersh; and at the same time he himself wormed his way into the Sunnoad's quarters, murdered him and donned the golden cloak, to take his place.

Fozdak had long had a feud with Sunnoad Ahim Trarv 77062, but it is unlikely that the killing was pure revenge. It is more probable that Fozdak meant the impersonation to last, and to take control of Syoom in the chaos that soon ensued.

For the mascon birds, as they shot out of the surface of Ooranye and into the atmosphere which to them was like a deadly vacuum, broke the mountains of Jersh in their throes, causing volcanic outbreaks and signalling to the waiting Fyayman forces that it was time to invade. The latter did so in force, and this, combined with the havoc caused by the great birds, meant that this day, 13,324,486 Bi, ended with an *eomasp* and was followed by Day One of the Polonium Era.

Fozdak's most evil act, however, would have been repudiated even by his Fyayman allies, had they known of his plan. For he had rediscovered the long-lost and well-lost Corruption Ray, last heard of in the dawn of history in Era 7. To make sure of the chaos out of which he planned to forge his own regime, he released the Ray, in more concentrated form than ever before. Full public awareness of this event – hastened by repentant confederates of the master criminal – brought the Polonium Era to an end when it was only two and a half hours old, whereupon yet another *eomasp* disturbed the clocks of Syoom. Thirty-two more minutes (the Astatine Era) the Ray blazed at full strength but in so doing betrayed its location and was destroyed, and Fozdak driven into hiding. The end of the broadcast brought on a further *eomasp*, this time of relief, and then another, 1 day, 2 hours and 40 minutes later, after the influence of the Ray had been shaken off sufficiently for the horror to fall below the threshold of despair (this short period of recuperation counts as the Radon Era). None too soon the recovery had come. Fyayman forces were advancing. Syoom was being invaded. Morale needed to be at its height.

34: Invasion

The Francium Era, Era 87, lasted for scarcely more than a generation: 11,496 Uranian days plus 24 hours; equivalent to 39.35 Earth years. It was sometimes looked back on as Syoom's Last Stand, before the era of subjugation which followed. It was an individualist's era *par excellence*. The Sunnoad had been murdered and no successor had been chosen; much other authority had also disappeared, much organization broken down; the defence of Syoom was left to personal initiative. The only reason the "last stand" took as long as it did, was that the invading Fyaymans had been almost as damaged as the Syoomeans by the nightmarish broadcast of the Corruption Ray.

For some thousands of days the demoralising effects of this ray prevented a new Sunnoad from being chosen. It was felt, with irrational fervour, that no such election could wholesomely be held while the villain Fozdak remained at large. Finally the man was tracked down and killed, but by that time Syoom had been without leadership for thousands of crucial days.

When preparations at last went ahead for the election of the 77,063rd Sunnoad, it was realized that occupying forces held so much of Syoom that a normal peace-time election was impossible; and as for a wartime election, for which different procedures applied, it was thought that the mandate of Fate did not at present favour any one candidate to a sufficient extent. The preparations were called off. Syoom was rudderless.

The news spread; despair ballooned; an ***eomasp*** ended the Francium Era.

The "last stand" was over and the era of subjugation had begun.

35: Tu Rim

Character of the Radium Era

Era 88 lasted 3,889,328 days. This amounts to 158 Uranian years, equivalent to 13,310 Earth years.

Because of the sketchiness of this summary it often happens that we devote more attention to the transitions between eras than to the eras themselves. And so it is on this occasion: we must glide lightly over the Conquered Era, and zoom in upon the extraordinary character who brought it to an end.

It was not in fact an utterly "Conquered Era". Though in most cities Ghepions seized control, in alliance with the Fyayman invaders or otherwise, in belated revenge for the pogroms of Era 81, and enslaved or dispossessed the human inhabitants, this did not happen everywhere. Thanks to the rear-guard action by fighters of the era of "Syoom's Last Stand", four great cities were never conquered: Vyanth, Lysyon, Pjourth and Skyyon itself. They persisted as islands of human rule in a sea of **kalyar** and Ghepion and general Fyayman domination.

It is also true to say that as time went on the Nenns won back a lot of ground (though they could not yet reconquer any of the lost cities), until by the end of the era, while the Ghepions still possessed twenty-one of the twenty-five great disc-on-stems, free men mostly occupied the plains, the forests and the mountains between them.

Of course, this was not a time of perpetual conflict. For those who lived in the middle of the Radium Era it must have seemed the natural order of things for free men to live on the land and in the lesser towns, and for Ghepions to hold most of the cities.

The Invaded Soul

The sunnoadex was revived early in the era, and it endured under restrictions. In the last few hundred thousand days there was something of a Renaissance of Syoomean pride and culture, and a feeling grew that the great days would soon return and the lost cities be reclaimed.

The man who, more than any other, actually accomplished the reconquest of Syoom, was perhaps the most controversial character in Uranian history – even more so than Fiarr Fosn 723 or Nalre Zitpoidl 4854. Many Uranian historians believe that Sunnoad Tu Rim 78860 could not have been a man at all; to achieve what he did, he must have "sold his soul" to a Fyayman power, or in other words, agreed to a partial mind-switch with a more powerful entity.

We take the view that Tu Rim was merely a man of unusual ability, who was tempted and mislead by that ability into over-reaching himself.

He did reconquer the twenty-one lost cities from the Ghepions, and this must always be counted in his favour. However, he did so in a manner which served his own power, and he tried to convert the traditional privileges and aspects of a Sunnoad's reign into a despotic rule. He had excuses, but none were good enough to satisfy his nemesis, which happened to be none other than the second incarnation of Taldis Norkoten 64702 – the famous Sunnoad of the Osmium Era.

We can visualise the ex-Sunnoad as playing Juarez to Tu Rim's Maximilian – except that Norkoten had no interest in supreme power this time. All he aimed at was the overthrow of Tu Rim and to free the sunnoadex from the shame of despotism; and this he did. Tu Rim fled, was deposed; Norkoten convened a conference to discuss ways in which to prevent this story from ever happening again. After much debate it was decided that the best way to ensure the future innocence of the sunnoadex was by means of a taboo – a powerful symbolic prohibition. It was therefore agreed and proclaimed that never again could a Sunnoad make his home in Skyyon. Never again could a Sunnoad even spend a night in Skyyon. Henceforth the Sunnoad's Palace would be used for other purposes – as a city hall, a Noad's residence, a museum. Henceforth the Sunnoad must be content with having his official home in a hut (well-appointed, to be sure, but shaped like a hut) in the village of Melikon, 90 miles outside the Sunward City.

Some time was spent in discussing how this measure might be put to the people of Syoom for their confirmation. But as the news spread, it was met with such satisfaction and calm joy and acceptance, that the air trembled with an *eomasp*, and this transition to a new era was regarded as more than adequate confirmation of the rightness of the decision.

36: The Actinium Fulfilment

The Actinium Era – Era 89 – lasted 11,176,884 Uranian days, or 456 Uranian years, equivalent to 38,319 Earth years.

In character and outlook it was the last great "pure" Uranian era, before our present era of space travel and interplanetary contact caused that subtle change of atmosphere brought about by the immigration of Terran off-worlders.

To a remarkable degree, Era 89 was also the epitome, the summing up, the fulfilment of all earlier eras. Just as the blood of fourteen thousand lifetimes of humanity flowed in the veins of the Actinium Era Nenns, so did glimmers from the past light up their present culture with some of the brilliance of the Phosphorus and the Osmium, the daring of the Vanadium and the Praesodymium, the mystic glow of the Argon and the Cobalt, the heroism of the Rubidium and the Francium, the wisdom of the Zinc and the Gold, the moral, mental and physical hues of 88 ages in all their variety of experience.

Blending with these were some new ingredients, as follows:

Firstly, the approach of Uranian Year Zero. (See "Systems of historical dating in use on Ooranye".) At the start of Era 89, the UTU countdown stood at -456 Uranian years. This meant that the Year Zero was still so many lifetimes in the future (remember, one Uranian year, at 84 of Earth's years, is a longish lifetime) that it was hard to relate to it personally. Yet, as the number gradually crept down, it became food for thought in idle moments, especially as the lengthening Actinium Era began to seem the probable last great era befor the Zero. Reflective minds began to wonder what the final shape of society might be like, as Zero approached, and how that might affect the outcome of whatever stupendous event was destined to happen in that year; and what one's own self might personally contribute to the push of that outcome.

Secondly, towards the end of the era, during UTU-8, there occurred an event so striking that, had it not been for the UTU countdown being so close to its end, would surely have caused an *eomasp*. This event was none other than First Contact with us, the Terrans. From Day 11,002,739 of the Actinium Era, our scientists in their orbiting ships began to survey Ooranye and converse with its inhabitants. As days went by and they did not land, nor offer to bring any Uranian aloft, it became apparent from this stand-offishness of ours that we were enforcing some sort of blockade of the planet, or else skirting some invisible barrier. This, in turn, gave Uranians a clue as to what Year Zero might bring. Year Zero might well see the breaking of the blockade or barrier, followed by *their* achievement of space travel, their challenge to Earth! Meanwhile long conversations and exchanges of ideas took place over the radio. Earth history, language and ways of thought began to tinge the culture of Ooranye, and vice versa.

The crisis which *did* cause the **eomasp** which brought Era 89 to its end, occurred when UTU-0 arrived without any accompanying drastic event. People had been waiting with bated breath for a world-changing cataclysmic *something*, yet life went on as before. Sunnoad Iyen Noom 80525 and his advisors knew that matters could not be allowed to rest thus. Fate evidently was waiting for the Nenns to act. So the Year Zero event would have to be caused deliberately. The people of Syoom must do something so big that it could not have been dared at any other time. Only thus could Year Zero be fittingly marked.

By this reasoning, the decision was made to try to succeed where Fiarr Fosn 723 and the Great Fleet of the Phosphorus Era had failed.

37: The Assault on Arclour

Arclour is the fabled Starward Polar region of Ooranye, antipodeal to the Sunward City, Skyyon. The Starward Pole has traditionally stood for everything that is utterly remote, mysterious and unattainable. Sunnoad Fiarr Fosn 723 had intended to reach it but although he had commanded fifteen hundred airships his fleet had been destroyed many thousands of miles short of his goal. For hundreds of millions of days since then, the legendary disaster had appeared to confirm that Nennkind was not destined to penetrate to Arclour. Nowadays, however, Uranians – like Terrans after the first moon landings – have got used to knowing that what *used* to seem unattainable has now been reached.

Because it is far too soon to assess the full significance of these tremendous happenings, any proper account we might try to give of them would lack perspective. Everybody knows the bare outline of the events which ushered in our present era: how the Second Great Fleet did succeed in reaching Arclour and its ultimate *sivvan*, and how that discovery retro-triggered our retro-Fostering of Ooranye, that is to say, the grafting of Ooranye's true history onto the history of our solar system.

So if the Fleet had not reached Arclour, the First Terran Contact eight Uranian years previously would not have happened either. The future re-writes the past.

Otherwise the world of Ooranye would be known to us still as the lifeless gas/ice giant Uranus, remarkable merely for its odd axial tilt, whereas now that tilt, and the lifelessness, *never have been*. Shunted, grafted retrospectively onto this reality is the *real* Uranus, become fully itself. *That's* what we accomplished, that was our half of the pincer which adjusted reality, the other half being the triumph of Sunnoad Iyen Noom 80525 and the Second Great Fleet.

The Assault on Arclour also broke the barrier – the ontological membrane – which had separated Terrestrials and Uranians since First Contact. Henceforth in full co-dimensionality a limited number of adventurers from each planet have been able to visit the other. Earthmen and Nenns have met face to face at last.

A few remaining details will round off our sketch of Uranian history.

The actual *eomasp* which ended Era 89 was caused by the wave of emotion which accompanied the departure of the Second Great Fleet. But the short era which followed – the 8 days, 9 hours, 20 minutes of the Protactinium

Era, the duration of the voyage to Arclour – counts as Era 91, not 90. Why is this so, and what happened to Era 90?

Exactly when, in other words, was the Thorium Era?

The peculiar whisper in the mind, experienced by so many as the fleet set out, and some unusual dreams, which came to innumerable Nenns all over Syoom that night, powerfully reinforce the following conclusion:

The Thorium Era never happened. But it could have, and, on another time-track, it did.

Sunnoad Iyen Noom has since admitted to chroniclers that it was only at the very point of departure that he made up his mind on a vital point of tactics. He decided that the ships under his command would, if they were forced, do what Fiarr Fosn's fleet had not been able to do – namely, use the vibrational mode of inter-molecular transport which had been invented in the Bismuth Era. Due to its enormous expense it could only be used once by a fleet of this size, and if that use were to prove inadequate, the airships would be trapped and doomed. But the gamble – in this universe – was taken.

The mode was used at one stage of the voyage, shortening it by a few per cent. More importantly, it circumvented ambush by Fyayman forces.

According to the Thorium Whisper, in another universe this measure was not taken at all, and Arclour was never reached, and the Terrestrials never landed, and the continuing era was indeed the Thorium, with a history very different from the path on which Ooranye is now launched. In *that* universe, for one thing, there are no Terrans...

Meanwhile in our universe, as we write, we are now in Era 92, the Uranium Era. It is the last, say the people of Ooranye, and it shall continue six times as long as all the others put together. Thus it shall constitute the remainder of this Great Cycle of 100,000 Uranian years, or 8,400,000 Earth years, of which about 1,200,000 Earth-years have now passed.

Our friends on Ooranye tell us, good-naturedly, that the days of Earth's pre-eminence will soon be over and that leadership in solar system affairs is about to pass, inevitably, to their own giant world.

However, we wonder just how soon is "soon" to Uranians.

Besides, although Arclour has now been reached, Fyaym has not been conquered, and perhaps never will be. Can the Nenns dominate the solar system if they cannot even subdue their own planet? And yet this may be the wrong way of looking at it; perhaps Fyaym will always be needed to keep them fit for adventure; perhaps the great wisdom of the Nenns lies in *not* crowding their horizon.

102

Prologue to the first edition of the Gleams

...Anonymous letter of thanks beamed from the Terran Literary Guild to the Vyanthan Bards, 31ˢᵗ August 3604:

May I add my own insignificant voice to the countless messages of congratulation which must be raining down through the barrier between us and your world.

Your gift, and the promise it brings of an unending stream of further delights, have at last begun to slake that millennial thirst which we Terrans have suffered ever since the so-called "end of history" in our Year 2330.

Of course, history never really ends while people remain alive. But the Discontinuity of 2330 – the dissemination of the Replicator all over the Earth – the abrupt and complete end of all the old economic struggles for survival – meant that the word "economy" thenceforth had to be redefined with a purely psychological or spiritual meaning. You of Ooranye, experienced though you are in almost every type of adventure, have never had to face *that* one! So perhaps you could spare a thought for what it has been like for us, ever since that day in 2330 when the practical pressures disappeared, and Terrans were left without needs, except the crying need for purpose in life.

But what's the point of trying to explain? I don't suppose you Uranians have ever felt a lack of purpose or structure or meaning. *Your* challenges are so much more external than ours, that we can't reasonably expect you to imagine what it's like for us. If I were to tell you that our adventures arise from our shortcomings alone, you'd most likely shrug in contempt. The fact is, in order to make our case to you, we'd have to translate certain terms which your world never needs, and our knowledge of your languages lags far behind your knowledge of ours.

That reminds me: pay no heed to any carping historians or geographers who aren't comfortable with the way you render some of the notions in your stories. You've done well to tailor them to what we can comprehend. That's the way to do it. Don't overstrain the reader. Over-simplify if necessary – we all do it, quite rightly if the alternative is total failure of communication! Long may you continue in this vein.... We want more than Gleams!

Reply from the Vyanthan Bard, Day 11,014,471 Actinium Era:

...some day in the centuries to come the barrier you mention will be no more, and our two peoples will meet face to face. Reality looks forward; destinies have greater weight than causes.

And finally: why do I call the following batch of six stories the Gleams? Because our history is so long, 1,200,000 of your years, all I can offer in this first volume is a few shafts of light, a half-dozen gleams to illumine tiny fractions of the vast canvas. Of course many, many more stories are in the queue to come, and each will shine another ray. But these first six little views will always be *the* Gleams...

Nitrogen Era:

Basilisk

1: Ethical Action

At certain priceless moments, a faint line, which appeared as an actual silver thread before Veppora's mind's eye, strung her days together like jewels on a necklace. It meant opportunity. Hope.

She vaguely knew that if it were not for this visionary thread she would simply be marking time until she died. An "old maid" in late middle age, she was tolerated by her nephews and their families, and also got on well enough with a few unmarried women whose situation was like hers, but that was all the personal comfort she would have had – were it not for the thread...

It gave meaning to her life.

"I'm sorry, Veppora," broke in the voice of Gizwa, her niece by marriage. "The flatcar's broken down."

Veppora went white. The knife with which she had been slicing vegetables clattered to the floor. "Oh, but I *must* get home to my meeting." Her homely face sagged; her cheeks quivered.

"I'm really sorry," repeated Gizwa.

Gizwa's husband Bzurth entered the kitchen and said, "Yeah, most unfortunate. But stay overnight with us, won't you? We've got..."

Neither of them understood. Bzurth's chunky face, and his wife's matronly bloom, became figures seen through a blur as for a few moments Veppora came close to fainting, but she drew herself up and spoke: "I am sorry also. I *must* be at my meeting on time. Could not any of the neighbours...?"

"I looked," said Bzurth. "Their cars aren't there. Still at work. And by the time they get back it will be curfew..."

"Then I must set out at once."

They could not dissuade her, though Bzurth did point out that the Noad had imposed the curfew for good reason; that with rising levels of crime and sedition, the city of Narar was no place for a lone woman pedestrian at the hour of evenshine; that he, Bzurth, would accompany her except that if on the way back he got caught –

"Please don't argue any further," Veppora said primly. She laid a hand on his arm. "Of course I won't hear of you coming with me. Gizwa needs you here; you have other guests coming. Don't put me in the position of being a nuisance. It is *my* decision that I set out immediately."

Her hosts glanced at one another. The glance said: yes, we've said enough, let her go.

Veppora was not an adventurous woman; she was merely stubborn. As she emerged, in hat and shawl, into the red gully of Pnarash Street, her mind grasped anew that thread which guided her steps. Now she pictured it more like a rope, pulling her along the pavement past looming walls, sinister alleys and knots of loitering youths, towards the sanctuary of her home. The thought braced her, made her feel fortunate… more fortunate, though also more lonely, than her friends and kin.

"They take me for granted, of course," she thought, "but there's more to it than that." Indeed, they riskily took other matters for granted too. All their daily lives were lived on the unacknowledged brink of doom. But whereas she tried, in her small way, to pull back from it, *they* pressed on with their little affairs as though civilization had been guaranteed a future. As though the darkness outside the city walls did not squash inwards.

Yet today Veppora hummed contentedly to herself, her silver thread of purpose shining brighter than usual. This evening, she suspected, would bring the one sufficient triumph, to content her for the rest of her life. She would have "done her bit", and after that the line, the thread, the secret silver wire of opportunity would pass on to another link-person, while she herself would be left with the satisfaction that she had not lived in vain. Yes, to *have held* the thread would suffice for her.

Therefore it was especially vital that tonight's meeting should go ahead. The signs were good. She had managed to arrange for a foreign guest, a travel writer of some renown, to come and speak. To have booked the Lady Hyoen Freld of Jador was quite a coup, giving extra shine to the thread of meaning.

Who knows, Veppora mused, I might induce this Freld woman to set up a branch of Ethical Action in *her* home city, which would mean I could truthfully claim that notice has been taken of my little club elsewhere. A heady thought. Today, two cities; tomorrow, who knows? All of Syoom – the civilized world – may one day look back to this as the most important Ethical Action meeting ever!

But only if I get there.

The air was dimming towards a face-blurring dusk. Veppora hesitated at the sight of the tree-lined vista where Pnarash Street debouched into Kensh Avenue. The space was wide and sparsely lit, and pedestrians were few.

If she could cross the avenue boldly, confidently, and preferably at an oblique angle, she would reach the side-road she wanted as quickly as possible... She had heard stories of people being mugged, or worse, in this district. A half-dozen youths were scuffing their boots against the kerb some fifty yards away. They were in the direction she needed to go. She must advance, no matter what rasped at her insides.

As she cringed past the youths she heard one word which made her skin tighten painfully: "cur-few, cur-few" – the taunt aimed at her: implying, *we* can dodge it, but don't *you* dare. Yet she got by, and heard no following footsteps. The yobs receded. So why did unease still grip her shoulders? Something in these darkened streets still nudged and twitched her mind more disagreeably than any common fear. Well, what could it be?

As if she didn't know.

The old question:

How do you know that if you succeed too much, Dmara won't come to you?

It didn't help to say: Dmara can't move; Dmara is only the name of an old ruined city, and of the dried-up lake beside it.

It didn't help, because enough vagueness hung around the name, to make one feel that something about it *could* reach out.

Veppora adhered to the widespread popular belief that the cradle of evil was locatable. She, along with millions of other Uranian humans, had no doubt that it lurked in the dead city of human origins thousands of miles away on the other side of the civilized world. To this belief she added her own personal conviction, that it was the duty of all living city-governments to co-operate in mounting an expedition aimed at eradicating or exorcising Dmara. This should be done once and for all, decisively: the horror wiped out.

Not for nothing was Ethical *Action* the name and watchword of her organization.

Ridiculous, that it had been left to her to set up this pitiful little club... That thought knocked her pride, caused her steps to falter in bewilderment... For an instant she would have willingly abandoned all her life's work. That was a crazy thought. It couldn't be right! She reproved herself: "It's *not* a pitiful club. Somebody has to start somewhere, and I've had some good responses..." But that (right now) was no comfort, in fact it made matters worse: for on this particular evening, as she stumbled through the dim streets of Narar towards the spacious haven of Nowan House, she began to wonder whether she had done the right thing in asking that prestigious foreign wordsmith Hyoen Freld to address the meeting tonight. *Has it ever occurred to me before now that I might actually SUCCEED, and if I do, I may rouse something too big for those involved to endure?*

After all, the thing we dread is real; it is out there; it is not asleep. If international pressure is brought to bear on it, it will surely retaliate. And might it even move before then, against those who locally raise the alarm – might it move against me? Skies above, what have I done?

She felt a craving for her own walls around her. By the time she finally reached her house unharmed she was shaking with relief. She drunkenly burst in, locked the double doors behind her and pressed the master switch which put on all the lights. Well – a drink might be sensible, at that! She lurched upstairs to her bedroom where she poured herself a glass of secret strong stuff, thankful that no one had yet arrived. Gulping, she reflected that the only thing which really mattered was results.

Everything was back on course now. How fortunate to have inherited a mansion of this size, and how comforting to have a steady objective as regards its use. An aim which was so grand, it was in no danger of being realized too soon. If it ever *was* realized, she'd be either dead by then, or so old that no one would expect… humph, never mind. Must hustle. Downstairs again, to prepare the lounge.

The richness of the lounge soothed her: its carpeting, its panelling, its lamplit glows. Medicine for the mind. She went around straightening chairs, plumping cushions, and putting a pile of spare notices on the little table by the door – copies of the ones sent out some days back:

> Date and time: third hour of evenshine, Day 20,867
> of the Nitrogen Era
> Venue: Nowan House, Ungezazz Street, Narar
> Guest Speaker: the Lady Hyoen Freld of Jador
> Veppora Munoo to take the Chair.
> Visitors welcome. Overnight accommodation available.
> Members are urged to make every effort to attend.

Proudly she thought: "I successfully made my *own* effort to attend –" That walk through the streets had been no joke.

The guest speaker was the next to arrive. Younger and slimmer than Veppora, the Lady Hyoen Freld turned out to be quite short in stature but she stood straight and business-like. Her eyes, dark beads of restless glitter, gave her a forceful presence. Her tone of greeting, however, as she shook hands, was kindly and appreciative. "I am most grateful for the opportunity to come and talk to you. How odd that it has taken me so long to make my first visit to Narar," the lady smiled, and went on, expertly speaking the Nouuan tongue in lofty style, "I suppose that the pattern of my roamings has depended too much upon the convenience of the moment. Well, here I am at last, and high time I had a look at your city."

Veppora was a touch irritated by the blithe assumption that anyone with enough money could still roam around Syoom the carefree way folk used to do. All right, 'Syoom' was supposed to denote 'the civilized part of the world'. And all right, Hyoen Freld doubtless had a lot more money and a lot more luck than most people. *But some day, your ladyship will find that the supply of both has run dry...*

In fact – decided Veppora there and then – when I introduce her I shall give her the common title 'sponndar', and none of this 'Lady' business, and she can like it or flunnd it.

At the back of this assertive twitch there crouched Veppora's newly re-awoken dread of success. She had always been apt to shy from any over-clear image of her aims. Now the presence of a likely agent brought the vision uncomfortably close to focus. *This chic smartie just might go further than I bargained for, in a spurt of precipitate action...* Astonished at the inconstancy of her thoughts, Veppora was glad when other guests began to arrive. It was a good turnout. About thirty people eventually settled themselves on the armchairs, the couches and the cushions in a semi-circle which faced the great wooden desk; soft light from the pillared lamps poured gentle gold over the scene, and Dmara and its horrors seemed impossibly far away. The clock struck the hour. Chatter died down.

Veppora, her mood lightened, took the Chair and began, "It is my privilege to introduce sponndar Hyoen Freld..."

Soon, though, she was thinking: *Whatever I expected, it wasn't this.*

Right from the beginning of the guest's speech the meeting was given a new slant on the problem of evil. Very un-traditionally they were all soon laughing as if evil could be reduced to buffoonery. "You won't believe this," Hyoen Freld told them, "but recently the Jadorian Government introduced a slew of Well-Being regulations, including penalties for anyone who told a joke within hearing of someone chewing a *spikko* fruit, in case the hearer choked with laughter..."

Funny anecdotes, thought Veppora in wonder. *A mere laugh. And there I was, worrying...*

And yet I'm right about one thing. As soon as I saw her, I knew.

For on reflection Veppora understood that she had recognised Hyoen as the person who was going to pick up the silver thread. *When she does, I shall be able to relax. The narrative will have passed to her and it will be in good hands.*

"…and likewise recently," Hyoen Freld went on, "in my home city of Jador, a campaign has begun to replace our ancient system of measurement with a set of polysyllabic terms having no evocative or descriptive power, the sole merit of the new system being that it facilitates multiplication and division by powers of ten. As though measurements were used only for calculation, rather than as descriptors. Thus instead of inches we're told to use *foopisnargles*; instead of yards, *snargles*; instead of miles, *kruntisnargles*. I'm not making this up. Wait," she held up her hand to control the audience's incredulous mirth, "till you hear how the authorities where I live are also mucking about with the measurement of *time*." ('Mucking about?' A lady should say *tampering*, Veppora's inner censor protested, but the guest surged on; she could get away with anything –) "In order to make citizens work harder and use their hours better by getting up earlier, our government has told us we must all put our clocks forward one hour –"

"Ah, come on!" said several in the audience.

"I'm serious! They really believe that the only way to get us Jadorians out of bed is to pretend that it is one hour later than it really is! But I see you're having trouble accepting all this," Hyoen went on as heads shook while bodies continued to heave with mirth. "All I can say to that is – come to my city and see and hear for yourselves. Meanwhile – do you wish to hear more?" ("Yea, yea," responded the delighted audience, eager for more farce.) "Very well, one more tall tale that happens to be true. It's about the way we Jadorians speak. We have a growing habit of using the word for 'she' as a polite form of 'you'. And more serious still, I hear reports that the simple past tense is dropping out of use, so that 'I have gone', for example, is replacing 'I went', as in 'yesterday I have gone to visit a friend'…"

Hyoen's voice suddenly drooped to a more serious tone.

"All this," she remarked, "is, of course, too barmy to be natural."

She paused, and glanced at the Chair. Veppora gave the right verbal nudge:

"If it isn't natural, then…"

"Something," said Hyoen, "is rotting our minds."

The audience had frozen in captivated suspense. Veppora experienced a sense of glad surrender, as a tired business-owner may feel willing to hand over nen's enterprise to a young, able, energetic successor. This is it, this is the moment, she thought objectively, this is the point in the story where Veppora hands the thread to Hyoen.

Meanwhile the speaker continued:

"The *something* has been given a name. We call it the Corruption-Ray, or C-Ray for short. I dare say you may have heard the theory…"

(The thread having passed to Hyoen Freld, the narrative shifts to her point of view. Sensing the pressure, Hyoen falters, noticing signs of impatient dissatisfaction in her audience as their lips murmur *no, not that nonsense, is that all, that C-Ray fantasy stuff…*)

"…although the fashion is still to decry it and to posit alternative explanations. I have heard, for instance, that some of you people pin the blame upon spooks from Dmara – but I say, *forget Dmara.*"

Hyoen Freld's gaze panned around to see how they took that last bit. She noticed that the lady in the Chair, Veppora Munoo, seemed delighted, really delighted at the phrase, *Forget Dmara.*

The rest of the audience, though, seemed disconcerted rather than pleased… Well, any change of outlook tends to be a bother, Hyoen well knew. But they did all continue to listen as she flowed on.

"…Whatever our differences in theory, at any rate your aims and mine coincide, as do some of our beliefs. You and I long for a better world. You and I agree that the source of contemporary evil is to be found in some *place.* So next we must ask, which place? Wherever the culprit's headquarters may be, it must house a modern group of scientific criminals engaged in an international conspiracy. Yes – forget Dmara! Dmara is a cover, a distraction, an excuse. We face a plot by real flesh-and-blood people who aim the C-Ray at our cities. How to find them, how to defeat them, I have no idea. That's why I seek support wherever I can; I hope to be speaking with your city government soon." (Audience reaction still mixed… some nervous titters…) "Thank you for listening to me."

"Thank *you*, Lady Hyoen," said Veppora, who to herself commented: *I need not have worried about the dangers of success. This woman isn't going to get anywhere with our government. So if she does stir things, it won't be here. No, thank goodness, the deed will be done a long way from here.* "Questions from the floor?"

A portly bespectacled man put his hand up.

"What I'd like to know is, how are these C-Rays aimed? From towers? Airships? And how come nobody has traced them yet?"

Hyoen smiled tightly. "The rays belong to that type of radiation known as heavy-light. As you must be aware, heavy-light can travel in arcs. The trajectory of the C-Ray, we believe, is like that of a surface-to-surface missile. It needs no tower or airship platform. It could be launched from anywhere to anywhere."

A woman gowned in bejewelled velvet asked the next question in a tone of formidable doubt. "Those who fire this… thing – what could be their motive? Living in hiding, as they must be, what's in it for them?"

"Their motive," replied Hyoen with a snap in her voice, "is to deprive people of their roots."

"How?"

"How? By destroying their network of cultural referents. I say this because of my experience in Jador. Anything well-established, anything of good quality, is a target."

"Yes, but why?" insisted the velvety woman.

"To undermine public spirit, of course; to weaken the state, so making it more vulnerable to conquest or control by whomever is mounting this operation. Have no doubt, when matters have gone far enough, they'll come out of hiding and show their hand. But by then it'll be too late for Syoom."

A hush fell, with few smiles. The bright little flowers of amusement were fading in a desolation of sombre thoughts.

Her questioner tried again:

"Do your compatriots, sponndar H-F, agree with you about this conspiracy?"

"Those who agree, as yet, are few, and none are in positions of importance," admitted Hyoen. Even more frankly she added: "My supporters are mere drops in the bucket, so far. If you want a reason to disbelieve, that's certainly one."

Veppora interjected:

"And so you came to Narar,"

"Yes, I have come to Narar. This is my last throw." Hyoen softened her voice. "I dare say you will agree, rather than take offence, if I assert that your city is in some respects further than mine along the road to social decay." She saw assent in their faces. No one was prepared to argue that one. It was the underlying reason they huddled here, in this bright room with the comforting lights and companionship. "I had thought," she went on, "perhaps to bring one or two of you home with me, as witnesses to warn the people of Jador of the future of crime and hopelessness that lies in wait for them. Then it also occurred to me that the reverse was likewise true – that I could use the example of Jador to warn Narar. For some of our Jadorian

112

idiocies have not yet taken root here. You've proved that, by laughing at them."

Faces brightened at that, whereupon Veppora issued a kindly rebuke from the Chair:

"My feeling, sponndar H-F, is that it is all very well for you, having lived all your life in the relative freedom of Jador, to complain about minor silliness such as tinkering with measurement and clocks. What you have yet to realize is the degree to which we in Narar have to put up with *real* oppression. For example, here, if the Noad deigned to glance at our humble little club, he could imprison us all tonight, and keep us imprisoned without trial. Fortunately we're way beneath his notice – but perhaps you can try to understand why we have been entertained rather than enflamed by your speech."

Hyoen bowed her head. "I am aware of the oppression you speak of, sponndar V-M."

"And now that you have gauged the sense of our meeting – what will you do next?" (Veppora, her silver thread of purpose gone, asked this only out of mild curiosity. She welcomed a new blankness in her own mind. It had replaced the terrible fear, the dread that she might get what she had asked for. Now the chance and the hope and the terror were all gone. All handed over. What a relief.)

"It has just occurred to me," said Hyoen Freld bitterly, "that your oppressors may not be too stupid, they may know how to think…. I realize that your Noad is supposed to be a mere dictator, but –"

"Oh, you'll find he's a clever man," interrupted Veppora. "Politician to the core. Yes, you'll find that Vroonwik Clarm is a master of the Bleak Arts."

2: The Button

Thebb Clarm paused with a large spanner in his muscular grip.

He listened for a moment, his senses on the alert. A door had slammed.

Happiest when tinkering under the dim ceiling of his cavernous workshop, he was not so consumed by passion for his hobby as to neglect the arts of survival.

He was a constructor of hover-rafts by preference, but a politician by necessity. No member of the ruler's family could avoid politics. This being the case, any scrunch of footsteps on the gravel path outside –

Those steps, though, sounded merely like Smim hurrying his way... but why was she in such a rush? The door opened. Yes, it *was* Smim and as he looked at her leggy, tousled figure in the doorway, Thebb smiled in tolerant contempt.

Whatever it might be, that had brought his woman-of-the-moment scurrying to his shed, it wasn't any regard she felt for him or for his hobby... that much was certain.

"Thebb!" she screeched. "Five men in your front garden!"

He gently replied, "Thanks for telling me, Smim. Send them round, will you? I'm not going anywhere."

She really did look scared. Did she, he wondered, care for him slightly after all? Of course she had been placed in his life to keep an eye on him; on the other hand, it was a lazy enough eye. In fact the vacuous Smim appeared to show no interest in whatever he did. There was something so cheap about her, as to reassure him that his great-uncle could not possibly consider him much of a danger to the state.

And so the easy-going Thebb had never got round to looking very hard for something better, once Smim Lerank had trickled into his life.

She darted back out of sight as other, heavier footsteps tramped on the gravel. A guardsman pushed his way in through the shed door.

"Come right in," invited Thebb, redundantly.

Another followed, and they stationed themselves on either side of the entrance. Then in strode a younger man, as young as Thebb himself, but whose piercing eyes brooded as if prodding the scene with invisible wires.

Beyond him, through the still-opened door, a third and fourth guard could be seen, who remained stationed outside. Thebb smiled at these excessive precautions. He straightened himself, still gripping the spanner. "What can I do for you, Advisor?"

The Noad's Advisor, Ob Solm, bent his frown at the partly disassembled raft which overspread much of the shed floor.

Thebb noted his gaze and said, "Yes, your arrival has just broken some trains of thought concerning the optimum volume-to-drive ratio of the rear-port buoyancy tank –"

"Interesting," drawled Ob Solm. "But, so I would think, marginal to the needs of the State..." His scrutiny swung back at Thebb. "Have you not thought of using your talents to further the Noad's plans? Does the Navy of Narar not interest you more than this tinkering hobby?"

"You mean airships."

"You say it boredly."

"Let me tell you, Advisor, that dozens of rafts like this could be built for the cost of one airship. Besides, skimming close to the ground is much more useful in Unnesp's terrain. More exhilarating too, than floating half a mile up –"

"That," cut in Ob Solm, "is your opinion."

"Which is why I voice it," shrugged Thebb.

"The Noad takes a different view."

Thebb nodded quietly, having had plenty of arguments with his great-uncle on this theme; arguments which (so far) had remained safely less energetic than quarrels.

What the young hobbyist really wanted to do was to put some of his working models to the test. And the only proper test was a voyage into the wilderness. Noad Vroonwik, however, had flatly forbidden Thebb to go exploring.

He'd thought of going anyway – but really he was stuck. As one of the ruler's close relatives, were he to leave the city without permission there would be hell to pay when he got back. Politics! His heart wasn't in it – but his fortune was.

He did not yet feel real danger. All he wanted was to be let alone to tinker. Surely that was not too much to ask, even in today's sad world.

"So, am I due for another lecture?" he smiled at Ob Solm.

Then he wondered if perhaps he had gone too far. He noticed the guardsmen flicking expectant glances at their boss.

"What's in that bin?" demanded Ob Solm in a sudden drab voice. A jerk of the head towards the back of the workshop left no doubt as to what he meant.

Thebb turned. "Gvo crystals."

Ob Solm strode over to stare down at the heap of what looked like magnified orange sugar crystals. "A valuable hoard."

"Accumulated legally; I can prove it," said Thebb, now somewhat on the defensive.

Ob Solm turned his head back with a glare which could discompose the most guiltless; eyes which made Thebb want to wail, *I've got nothing to hide!* All right, in today's resource-poor world it would have been far better not to have been caught with a whole bin of gvo, legal or not, but – thought Thebb despondently – politics was ultimately about what you could grab for yourself; Vroonwik knew it; Ob Solm knew it; and he, Thebb, needed the crystals for what he was doing.

Ob Solm remarked, "You're looking unhappy, Thebb Clarm." And he gave a signal to the guards.

One of them, in turn, signalled out the door.

A third guard came in carrying a dark grey cubical box with a lid and metal hasp. As the box neared, Thebb's emotions reared, plunged, squirmed away from the lip of panic with a lunge at the idea that the box must be nothing to do with him – must be merely one of those admin monitors which Advisors insist on trailing around with. "Actually," he hastened to say, "my dream for a long time has been to be able to do without gvo."

"Really?"

"Really. I have been experimenting – admittedly in a small way – I have no assistants, no state resources, it's just a hobby – experimenting, I say, with an alternative source of buoyancy-light."

"And what is that?"

The grim thought came that if Vroonwrik had finally given orders to eliminate him, he would have told Ob Solm to get all possible information first. In which case the longer a full confession could be avoided, the better... On the other hand this thought must be mad. Old great-uncle Vroonwik didn't love him – didn't love anybody – but neither did he hate him...

"The ell-light of the *vheic* plant," explained Thebb more calmly, "like gvo-light, is buoyancy-light. If vheic-light could be trapped in a chamber, well... that would really be something. Just think of it," he went on, accelerating into confidence. "No more dependence on gvo, at any rate for transportation, so we could cock a snook at the gvo-merchants; their international stranglehold would be broken and we'd earn the thanks of all the cities of Syoom. Picture it." Thebb, as he warmed to his theme, was able to use his flood of enthusiasm as a fear-extinguisher. "Instead of a world dependent upon rapacious and elusive gvo peddlers you'd get a world dependent upon farmers, reliably rooted in their lands, dependent in their turn upon protection by the cities. A different set-up, far healthier for all of us."

"Well! Quite the political engineer! You *have* thought about this, haven't you?"

"Don't call me a political engineer, Ob Solm," pleaded Thebb. "I just live my life. I have no idea how to guarantee the people of Narar enough to eat, let alone solve the crime-wave and defeat the pirates in the badlands of Unnesp, or whatever... no, I just live."

"Quite successfully, judging from the size of your house and the time and money you devote to your hobby. Enough of this." Ob Solm made a gesture to a guard, which Thebb did not catch – he misunderstood the phrase *enough of this* to be a sign that Ob Solm was about to leave.

And so Thebb made the mistake, for some seconds, of ceasing to watch his enemy, and of scowling at the floor instead while glooming over the Advisor's taunt – for taunt it seemed – about Thebb Clarm the wealthy pottering dilettante.

He had an answer, the one possible answer: *What else is there?* Nothing else. Nothing for a great-nephew of the Noad, except to take whatever advantages he could in exchange for the dangers of his position.

Those dangers would markedly increase if Noad Vroonwik Clarm and his henchmen ever got the false idea that Thebb was as interested in tinkering with the mechanisms of society as he was in those of his hover-rafts... using the masses and the interest-groups to advance his ideas and himself.

He had no desires in that line. It would be futile to have them, anyway, in these days when civilization was going downhill towards a crash. All sensible people knew this. In fact, come to think of it, some Professor at the University was actually saying so, and they hadn't yet taken *him* to task...

Thebb looked up, intending to make this point as a parting shot. Then he saw his mistake. The visit was not over; the guard with the big box *(why didn't I twig about the box?)* came forward and Thebb's jaw slackened in dismay. Words no longer came when he needed them. Click – another guard had the box open.

The Advisor reached in, all the while keeping his eyes fixed upon Thebb's face.

Now something small and grey was lying in the palm of Ob Solm's left hand. A metal ovoid with a button on its top.

"What's that egg for?" rasped Thebb.

Ob Solm's eyes blazed close now as he pushed the thing under the other's nose. Thebb's thoughts were sent scatty – *Vroonwik doesn't like long arguments – he hires Ob Solm to snip them short* – as his mind bumped down a rough slope towards a pit of no return, of ultimate obedience.

"This," the Advisor was saying, "is your opportunity, Thebb Clarm. The Noad is honouring you. He is giving this to you *first*. Will you accept? If you refuse, the offer will go to Knef Krateen."

Vroonwrik's other great-nephew, Thebb's cousin and chief rival for the succession to the noadex of Narar... Knef Krateen whose one idea was to expend the entire resources of the State upon an airship navy... Knef Krateen the would-be admiral of a fleet to boost Narar's power against the day of collapse when the supply of gvo crystals finally ran out all across Syoom... the sort of man the Noad could believe in, and whom all the citizens might end up believing in as a revulsion from despair when the general darkness fell.

"Press this button," urged Ob Solm, "and Knef Krateen will die."

Thebb's lips parted in eager thirst for this suddenly beautiful idea. Typical enough of Vroonwrik; the starkness of the choice, to obliterate or not, placing the life of a hated rival at the mercy of one jab of the finger.

The Advisor's voice clanged on: "If you do not press it, the equivalent choice will be offered to him, you see. The Noad is weary of trying to choose between you. And you cannot *both* be allowed to live, weakening Narar as each of you strives against the other."

Thebb looked up and had to believe. Those eyes fixed upon him drowned all questioning. He did not think to ask how the box would work. Details merely. Nor did he ask why Vroonwik had chosen to sort out the problem this way. The style was typical enough.

All he knew, now it had come to this point, was that he could not bring himself to press the button.

3: The Noad

Hyoen Freld was scarcely aware of her own fidgeting as she smoothed down her skirt for the third time and repetitiously patted her hair, but when she caught herself standing up and sitting down again almost immediately, she angrily told herself to keep still. It was too late for nerves and doubts. She had committed herself. Here, in the anteroom of an office in the Palace of the Noad, hesitation was for weaklings; one might as well play one's last card and get it over with.

By all accounts Noad Vroonwik Clarm of Narar was a fairly nasty piece of work – indeed quite apart from personal rumours one could hardly absolve him from responsibility for his regime – and yet, Hyoen told herself, he must have some common sense. It was essential for survival.

Besides, since all the so-called good people to whom she had applied had proved useless, she could hardly be blamed for turning to a bad one…

And the fact that she had been granted an audience after a mere couple of days was promising. Most likely the Noad realized that it was in his interest to encourage visitors who, if nothing else, were apt to bring in much-needed crystals into his realm…

The inner door clicked open and she jerked to her feet. A formulaic voice announced, "The lady Hyoen Freld may now approach."

Jaw set, she marched into the office.

And stopped at the sight of the Noad who sat behind a crude, un-elegant desk of dingy wood. The only smart furniture she could see was a modernistic computer-terminal, a rare sight in an age when advanced technology was becoming prohibitively expensive. Otherwise the office was drab. Noad Vroonwik Clarm lolled and creaked in his inflated swivel-chair.

"Siddown," he said, motioning her sloppily to a smaller, tubular chair. "Why have you come to me, Hyoen?"

At least he did get straight to the point. She noted that he was a large man, somewhat jowly but all in all not an ill-looking animal. Pursuing an earlier thought, she decided that although she could not hope to find honour here, she might at least expect intelligence.

She replied, "May I be candid with you, Noad V-C?"

"You may. Only worry if I start to yawn, for then you can expect to be thrown out of my office shortly. Though I don't look it, I am actually a rather busy man. But I allow myself the occasional amusement, so – amuse me! Candidly or otherwise."

Hyoen said, "I will take you at your word, Noad V-C. I am here because I have something vital to say. I –"

"Have you already said it in Jador?" the Noad interrupted.

Disconcerted, she forced her whirling mind to focus upon the perception that the Noad must be used to people coming to him with all kinds of tale to tell. Therefore he must have developed a habit of mind that leaped impatiently ahead of the tellers. Must watch out for that, she thought; he'll be apt to categorise what I say before I finish saying it –

Controlling the rising heat of her temper she said:

"Yes, Noad Vroonwik, Jador has heard. Heard but not listened. The *relatively unsullied* cities have no idea of their own as to what's going on, and do not believe me, whereas the *thoroughly corrupted* ones don't care anyway."

"And which group do we come in?"

"You of Narar are in an intermediate category – partially gone bad, but still with some sense." *That was telling him!*

The Noad's eyes bulged, his cheeks puffed and he burst out laughing. "I'd like to have you on my Board of Advisors!" he hooted. "Love 'em to hear you!" He gasped and wheezed, and it flashed across Hyoen's mind that this ruler might not be in the best of physical health. "So tell me what's up," he encouraged.

She braced herself. She did not like being laughed at and she was much afraid that she'd get the same reaction which she had experienced so many times before – as though she were some crank. That would terminate this last precious chance of a hearing. But there was nothing for it: she had to plough on with the truth.

"The Corruption Ray," she said. "That's what's 'up'. You have heard of it, perhaps, as a hypothesis?" Seeing him nod, she went on: "I have statistical proof of its existence, proof that it is being aimed at the cities of Syoom. Not equally, and not all at once. Some cities have fallen to a lower state than others. Some are hardly touched…"

"And mine is pretty bad," said the Noad gently.

She gave him a sharp glance and was disturbed at a vision of apathy which was not at all what she had expected. What *had* she imagined his reaction would be? Disbelief, anger, or the faint possibility of sudden conversion and support. Not this glimmer of sadly resigned wisdom. False wisdom. She refused to accept it.

"You're a *leader*," she snapped. "I am asking you to lead. The civilized world is in crisis and somebody somewhere has to be the first Noad to recognize the fact. It could be you."

"Hmm, bossiness with backbone," he smiled. "Suppose I did agree. What," he asked in a mildly interested tone, "would be your next demand?"

"Send out warnings with copies of the evidence. Subsidize more statisticians to make the case even stronger. Form a coalition of cities. Mount an expedition to find the perpetrators of the Ray. Destroy them and it!"

Another "Hmm…" and Vroonwik Clarm leaned back in his chair. "This has been quite a morning, Hyoen. Have you heard of Professor Himbock Thiams? Author of *The Impossibility of Ethics*? Well, I'm supposed to make a decision on him in the next few hours. My advisors tell me I have let him go on too long. They may be right. You listening, Hyoen? You getting all this?"

"I'm listening, Noad," she replied, hanging on to her own guide-rail of purpose with each sway and lurch of this roller-coaster interview.

"The Professor's statements," the Noad went on, "about mankind being on the way out, and everything being futile, and so on, are, on one level, mere expressions of fashionable opinion. But coming from *him* they may cause more harm than the average. I muse make a pragmatic decision as to when the time has come to say 'enough is enough'. A few useful fools still exist who preach public spirit and so help to keep the State minimally functional. Himbock is busily undermining them. I am getting tired of it." The Noad leaned forward again, resting his chin on one palm, and regarded Hyoen obliquely. "You see the sort of thing I have to put up with? No, of course, you don't. Hmm… let me tell you some more about what I've got on today. Then you'll see what my life is like." His face brightened at this whim of his, this

120

neatest of ways to silence her: for his own predicament was the effective answer to her requests. And she, meanwhile, guessed that it might, as a bonus, be a relief for him to unburden his soul to a visitor.

Despite some sympathy, she recoiled as he spoke on. She found herself listening to an account which sucked her deeper and deeper into the madness of power.

"Today I am due to pronounce sentence upon my favourite nephew," Vroonwik continued. "You know, I get my worst pressures from members of my own family. Sad, but there it is. It had become obvious that either Thebb Clarm or Knef Krateen had to go, for Narar is not wide enough for both of them and I am determined not to leave a legacy of civil war. Therefore I sent my hypnotist, Ob Solm, to each of them – Thebb first – with the button to press: the button that is supposed, when pressed, to kill one's rival. Sounds fantastic, but in Ob Solm's presence one believes it. And yet Thebb refused. Whereas Knef Krateen went ahead and pressed it – so Knef, I must regrettably conclude, is the man who has the stuff in him to rule when I am gone.

"So there you are, that's one sad sample from my in-tray. What else can I tell you?" As he spoke he shuffled some plastic sleeves around his desk. "Here, this is interesting." He picked up a folder. "Take a look at that." (Gingerly, Hyoen reached for it.) "Open it."

She did so and saw the minutes of a secret trial. On the front page was a photo of a young man with a sullen stare.

"Political opposition?" she queried.

"No, just vandalism. I became curious to know why this lad had destroyed a tree in one of my parks. I had him brought in for questioning. I told him he would be released on one condition: he must give a good, convincing reason why he destroyed my tree. And you know what? Not even to save his life, could he give that reason!"

She sat clamped by a chill of dull horror.

"What do you intend to do to the boy?"

"It's been done. I've had him put down."

For a while there was silence. It was broken by the Noad, who began a rambling soliloquy. "My people are evil, Corruption Ray or no; and I reckon that no Corruption Ray is needed now, if it ever was; we're doing a good enough job of undermining Narar ourselves. But in any case I wonder if perhaps it might be a good thing after all that the Ray should shine and toughen us, dirtying our minds to suit us for the dark days ahead. That nuisance Professor Himbock is doubtless right in assuming that we are in the final stage of civilization. How could we not be? When the gvo-crystals finally run out, the cities are doomed and most of us will starve. A remnant will retreat to what is left of the forests. That will be that. Not in my lifetime, I hope. For the time being the thing to do is to grab a comfortable berth and defend it against all comers. That's what Thebb should have done, and that's what I've done. Though actually the noadex is not very comfortable. I would prefer to be like you, Hyoen Freld: a rich traveller who has time to saunter around offering impractical advice. But I'm not complaining. You have given me some rest from my usual round. You have lent me an ear –"

Hyoen saw that the communicator light had been flashing for some seconds. Now the buzzer purred; the Noad with a sigh picked up the handset. "Yes…? Ah! Go on… Yes… just a moment." Cupping the handset the Noad smirked: "I mentioned a certain Professor Himbock, didn't I? Well, this looks good. Himbock's not keeping his head down any longer, it seems. With luck, this can be turned around." Once more speaking into the phone, he commanded, "Continue!"

Then as Hyoen watched, the Noad's smile grew ever broader, until he heaved backwards and laughed, "Oh *no!*"

4: A Glass of Water

Tlall College was an island of mellow, scholarly calm. Its creamy stone was attractive to the eye amid the dingy quarter of Hwain.

The so-called slums of Hwain were not really much worse than many another district of Narar, in these days when a blight of drowsy hopelessness lay over most of Syoom, but the contrast of atmosphere, between the intellectual stimulation inside and the social decay outside the College walls, made the outside into something which (for philosophy student Jarchon Whepp) didn't bear thinking about…

Jarchon therefore simply put off thinking about it.

A smooth-faced, flippantly handsome youngster, he had the reputation – oddly, in view of his shallow personality – of being brilliant as brilliant at his second subject, philosophy, as he was at his main field of study, engineering. But maybe (said some of his critics) this wasn't so odd after all: the kind of intellectual pyrotechnics Jarchon was good at were nothing more than the kind of silly game chosen by the idle rich when they happened to have brains as well as money to waste.

In actual fact he was not that rich; he merely looked it. Moreover, outside of seminars and debating halls he was quite mild-mannered. Nevertheless the fact that he obviously *could* show off if he wanted to, gave him the reputation of having done so. This was a little unfair; after all he was merely one of many who adopted a public persona as a defence against a reality going to pot...

His Director of Studies, Ryel Nound, hoped that Jarchon would be on his best behaviour today. The scheduled seminar was due to be graced by none other than the illustrious Professor Himbock Thiams.

Ryel noted, approvingly, that during the preliminary chit-chat while glasses of liqueur were being handed round, Jarchon was listening with polite attention to Himbock's affable remarks amid a circle of respectful students. And a few minutes later, as the Professor began his introductory address to the seminar, Jarchon, having got the seat next to him, seemed (thank goodness) quite rapt.

Himbock was saying what he had often said before: that humanity was in its dotage and that rational people ought to come to terms with their species' old age, just as an individual must resign nenself to senescence.

"Partly," the Professor went on, "this involves doing away with wasteful emotions like indignation and surprise. Humanity is so old, has been through so much, that what with one thing and another we've seen it all. There's nothing new, and it's simply silly to get angry about injustice from others, or guilty about any injustice that flows from oneself. Good and evil are shared around. Whatever we do, those two attributes reach their own levels, like gases in an atmosphere. You may call this cynicism, but if so, cynicism can no more be evaded than the law of conservation of energy. And just as that law, of conservation of energy, has been expressed mathematically and can help us to model physical realities, so it would be an achievement in our lives if we could schematise the law of cynicism. Perhaps we can make a start today?"

Himbock paused, and beamed benignly around the oval table. That table, heavy and covered with velvet, and the fine leathery smell of old bindings pervading the room, lent such comfortable dignity to the scene, that to an impressionable scholar it might not matter what was said – the college atmosphere prevailed over the sense of the words, which murmured like a shallow brook through the wisdom of past, present and future academia.

"How would we make a start, sir?" asked Cuelna Dewsplir, a hurriedly scribbling girl.

The Professor bestowed a kindly glance upon Cuelna. "Let's begin," he suggested, "with possible guilt feelings. Do any of you have any twinges of conscience about your privileged position here? Attending this elite college – which incidentally, between you and me, has dumbed down its entrance requirements quite a bit, but still retains most of its prestige – attending as I say this college and enjoying this comfortable environment that's in such contrast with what you can see out of the window – well, anyone for guilt?"

Following that cue, they beheld the distant huddled dwellings of Hwain quarter. It was a vista of ramshackle, tottering drabness. The older structures were constructed of good materials, but even the best of them were in disrepair. Energy was lacking, wealth was lacking – the energy and wealth which came from gvo crystals, of which the supply was fast disappearing as the great Dzolm, the Sun-Egg near Contahl, neared final depletion.

The Sun-Egg had been civilization's source of energy for over two hundred lifetimes, but everything must come to an end eventually, and that clear prospect was depressing human culture – more so than any economic lack that had yet occurred.

"Well?" the Professor prompted them again, for the uncomfortable silence had remained unbroken. "That view through the window: does it make you morally uneasy, or not?"

"It does a bit," confessed Cuelna.

Perhaps the Professor saw something fetching in her earnest, bespectacled face, for he smiled as he said, "In that case, let me tell you that you are wrong to feel uneasy. You don't need to feel any guilt at all. That's why I am here – to explain this truth. And that's why this seminar is entitled 'The Ethics of Determinism'." He paused to sip from the glass of water in front of him. Some of the students did the same; they all had glasses of water, for this was serious stuff; later would be time for liqueur but right now let plain water accompany the display of no-nonsense intellect.

"How much," the Professor continued, setting his glass down, "do you people understand so far, of what I have said in the articles and books which I've seen are on your reading list?" He chuckled. "Eh, come on now. Time for *your* contributions. What do *you* grasp of the Ethics of Determinism?"

The silence threatened to lengthen again; then all eyes swivelled gratefully to the opening mouth of Jarchon Whepp.

"I grasp that there aren't any," he said, dryly.

Oh-oh, thought Ryel Nound. That's all right if you can keep it there, Jarchon. Just don't overdo it.

Himbock was nodding, lips pursed. "If you like to put it that way, yes. If you wish to define 'ethics' as the mysterious operation of a supernatural conscience, un-determined by physical laws, then yes, there aren't any.

Since every event has a cause, nothing *can* happen except what *does* happen. That goes back to what I said previously, that indignation is a waste of time…"

As the Professor continued his speech Ryel Nound relaxed. He felt grateful now, and contented. *Good for Jarchon, he's actually helped things along; I thought for a moment he was going to make a bit of trouble but really, come to think of it, it's natural that he should get on well with the Professor. Nobody is likelier than Jarchon to agree with Himbock that it's no use bothering or caring about anything. Nobody should be more pleased than he, at hearing such perfect justification for pleasing oneself and having as much of a good time as one can.*

Jarchon Whepp, however, existed on a plane quite unconcerned with his Director of Studies' wish for a quiet life.

Nothing in Jarchon-land at this moment was quite so strong as the whimsical impulse which caused his hand to reach for the glass of water in front of him. Nobody guessed what was in the student's mind, no one could tell what he was about to do, though afterwards they wondered why they had not foreseen what it would be. He always did have an iconoclastic streak, did Jarchon; as a rule it manifested itself not in serious anti-establishment speeches but rather in a mocking literalness, a propensity to use his opponents' own words against them – and *that* is why they ought to have foreseen.

Jarchon calmly lifted the glass of water and poured it over Professor Himbock's head.

A strangled gasp arose from all around the table. Himbock flapped and sputtered. Ryel Nound, choked by shock, could not get a word out. It was so hard to believe one's eyes. Could even Jarchon have done this, have really *poured a glass over the Professor?* Himbock lifted his arms, aghast over his wet suit… "What djis – what djistdoo?" he gibbered.

"It was inevitable," Jarchon shrugged.

"Whaaa…"

"It was determined," Jarchon explained. "The fact that I did it, means I could not have done otherwise. Could I? Come on, Professor, calm down – what are you so indignant about? Indignation is a waste of time –"

"Now look here, Jarchon –" began Ryel, and stopped.

Himbock's wet features had sagged further. The others all now witnessed the unmistakable kind of appalled calm which came over the Professor – the awful clang of inner truth, which also, at that same moment, came upon Ryel Nound.

Ryel could not help it: he began to grin, and grins flickered round the rows

125

of other students' faces likewise, their thoughts wheeling to alight upon the un-suppressable awareness that a perfect hit had been scored.

Nobody was ever going to forget this...

5: Recruits

"...Can't affort to put the University people's backs up too much," the Noad was explaining. "So I'll have to let them expel Jarchon, pity though it is to punish such a hilarious deed. But I have an idea..."

Hyoen was sitting very still, trying with all her might not to allow herself to be taken in. Belatedly she appreciated the force of the Noad's charm; he had a way of getting round people. Indeed he had expertly flattered her self-importance and her intelligence by giving her some of his time, confiding in her and then recounting to her the tale he had just heard over the phone. At any moment she would hear the price he would demand in return. And she was going to pay that price. She would choose to let herself be used by this Noad because she had come to the end of her resources as an individual. She'd get no further in her mission without state help of some kind; it was as she had said at the Ethical Action meeting: the good ones won't listen so she must get help from the bad.

"Hyoen Freld!" His tone made her jump. "Are you all right?"

She unfroze and said, "I'm wondering what you're after, Noad."

"A mutually profitable agreement." He breezed on: "There are some people whom I need to get rid of, and you are going to help me do it. In fact you're just what I need. Come," he stood up. "Pull yourself together and we'll sort this business out."

"Where are we going?"

"To the house of an honest man," said Vroomwrik with sudden grimth.

He put out his arm, sweeping her along by his side. Out of the office and along a corridor, in which staff members straightened respectfully as they passed, he strode and she trotted to keep up with him, dragged in the current of his authority. She recognized, but could do nothing about, the psychological pressure he was exerting.

During the walk to his flatcar the Noad spoke orders to officials whom he beckoned to him briefly. They listened and fell back to do his bidding, whatever that might be; Hyoen gleaned the impression that he was making sure that various people would be gathered where and when he wanted them, as if he were moving units around on a game-board. Then, sitting with him in the back of the flatcar, she heard him tell her with complete assurance that he was appointing her to lead a mission, fitted out by himself, against the Corruption Ray – precisely what she had wanted all along – more than she had dared hope –

Yet she felt chilled rather than elated. There'd be a catch.

Sure enough, it soon transpired that the mission was to be financed by means of the confiscation of property from the Noad's nephew, Thebb Clarm. "He won't be needing it any more, where he's headed," added Vroonwrik Clarm.

A shudder wrenched Hyoen partly free.

"Noad V-C, don't expect me to believe that you would kill your own family."

He smiled at the scolding, at the way she blanked her horror by telling him off.

"Oh, so you think there's something specially bad about killing a relative rather than a stranger, eh? One's own flesh and blood is of more value than the rest of humanity – is that your idea?"

"No, but…" her voice petered out.

He growled, "I know what I'm doing."

Minutes later the flatcar swished along a drive. It stopped outside a large house. The Noad emerged and so did the driver. Hyoen, shakily clambering out after them, was interested to see no guards. No armed men were in sight apart from Vroonwik Clarm himself and the chauffeur. *No other witnesses*, went one dark thought, but a lighter thought went the other way: *not enough fire-power to risk the deed*. And really, at no time during the car ride had she managed fully to believe that he was bringing her along to watch an actual murder.

Then a guard did appear, as the front door of the house opened to reveal the man saluting upon the threshold; the Noad in response pointed to a large shed beside the house and tilted his head inquiringly; the guard nodded – whereupon the three men drew their lasers and approached the shed door. It was all quite business-like, Hyoen perceived; this was Noad Vroonwik coping with a run-of-the-mill managerial problem. The guard kicked open the shed door…

The Noad called over his shoulder, "Come on, Hyoen. Meet the recruits I've gathered for you."

He spoke lightly, making it obvious that no matter how much their lives were stamped by his decisions, the outcome would be their problem, not his.

All he would say, as she edged past him, was: "You'll take this bargain, I think."

It was quite true, she thought as she walked in through the doorway.

The workshop was patchily lit by adjustable spotlights, mounted upon the shelf-table all around the side, and by glows from ornamental cubes illuminating the upper shelves. And in a corner beyond the forty-foot hover-raft which occupied half the floor space, stood a tub three-quarters full of gvo crystals which cast an extra splotch of orange brightness onto the ceiling immediately above.

Three men waited by the raft.

One of them seemed at home in the workshop. He wore a stained overall and tools clipped to his belt. He was about Hyoen's age, with the clouded face of one who has lost a long battle. "I am Thebb Clarm," he said formally. "The Noad has granted me my life, if I keep to my side of the agreement. So you can expect obedience from me."

Hyoen forced her head to nod, to swallow the idea that this man was subordinating himself to *her*.

Vroonwik's voice boomed from behind: "Good, so I'll leave you all to get on with it, then!" His departing footsteps scrunched away; Hyoen gazed back in stunned fashion. Through the still open doorway she saw that one solitary guard remained stationed there, obviously to ensure that the order for exile was carried out. For this was the whole point. This was the beautiful method of ridding the State of a whole clutch of nuisances in one neat parcel.

Well, nonetheless, it *was* a mission. Conscious of her need to assert the control she had been given, Hyoen turned back to Thebb and asked with formal courtesy, "And will you introduce me to these sponndarou?" – reminding herself as she spoke, that on this voyage "sponndarou" ("laser-bearers") would most likely *not* be a mere honorific.

"This young fellow is Jarchon Whepp, who did a bad thing in college, which is why he is coming with us –"

"I know about that," Hyoen smiled.

The youngster, who had been lounging against a workbench, performed a sarcastic bow.

"And this," continued Thebb with a gesture at the third figure, a small man in a rumpled suit, "is Professor Himbock, who – so Jarchon and I suspect – is to accompany us as a spy."

If only, thought Hyoen, I had not smiled at the mention of Jarchon's prank – for here was the victim of that prank... Embarrassed, she risked a proper appraisal of the Professor to whom she was being introduced. He had a wizened and bedraggled look about him. Plainly, the shock which had uprooted his life now caused him to wince from all contact with his present unwelcome environment: he huddled with his arms by his sides, and seemed to shrink inside his clothes. At first, when he failed to make an immediate response to the accusation of being a spy, Hyoen wondered if he had been rendered mute. But then he said in a dead voice, "Yes, I was asked to keep an eye on things. However, I shall bear no tales to the Noad."

"And why," asked Thebb, "should you expect us to believe that?"

Himbock shrugged:

"Because as a matter of fact I am not bothered about ever returning to Narar. Drop me off at any big city we come to – anywhere I can get a university post – and neither you nor Vroonwik Clarm will hear from me again, I can promise you."

"Ah. That, if true, does rather change things," conceded Thebb.

Jarchon Whepp, intervening, drawled: "Does it? So far as I can see, it doesn't matter one way or the other. Let the Professor spy all he likes, if he gets the urge – what can he tell? What could we be plotting? A coup? By blundering around Syoom on a raft? Not that I mind going on this pointless jaunt. But only because it beats sitting exams."

The ex-student did not seem to mind the unappreciative silence that followed his speech. Hyoen recognized the type – one who would never be dislodged from his breezy ego – and she decided not to worry about him. The lad's shortcomings weren't the sort for which fate would exact a penalty. The expedition would not get crushed any sooner, or any later, for the falsity of that word "jaunt".

They spent the early hours of the afternoon packing and arranging the raft, storing and checking vital equipment, and arranging four blockish tents called *runks* on deck, one *runk* per person. While they worked Hyoen spoke about the mission. The others listened obediently, but did not say much. Exile, especially in these darkened days, was a terrible fate; the two listless older men simply did not have the heart to show interest in where they were going or in what they might be called upon to do. They worked like automatons, leaving the thinking to Hyoen. As for the ex-student, he fetched and carried with a smile on his face. Obedience to orders was a whimsy he was prepared to indulge. Fate must after all be humoured. Fate apparently knew no better than to take this bizarre liberty with Jarchon Whepp.

Presently an official sent from the Noad came to chauffeur Hyoen back to her lodgings, waited while she packed a small case with her belongings, and

129

then returned her to Thebb's workshop. Otherwise there was no more word from those in authority. The single guard watched silently.

Thebb Clarm roused himself to make one surprising statement. "I must," he said, "take these sculptures with me."

"What sculptures?" asked Hyoen with an automatic flinch at any unknown factor.

Thebb showed her the objects, which she had thought of as mere ornamental lights – the beautiful glowing cubes and other geometrical shapes ranged on the upper shelves.

He explained: "I cannot bear to leave them. My young brother, Rawm, made them. My late little brother, who made the mistake of retreating too far from politics into his art. I can't leave them to be thrown away or sold off."

"Pack them in a box," nodded Hyoen.

Finally they named the raft the *Rawmdeck*, loaded its fuel chamber with gvo crystals, and stored the balance of the crystals in the aft bunker. Now the *Rawmdeck* looked like a scale model of part of a drab housing estate with the *runks* instead of buildings and the steering-post like a semaphore up front. The guard, seeing that they had finished, walked smartly up to Hyoen.

"May I report that you are ready to leave, sponndar H-F?"

"You may."

The guard went off to one side and spoke into his transceiver. He then told them, "You must be out of the city before evenshine."

"That suits me," said Hyoen. She looked round and surprised a wan grin on the face of Thebb Clarm.

"I like the way you put things: 'That suits me'."

Approval? Irony? Or had he spoken in bitterness at her easy take-over of his property and his life? Hyoen brusquely postponed the question. The thing to do was to get away from Narar while the going was good. In that sense, the Noad's orders *did* suit her.

6: Dark-Age Syoom

Thebb Clarm pressed a button on the wall of the workshop and with a mechanical sigh the main double doors swung open. He then stepped back onto the *Rawmdeck,* where the other three members of the expedition were already seated; he went over to the helm and switched on the engine. A hum in the fuel-chamber: crystals were being devoured, and in the process they began to release

130

their force of levity; the raft lifted off the floor. Thebb pressed another switch to erect the windscreens. Then he pushed the steerstick and the vehicle began to move forward.

It was the supper hour, as he manoeuvred out through the doors, along the drive and into the street. People were going home or were already at home. Those few who remained on the pavements stared as if through invisible bars at the curious departure of the hover-raft. Some rumour had begun to spread, about the sentence of exile passed upon Thebb and Jarchon. As for Professor Himbock – the bystanders might not be so sure what he was doing on the raft, but a learned man might after all take it into his head to accompany an expedition. Or did people know more? Had the story of the water-pouring already got around? Were some of the pedestrians whom the raft overtook, grinning as their heads turned?

The raft floated out through a gate in the city wall, into suburbia. Then the houses thinned out; the underlying cork-like plain became visible in larger patches. Outcrops of unworked stone became more common. The definable road disappeared. All these signs told the voyagers that they had left the city of Narar.

Thebb increased speed to the maximum: fifty miles per hour. Still he kept silent. He did not ask for directions. His two compatriots were likewise taciturn. Affected by their mood, Hyoen, too, postponed utterance, as she at last began to view exile the same way they did, as a terrible blow; not yet personally, for it had not happened to her yet, but she knew it might.

They skimmed through the farm belt. Fields here glowed a beautiful orange. It was a fine colour for landscape painters but not as good a sign for the economy as bright yellow would have been; the worth of the *vheic* plants was diminished, and the purplish sky darkened, by fat pests in the form of wardrobe-shaped clouds hanging low to feed upon the *vheic*'s emissions, weakening the plants' yield.

"Your territory," ventured Hyoen, "could do with a sky-cleaning."

"No navy," muttered Thebb.

"Why doesn't Vroonwik build one?"

Thebb shrugged. "Politics. Money. I don't know. He probably will, now."

The gloomily beauteous farm-belt was left behind as fields petered out into scrubby stone badlands, where ancient lava had been whipped into a frenzy and then frozen into a knife-sharp jumble of arcs and spirals. The area looked impassable on foot, and hazardous enough even from the perspective of air transport at points where the rock-tips reared like frozen flames, but the *Rawmdeck* had sufficient altitude to clear the obstacles.

According to what Hyoen had heared, this region of tortured terrain had played a varied part in the history of Narar, sometime serving as a defence, other times as a threat. Apparently these forbidding lands were not completely uninhabited. Predictably, they were the haunt of outlaws – though Thebb appeared confident that four sponndarou on a raft going fifty miles per hour could defend themselves against anything they were likely to meet.

At some stage, Hyoen knew, she must dictate a change of course, but perhaps she had better allow their pilot to get them through these badlands first... This excuse to postpone the exercise of authority lasted about one hour. After that, the country became easier and soon the only thing visible on all sides was the normal plain, the endless granular *gralm*, which formed the solid world-ocean of Ooranye. It was not utterly uniform, being sparsely strewn with occasional crags, hills or mountain ranges which poked up through the gralm. But it was no longer true that the pilot need give all his attention to the steering.

Hyoen touched Thebb on the shoulder, pointed a bit to the right, and it was as easy as that. He simply nodded and obediently turned the helm, ceasing to turn when she touched him again. Perfectly, though listlessly, he had adjusted their course as she wished.

She liked this quiet co-operation. Nevertheless, it was necessary also to speak. It was important to convince Thebb to follow her with wholehearted, keen intelligence. Of course he was supposed to obey her anyway, according to the terms of the agreement by which Noad Vroonwik had spared his life – but Hyoen was not stupid enough to believe that her authority would survive long under its own steam. She had no means of coercion, no real hold over the three men who were speeding beyond their Noad's reach.

She raised her voice above the wail of the wind:

"Thebb, I need your co-operation."

"In what?" he bawled back.

The others, she sensed, were edging forward.

She filled her lungs and spoke out:

"Your Noad has sent you away as punishment – yes – but there is more to this voyage than punishment – it is an assignment, a vital mission."

"Depends," he retorted. "On whether we can see it the way you see it."

"Initially," she pressed on, "my plan is to get us to Jador, my home city. There I can impress the authorities with news of your Noad's support for our mission against the Corruption Ray – you *have* heard of the Ray, haven't you?"

"I've heard the theory, yes."

"Much more than a theory... never mind, I'll coach you when the time comes. The point is, we haven't yet got enough crystals to go looking all over Syoom, so we have to call at Jador first, get support from there."

Thebb smiled bitterly at the mention of the crystals, which represented the greater part of his life's savings. But he merely said, "Destination Jador, very well" – obedient though sullen.

Hyoen continued, "It's about six thousand miles, at our top speed it should take one hundred and twenty hours, that is, four days of continuous travel... but I must ask, can we do it that way, or must the *Rawmdeck* stop at night?"

"The *raft* can go non-stop," shrugged Thebb, "but can we?"

But his real meaning was, "can *you*?" This she could tell, and she realized the importance of the question because it suddenly came to her that she was terrified at the idea of stopping out here, night or day. Up to this point she had not considered it. Airship travel was the kind she was accustomed to: up amongst the clouds, floating and dozing her comfortable way from city to city. As long as you had the money you could do it that way, sticking to your cabin, unaware of the enormity of the world. By contrast, down here, viciously close to the ground, where the plains tore past a bare yard beneath the keel and the raft was thumped by rebounding winds, the truth threatened to hatch in her mind. And at night, stopping would be worst of all. That idea of being exposed on the dark plain... no!

"We won't stop," she declared. "We'll take it in turns to pilot. Surely, any of us can steer in a straight line."

"Yes, that part's easy enough."

It was arranged among the four of them. Hyoen, when night fell, took the first watch. She had skill enough at steering, to skirt the odd isolated crag. But in order to be able to do that she had to keep the bow light on, thus risking the advertisement of their presence to any prowler of the wilderness. She preferred this, though, to the thought of parking in the plains. In the darkness beyond and around the bow light's beam, the hum of the motor and the roar of the wind blended into what seemed to be a real, shouting voice, as if the world were giving tongue to warn the voyagers of obscure and terrible fates in store for those who intruded in the wastelands. Standing nearly four hours peering into an inadequate cone of illumination and imagining what shapes might suddenly appear ahead, Hyoen grew so rattled that she hardly slept after her watch was over.

Thebb, for his part, knew that whereas the night voyage took its toll on all of them, the strain was worst for Hyoen; patiently he endured her brittle manner towards him the next morning.

"Demoralisation, everywhere," she chattered, standing beside him as he steered. The return of daylight made it effortless to man the helm; he could easily put up with the flow of her voice as she complained on and on: "We're up against it. Cynicism. Both social and political. Complete selfishness shown by every regime. Jador's as bad as any. I admit it. Every bit as bad."

A pause. Thebb felt he ought to say something. He began, "Then what's the use..."

"*But*, let me finish, *but,* when they see the evidence we'll bring! Ah, *then.*"

"Just so I know what you expect of me," Thebb politely enquired, " – *what* evidence?"

"Don't take that tone," she snapped at him. "You are the nephew of the Noad of Narar. If we can't use that... Your trouble is, you have no faith."

"I have hope, though," he said with a thoughtful glance at her. "My own individual hope."

"What good is that?"

He started as if to speak, then looked away. As if reconsidering his words he began again: "Individuals can always carry on and on, until in the far distant future the wheel of fortune may turn and a fine society be reborn."

"Not so long as there's a Corruption Ray, it won't."

That dampened the conversation.

After a long pause Hyoen insisted, "Someone, somewhere, is aiming this evil thing at all of us, and nen – whoever nen is – must be stopped. Thebb, will you share my hopes in this?" She put forth her best smile; she placed a hand on his arm.

"I can give it a go," he assured her. "But don't be too surprised or upset if our efforts go down the drain. Whatever happens, our soul-stuff recycles, does it not? Maybe into a more fortunate species later on."

"Are you mocking me?" For this seemed almost a caricature of the decayed reasoning of despair.

"Not precisely. I suppose I am resorting, for want of anything better, to the cheap melancholy talk I used to hear from Smim." He spoke with bite, because the effort of coping with Hyoen, though he was beginning to regard it as an honour, was also beginning to fray his nerves.

Of course she immediately asked what he meant and he then explained to her that Smim was his woman whom he had left behind. Hyoen said, "And you never even said goodbye to her? Don't you care what happens to her?"

"I want her to be disgusted enough to forget me."

"That's unkind!"

"No, it's kind. She can then go find herself a successful man. She's not like you, Hyoen, she can't make her own success."

"Hah! I am glad you think I am successful."

He said earnestly: "You are at least trying to grab at something connected with what's going on; that's the great thing, to be political and not just private, if one can manage it. I can't – not any more. It's such a temptation to go private. It's the fatal step, which I took. One ought to live and die with some clutch on events – otherwise life has no meaning."

It was a more vehement speech than he had intended to make. She, however, did no more than put her hand on his for a moment, before pacing away.

Later, in conversation with Jarchon, Thebb broached the question of what to do the next night – asking that the subject be broached with proper tact. The ex-student nodded and said, "I'll see it gets sorted out. She'll agree, never doubt it."

Jarchon's smoothness, reflected Thebb, has its uses. Sure enough, that evening, as Thebb steered while the others sat and ate their rations, Jarchon made the casual remark: "I don't think any of us really want to try to sleep through another night of howling wind." He went on, with no contradiction from Hyoen or the Professor, "So we *do* want to park this time." He looked neither at, nor obviously away from, the leader, and every moment in which she did not speak was a gain for his point. "There are various schools of thought among hover-raft travellers in these parts. Should one settle for the night in the open plain, or close to a forest? I suppose one could argue about it forever."

"I don't want to argue forever," said Hyoen testily; "I'm tired." She had given in. "Let's camp close, but not too close, to a forest." And so it was decided.

Himbock had hardly uttered a word during the trip so far, though he had done his share of the steering, but now he said, "I can take the first watch."

The *Rawmdeck* settled a hundred yards from the next sizeable forest. The air was darkening from evenshine to anyne; the dark green of the treetops nearby was deepening to black. Hyoen fell asleep in her chair before she even had the energy to get inside her *runk*. Himbock entered his tent. Thebb and Jarchon stepped quietly off the raft, glad for a stroll.

Jarchon said, "Our leader is not so full of resource as she likes to make out."

Thebb glanced at him and was satisfied that the words had not been harshly spoken. He replied, "We seem to be her last hope. And I think deep down she knows she'll get nowhere with this mission."

"Oh, well," said the younger man, "she's got an idea and she's trying it out. Good luck to all triers. But how long are you going to stick with her?"

"As long as she needs me. How about yourself?"

"Oh," said Jarchon airily, "I'm not bored yet."

The night passed; the air brightened into the 20,871st day of the Nitrogen Era.

It did not seem such a Dark Age while they sat at breakfast on the parked raft, with the breeze from the limitless plains fanning their faces and the treetops of the forest close by. Hyoen, now bright-eyed and refreshed, said: "I'm so glad we stopped here. Perhaps," she added shyly, "you men might accompany me on a short walk?"

"You're the boss," said Thebb, "but let me stay behind to guard the raft."

He watched the other three hop down and stroll across the gralmy plain in the direction of the forest: Hyoen with Jarchon on her left and the silent Himbock on her right. Hyoen, it seemed, had quite swung away from her previous mood of apprehension.

Thebb saw them approach to within perhaps forty yards of the trees when he beheld an abrupt shake and rip in the higher branches. Through that gap protruded a head. It was of gleaming cartilage and revolting size: two yards wide at least, and split by a down-curving, lipless mouth. The mouth undulated like the base of a curtain, to reveal serried fangs – in fact the creature seemed to be almost all mouth. The eyes were mere dead black spots in the smooth face. Pincers then appeared, and pushed the branches further apart. Next, the enormous head, and the meagre body behind it, toppled out of its perch, and fell in a rolled-up state, a vast stony ball, which crashed onto the ground. A cable still seemed to connect it with the trees, however. Thebb stared dazedly at that cable. He tried to think, while he drew his laser with one hand and started the raft's engine with the other.

He had no real hope that he could advance in time to help his companions. Drearily aware that he was out of training for a fight, he was above all appalled at his own lack of knowledge. He had never heard of this monster. It was intensely embarrassing to encounter such stark proof of his ignorance. As that thought sank deeper, as seconds ticked by in slow motion, the monster was unrolling, revealing its body plan, bristling with open-and-closing pincers. Thebb gunned the motor; the raft lurched forward; but then he saw Jarchon *waving him back*.

Though he did not understand, Thebb reversed the steerstick.

Hyoen was crouching out there, taking pot shots at the thing with her laser in bolt mode. The bolts were pinging off its body surface, making no difference at all, but she did not seem able to change her tactics; she simply continued to fire, in frozen panic. The other two, however, behaved as though they knew precisely what to do. Thebb was close enough now to overhear their words.

"Umbna-jorraynt," observed Himbock in an academic tone.

"Still hyphenated," agreed Jarchon. He added brightly, "Shall we make it just an umbna?"

"That would be best," the Professor agreed. "You circle round... watch for a chance to cut the cable. I'll keep its pincers off."

Jarchon ran and dodged as he ran. Leftwards and to the rear of the monster, his course left Himbock free to approach it from the right, waving his laser almost in its face.

Watching all this, Thebb got off the raft, came up behind Hyoen and put a gentle hand on her shoulder, telling her to stop her incessant firing lest she hit their companions. "Let the experts deal with it," he murmured. "We're outclassed here." *You fear the night and its bumps; I have feared that more complex outrage known as day; meanwhile, however, I think we are growing into a team.*

Himbock stepped aside from a flopping pincer which almost plummeted onto his head as the creature subsided. The struggle was over. Jarchon emerged from behind the inert mass. "It's just an umbna now," he affirmed.

"Don't stand too close," Himbock warned. "A specimen this size won't remain stupefied for more than a minute."

"In that case we'd better be going."

The conquerors led the way back to the raft, Thebb and Hyoen following in humble silence. Thebb did not need to be told to start the engine and pull out as soon as all were aboard. New despondency dug roots into his mind during the cheerful post-victory comments swapped by Jarchon and Himbock.

Hyoen, like Thebb, was unreconciled to the shock of it all. "Tell me, for Sky's sake," she burst out as the *Rawmdeck* accelerated, "what *is* an umbna-jorraynt?"

"One end animal, the other end plant," answered Jarchon. "Sometimes the umbna snaps the link between them and strikes out on its own, but this one hadn't, yet. So I helped it on its way. You could say I did it a favour, helping it towards freedom."

"But what in the world does a thing that size live on?"

"The very occasional traveller," replied Professor Himbock. "Umbnas can wait tens of thousands of days in stasis between meals. Which is why, when they do wake, they're quite determined."

7: Kasproueh

Thebb awoke in such a state of depression, so unable to face the day, that he lay still while he yearned for sleep to reclaim him. Because he made no move and no sound, through the fabric of his *runk* he overheard voices which might otherwise not have spoken.

"...a case of nebulation," Jarchon was saying.

"Aaaah, no," Hyoen's voice responded.

Jarchon insisted, "It might well prove so. He hasn't been his usual self, the last few days."

"I think it was the umbna-jorraynt that unnerved him," said Hyoen. "It certainly had that effect on me."

"Yes, but you got over it. Thebb has sunk into a kind of permanent stupor. That's why I reckon it's nebulation..."

Nebulation? Might he really have succumbed to the mental cloudiness, the leakage of identity which can overcome the unwary out in the plains?

They can't understand, mused Thebb sadly. *In fact, the truth is far simpler.*

He spelled it out in big letters on the blackboard of his closed eyelids as he listened to his companions discussing him.

He had wasted his life.

He was nothing.

He had always been nothing.

No wonder his great-uncle had finally exiled him: Thebb could now see clearly that he had fooled himself all his adult life, imagining that the business of attending committees of this and that, wielding a certain minimum of patronage and exercising occasional influence that came to him from Vroonwrik's coat-tails, might make him, Thebb, a citizen worth the name. Complete waste of time, to fall between two stools, the politician and the engineer. And to think that if only he'd followed his own bent, he might instead have become a *proper* engineer, perhaps a real inventor... instead of a failed politician who took refuge in his workshop whenever he could spare an hour.

Admittedly he'd had his reasons. Survival. To keep a finger on the political pulse had seemed to him the only way for a member of the ruling clan to stay alive. Besides, if he *had* risked all for his true vocation, he might still have failed, have ended up as isolated and ignorant as he was now.

But at least he would have had more *fun*.

While he lay, cheek on pillow, intuition spoke to him, taking on a whispered voice-of-the-world: *You think you're in a bad way now, but wait till I hit you with some real misfortune. I, Ooranye, have you exposed. You're out on my plains, where anything can happen.*

He gave a start. A shiver at the voice. Only a bad dream? Had he dozed off again?

Too easy, that. Call it a dream, but – dreams, after all, can be advance warning of the truth. A probability run. Distillation of what's likely.

Sure enough, bad news arrived over breakfast.

Rawmdeck's communicator buzzed and the four travellers looked up from where they sat around a trestle table near the stern. Hyoen half-rose and sat down again when she saw that the others kept still. She said, "Shouldn't we answer?"

"Hmm…" shrugged Jarchon, "might as well, I suppose. If someone has beamed us, the damage is done."

Hyoen, looking thoughtful, rose again, and this time walked to the box near the helm.

The others saw her stoop over the dial, listen, and then straighten indignantly. "What!" Next, her shoulders drooped and finally they heard her say, "Thank you, Olmiroa, for telling me. Goodbye." She wobbled back to the table, as though she had been dealt a blow that loosened her joints.

"A friend just called to warn me," she explained, slumping back in her chair. "My property, all my wealth has been confiscated by the government of Jador. My city," she concluded in a listless calm, "has beggared me."

A few days back Thebb would have known how to retort: "So it's your turn now", or some comment to that effect. But now he was not capable. All he could feel was the weight of sympathy, for they were all sinking together…

Jarchon said crisply, "Why?"

Professor Himbock supplied an answer. "Jador like most cities has rules on citizens' foreign expenditure. I expect Hyoen has exceeded her allocation. That is to say, Hyoen, the amount of wealth you are allowed to take out of your country…"

She sighed, "I have heard of some such rule."

"You should," the Professor said. "It carries stiff penalties."

Jarchon patted her on the shoulder: "But you didn't think it would ever be applied to you."

"Whereas," the Professor added, "it's *because* it's you, that they've applied it. Obviously."

139

"Do either of you realize," Hyoen glared round the table, "what a disaster this is? The mission we're on is rendered vastly more difficult if I can no longer get to my money –"

"I think," said Jarchon most gently, "we should be more worried about something else. Your friend was most unwise to send that message across the plains in times like these. This isn't the Lithium Era."

"She felt she had to," insisted Hyoen. "Olmiroa felt she had to warm me against returning to Jador. I might face a prison sentence. The government has changed…"

"Governments, everywhere," remarked the Professor, "are lurching towards greater controls." He nodded wisely at his own words.

"Meanwhile let's be brisk," Jarchon said, "in putting some distance between ourselves and this spot."

But it was hard to force themselves to clear away the breakfast things and make ready for departure with the proper urgency, hard to believe that the empty, silent horizon, which had encircled them without harm for days, would change face so soon. Yet they had had been underway for barely an hour when it became apparent that their luck had run out.

At three points of the compass, steadily growing dots appeared between ground and sky. It was their even spacing – one hundred and twenty degrees apart – which in itself was the worst news.

"Three rafts. We're boxed in," gloomed Thebb, though at this most inconvenient time he felt intoxicated all of a sudden by the limitless possibilities of the plains; he could not help but admire the scene which seemed poised to destroy him.

Hyoen, who sat at the telescope mounted on deck, reported: "I can see about ten men standing on each raft."

"Pirates, I dare say," said Jarchon at the helm. "How far are we from Jador?"

Himbock replied, "About five hundred and fifty miles. Too far to summon help."

"Naturally," said Jarchon. "Otherwise we wouldn't be seeing this. But maybe we should transmit anyway, for others' sakes."

"Or," suggested the Professor, "we could use the possibility as a bargaining counter."

"Hyoen is going to transmit," Jarchon nodded as the lady jumped up and ran to the communicator. "She's in a real fury."

They watched her, imagining the acerbic reproaches she must be hurling at her home city, which had so carelessly broadcast their location. Then when the enemy rafts had approached to within a few hundred yards, and the insigne on the nearest could be made out, she fell silent and joined the others as they waited, lasers in hand, for their foes to make the next move.

The *Rawmdeck* and its trio of enemies were now all travelling in formation. One of the strange rafts edged closer. A man on its deck held up his hand in a "stop" signal.

Hyoen said dully, "We had better obey."

Jarchon accordingly brought them to a halt, and they sank to the ground. The other rafts settled likewise, positioning themselves like surrounding siege-works.

Within minutes Hyoen, Thebb, Jarchon and Himbock, their lasers confiscated, were "guests" seated on low chairs on the deck of their captor's raft. Under strong guard, they faced the reclining chief: a lanky, stringy man with a face of red leather and a drooping silver moustache.

"I," he told them, smiling up at a point in the sky, "am Metek Kasproueh, gvo merchant. Merchant? Well, I pay when I have to." And he laughed the revelling laugh of one who knows that his audience's desire to wring his neck must remain forever unfulfilled.

His face shining with false cheer, he called for a bottle and glasses. His captives did not speak. They all felt the same – that to speak would put them at an even greater disadvantage.

Before long they sensed that it would have been easier to deal with a pirate who knew he was a pirate. This jovial madman seemed really to think of himself as imbued with the rank, prestige and importance of a nomadic merchant prince. He spouted on about his "business" although it was perfectly obvious that, while they sat and listened, the *Rawmdeck* was being robbed of every gvo crystal in the tank and storage bin.

It seemed likely, from his speech, that he had been a real trader once, a member of the guild which mined and distributed the gvo crystals to be found in the *Dzolm*, or Sun-Egg, the mountain of treasure – what was left of it – close to the ancient city of Contahl.

He boasted as he cocked a twinkling eye at them: "If I had been Noad of Contahl when the *Dzolm* was discovered, you would have seen a difference, oh yes. Never would *I* have allowed people like myself to get in on the act! Imagine, a whole mountain of gvo in one's own back yard... Fools say that Contahl could never have retained control of it; that the other cities would never have stood for that; yet the same fools *do* stand for the entire lot being monopolized by *us*, the princes of commerce! Anyhow, it's nearly all gone now." His tone veered towards maudlin sadness. "I've been there recently and, you know, the Sun-Egg now looks more like a field of rubble than a mountain. The gvo is nearly gone," he repeated, dropping his rambling voice to a whisper. "One or two more lifetimes to go, and then, lights out – the end of history." Kasproueh's head jerked. He whooped, "Enough of this gloom. Let us drink to – no matter what – how about the vanishing remains of the *Dzolm* – though as you know, haha, I prefer to purvey *negative* energy." Another, louder whoop. The captives thought it best to raise their glasses.

At no time had the pirate made eye contact, and his remark about negative energy made their flesh creep. Each one of them had at some time heard the folk tale about the renegade gvo merchant who carried nightmare for sale in his bags; from that it was but a step to the next thought: what might Metek Kasproueh do, if he knew of that tale and decided to play up to it? Thebb dumbly licked his lips as if probing the taste of fear; he could not detect the cause of it in his field of view; the fear was wider, deeper, as if Kasproueh was merely an agent of an invisible paw raised more vastly above all their heads. Kasproueh himself was hardly anything, thought Thebb. A verbose thug, a boring idiot.

But sufficiently deadly.

He had them escorted back to the *Rawmdeck* and then, without another word, with nothing but a contemptuous wave of the hand, he returned to his own raft, and he and his followers left Hyoen's party with an emptied fuel-tank, marooned weaponless on the plains of Ooranye.

Marooned. The word with a worse sound than *exile.*

8: The Decision

Thebb ran his eye down the paper they had brought him to sign. Then he gazed at them, mouth agape.

"You want *me* to lead?"

Oh yes, they meant it, all right. This was no dream. Hyoen gestured with the upturned palm of her hand, a manual shrug as if to say, what *else* did you think the words of this document could mean? The paper, drafted in official style, would count as an Instrument of Succession if, by some miracle, they ever got back to Narar.

In other words, Hyoen was resigning her position. She seemed not to think that any comment was necessary. Her failure, in her own eyes, was so obvious, she saw no need to speak.

Thebb thought it pretty obvious too. He could well understand her feelings of dejection. Guilt, no doubt, at having answered the radio signal which had allowed Kasproueh to home in on them... and then the deeper consequence: the total failure of her mission. Fate had surely snubbed her in a big way. The slob, Metek Kasproueh, had not even offered the chance for a fight; he had cleaned them out and gloated over them and left them, and now poor Hyoen had finally taken on board the awful truth. The world wasn't nice; it was the lair of forces which trampled and squashed.

As for Jarchon and Himbock – Thebb's gaze turned to them. They were a somewhat different case. However, their stance – close to Hyoen, supportive – showed they were solidly in favour of her decision. Hmm... The youngster, Jarchon, must want to get back some day. He wouldn't want to get into any more trouble, wouldn't want any awkward questions asked about the change of leader: so when Hyoen resigned it must be made clear that Thebb Clarm, great-nephew of Vroonwik Clarm (and thus the natural choice) had legally assumed the responsibility for the take-over. Hence an officially worded Instrument became vital. As for Himbock, he doubtless did not care who led, so long as it was not the unstable Hyoen who might get them all killed...

But it was all crazy anyway! They were marooned, finished – so what did it matter which of them was leader?

Without transport, almost nobody out here, even if armed, could expect to survive long enough to reach a city on foot. And if they did by some miracle cover the five-hundred-plus miles to Jador, they would most likely end up in prison. Cities were becoming more suspicious of strangers; Hyoen's losses by confiscation were part of a trend. She might well turn out to have been the last rich traveller in the old style...

Yes, the mission was doomed and their chances of life were poor.

Thebb, however, signed the paper.

As he did so he watched their faces and suddenly had a glimpse of the real, underlying reason why they were putting him in this position.

It was an awkward moment: a bitter laugh almost bubbled out of his throat. *They were superstitious.* For all their rationality, they clung to a belief in the power of leadership of a ruling clan! Of course they would not admit it. No more than Hyoen would have admitted to a belief in the ghostly exhalations of Dmara... but the fact was, they really did believe that he might get them out of this.

How ironic. On one occasion Hyoen, with a sneer, had trashed the notion he'd tried to express, that the international criminals who aimed the Corruption Ray at the cities of Syoom might somehow be using the Dmaran exhalations. And now she and the others were indulging in the considerably more far-fetched belief, that he, Thebb Clarm, might extricate them from the mess they were in.

Thebb heaved a tired sigh, tired of life itself but even more weary of arguments – so he decided to play along. He had put his name to their paper; very well, he would do what the paper said. He would lead them.

After all, the sooner the inevitable disaster occurred, the sooner he would find rest.

And after that, after death, would come the second chance in the second life. Preferably far down the river of time. Beyond all influence of this unfortunate period.

Long ago, he used to tell jokes, and now the uppity inspiration brushed his thoughts again; how odd it felt, yet how compelling – he was co-operating with the joke, he was readying himself to play the part expected of him! Something fizzed in his head: *lremd* was the quality which Fate demanded of leaders.

Lremd, the gift of being in the right place at the right time. The inbuilt radar which enabled a person to weave nen's way around the themes of life in a triumphant manner. Surf the waves of destiny with decision-making skill –

Thebb's blood ran cold at a sudden rent in the mists of doubt.

Hyoen touched his arm and said, "Are you all right?"

The others watched in silence.

Thebb said, "Wait." He went to his *runk* and dragged out a box. "My brother's sculptures," he panted. Yanking the box towards the raft's emptied fuel tank, he grunted: "Give me a hand with this."

Jarchon ran to him and helped to haul the box. "Do you have an idea? Will it work?"

"I have and it will."

He reached the tank and turned to face his companions. "I have been experimenting with *vheic* fuel for some time."

"I know there has been talk," Himbock said, "of it being used as a replacement for gvo when the Dzolm runs out, but…" He paused as Thebb began throwing the sculptured objects into the tank.

Beautiful geometric shapes, glowing with blue and gold ell-light from the vheic plants gathered and compressed long ago by the late Rawm Clarm… the others stood around awkwardly, letting him do it, waiting to see if the sacrifice of art would bring its reward.

The motor, often tinkered with, modified and adapted, now accepted the offering. When switched on, it roared louder than ever. The voyagers' outlook was transformed. No longer marooned, the raft soon sped away across the plain.

"Lucky for us," Jarchon remarked, "Kasproueh wasn't interested in art."

"They were just tat to him," nodded Thebb, staring at the horizon ahead. The sacrifice of his brother's work had keyed him up, as if he had signed a strict contract with Fate. "I am betting that there is a link," he added after a while, "between two stories we've been hearing."

"Oh? Which two?"

"Can't you guess?"

But the ex-student did not want to guess, at least not out loud, so Thebb voiced the connection: "Between the folk-tale of a renegade gvo merchant who sells negative energy, and the origin of the Corruption Ray."

Jarchon whistled at this. "Let me go fetch the others." He went to summon Hyoen and Himbock who were currently standing at the stern observation posts. When all were gathered round, Thebb told them:

"The time has come to follow the right trail. A line of evidence which has been around a long time. Let us start by considering Metek Kasproueh. What can we know about him, from what we have seen and heard? Let's build up a picture by induction. Any fact will do. Come on: observations about Kasproueh, please. Hint: note how I name him."

Himbock in his dry voice said, "In calling him 'Kasproueh' rather than 'Metek' we are following the example of his subordinates, whom we heard addressing him by his second name. That places his origin at Ao or Innb, or possibly Nuvium, all cities where second names predominate. Will that do, as a crumb of information?"

"Here's another crumb, if you will," murmured Hyoen: "it would make more sense for gvo merchants to be the culprits, in any case. Am I making sense?"

"You are," nodded the Professor. "Gvo merchants, of the worst kind, would have an interest in undermining city governments. In the power vacuum that ensues…"

"Crumbs here and crumbs there," interrupted Thebb, "all lend support to my idea."

"Which is?" Jarchon and the others leaned at Thebb as they stood around the helm on which he, Thebb, rested his hands.

Well, *he* was impatient as they, or rather, more so, he thought groggily. Leadership-fever – a thirst for justification – could only be soothed by the balm of success –

"The perfect hideout for the users of the Ray," he began, "is to be found in the part of the world we've just mentioned. A particular location shunned by everyone else for superstitious reasons."

145

"If you mean Dmara," said Hyoen, "there are practical reasons to shun it. Radiation, disease…"

"Not after all this time," Thebb shook his head. "Let us be honest. It is simply that none of us like the idea of going to Dmara."

And if *he* was honest he must admit that part of him still hoped they would talk him out of it. But no, they apparently believed in his star. Perhaps he was beginning to believe in it himself.

9: The Vomdo

So the days passed and they approached that unfrequented region of Syoom roughly mid way between the cities of Ao, Innb, Nuvium and Pjourth, several thousand miles from each, a desolation which contained the dry bed of the prebiotic lake from which humanity had emerged at the very start of Era One.

Superstition, repeated Thebb to himself as he pulled back the steerstick to allow the raft to settle, close by the lip of the ancient shore line. *A psychic reek so strong I can smell it.*

Groves of giant grasses, the size of trees, waved their pods in scattered clumps on the plain, but nothing whatsoever grew on the dead lake-bottom itself. That great hollow was wanly blotched with chemical stains. It had a poisonous sheen. Its streaks and blotches of grey, brown and metallic blue were partially hidden by drifting, ragged mists.

Exploitable superstition, ruminated Thebb.

Professor Himbock muttered, "Not sure I ever wanted to see this. But now I'm here, well, it is something to see."

Thebb nodded. "The *sivvan*, the Lake of Origins. Yes, here is the source of what we are."

One could not disbelieve, standing here. Could not deny the ultimate source of the physical nature and the minds and the senses of all Nenns – all of Uranian Man back to Lrar Verzak himself who had crawled out of the waves on Day One of the Hydrogen Era.

The few hundred *verzaknenns*, the First People, had not been born of woman but had come directly from the *sivvan*. Now the place was dry, having produced nothing further since that morning of the race, a thousand lifetimes ago. Still, with such an aura of the ultimate, it was hardly surprising that legends persisted –

Legends of *emanations* from the long-dead lake.

For the belief was universal, that the sivvan, as it had dried up, had gone bad.

"I assume," said Himbock in his dessicated tone, "that we must next locate the ruins of Dmara."

Thebb hastily objected: "We ought to stock up on provisions first." He pointed backwards with his thumb. "Maybe glean some food from those groves."

It was no use. Jarchon, supporting Himbock, said: "That would just be wasting time."

Hyoen explained remorselessly, "We ought to find supplies where we're going, anyway. If, that is to say, our thoughts have led us in the right direction."

"Very well," sighed Thebb, "let's get on with it. Ha, well. I suspect we ought not to approach under power. We had better walk."

The others jumped off the raft with alacrity. It was odd how the mere fact of having reached this dread shore had galvanised them. From their previous fatalistic gloom they had zoomed into... what? Gloomy *optimism*, if you could imagine such a thing. Not even the sight of the extinct sivvan had dampened their new faith that fortune and vindication were close by. Thebb had to admire their attitude. He renewed his decision to stay the course.

A leader, he reminded himself, ought to lead even when leading really meant following.

Just over five minutes on the raft brought them round the spur of a little headland into view of what was left of the First City.

Despite the public urgency of their mission it was natural for them to stop and stare for some minutes of personal contemplation. So they stood still in awed silence, till Thebb bade them advance again.

With cautious steps, their thoughts hovering between the hugeness of Time and the smallness of what their eyes actually saw, they walked into the city of Damara.

It was a jumble, about half a mile in extent, that had the appearance of litter strewn by careless giants. Metal boxes, house-sized, lay crumpled or mangled on the shore. Amongst them were a few which had resisted the damage dealt by storms or war; their tidy emptiness was even more forlorn.

Some distance inside the wrecked city, the explorers came upon a more modern structure. This round-edged stellated cuboid they recognized straightaway as built in the style of Innb. Thebb's companions looked at him, complimenting him with their shining eyes, for the process of deduction by which he had led them here. The clincher, was that in front of this modern building was parked a standard model Xennat mobile gun.

The thing's snout was pointed at a meaningless angle at the empty sky, but the presence, unattended, of such a weapon told an obvious story. The users of the Ray had at first arrived prepared for opposition, but after thousands of days had gone by without any challenge to their hideout, they felt themselves secure. That was why no one was guarding the gun; why no one hailed the approaching explorers.

Lasers drawn, believing in the advantage of surprise, Thebb and his followers entered the Innban structure through an archway.

Jarchon swept the scene with expert eyes. He was the one who knew architecture and – Thebb had learned by now to admit – knew a whole lot more structural engineering than Thebb himself.

"Over there," Jarchon pointed. "The cradle for the launcher."

They ran to it and took up position around it. A diagonal upward flue, set in a bowl mounted on a platform with thick springs, the thing was a cradle indeed, one in which something heavy had rested. Some gun-barrel far more massive and peculiar than the Xennat.... but gone now. Taken away.

It was a moment of let-down and Thebb felt all the pangs of a new kind of disappointment. He had just recently dared to hope that they might have come upon the main apparatus of the Corruption Ray, at a lucky moment when its users were absent. But of course that had been too much to expect.

Now, where was Jarchon? Thebb heard a shout. The fellow appeared to be capering about among some glowing screens in another corner of the immense hall. Half a dozen of them – vidscreens – lined up diagonally in front of each other, and Jarchon was rushing hither and thither to adjust switches as though it were a matter of life and death. Next, the ex-student plumped into a swivel chair before a nearby array of switches and dials, then waved to his companions to gather round. Together with the other two, Thebb hurried forward, frozen-tongued with disquiet. Odd to see Jarchon trembling.

Peculiar, also, the first screen's image, or rather its periphery.

Jarchon grew calm enough to speak.

"I think we can look. For a moment I thought they'd gone out of phase –"

"What are you talking about?" rasped Himbock.

"Not sure I'd like to say." A wild grin. "Look at those frames…"

Thebb peered forward.

The vidscreen showed a picture of a picture of a picture: nested images, one inside the other. Odd.

Himbock cut in: "The object of this arrangement is, evidently, to interpose layers of relayed transmission between viewer and object."

"Between us," Jarchon explained, "and something out there."

"Ah-hah," nodded Thebb. *And you, youngster, have made sure that all the relays are properly in line, so that all interpose.* Thebb gave silent tribute to the ex-student, but also wished – and knew he wished in vain – that this entire building and the vidscreens inside it could have nothing to do with any source material for the Corruption Ray.

Duty bound, he looked at the nested images.

The inmost one showed part of the dried-up sivvan shore. More precisely it showed an inlet, or what would have been one if the lake had still existed.

No way of telling how far away it was. But it could not be further than a few miles; the lake wasn't that big. And that flat gleam, in the centre of the inlet, must be a mere *pool...*

Just a little pool, ten yards across perhaps?

"So," breathed Hyoen, "not quite all the lake has gone."

Nobody answered her because they all became paralyzed by the sight of what was happening on screen. The stagnant water had begun to ripple. After a minute or two the surface broke. A black and glistening object reared out of it, and unfolded in the open air. The four watchers immediately understood the purpose of the arrangement of relayed transmissions. What they were seeing, if perceived directly, would have blown their minds.

The thing shook the drops from its scaly skin and from its black wings as it rose out of the liquid. Undeniable evil bulged from the head. Blurry eyes and sagging mouth offered a message dismaying beyond all reason. No use to say it was "only" this or "only" that. Certainty flooded the watchers: this was...

They knew, but did not want the thought of it to form.

A thing that should not be. Should not count as real, anywhere in our universe. But it was *here,* a nightmare trespassing in daylight, as it clambered and waddled out of the pool and fully onto the shore, where it strutted, turning its eyes this way and that.

The vidscreen panned automatically to keep it in view. Appalled, the humans could not take their eyes away from the revelation, that evil is not a principle, evil is *this,* the jeer of physical presence of what should not be.

"The vomdo," breathed Thebb.

"I don't believe it!" shouted Himbock.

"There it is," Thebb shrugged.

"But – an evil beast? Absurd!" cried the Professor. Outrage shrilled his voice almost into a squeak. "Work it out! If an animal gets responsible enough to choose between good and bad, well then, it's no longer an animal; so –"

Jarchon interrupted, "It's an animal, all right. Look at its tiny bird-size head. Can't have more than a tiny brain."

"Speak for yourself!" came the sputtered reply.

"Hey, calm down, Professor," Jarchon soothed; "we've been getting on quite well, you and I. You know better than to renew our past differences now."

Himbock after a few ragged breaths subsided and managed a gentle smile. "What will you do about this thing, this legend – pour another glass of water over me?"

"No glass handy, but I can point out that according to *your* philosophy good and evil have no meaning anyway –"

Thebb intervened, "This is not the time to argue. We've learned one thing. The vomdo is no myth."

None of them could deny it. The screen's display matched perfectly with the legendary creature which killed with its glance.

Without a doubt the sight of it would have killed them, had they come face to face with it in the open air. Their minds finally admitted this truth. You could reason it away, but –

A sudden *whupp* made them flinch anew.

The image on screen underwent a kind of in-folding compression, too fast to follow, but leaving a sense of what had occurred. The compression became a dagger of light. It plunged downwards and for a second the screen went dark, before winking back to normal. Simultaneously they heard a clatter.

A solid object of some sort had fallen. Out of a chute? Into a bin? The sound suggested these things.

"Another bit of ammunition for the Ray," commented Jarchon, his voice weak but airy.

"What?" demanded Thebb, as often dismayed at his own slowness.

"I suppose there's a big box of it somewhere around."

"Of... ammunition, you said."

"Yes, might as well use that word."

"But – " A helpless sound.

Jarchon continued, "As for how, I'd guess some pattern-recognition programming – at any rate you can bet that if we knew *all* of psychology we *could* draw evil with a pencil."

"Then," said Thebb, "we know enough. We must destroy this thing."

A pause.

"Destroy the installation?" queried Jarchon.

Another pause, by means of a little silence to say "no, not that". Atop this cushion of delay, Thebb gave the order in clear:

"We must destroy the vomdo."

He expected argument, because they all knew the legends. But this did not happen. Jarchon nodded quiet assent. Hyoen moved closer. "We'll find a way," she reassured Thebb, brushing into physical contact, signalling affection and support when he needed it most.

Thebb Clarm thought: "Here is a reason to live past the nightmare." With immense pride in his band of followers he began mentally to phrase the order which would commit them to action, but a softish sound made him turn, to see the Professor backing away.

Himbock's face was pale grey and twisted with a scowl from behind the laser he was pointing straight at them.

"What are you doing, Professor?"

"Stay where you are, all of you," Himbock winced, continuing to back towards the exit.

10: Sacrifice for a Sideshow

Once again it was proved to Thebb that Jarchon's mind moved – when necessary – faster than his own.

"You can't, by yourself – let me help," cried the youngster, twisting out of his chair. He rose and began to stride with decision towards the Professor.

Himbock stared blankly – then sheathed his laser. "Can't deny it," he muttered. "But the rest of you must at all costs stay here."

Thebb and Hyoen watched the two of them leave the building.

"I see," he said to her, "but I always see too late."

"No, Thebb, don't say that about yourself. You have played your part. You've been like a carrier platform, a human raft, to bring us all here. You did it by making the correct decision, the crucial decision, several days ago – certainly not 'too late'."

And her head came to rest on his shoulder; her arm stole around him, squeezing, comforting.

She continued, "Nnow that you have brought them this far, they are – you might say – taking off from the 'carrier platform' on their own."

"Do you know," mused Thebb, hugging her in return, "I have a mind to employ you for the rest of your life, to say this sort of thing."

After this proposal, they nested in each other's arms in blissful understanding for perhaps a minute; then he walked her to the window. From there they gazed at the Xennat gun parked outside.

He murmured, "Do you think they know *all* the legends?"

"Of that I am sure. Otherwise you would not have let them go."

He laughed in wonder at her confidence in him. Then he was able to realize that she had done him justice. "You're right there, at least."

They watched as Himbock climbed into the cockpit of the mobile gun. They saw Jarchon follow and begin to check the controls. Then the two men appeared to be having an argument which lasted a couple of minutes, after which Jarchon made an arm-spreading gesture and climbed down.

The ex-student wandered back towards the building where Thebb and Hyoen waited.

Meanwhile the mobile gun, with the Professor at the helm, began to crawl away on its treads. Slowly it wove its way among the ruins, out towards the open lake shore.

"He told me," said Jarchon upon re-entering, "that there was no point in both of us risking our lives."

"Welcome back. He was right," said Thebb.

"Sure about that?"

Thebb reinforced his reply with all the firmness he could muster: "Wait and you'll see. Keep watching the screen."

The multiple-relay vid was once again tracking the vomdo. It now showed the nightmare creature waddling in a different direction, back towards the pool whence it had come.

"Good," said Hyoen, "that'll give the Professor more of a chance. He won't have so far to circle…"

"Ah, you're right, he *has* to circle," nodded Jarchon, "to come at it from directly behind; otherwise he has no chance at all…"

"Yes but in any case," broke in Thebb, "he has no choice but to fire while he's still on this side of the teletransmitter array."

"You mean –" said the others, simultaneously.

"He must know he can't afford to get actually within sight of the thing. Whether behind or in front of it. It could, probably would, turn in an instant."

"How then will he aim the gun?" quavered Hyoen.

Jarchon tried to reassure her: "He told me just before I left him, that he had reasoned out where the pool must be. *That's* where and when he must make the kill."

"Let's assume," said Thebb, "that not only he, but also the people who left the Xennat gun knew what *they* were doing. If the scum have any sense they'll have equipped it with extra powerful shells…"

Hyoen nodded disgustedly, "…in case the vomdo turned against them."

"Not understanding," added Jarchon in a murmur, "that with the vomdo there's no safety."

Queasy silence fell. The prickly moments dragged on. And then they felt the floor quiver.

Seconds later came the roar of an explosion and the TV screen flashed white for an instant, after which it imaged grey, billowing smoke.

The televised smoke gradually cleared to reveal a hole in the ground.

Thebb, Hyoen and Jarchon all thought the same thing: *this has to be enough. The shell has burst and the monstrosity has been obliterated.*

They filed out of the building, returned to the *Rawmdeck* in a solemn daze, and Thebb started up the raft. No thought remained to them but to skim along the dead shore and look for the Professor. After about five minutes they found him. He still clutched with one hand the wheel of the mobile gun, well out of sight of the target on which he must have scored a direct hit.

"Look at his poor face," whispered Hyoen. They all stared at the wizened countenance. "What was it like for him, what must it have been…" The others offered no comment, but Hyoen continued to try to hack her way through her thoughts aloud. "As though he saw it coming, despite the distance –"

"No," spoke Thebb at last with a firm shake of the head. "He was dead the instant he fired. The terror was momentary."

"Backward-causation," murmured Jarchon.

"And," added Thebb, "he must have known it was likely to happen that way." Since they were going to have to live with this memory for the rest of their lives, it was important to spread such reassurance. He looked to Jarchon for more confirmation.

"Yes," nodded the ex-student, "he went in for it with open eyes. Er – you know Himbock and I were, let's say, opponents… I mean, everyone's heard the story of our, er, dispute in college; yes, well, in the end he must have learned his lesson from that."

Hyoen demanded, "What precisely do you mean?"

"I mean," and Jarchon's voice strengthened, "that the Professor, once he decided to accept the idea of absolute evil, went all the way. No more believing contradictory things with different halves of his mind. He accepted, really accepted the entire legend as true. Including the part which states that the *vomdo* is so noxious, that any direct connection with it - *any* connection, even a backward-causal one – kills. To be the cause of its death, though

153

remotely, was enough to kill the Professor wherever he was. No shielding can suffice against backward-causation."

Thebb's voice rang out next. As if he were speaking to history, he announced: "Whatever happens from now on, he shall not have died in vain. We may or may not find and destroy the users of the Ray – but *we have destroyed the source of their ammunition.*"

The three adventurers stood for some silent minutes gazing down into the crater gouged by the shell blast. It had not only killed the vomdo, it had also destroyed the pool, vaporising the final remnant of the ancient waters of Dmara.

11: Veppora Munoo – again

In a quiet room in Narar, an old lady opened an envelope and extracted a letter. Her eyes grew rounder as she skimmed the pages.

"...The C-Ray users are working on borrowed time... After their current store of encapsulated evil is exhausted they will get no more... Henceforth we are fighting merely the quotidian evil in man."

She felt a tingle as if a spark from that electric current of purpose which used to shimmer its way through her life had blown from far to touch her skin.

She dried some tears and whispered –

Thank you, Hyoen, for thinking of me. Now to believe, if I can, that the nameless is dead.

– And burned the letter.

The Shears of Night

1: Flocking to the City

Night. Look down and see a dark plain crawling with lights. You are to understand that each light is a skimmer at close to top speed. It's only the size of the picture that makes them seem slow.

We control what you see; we ensure that you understand, when we so direct you and not before. Otherwise the thing is equivalent to a lie – and we can prevent that, by force if need be.

Since the days when we were simply writers and you no more than readers, the relationship has progressed. Having placed yourselves in our hands, you must allow us to do what we like with you, till the tale is over. You are the rider on the Ferris wheel who cannot get down till the turn is completed. And think now, since we know about Ferris wheels, since we know *your* world in such detail, how utterly we must be masters of ours – so give in; accept our direction; do not struggle when a horror makes its approach.

The skimmers are converging upon a city in concentric waves, like reversed ripples in a movie run backwards to show a stone un-thrown from the water; an effect unseen in nature but common enough in human affairs, for example when hordes are hastening to witness a trial.

You will not forget, during the telling of this tale, to give us credit for being truthful about ourselves. We story-tellers are natives of Ooranye, and as such we are honour bound not to "whitewash" our world: indeed our judgements are severe, in fact we're judges of judges, here where we sit at our safe distance from the Phosphorus Era. But in the late days of that era, it was Vyanth that was the judge – Vyanth the richest and most populous of the great disc-on-stem cities of Ooranye.

Surrounded, for hundreds of miles in every direction, by the bioluminescent glow of cultivated fields, it itself outshone those farmlands, concentrating into itself the garnered light that was its wealth. And on

14,620,509 P, it had swept even more brightness than usual into its embrace.

We can make you see all this with your own eyes. For we now push you back across the span of ages, precisely to noon on Day 14,620,509 of the fifteenth era of Man on the giant planet, Ooranye.

First we force your eyes to stare at the pedestrians on the city's rim. There they stand or stroll, there they chat, close to the edge, fifty yards above the surrounding plain. Then we swivel your sight to focus upon the watchers on the central towers. Aligning your brains, we next force the watchers' sight into yours. Now you, like they, gaze at the pellets of light which are approaching over the plains.

You partake of the knowledge, that each brilliant dot is the skimmer of a foreign observer. They're flocking here so as to witness the treason trial of Mulvu Xy, saboteur.

At the mention of that name – Mulvu Xy – we cause you to share the appalled, fascinated hatred of the people for the traitor in their midst.

An obscure nonentity before his crime was discovered, Mulvu Xy had then soon become the most notorious man in the known world. Still little more than a name, though. Most people had never seen him, never heard him speak.

We the back-haunting chroniclers can take you to see him this moment as he waits in his cell, but there is a difficulty: even if we allow you to read his thoughts, you won't be greatly enlightened. A scrawny, unkempt man with pointy features, he sits back in his armchair, smiling faintly as if the impending horror were a ridiculous mistake, and in his mind there is the certainty, "I can get out of this."

His accusers know better; know that he had no defence and no allies. He is surrounded only by enemies filled with righteous disgust.

(And we, with our special hindsight, can confirm that he shall not be rescued, nor acquitted.)

So far, though, Mulvu Xy, despite the doom that faces him, shows good spirits. He evinces no resentment, makes no complaint about any unfairness or harshness in the circumstances of his incarceration. Indeed he is comfortable enough, for the time being; the authorities are quite gentle in a way, quite lax as they serenely trust in the strength and power of their city. The government and people of Vyanth are willing for everything to be done openly; no precautions have been taken against espionage, no obstacles raised against publicity, and only the usual moderate measures are in place to safeguard the prisoner – it being correctly assumed that no one will want to rescue him. All extra efforts have gone into preparations for the great welcome which greets the spectators from foreign lands.

Throughout the city, scattered at various heights like birds' nests in a tree, the illuminated hostelries, each on its own platform, flaunt their rooms and gardens.

Guides, stationed at intervals of sixty degrees around Vyanth's rim, attend the landing-parks beside each of the *ayashou* – the airstreams which hoist incoming traffic onto the six main reception spaces. Like a two-way fountain each *ayash* continually spurts traffic up from the plains onto the raised city floor, and down in the reverse direction. Currently the incoming stream is by far the denser of the two sparkling lanes, as Vyanth blazes against the purple sky, imperiously welcoming the nations.

To those who journey towards it, the city's glittering power first appears across a distance of over a hundred miles, as the summit structures, the aerial docks and spires, rise over the horizon. Minutes later as the incoming skimmers hurtle closer their pilots behold Vyanth's concave-sided stem rising into view, like a sleeve and hand, bearing aloft the five-mile disc piled with multi-coloured forms: the lit hostelries, the branching walkways, globular palaces and helical towers.

Glorious reassurance for anyone at the end of a long and lonely voyage! Visual proof that humanity is able, even upon this vast and forbidding world, to build an unconquered haven for two million people.

And somebody has tried to destroy it. All the more do the visitors treasure the sight of it now. Many of these feasting eyes belong to reporters – those who might have been expected, by some defendants, to spread fair words, if anything might be said in the prisoner's favour.

But the reporters, who in their home countries could have shown independence of mind, are here overawed by the splendour of the giant city. Even before they arrive upon its rim, they submit to its mind-set. Amid the vast influx of spectators the most rugged individualist is no more influential than a mote of dust, and we make this submission comprehensible to you the reader as we pull you through the incoming throng, to manoeuvre your invisible eye alongside one speeding skimmer among so many, to show the truth of what we say through the example of reporter Jad Lael.

Jad Lael is a chronicler from distant Pjourth who has skimmed over thirteen thousand miles to be present at the treason trial. The journey has taken him eight days.

Outwardly you see him, astride the vehicle, a wiry young man who eagerly leans forward with rapt gaze fixed upon the glow of his destination. Then we make you, Terran readers under our control, look inward, to share the awareness inside his skull –

Not such a shock as all that, is it? You meld quite swiftly, thanks not only to our skill, but to the context-awareness of Uranian humans.

Consider: they have never known any other world than their cold, dim, giant planet. Their species evolved there; they have no biological connection with Earth humanity despite close similarity in appearance. It would be natural to assume that their world is their norm, that therefore it can't seem unusually large and cold and dim to *them*. And yet this is not the case. With that part of their minds which can lift their awareness above context, they know their own "norm" to be extreme, just as you do. By some objective cosmic standard they judge themselves to be immersed in some extra-vast mystery, which is your opinion, too. On this special level of their minds, therefore, they are not "used"to their situation; they are in a state of wonder, just as you are.

Thus the importance, to their restless souls and yours, of the reassuringly mighty, glowing city of Vyanth.

Like all educated Uranians, reporter Jad Lael understands that one must not expect too much of Syoom – the so-called area of civilization – which is, basically, a statistical concept. "The lands in which you have an over-fifty per cent probability of surviving a thousand-mile journey alone" – that is the strict definition of the area. Well, he has survived thirteen thousand on this particular journey. An instance of how the safety-percentage can soar well above ninety in good times. Yet, of necessity, patrols remain frequent and city-defences alert; for you can never take the resulting "civilization" for granted.

He reflects on this as he nears Vyanth, because here is a brilliant exception, an oasis of confidence, of glowing belief. The confidence trickles right down to the lower levels of his mind.

There it stops short of the bedrock, the stoppage point at which the people of Ooranye remain aware that they will never tame their world. Though they have evolved on it and know no other, they will never understand it. Jad has had plenty of personal experience to support this mood of pessimistic awe. All wayfarers know that they share the cold dim global vastness with so many bewildering forces and intelligences that the way of wisdom becomes the way of parrying, dodging, fielding, coping pragmatically with what one can not hope to understand.

But cities are havens – muses the elated Jad Lael as his skimmer begins to rise in the grip of the *ayash* –

He sees further as the airstream lifts him higher until it treats him to a view of the entire extent of inner Maelv, the Bright Realm over which Vyanth reigns. In these exceptional lands – tended by hundreds of lifetimes of genetic engineering – the glow is constant: the bioluminescence does not pulse: the *vheic* crops do not dim and brighten in the thirty-hour beat which prevails elsewhere to define the cycle of day and night upon Ooranye. The exceptional empire of Vyanth shines uninterruptedly.

The brilliant vista is so strong a challenge to the vault of night, that even the bedrock of pessimism quakes, far beneath Jad Lael's vision at the summit of the *ayash* arc –

But no. This heart of empire looks splendid, but even so, you simply cannot spread civilization all over such a world as Ooranye. The planet is too big, too intractable.

Civilization, moreover, means more than security; it means a shared system of values, and above all it ought to mean human solidarity in the face of the unknown. Jad reminds himself, in that culminating moment, of why he is here. Mulvu Xy has been accused of attempting to wreck a city. So you can't even rely upon human beings... though surely no one man, however malevolent he may be, could inflict mortal damage upon this great ally against the darkness...

Past the summit of the airstream trajectory, Jad begins his descent towards the metal disc.

The compressed moment of vision is over, leaving him with a moral jumble of gratitude, sorrow, joy and dread. All local triumphs must come to an end some day. But one can hope that the current brightness will prove sufficiently robust, that it cannot cease by the action of a single traitor –

Instead, what *would* most likely cause the end would be a failure by the crop-scientists.

He has been hearing talk of this. Agricultural experts aren't forever going to be able to keep one step ahead of mutations in the crops. When their efforts fail, the continuous glow will give way to the natural pulse of the wild; the city's resources will be halved; Vyanth will become poor and vulnerable to attacks from Fyaym – the antithesis of Syoom.

Fyaym – the "land under fifty per cent" – the area in which you have a *less* than half (usually a *much* less than half) chance of surviving a thousand-mile journey alone.

When that sad day came, Fyaym will bite a chunk out of Syoom, and the Phosphorus Era will be over.

Jad Lael is happily convinced that he will not live to see that day.

The *ayash* brings his skimmer gently down to a hovering rest a yard above the *oalm* or landing-park upon Vyanth's rim.

He alights, his cloak flapping and billowing in the eddies from the *ayash* and the winds from the plains. Scores of other arrivals at the same moment are likewise stepping down from their aerial canoes. Each traveller's first task is to see where nen's vehicle may be stored. A guide stands by, repeating the words of welcome, "'Mjard. Here for the trial?" Almost always the answer is "yes". Jad Lael gives this answer, whereupon the guide continues:

"Starts at noon. Palace of Justice two miles down Radial 3. You can park your skimmer in the vaults next to the Palace."

"Thank you," says Jad Lael, noting the direction of the guide's pointing thumb, "but I prefer to walk."

"That's what I would do," agrees the guide. "Get used to the dazzle."

Jad Lael wonders a bit about last phrase. However, it never crosses his mind to prolong the dialogue. He is too well bred for such crassness. When you're in a queue of events, you don't request further explanation; you go in for brevity so as not to hold up the plot. If you're a good Uranian, that is. For we of Ooranye are able to boast the quality of *lremd*, of steering without bumping. (Of course, we have heard that you Terrans have your own way of doing things, but we do not understand how – without *lremd* – you can possibly shape your lives into proper stories.)

Jad pushes his vehicle to the city's very edge. Here he finds the skimmer-bank into which the aerial canoe can be slid. He obtains a key and registers the craft's number, then happily turns his back on the rim and heads inward.

Down Radial 3 he strides, heading for the hot brightness of the city's hub. Pleasurably awed, he passes deeper into the polyhedral jungle of Vyanthan structures, immersed in the bath of radiance from metal hostel-trees, residential mounds and dangling palaces, overlooked by office-towers and airship docks, and threaded with the sparkling traffic-lanes which are bearing swifter travellers in the same direction. The thrumming dazzle never quite squashes his sharp reporter's instinct. *When I'm back home,* he tells himself, just once before he forgets –

I shall remember one critical thing to say. Vyanth is a great place – but I wouldn't exactly want to <u>live</u> here.

2: The Courtroom

The air cracked with random coughs, rustled with swishing cloaks, hissed with the shuffling of papers and droned with formalised voices. Over and above these human-scale sounds could be heard the odder whispering crawl of a moving beltway. It forever circled the central arena of the hall, as if to illustrate the unceasing grind of the wheels of justice.

The beltway was elliptical. The prisoner sat at one of the foci; the judge at the other.

The prosecutors had no fixed abode. One by one they were wont to detach themselves from a central knot of officials, step onto the beltway and orbit both prisoner and judge. Like comets around a sun they approached the prisoner, swung past him and receded.

Woe betide the prosecutor who did not time his speech to pack the maximum punch at the instant of closest approach to the target. Those who made the tactical mistake of being either too long-winded or too concise were sure to be rebuked when the continuation of their orbit carried them past the judge. So, pressure was on the accusers as well as on the accused.

However, the general atmosphere in the packed hall was one of unrelenting hostility towards Mulvu Xy – every Vyanthan spectator chewing the question, *how could such a monster have been born of woman?* Less partisan were the foreigners, perhaps thirty per cent of the crowd, but even they were swayed, their wits submerged and almost uprooted by the deepest currents of emotion. Take, for instance, Jad Lael of Pjourth. He had just about "gone native" during his walk down the avenue to the courtroom. And he was the sort who might, in other circumstances, have been of service to the prisoner; the helpful knowledge was there, in Jad's head, but the memory of it had been cut off, and even if it had not been, no opportunity now existed to share the crucial facts.

Jad sat squeezed between an aristocratic lady from Nemyurur and a mountainous soldier from Contahl. His other immediate neighbours on the benches, he noted from the cut of their cloaks, were native Vyanthans. But with every minute that passed, he blurred these distinctions, thinking more in terms of "all of us" versus "him".

The prosecutors droned on with the extraordinary list of apparently motiveless crimes.

"On 14,620,451 P you endeavoured to engineer a power-drain in the vaults."

(Imagine if that had succeeded! Jad and the Vyanthans pictured it the same way. The treasure wiped out – resources depleted – freedom of action lost, both political and military – Fyayman pirates jump on our trade-routes the day after –)

"On 14,620,489 P you keyed a program for randomising the schedule of the freightways."

(Imagine – economic paralysis – transport arteries clogged – city grinds to a halt –)

And then the worst so far:

"On 14,620,502 P you broke into Wayfarers' Hall. There you were apprehended in the act of *shuffling the signal-blocks of the Patrol.*"

(Imagine if that had not been prevented! Wayfarers' memoranda erased – dance of efficiency interrupted – intuition lost – knowledge of wilderness declines – safety statistic falls below 50 – encroachment of Fyaym upon Syoom – darkness falls on Maelv –)

With a united frown the accusers pressed their charges, and the spectators in the hall added their own dark incredulous stares, and noisier detestation rumbled from the crowds who were gathered outside in the octagonal Clears, where the trial was displayed on public screens.

Mulvu Xy sat flanked by three guards to either side, at his focus of the central ellipse. His face was fringed by an untidy beard. He looked peaky and haggard, and his skin had blanched to a paler grey than that of most Uranians. Yet, considering what was likely to happen to him, he appeared to have his nerves well under control. While the accusations were hurled at him with wavelike regularity by the orbiting prosecutors, he assented to them monosyllabically, one after another.

The crowd would have been further amazed, had it been able to see into his mind. For what frightened him the most was not the panoply of the law or his own probable fate, but rather a pretty little memory, sweet and uncanny, which had carried him many times through the hours of his working day, making those hours fly hazily until his work was done.

The facts were scattered, and can only be brought together by our hindsight – lacking which, the audience heard, at first, only a senseless litany of misdeeds. Perhaps some sympathy for the prisoner might have touched them if at that stage he had been accused of some single, comprehensible enormity, but the spate of vandalism hardened their hearts, and their looks increasingly scowled the message: *you deserve what's coming to you, O soon-to-be-Interrupted Mulvu Xy.*

The opinion hardened, that the euphemistically termed *Interruption* was the only fitting doom. This view was congealed into an immoveable clot by the last of the prosecutors: Gnaevona Hekka, the Summariser.

A slim, glittering figure, she began to speak as she glided forth onto the beltway, and her speech amassed conviction in all who heard, so weighty was her argument, so clear her conclusion that the misdeeds of Mulvu Xy were all aimed at *Interruption*, and *Interruption* must in turn form the penalty. Finally:

"You," she pointed at the accused, "were out to cause a discontinuity in the city's metabolic flow; to snip the thread of its life."

What an art it was – gaped the audience – what an art, to marshal what you had to say, choose your moment to step onto the Track, time your piece so that the pith of your argument is spat towards the prisoner at the point of closest approach. And how effective it could be, especially when the prisoner could not resist the temptation to answer back with a proud, futile admission –

"I had my reason," croaked Mulvu Xy.

"Tell the court your reason," Gnaevona called over her shoulder, receding from him now.

"Perhaps," complied the prisoner hopefully, "it will not be a waste of breath to tell you." He knew that the moment of maximum danger had arrived. They were listening, to allow him to condemn himself. Very well! His words tore the air:

"I voice the name not of Vyanth but of another, more tragic city – Hoog!

"Remember the hive-mind of Hoog, detected far too late? Remember the grief it caused? Hard to imagine, that there must have been a time when it was young, incomplete, intermittent, deducible in moments of reflection. Easy it would have been, to snuff it out then! And perhaps some people did think of doing so. Perhaps some Hoogans' thoughts, wandering by chance, found evidence of superhuman efficiency, of economic co-ordination far out of the ordinary, of excessive hours lost in trance, which could only mean that their city was evolving into a conscious organism. If those early thoughts had been voiced –

"But they weren't, and nothing was done. Inexcusable. Any psychologist can tell you that consciousness is triggered by patterned complexity – and there comes a moment when a city's awareness is *switched on* by the routines of its human components.

"Apparently, however, although you admit it happened to Hoog, you can't bring yourselves to admit that it could happen here. In fact I suggest your minds *can't* form the thought – it being already too late." Mulvu slumped in his chair and ended with, "I, however, did form the thought and I decided to act, to interrupt the pattern while somebody still could."

A moment's silence gave way to a multitude of buzzing whispers. The next move was up to the judge. This was none other than the Noad – the Focus or Head of State – who was always ex officio judge in cases of treason. Fiarr Fosn, Noad of Vyanth, grey-cloaked and cadaverous in the glare from the hall lights, rose to look round at the "jury" – namely, the expressions of the audience – and then to deliver both verdict and sentence. His youngish, stern features faced the sea of eyes, and as he gauged the mood of the gathering the invisible crackle of their mutual regard bounced between him and them with an intensity which reflected his responsibilities in moments like these. His power hemmed him on all sides. His word was final and therefore it had to be right. His people were convinced that he was a great man – and so he was forced to be, by the inward-stabbing rays of their expectation which transfixed him with the compulsion that every word he spoke must be perfect for this moment.

"Mulvu Xy," said Noad Fiarr Fosn evenly, "you have obliged us with the last piece of your mystery. I thank you for simplifying the case in this way. But your argument is invalid. The workings of any large city are bound to be systemic. They are thus always vulnerable to the kind of superficial comparison which you have made with the case of Hoog.

"And speaking of vulnerability, the signal-blocks and memoranda which you scattered – you actually kicked them around, an unforgivable act – are of course open to such vandalism any time of the day or night. We cannot protect them by guards, for we do not operate them consciously. The trance state which you deplore, in the belief that it is evidence of our submersion in an urban group mind, is actually the only method by which such a complex system could possibly be maintained. We rely thus on instinct, and we have faith that the instinct is wholesome.

"It remains for me to pronounce what shall be done with you. Justice usually demands that the ill-doer's motive be taken into account. Yet we cannot set the precedent of excusing or pardoning a deed like yours, a crime against the greatest fortress of light in our dim world. It was sheer luck that you were stopped before the harm you did became irreparable. To attempt such damage is to threaten more than Vyanth; it risks more general woe to the entire thin-stretched humanity of Syoom. The problem therefore is not how to temper justice with mercy, but how to conceive of a sufficient deterrent against any repetition of such an atrocity.

"Fortunately, in *your* case it is particularly easy to make the punishment fit the crime. Mulvu Xy, I order that thirty hours from this moment you shall be *Interrupted*."

A sign breathed through the hall. The audience once again felt nourished by its own trust in the Noad. Reassurance, as well as justice, had been achieved.

And what of the light they could not sense, the bath of radiance which impacts the scene from *our* eyes, the hindsight of future knowledge and understanding?

We happen to know that the judge was right in his argument: Mulvu Xy had been wrong to equate Vyanthan efficiency with sinister Hoog.

But as for the punishment… no. That was a wrong idea.

3: The Visits

Mulvu Xy lolled in the short-term comfort of his cell, maintaining his equilibrium, he knew not precisely how. His hands gripped the wooden arms of his chair more tightly when he heard voices outside the heavy door. He could not make out the exact words, though he recognized the woman from the sounds… He did not wish to see her just then, he wanted to remain alone for he was busy trying to work something out, something confusing: he was beholden to a power – a force – a kindness which scared him at the same time that it bolstered his hopes. We in the far future cannot reach back to tell him, that it is the innocent murmur of the city itself, trying to comfort him with proof of its own harmless infancy. Perhaps it is just as well. How could he have understood? Most likely he would have taken it as proof of the existence of a mature, dangerous group mind.

…Meanwhile outside the door, the generously proportioned Ommwa Plenn – the pale blonde betrothed of the condemned man – held herself straight as her uneasy escort explained the rules. She was determined to confront tragedy with a no-nonsense air. With a curt nod she assured the guard: "In my view it is actually fortunate that you and your men shall be listening to every word which passes between that idiot and myself. Not only do I need to knock some sense into him, but I need it reported that I have done so. Then and only then, perhaps, can I appeal to the Noad." The guard bobbed his head and ordered the rest of the detail to fan out. They took their positions round the platform which ringed their destination. Each man armed his laser at the door of the great sphere. Their chief thumbed the entrance switch.

The door slid open. Mulvu rose, smiling. "Glad to see you, Ommwa," he said with a hand-squeezing gesture in lieu of being allowed to touch her. "And you, sponndarou [gentleman warriors], make yourselves at home and help me share this luxury, which I am unaccustomed to, and which is making me feel bad."

"So you should feel bad, you freak," stormed Ommwa, advancing upon him until the chief guard stepped forward and took hold of her arm, halting her a couple of paces from the prisoner. She ranted on: "Giving the Noad no choice but to treat you like an exhibit in a zoo!"

"You understand a lot of things, don't you, Ommwa?" nodded Mulvu peacefully. "About the rarity, the unnaturalness of crime, here in Vyanth."

"Oh yes, I understand things, I just don't *bother* about them the way you do." Her voice went gruffer, quieter, and there was a quaver in it now. "Retract, Mulvu! Claim temporary insanity – even if I know it's permanent – and throw yourself on the mercy of Fiarr Fosn. Please."

"Ommwa, believe me, the Noad won't weaken; he can't."

"He's human! And he knows we were to be married in thirty days – in thirty days," she repeated, "we two were to stand in front of the Jommdan mirror to make our vows." She checked herself, quelled the wail in her tone, and made it hard once more: "But for your stupid, selfish, incomprehensible –"

"We'll still stand in front of that mirror, one day," soothed the prisoner. "At any rate, *I* intend to keep the appointment."

She glared at him in frustration.

He went blithely on: "Our troubles, I suspect, will be over by then. No one can be Interrupted twice for the same offence, you know."

Rage and admiration mingled in the look she gave him then. She quivered, for part of her wanted to hit him – and the guards, sensing this, closed in. At that point a diversion occurred.

A second visitor stepped in through the swishing door, accompanied by yet further guards. Tarl Hemmg, a tall, craggy, middle-aged wayfarer, greeted both Mulvu and Ommwa as friends. Bluntly he addressed Ommwa:

"Have you told him about the petition?"

"I was leading up to it." Her tone became, for the first time, defensive.

"Petition?" demanded Mulvu in an ominous voice. Suddenly it was as if he had not been fully awake before. A new harshness glared from his eyes.

"Yes," she began, "we have collected –"

"Don't tell me," and the prisoner's voice shook, "I can guess: some softheads want to dilute the power of the law *even though they believe that I was justly condemned*. If you or they think that I shall ever accept a *pardon* – think again!"

Ommwa drew breath to shout him down. Tarl Hemmg pinched her arm. "Let me try telling him," he whispered.

Mulvu, observing this by-play, snorted: "The philosopher!"

"Yes, the philosopher," Tarl stated. "Let me ask you – even if you don't immediately understand the significance of my question –"

"Go ahead," growled Mulvu.

166

"It concerns a line of research which has more or less petered out, and I wonder if you understand why. I'm talking now about: matter-transmission."

"I fail to see the relevance. Matter-transmission? What —"

"Every time it has been tried," Tarl ploughed on, "every single attempt from the Lithium Era onwards, it has always been abandoned before it could ever become popular as a personal transport system. Do you realize why?"

"The expense, I suppose," shrugged Mulvu. He felt a petty headache coming on, almost a welcome ailment, a fog of kindly triviality. These people who had invaded his cell — it wasn't worth worrying about them. The only development he need fear was some new avenue of insight which could disturb the balance he had achieved, the balance which was all that kept his courage up as he awaited his doom. Insight? It hardly seemed he need fear *that* from this silly conversation... but this thought was interrupted by Tarl's angry reply.

"Expense! If you think *that* was the reason, you don't know *flunnd* about it." Tarl's voice became dry as crunchy bone. "Think about it for thirty seconds, will you?"

Mulvu put on a thoughtful expression and counted off the seconds with sardonic patience. "Sorry, time's up and I still don't get it."

"So maybe you think it *was* a viable idea. Matter-transmission: a convenient, fast way to travel? Just scan the body, particle by particle, then dissolve it and beam the information to a receiver, a few thousand miles away perhaps, where it builds an identical body, identical to the last molecule and the last memory, and you assume the person at this other end is the same person! You'd go in for that, would you, Mulvu Xy? Without sparing a thought for the implications? The *old* body which is vaporised in the transmission chamber — it somehow passes its identity on, does it?"

"I see now what you're driving at," admitted the prisoner, and scratched at his beard.

"Then you see how serious this is? You get the analogy? You see that Interruption must be death?"

"Not necessarily. Perhaps the soul — the qualitative dimension of man — survives as if carried along the beam."

"Wishful thinking."

"Not if this 'soul' is linked to a brain-pattern in a way that's independent of location." Mulvu actually grinned; he quite enjoyed this type of argument. "In which case, there'd be no interruption of identity after all. Hmm... so what I'm saying — what you've led me to see, though you didn't mean to — is that matter-transmission might well be harmless, since disintegration followed

167

by reconstitution would not be equivalent to identity-interruption... an interesting point."

At which Ommwa and Tarl gave up.

The visit did not quite end then, but both visitors realized that they could not defeat the courage of the little man who sat there debating the "interesting point".

The furthest he was prepared to go, was to write a letter to Noad Fiarr Fosn expressing regret for the destruction which he, Mulvu, had tried to cause. He would not admit that he had been wrong, but he did admit that the decision to damage the great city of Vyanth had been a painful one... "The part of me that admires beauty above all else," he confessed near the end of his letter, "makes me glad that I was defeated." And then he spoilt it all by adding: "Illogically glad – for I know my plan was right."

After this, just one more task was left to him. Another, far more important letter remained to be written.

4: The Letter

My dear Self,

They are coming to fetch me in four hours. This leaves me time to write this to you – to the Me who will be rubbing his eyes and looking around in freedom on the morrow.

Of course these words *may* be unnecessary, but just in case your sense of identity needs a nudge to make it fall into place, I attach a summary of the arguments which ought to convince you that one's self *can* bridge the chasm of interrupted consciousness. Cast your eye over it now. Done that? Good. You must now surely sense the continuity, at a deep enough emotional level. *The mind is transcendent.* And please don't dismiss this as wishful thinking; don't get too tough, Mulvu Xy. Give positive thinking a fair chance. Consider: if I have sufficient confidence to dodge the terror which would otherwise seize hold of me, surely you, my dear self of tomorrow, can achieve the same. And the proof that my confidence is real, is that I have made no effort to escape. As a matter of fact, certain opportunities of escape *were* offered to me; yes, there are some sensitive souls in the Noad's entourage, even including one member of the corps of guards who has hinted to me of ways out of here. Ways by which certain personnel might be hypnotised, ways by which I might be smuggled out, disguised as a reveller in the night; for life in this city is getting heated, and some have whispered to me that the Noad himself would not object if the Interruption were itself interrupted; does that mean that the logic of retribution has rendered him faint of heart? It's possible; Noad Fiarr Fosn seems to me to be staggering under an invisible leaden cloak, namely the future that weighs on him: he's an over-achiever, young for the post he holds, and I'm not the only one who suspects there's no ceiling to his ambition; some day, mark my words, he will leave Vyanth and grasp a higher destiny – but meanwhile he could do to be bled of some pressures here... such as squeamishness about what must soon happen to me. Well, I shall not oblige him by entertaining any cowardly notions of escape.

I am a patriot to the last. I will take what is coming to me – in the name of the good old laws of Vyanth.

See you tomorrow – in the mirror.

Mulvu Xy.

5: The Punishment

Some dark mauve polygons of visible night loomed above Kioll Octagon where the multitudes waited to see justice done; but two-thirds of the sky was hidden, for the glowing lattice of city structures heaped itself highest in this central zone. Nevertheless, the very brightness, the throbbing vigour of the cityscape itself, brought contrastingly to mind the dimness beyond... the dimness, Jad Lael reminded himself, into which he would soon depart. He had achieved little on his visit to Vyanth. As a reporter he had learned no more than anyone else about the trial. Well, he was no investigator, merely a humble observer and chronicler of a public event. His one remaining task was to record the punishment of a traitor, execution of whose sentence was about to be carried out.

He and the rest of the crowd encircled a space with a platform at its centre. A bed had just been wheeled up onto the platform and now the mood of the crowed tautened. Dissatisfied with his own efforts so far, Jad Lael began one last attempt to get a special angle on the event which was about to occur: he elbowed his way towards what looked like a small knot of friends of the condemned man.

One tall, bitter-looking fellow was jogging up and down, to keep warm or to contain a desperate impatience, but he subsided as he noticed Jad pushing towards him. The man nudged the woman who stood next to him, and put an arm around her shoulders. They both faced Jael.

He said in a low voice, "Jad Lael, reporter from Pjourth. I saw you two at the trial. Can you tell a stranger what is going on?"

"I am Tarl Hemmg, and this is Ommwa Plenn. What do you find so hard to understand, stranger?"

"The jargon of punishment here. Why do they call the death penalty 'Interruption'?"

Tarl grimaced, and quoted, " 'When in Vyanth, think as the Vyanthans think.' The body of Mulvu will continue to exist; after eight hours it will be inhabited again. That's their excuse for not using the word 'death'."

"Look," said the pale woman, "here he comes now." A slight, lonely figure had been pushed up onto the platform. They watched as he was shown to the bed and was signalled to lie down.

With a sob the woman continued, "Look, Tarl, he's hesitating; he's not so brave after all – he understands really."

"We can't be sure of that, Ommwa," soothed Tarl. "His stance may be political, even now. But he's too far away for us to read his face. You'll have to take his courage on trust."

"Ah, but I knew," she muttered, "I knew all along, that at the end he would see it was all for nothing."

Jad Lael, stung with pity, intervened with a suggestion he knew was no good. "I can at least take back word to Pjourth, that an injustice has been done."

They shook their heads. "Thank you, but no," sighed Ommwa. "He would not have been interested."

Tarl said, "Hush!"

The condemned man was making his speech from the bed. His words drifted across the Octagon in an amplified blare. "…wider perspective… I can now see… part of a to-and-fro… no complete hive-mind yet… apologise for acting too soon… you people must look to the future…"

Then he stopped, for otherwise he would have been silenced by the hooded pharmacist who now approached the platform.

The pharmacist bounded up the ramp. Ommwa and many others turned their faces from the sight.

Tarl swore violently, "The stupid *narp*, for a moment I believed he had repented…"

The hooded one extended a fist. The fist opened, to show that it contained no last-moment pardon, but instead the dreaded little white capsule. The other hand reached forward, holding a glass of water. The crowd caught its breath as the prisoner obediently took both objects.

After it was all over, Jad Lael carried the scene in his mind's eye, away with him as he walked to Vyanth's rim, slid his skimmer out of store, mounted it and manoeuvred himself into the *ayash*, soared up and out and then down to skimming level and sped away across the plains.

The zenith was black with night, but for some hundreds of miles the lower air remained lit as if by day, stained bright with the glow from the rich fields of inner Maelv. "When in Vyanth, think as the Vyanthans think." In the encompassing glow of this empire the precept was easy to follow, even for a traveller from the other end of Syoom. In fact it was hard *not* to think as a Vyanthan, after having spent an entire thirty-hour cycle of day and night under the influence of that city. It made it seem a normal way of living one's life: to keep awake the whole time, in a state of never-ending uninterrupted consciousness, albeit muted by the trance of work-routines...

At length, however, Jad Lael reached a shimmering boundary, a wall of pallor between bright air and dim. He shot through this Attitude-pause at two hundred miles per hour. Suddenly he found himself back in the ordinary night air of the wider world.

The memories in his head took on a modified meaning.

The change made him laugh.

Pity he hadn't stayed a bit longer to greet Mulvu after he'd woken up! So much for the Vyanthan penalty for high treason! All that emotional agony, and then... but of course anything, even a harmless thing, can serve as a deterrent if people are sufficiently scared by it. So, if Vyanthans spend every moment of their lives in that opinion, it must fulfil their requirements for law and order, to punish a traitor with a sleeping-pill.

The Open Secret

1: Public and Private

A flimsy base constructed of aluminium and plate glass, Sector HQ had no need of stout defences. Expendable, it would be abandoned long before the enemy reached this portion of scrubby plain thousands of miles from the battlefront. Therefore the anxieties which gnawed at the base's personnel were strategic, not tactical; large concerns rather than hot anticipation of immediate attack.

However, today the officers of the General's staff had begun to notice that their commander was moodier than usual. It was puzzling. It seemed unlikely that the military situation could alone be to blame.

Admittedly, the fall of Skyyon was disturbing: it made one queasy to think of the polar city conquered with hardly a blow being struck in its defence; the seat of the Sunnoad, the Noad of Noads, overrun –

Almost unbearable to watch was the film taken of those last hours, in which laden hover-barges dropped like tears from the city's rim to the plain below, bearing away to safety the vital treasures and archives of civilization.

Yet the loss was retrievable, indeed it certainly would be retrieved if all went according to the long-term plan for victory; if, that is, the Sunnoad's gamble worked...

A mighty big 'if'. This thought went round and round in the heads of all those on duty at the base. All very well to repeat to oneself that the strategic withdrawal will coax the invasion from Fyaym into a trap of where it can be destroyed once and for all, and that this sharp medicine is better than the burden of a long war. A bold and considered strategy: yet there were moments when it felt like a walk upon rotten floorboards. And the stress must weigh most heavily upon those who saw the risks most clearly, namely the top commanders.

Especially, perhaps, omzyr Jovald Veon.

Tall and fit, with night-black hair and rugged features, he looked the part of General, but as the strain gnawed at him he was seen to tremble like a sapling. Up till today, he had managed with cool competence. His staff had gained strength and reassurance as they watched him second-guess the weaving, looping paths traced by enemy airships probing in widening circles through the spaces of Syoom... as they were still encouraged to name the land: "Syoom", "civilization", "the statistically comfortable area", defined as that portion of the giant world Ooranye in which one lone voyager has a more than fifty percent likelihood of completing a thousand-mile journey alive. At times like these one remembered the definition most strongly, and the more one doubted it the more one continued, in defiance of disaster, to use the beloved term "Syoom". The orders Jovald Veon gave to his captains were designed to maximise the chances of keeping Syoom real: in tightly coded messages he instructed them to offer just the right amount of resistance to the enemy ships, so as to convince *their* captains that the weak opposition they currently faced was the most which Syoom had to offer. Those orders had been masterly in their insight and precision − but then came the news of Skyyon's fall, and something odd seemed to happen to Jovald Veon.

The tension lines around his mouth grew tighter. His voice cracked as he gave his orders. He accompanied his words by futile chopping gestures, or, as if to restrain himself from such action, he plunged both fists into his pockets. Often he would stare out between the silver columns of the HQ building, like an artist or poet who waits for inspiration. And then the tremors would come upon him.

The truth, unbeknownst to his officers and secretaries, was that inspiration *had* come.

It was bringing him to a decision which, unsuspected by himself, would cause controversy down the ages.

The most unsettling emotion is hope, thought Jovald. *I never guessed that hope could be so threatening. Or that it could ever come close to making me forget my duty. But then, I never suspected, till this war started, that an enemy would hand me an excuse to say No to those of my own people who opposed me, and Yes to the happiness which they denied me.*

The fall of Skyyon could be his excuse − his personal excuse − to take action of his own, against his private tragedy.

He was quite certain that he could take everybody by surprise. Neither friend nor foe, neither superior nor subordinate, would guess until too late at his opportunity to act alone.

The route to his success lay concealed within his third duty: not strategy, not tactics, but morale.

Unlike any other war, this one, *as far as appearances were concerned,* imposed the duty not of maintaining but of depressing morale: for the gigantic confidence trick which the whole of Syoom was playing upon the Quonian enemy required the peoples of Syoom to put up a pretence of despair.

This in turn required tremendous attention to detail, plus an almost fantastic degree of discipline. The plan demanded that the public mood seem dismal and defeatist, and since everyday talk in the conquered cities and towns stood a good chance of being connected with the war, all such humdrum conversation formed a vast reservoir of deceit, vulnerable to the constant risk that the entire trick might be exposed in one moment of carelessness. So far, Jovald had successfully maintained a sham radio dialogue with the occupied lands. He had sent gloomy messages exhorting people to bear their lot with stoic fortitude; he told them to be ready for sacrifice and to be brave whether or not final victory was ever achieved – and putting it this way, he made it sound as though he did not believe in victory. Each report he received, he turned into an excuse to send more advice tinged with the message that Syoomeans must lower their expectations. He made the point that the previous era, just ended, had been one long unequal struggle to postpone the inevitable, and that it wasn't surprising, therefore, that the final fall of the Rubidium Fort had opened the floodgates of enemy pressure, resulting in the present invasion and perhaps the end of Syoom. "We must not complain if our light goes out, for it has shone fair in the history of the world. No culture is immortal. All great civilization have their term…" He churned out this lugubrious stuff and the population were playing along, intelligently taking their cue, and so far the enemy eavesdroppers had been completely fooled by the defeatist disguise, while in reality in millions of Syoomean hearts the fires of hope burned secretly bright.

Now, from fooling the enemy, Jovald Veon turned to fooling his own side.

Smoothing his face, he crooked a finger at his second-in-command, zynzyr Hyl Devadan.

"Yes, omzyr J-V?" said the zynzyr, stepping smartly forward. He had been watching the General as closely as he dared.

"Hyl, I need to explain something."

"Yes, omzyr."

"The fall of Skyyon," said Jovald, "will put a lot of extra pressure on the deception plan. It is, after all, a real disaster for us."

"I see that, omzyr."

"So, on the one hand we need to make sure that our simulated despair does not become real; on the other hand we need also to make sure that the *appearance* of it deepens. As would happen, were it real."

Hyl Devadan said, "Calls for finesse, sir."

"Indeed, we have reached the point of maximum danger. A situation in which fear and uncertainty may make some of our people fight too hard too soo, and give the whole game away. – Now then, Hyl, you know, do you not, that the Sunnoad has given me *this*." And the omzyr held up an orange glass object. It was shaped like a comb, with an inner purple shimmer. "You recognize it?"

"The signet of discretion," husked the zynzyr.

Jovald, satisfied with the look of awe on the other's face, carefully replaced the object in its pocket inside the folds of his cloak, and spoke in a lowered voice. "I showed it to you because I do not want to hear any counter-suggestions from you or anyone else."

"Counter to what, omzyr J-V?"

"I," emphasized Jovald, "have been given *absolute discretion* by Sonnoad Jad Darkal himself, and that is the proof."

"Discretion to do what, omzyr J-V?"

Jovald forgave the questioner; the business was outside normal experience.

"To cook up something special for the Quonians." The omzyr's face was a touch shiny with sweat. "If the Sunnoad can trust me, so can you."

"Of course, omzyr. Of course. But –"

"But?"

"Are you about to leave us, sir?"

"Yes; you are in charge of the base for the next few days."

The zynzyr paled.

The omzyr said gently, "I don't expect the enemy to push much further towards this spot while I am gone; they are veering to sweep up the heartland. But if they do come at you, well, you know the steps of the dance we've been leading them." His subordinate saluted and was about to step back, but held still as Jovald Veon mused, "Or call it a banquet, rather than a dance. I want to make personally sure, that the sauce is heated just right for this particular meal."

Left to himself, Hyl Devadan, still pale, drew himself up straighter to stand proudly at his new post in front of the winking status boards.

2: Vlamanor

So far as it went, the excuse that Jovald had given to Hyl was true.

When is desertion not desertion?

Answer: when you've been given Discretion!

Secret elation – knowing, at long last, that you had people just where you wanted them. Great feeling.... though accompanied by a croak, *perhaps I'm behaving monstrously.*

Jovald was a public figure whose personal tragedy was well known. To be famous on account of a one-in-a-billion fluke which had ruined his chance for happiness, was mortifying as well as miserable; not that he was too proud to accept sympathy – sympathy was welcome when it was offered on a friendly, individual scale – but he found it hard to exist as a curiosity for connoisseurs of misfortune, and he resented the humiliating, mawkish attention paid to his peculiar ill luck. Embittered, he found his professional success to be an inadequate recompense. Eventually he'd got into a habit of deriding his own abilities: what was the use of being acclaimed as a great general, as Sunnoad Jad Darkal's right-hand man, if all his brains and strategic sense failed in the area he most needed help?

Until this morning, that is.

Now all of a sudden an old daydream had materialised.

Achieve a coup which will force the bigots to allow you the woman you love? Today at last, that's possible! For the first time you stand a chance of turning their objections against them.

Jovald swept his doubts and hesitations under the carpet of willpower, and justified himself by due attention to all those practical matters where his interests and those of Syoom must coincide.

The first step was to get clear of the base building without alarming its personnel. He went to the skimmer-park and climbed onto his own vehicle. He bestrode it casually as if merely setting out for an inspection tour within the security fence. By the time he reached the main gate in the fence, he had a different story ready: he wished to have a look at the ancient Lithium Era cannon – the one local relic of a town which had long since crumbled to nothing. The cannon stood poking its huge snout at the sky a short way beyond the base's grounds. His genuine archaeological interest was already known to the people who worked with him. Tongues would not wag just yet.

He circled the cannon once and then, on its far side, set his skimmer in the direction of the city of Vlamanor.

The Quonian invasion was in its early days and although the enemy held Vlamanor, their rule had not been consolidated. So said the reports: and Jovald could reasonably assume that the Quonians had not yet established firm controls on the movement of population. They must still proceed by crisis management, relying on the reactive reach of their navy, on the fire-power of their ships and guns to quell disturbances, rather than on the preventative routine of meticulous patrols. They would not shoot at a lone traveller who wore farmers' garments, which Jovald now took from the storage compartment. He congratulated himself on the unconscious foresight which had led him to pack them.

Of course, once I actually get into the city I shall no doubt find that by this time there will have been some ugly incidents involving the occupiers and the civilian population. You can't have an invasion without nastiness. But at the moment the invaders are on their best behaviour, and such clashes will have been kept to a minimum. From my supervision of the airwaves I would have heard were this not so.

It was reasonable, therefore, to hope that he could avoid any unpleasantness until he had safely sent off his message to Ralath.

Thus reassuring himself that he was not an irresponsible idiot, the omzyr skimmed north-eastwards over the plain while the base which he had abandoned and the ancient sky-fingering cannon dwindled behind him. Soon he was utterly alone between ground and sky. The crowded emptiness, the silent voices, the packed solitude of the dim Uranian wilderness pressed around him with their phantoms of possibility. But though he scanned the horizon innumerable times during the next three hours, only once did he spot the floating skeletal tetrahedron of a Quonian airship, and its crew either did not see him, or did not think it worth altering course to intercept one solitary skimmer.

Presently the topmost towers and aerial decks of Vlamanor hove into view.

A somewhat bedimmed Vlamanor, it seemed. The visible portion, extending steadily downwards with his approach, showed fewer lights than in peacetime. Still, the city remained a beacon of glowing colour which dominated the plains around. Jovald began to discern the bright ribbons of traffic threading the geometric jumble held aloft by the concave-sided stem of *iedleis*, the ultimate metal.

Wonderful structures, these city stems and the floors they supported: forged to last for thousands of millions of days – many times the current length of human history; and to Jovald, momentarily struck with the comparative transience of human affairs, it seemed almost as if the present war and its outcome hardly mattered. One war could hardly dent the glorious tale of life on the giant planet Ooranye... so what then what of the affairs of Jovald Veon; what about his courting of Ralath Noom; did the fates of two individuals matter even less?

They matter, he said to himself, *because uniqueness matters.*

Two incarnations, just two lives to live, were all that most people had; and she and he were both in their second.

Even if we both turn out to be one of those rare cases who are granted a third life, the chances are vanishingly small that we will again be born contemporary with each other. It was quite enough of a marvel that it happened this time. For it to happen next time too, the laws of probability would surely need to be re-written.

So the conclusion must be: there will never be another me and another Ralath Noom at the same time.

Therefore, if we don't find happiness this time round, we'll have lost it forever.

Happiness! Amazing that an omzyr, a general commanding over sixteen thousand men, should dwell on personal happiness in wartime!

But it was the war that gave me the idea...

Continuing his approach to the city, he reached into the skimmer's bow compartment and took out a telescope, which he trained on the docking platforms that were spread in a lofty halo round the topmost towers of Vlamanor. Up there one of the Quonian tetrahedra could be seen drifting at its mooring. He wondered how many of the crew were still on board. Some look-outs ought to be there, watching the plains; the rest of the crew would have joined the city garrison.

Closer he skimmed, and entered the agricultural zone which crawled with moving lights as other travellers, farmers with their hover-drays as well as skimmjards like himself, plied the lanes between the fields of glowing vheic. Business as usual, in that respect anyway, and likewise the fountains of traffic riding the *ayashou* up from the plain showed that the normal method of entry to the city was still in operation.

Jovald eased himself into one of those currents. The nearest ayash took hold of him and he began to rise; a half minute later he had soared up and over the rim.

He settled onto the *oalm* or landing-plain. He had arrived.

Following the normal routine of a newly arrived traveller he slid his skimmer into one of the storage lockers, then, as was customary in Vlamanor, sought to exchange it for one of the smaller skimmers ('floaters'), suitable for use within a city. But the rental office was empty. On its door was a placard saying that the service had been suspended until further notice. It was the first practical sign that the city was under enemy control – its floaters no doubt reserved for use by the garrison. Jovald shrugged at the minor inconvenience: he did not have far to walk down one of the radial avenues.

Only a few people were to be seen on the rim. Further in towards the hub, the crowds became denser and during his stroll along the avenue he first began to notice a handful of armed Quonians mingling with the native Vlamanorians. He saw no swagger, no shrinking aside, merely a mutual aloofness, a coldness of natural resentment: it was, so far, a clean occupation because it was a clean war. And it was a clean war because the enemy were getting everything they wanted so far. As soon as this ceased to be the case – as soon as the invasion met with serious reverses – they would resort to more unpleasant patterns of behaviour *but,* thought Jovald, *this won't happen before we are ready for them...* Meanwhile he strode onwards and nobody looked as though they might stop him. He felt quite free to observe.

Most of the enemy floaters and strollers whom he passed on his way belonged to the more primitive species in the invading alliance: the Lotch and the Vraik. In battle they had shown themselves to be numerous and well-armed but not particularly well-brained. Leadership came from the Quonians, who had ample brain but, fortunately, were not so numerous.

Jovald reached a kiosk; his pulse thumped and joy upwelled in his stomach as wars and strategies receded from his mind. *A message-booth at last, in the right district. I've done it, I've got here, no matter what happens next.*

Shouldering his way into the booth he punched the number which he knew by heart. As he did so he prayed to the World Spirit that Ralath had not changed her job. His last news of her was a few days old... ordinarily not long, but during this tumultuous time –

The screen flashed on and showed the inside of a hotel lounge which had been turned into an office. There she was, sitting at a wide table with a group of other women. One of these rose to answer the call, blocking Jovald's view of the rest as she approached the screen, and he could not immediately tell whether Ralath, who was still sitting, had seen who he was. Dismayed at the twanging of his nerves he rebuked himself: surely an omzyr could cope with a screen call. *Faintheartedness at this point will have to be paid for with a lifetime of regrets.*

The woman said, "Protectors of Orphans at War. Who are you?"

"Omzyr Jovald Veon, despite not looking the part. May I speak with Ralath Noom?"

The woman blinked in disbelief. "This is a meeting of the Protectors – I –"

"I know of your great work," Jovald said agreeably, "and I shan't take up

179

much of Ralath's time. Just tell her to come over to the screen, will you?"
And he held up the Signet of Discretion.

He only held the thing casually, as if he were what it looked like, a comb
which he was about to run through his hair, but the woman recognized it and
gasped. A moment later she was off-screen.

Good, good, go on, fetch her, panted the mind and fizzed the blood of
Jovald, and then, as the face of Ralath at last blazed its beauty at him, his
heart thudded to a stop while his wits scattered, as happened every time,
caught off guard by that same old churn in the guts which had made a fool of
him so often in the past.

Heartbeat resumed as his mind reached for a defence which sometimes
worked – the trick was to find fault with her appearance. Secretly, he
reminded himself that Ralath was not perfect. Her teeth were uneven, for a
start. Her chin a little red…

"Jovald, are you mad? Speaking your name and rank like this in public?"
Her tone might have shrivelled his courage, except that her last word did
recall him to his senses.

She was referring, of course, not only to the unique social prohibition
which had long kept them apart, but also to the fact that one sure way to show
up on enemy monitors was to use the public vidphone system in an occupied
city.

"On the contrary," he breathed, "I am sane. I must stay public – if I am to
speak to you at all."

"Explain!"

"Will you meet me for lunch at the Embers?"

Time slowed around this pivotal question. Then it wobbled at a faster rate
as he saw her lips curl up at the corners. A wild notion came to him, that she
had guessed his whole strategy.

She said, "I *am* getting rather hungry. In half an hour – is that all right?"

3: Street peril

Well, he had done it: he had made the call. That particular operation was a
success.

He swung out of the vidphone booth and leaned against its side. Of *course*
the authorities had listened in. Gazing at his busy surroundings he imagined
the outward ripple of his "private" conversation through the city-scape and

beyond. By broadcasting his tryst he had ensured – if his calculations were correct – that he could now make his way to the Embers in reasonable expectation that he would get there unmolested: they'd want him to get there…

Nevertheless as he began to walk his senses were primed like those of a hunted animal. The city was dimmer than usual, with much of the energy that had been used for illumination now diverted towards the enemy's war effort; the business-corners and entertainment niches now had to function on reduced light. When he reached the inner ring called the Ezem, the circular avenue which revolves at the half-radius of Vlamanor, he found that the famous concourse still moved at its age-old speed, but shorn of its halo of brilliance. He stepped onto it and was borne past blacked-out mews that seemed enlarged by their obscurity.

Disappointment, when it came, was sadly complete.

One arm was seized above the elbow from his left side, the other from his right. Two grey figures had fooled him by their apparently random, separate approaches. Now they had him in a *reporznt* grip, the martial art that deceives by slowness.

Together they edged him into an alley. It was one of those spaces which gape like caves in the loosely heaped jumble of any Uranian city, but here, in an area subdued and bedimmed by conquest, the effect was more than usually speluncal. If any citizen had seen him being whisked away, nen would not protest. Had not the Sunnoad himself instructed his people to bear all insults and bide their time?

From the stocky outline of a third man who stepped forward, Jovald deduced rather than saw the coarse features of a Vraik.

The man flicked a torch on and shone it in Jovald's face.

"Hold him still, let's take a look at him…" The gravelly voice spoke recognizable Nouuan, though it crunched the syllables. "Omzyr, you were smart not to yell."

This gloat was echoed by a fainter snicker to either side of him.

The captive listened, silenced by his own dismay. Not only must he admit to himself that his hopes had been destroyed. Not only were his arguments, his guesses, his predictions junked. He must also face the fact that he had been selfish to an appalling degree – amounting to treachery. To let himself get caught like this was to invite disaster for Syoom. If they squirted him with truth-drugs how could he not reveal the Sunnoad's great plan? Only one way out was left to him. He must get killed resisting. He tensed for his act of final atonement –

And hesitated for a moment while he checked that this would not be yet another mistake.

He should be able to take these two oafs, though of course the third one, waiting out of his reach, would then get him for sure.

Almost happy that he was about to burst the bubble of his failed life, Jovald Veon stepped back and pulled his clutching enemies towards each other, so as to smash their crania together in the last second before their colleague gunned him down; but things went nauseously wrong.

He felt a *ripping apart* of what he tugged. Then he was the one who was thrown off his feet. As he fell, his eyes – now dark-adapted to the alley – registered that the two "men" were not, after all, men. They were *Lotch*, their bodies peeling into fluttering rags. Scraps of writhing leather, nightmare flexion –

Jovald rolled in an effort to evade the horrors and to draw his laser, but his every reaction lagged hopelessly behind the speed of change. The rags, before he knew it, had slapped together again into standing figures. These rebuilt Lotch cackled as their bony arms held him down on the city floor.

Close-up, he saw on their faces and necks the jigsaw lines which betrayed their nature, the man-mimicking colony of protoplasmic crusts which could pretend to be a single organism.

Meanwhile the Vraik, the human enemy, had stepped forward. He wagged his laser down at Jovald while he spoke to the Lotch, in his language or theirs, words that ended on a rising note.

The patchwork creatures made no answer. Intent on their victim, their features seemed to squirm and then dissolve. Worse things then began to happen as the despairing omzyr, befuddled with loathing, saw them lean close. Their now-faceless heads were *unfurling* like petals.

Jovald tried to cry out to the Vraik, *you at least are human, can't you stop this,* but what came out was a mere gasp. A remembered fact, that human brains were a delicacy to the Lotch, caused him to choke.

At that moment a cone of light flooded the scene and a hard voice rang out, freezing the Lotch. The voice lashed them again and they drew back, heads closing. Jovald lost no time in scrambling back onto his feet.

In unsteady relief he bowed to the fourth arrival.

Of all the Fyayman horde the chivalrous Quonians were the closest to Syoom's Nenns in appearance and culture. *If they were to conquer and rule us, we would merely lose our political liberty, not our way of life.*

The Quonian officer was short, stocky and helmeted. From this headgear the light came, a nimbus which enveloped the man's uniform in misty silver, signifying high rank among his status-conscious people. The two Lotch and the Vraik stood aside like children who fear rebuke.

The Quonian bowed back to Jovald, whose former optimism now slid back into favoured place as though he had never ceased to believe in his plans. Fate would – must – allow him to win.

Out of the corner of his mouth the Quonian spoke in acid tones to the Vraik, who replied submissively. The Quonian then switched to the Nouuan tongue as he addressed Jovald:

"Omzyr J-V, I am Quarin Yadqual, of a rank equivalent to yours, in the fleet of His Luminosity Quelm the Fifty-Ninth, Quonant of Quonia. I welcome your entry into His Luminosity's dominions. Allow me to state your position. Your arrival inside the territory of the New Empire has been taken to imply that you have resigned from the Syoomean Navy."

Jovald said nothing.

"Lesser powers," Quarin Yadqual continued, "in our situation would have defined you as a spy and treated you accordingly, but the Brilliant Folk scorn such reactions; we leave such attitudes of insecurity to the lesser breeds. So, you are free to come and go as you like, as a private citizen here in Vlamanor, henceforth under the protection of our laws."

"I thank you, sponndar Q-Y."

"It is no great matter. Obey the law and we will not interfere with your social life. I apologize for the crude behaviour of those who – due to the regrettable necessities of the moment – are allies of Quonia. And so I wish you good day."

"I sincerely wish you the same," replied Jovald. The day seemed the brighter for the haze of thankfulness in which he set off once more, knowing, and not caring, that Yadqual was gazing after him with a satisfied expression.

4: The would-be Corrector

For some hours Hyl Devadan had felt buoyant. He enjoyed the sensation of being in successful charge of sector HQ – success meaning the absence of disaster.

Enemy radio was easily overheard, and those of his monitoring staff who sorted through the chatter could confirm that Jovald Veon had been sighted in Vlamanor, merely as a refugee, not as a spy or prisoner. Hyl thanked the skies (or fate, or providence) for the laxness of the enemy.

However, he had the fighter's superstition that a run of good luck must be paid for sooner or later. The only question was, when and how heavy the payment would be. Broadly speaking, the longer the wait, the worse the penalty; hence he was almost glad when the communications officer uttered the words:

"A call on the red, zynzyr H-D."

Words that dried the mouth. Hyl Devadan did not need to be told that "on the red" meant that the call must originate from the flagship *Ayeis Dcifen*. Knowing whom he would see, Hyl strove to compose himelf as he turned to the monitor screen. As expected, it at first displayed part of the humming control-room of the airship which currently hovered in the vicinity of Toolv, away on the other side of Syoom; then that view was occluded by the head and gold-cloaked shoulders of a swarthy, young-to-middle-aged man with burning eyes and a hard jaw.

Jad Darkal 35480 was a warrior Sunnoad the like of whom had never before been known. He was acknowledged to be, in every normal sense of the word, a good man – yet his main interest in life appeared to be battle: fighting it, preparing for it, studying it.

It was as if he had been born to lead Syoom against Fyaym in this desperate time.

Or perhaps such men existed in all periods, and only now was one called forth to lead the Syoomean forces in their struggle; in which case the selection process for Sunnoads must be godlike in its prophetic wisdom; either that, or un-mathematically lucky.

Without preamble, Jad Darkal said: "I want Jovald Veon's report."

"Sunnoad J-D, the omzyr is not here. He has left on an undercover mission. At least..." Hyl hesitated.

The Sunnoad gave a grim nod. "You are thinking that it may not be undercover any more."

"You heard...?" probed Hyl.

"Not *heard*. Guessed. We're getting reports of reports. They lose coherence as they are relayed but they're enough to convince me that Jovald is up to something on his own, in enemy-held territory."

"I have heard he's been seen in Vlamanor, but, Sunnoad J-D, I have no more details as yet."

"Knowing that character, nothing will surprise me. If you learn more, inform me before you take any action." The Sunnoad broke the connection.

Hyl Devadan was thus left to wrestle silently and alone with fantastic thoughts of the omzyr's possible treachery...

...Meanwhile the debate continued on board the *Ayeis Dcifen*.

The Sunnoad, turning from the monitor screen which had shown Hyl's face a moment before, met the gaze of the wizened savant who was his counsellor and would-be Corrector, Marad Sydel.

"So then, Marad, will you seize this opportunity to say, 'I told you so'?"

Sydel gave a shrug. "At times you were wont to say, Sonnoad J-D, that to order the replacement of the omzyr might prove as dangerous as to keep him. Your reasoning was, you did not wish him to take alarm and flee with all he knows... yet now he appears to have done exactly that. So, yes, I told you so."

Jad Darkal, cryptically, said: "Then *prepare* to be worried." It was one of his phrases. Ever since his elevation to the sunnoadex he had experienced the almost indescribable sensation of (as it were) *inhabiting* himself – looking out from the top storey of a living mansion built from the lives of his 35,479 predecessors who had worn the golden cloak. "Jovald Veon," he remarked, "is a problematic tool. From the moment that I gave him Discretion, I realized that he might misuse it, but I am gambling that his grievance will work for our side, so that his gifts won't go to waste."

"But what will you *do*, Sunnoad J-D?"

"Right now, go to my cabin and lean into the latest stack of reports – and you're going to comb through them with me, sigh though you may, Marad; you must know I won't have you say afterwards that I covered up for the troublesome omzyr."

Marad Sydel bowed his head, hiding his thoughts. In addition to playing the part of a sounding-board, he had the secret ambition to be a Corrector: that is, one who gets away with coercing a Sunnoad. This most dangerous of all political games requires a special set of circumstances for success; the death penalty is the accepted lot of a would-be Corrector who fails to prove his case to his master – fails, that is, to convince him after the event that the coercion was justified. Correctors thus appear rarely in history. But this business with Jovald Veon had some promising aspects...

For just think – Sydel declaimed to himself in his imagined stance, as he addressed the imagined court of inquiry: if that omzyr in Vlamanor has gone to the bad, I shall be vindicated.

Later, more promising still, in the upholstered cabin the counsellor became spellbound at what he saw across the littered table: a really worried, brooding Sunnoad. It was a rare sight to watch and hear the man in the golden cloak soliloquize as he shuffled papers, as if he were delegating procedures to his hands while his mind tried to deal solely with destiny's terrible requirement to be *right*:

"What choice did I have?" murmured those lips, or so it seemed to Marad; he could pressure himself to believe that he knew exactly what the Sunnoad was thinking because he knew what the man *ought* to be thinking and therefore *must* be thinking, to fulfil the life-promise of Marad Sydel. "We cannot go into Fyaym to look for our enemy; Fyaym is too big, it's four fifths of the world. We'd dissipate our forces and come to ruin. No use." Jad Darkal was shaking his head at his own words. "The only other option is what I made us do." The voice became hushed; if only it were louder, instead of an almost whispered mumble! – but still it was guessable by Marad as it went on, "What *I* made us do... invite the Fyaymans into Syoom by a pretence of weakness," and now his eyes blazed all of a sudden – ah, thought Marad excitedly, this proves it all – nevertheless a glare made him flinch – *"ConVERT,"* the Sunnoad clearly pronounced, "the fall of the Rubidium Fort. Convert it from disaster into opportunity." The eyes faded back to dullness. As so they should. They must be resigned to the guilty truth. Here came the confession. "The responsibility is mine: I planted the stories which enticed the enemy to take his swift advantage; the invasion, in that sense, is my doing." Back and forth continued their mumbly see-saw. "And since I myself am guilty of so much, how can I not be lenient with the lesser tricks of Jovald Veon?" The lips ceased to move. With a sigh the Sunnoad looked up.

Then he really spoke.

"Daydreaming, Marad? Go on, finish that stack."

5: Deal at the Embers

As he strode up the crescent steps, Jovald knew what his advantages would be, and how he intended to exploit them beyond the hotel's arched entrance.

Though he could hear his heart thud in his chest, he was beyond hesitation. An expert sportsman, about to perform a difficult but well-rehearsed feat, need feel no confusion, and Jovald was in like case. Mind could discipline body to make it easy to saunter through a lobby, past reception and through glassy inner doors, into the rounded space beyond, the size of a concert hall – all he had to remember was to look like he owned the place.

Tables for two, for four and for eight were scattered around the Centrepiece where glowed the embers which gave the establishment its name.

Jovald could not immediately spot Ralath. She must be sitting somewhere on the Centrepiece's other side. He began to circle round, pretending all the while to relax in the cosy warmth of the embers' glow.

They are formed from a rare substance known as coal. It is rooted in deep time, in a previous Great Cycle of Uranian history, when the stuff was widely used for fuel. Supplies of it were depleted almost to nothing by the dominant species of that day. The substance itself was formed long before that; hundreds of thousands of millions of days before. It dates from a primeval, forested epoch which long pre-dates intelligent life of any kind on Ooranye. Good to know these things, especially as the hotel management prides itself on using real coal for its centrepiece, importing it from remnants of Fyayman deposits; they must still be able to get it – for today I note that all shines as normal, the fiery glow not faked.

"Nice shine, Thrello," he said as a man cloaked in black and white advanced upon him.

"Omzyr J-V, welcome back," said the head waiter, instantly recognizing him through his farmer's disguise. "Are you –"

"I'll find my way," smiled Jovald, and Thrello faded smoothly from his path. *That* had been an easy enough encounter…

Then around the Centrepiece *she* came in sight, waiting at a table for two.

Ralath Noom was on the cusp of middle age, with a fairly good figure, superb deportment and brilliant auburn hair. Her features looked somewhat stiff, making Jovald yearn to enliven them. It was like that with all her imperfections and drawbacks; they merely – confound them – intensified his adoration.

Nevertheless, her nod as he approached, and her quizzical smile, left him annoyed. And after some hundred and fifty days of separation he might reasonably have expected something a bit more intimate than a pert expression which seemed to say no more than, "Hello, what in the world are you up to this time?"

On the other hand, *he* was hiding *his* feelings; surely she could hide hers. And he was a commander, wasn't he? A respecter of discipline – so then, be fair – respect hers!

He sat opposite her. He placed his elbows on the table.

This is more like it, he thought next moment as she leaned forward and clasped his hands, and her face leaned close to his. *Skies above, you can never tell with this woman.*

"Jovald," she said in a caressing tone, "don't look at those characters at the table to your left."

"Uh?"

"The table near the window. Don't look. They're from the Clean Lines Society."

Maybe I'm the mystery. The mystery of why I bother with her. I really thought she was going to say something warm just then. Whereas in fact she's just playing games for onlookers' benefit. She just doesn't care, at least, not the way I do.

Ralath continued in a murmur, "Perhaps you know what to do with them. For me, the main thing is, you're here. It's been so long, Jovald."

She does care and I should never have doubted her.

Please stop see-sawing, O my mind.

He squeezed her hands and assured her, "I know, at long last, exactly what to do with the Clean Lines people."

"Are you serious, Jovald? Can I trust you on this?"

"You can."

Saying it once, though, wasn't enough. She found it too incredible. In an even lower voice she added, "You really have found a way for us…?"

"Thanks to the war," he murmured.

"I don't understand. I don't *understand.*"

He nodded, "Of course not. Not yet. But you will soon. Our friends over there are getting up, I see. Sit back and listen while I…" He broke off as three men and two women flowed forward to occupy the closest tables, turning their chairs round to face him and Ralath.

At the same time he noted the dark green uniform of a Quonian sponndar seated at a more distant table. This might turn out useful. Probably, thought Jovald, the Quonian has a voice pickup trained on the gathering around me; I hope so. It will make my task all the easier.

In the military and political sense, the Quonian was an enemy, yet as far as Jovald was concerned *the* enemy – in a far more important personal sense – was the group of fellow-Syoomeans close by.

One of the women, smartly cloaked and elderly, addressed him in a voice ripe with disdain: "Omzyr J-V?"

"I am he."

"And the lady Ralath Noom, of Hoog?"

Ralath nodded stiffly.

The speaker went on, "My name is Omwa Sisk, and I and my colleagues are –"

"I know who you people are," growled Jovald. "Every city I enter, I meet C.L.S. snoops." He fancied he could almost hear a "click" as the woman's haughtiness intensified.

"If that is so," she snapped, "no further introductions are necessary and I shall state our business –"

"That, too, I should know by this time." Jovald felt grim glee as Omwa Sisk bridled further. "But," he conceded, "I can listen once again, if you like."

Indeed I am willing – just once more. Little do they know that this is the last time. And yet, already, it seems, they begin to sense it. Delightedly he perceived the ebb in their self-confidence. Their blather must henceforth dwindle into reflex, an arrogant twitch unsupported by reality. The moment drew closer, the moment when comfort would be torn from them and they would be left to shiver in the icy blast of humiliation, failure and defeat. And the delicious thing was, they couldn't avoid it because they couldn't adapt. They could only go on repeating their one message. It was all they had to say. Even if they were to find out that he had something new up his sleeve, their entire position would continue to rest upon an argument which they had always considered to be rock-solid. *Unfortunately for them, I have mined that rock.*

Omwa was saying, "I don't know exactly how well the position has been made clear to you by our colleagues in other branches, but I shall enumerate the main points which cannot be gainsaid, concerning you two."

Ralath shifted uneasily, but Jovald shot a warning glance at her, and she subsided.

"Point number one," continued Omwa. "You are both in your second incarnation. You have never denied this, and it would be useless to being to deny it now, for both of you have confessed to blurred and distant memories in the characteristic second-lifer style."

"We don't deny it," said Jovald comfortably. "We are, as you imply, run-of-the-mill second-lifers. Like maybe five per cent of the world's population, this far into the Great Cycle."

Omwa, after waiting impassively for his words to cease, continued as if he had not spoken. "Point number two. There has been no skulduggery about your names. In both your cases, they were authenticated the usual way – namely, they were recorded as being the first sounds you uttered. Neither your parents nor anyone else made any attempt at concealment of these, your true names, Jovald Veon and Ralath Noom."

"Agreed! We are who we say we are." *This is going like a dream.*

"Point number three. There is therefore no reason to avoid the presumption that the Jovald Veon and the Ralath Noom in this era are the very same people as the Jovald Veon and the Ralath Noom who lived over a hundred and twenty million days ago, and married each other, in the Nitrogen Era."

189

"Except," said Jovald – *I had better make some objection, though I must not overdo it* – "the vast improbability of two people who knew each other in their first incarnation, actually returning so close in space and time that they also become acquainted in their second life."

"Statistical improbability," said Omwa, "is bound to happen, given sufficient opportunity. It would be more surprising if a few cases like yours did not crop up, in all the millions of combinations of lives in our world's history. Reasonable?"

"Reasonable," admitted Jovald, keen not to put her off as she approached her punch-line.

"Point number four. In that first incarnation you, Jovald, and you, Ralath, became the parents of..." She drew a sharp breath, then vomited forth the name: *"Liucgr Ell."* She then sat back and glared. Her face had gone red. Jovald wondered if his had reddened too. The obscenity of the hated name was enough to sicken and embarrass anyone. Liucgr Ell. Activator of the Corruption Ray. Liucgr Ell. The arch-villain of Era Seven. Liucgr Ell. The monster who had maimed whole cultures –

Careful, thought Jovald: I must be careful, now that I have reached this point. How can anyone maintain that there are two sides to *this* question? Yet debate I must. Keep a clear head. No one knows what governs the return of souls. However, in case there is any heredity to them at all – in case there is the slightest chance that Liucgr Ell may return if his former parents wed again – action will be taken. If Ralath and I have a child, observers either from the CLS or the government or both will insist upon being present at the birth, and if the infant's first sounds suggest the name of horror, it will – officially or unofficially – be killed.

Jovald's romance with Ralath had up till now been ruined by this threat. In vain he had argued that the CLS' concern was based on silly fears; that one coincidence did not make another; that there was no reason to suppose that Liucgr Ell would reincarnate via the same parents as before, any more than other second-lifers did.

People wanted more than arguments. They wanted nothing less than to be *sure* that the fiend did not return.

Jovald dared not ignore their determination. Suppose he did marry Ralath and they had a baby boy who at birth happened to gurgle something like "Loogr-Ell"? The risk was too great. And even if that did not happen, still the child would face a life of suspicion, in which people would continue to wonder whether perhaps he bore a mere *given* name, concealing a terrifying *true* name. Jovald by this time was thoroughly familiar with all the arguments.

Though he had not agreed to them, he had bowed to them because he could not subject Ralath to such tension and fear. He had given in to the busybodies, had allowed them to drive him away from her again and again –

Until now. Now he did something different.

Savouring the moment, he opened his right palm. On it the orange Signet of Discretion sparkled.

Into the stillness he sowed a seed by remarking:

"Syoom, admittedly, greatly suffered from Liucgr Ell. But there is little point in worrying about that now, isn't there? For we are a conquered land. Syoom appears to have no future any more. I therefore see no point in resisting the birth of Liucgr Ell."

"But the Sunnoad –" croaked Omwa.

"If the Sunnoad were here he would say the same. Otherwise he would not have given me *this*."

Next, sit back, let them stare more at the Signet. Watch as awareness blossoms in them.

He knew his opponents were not so stupid as to need any further prompts from himself. Members of the Clean Lines Society had learned, just like anybody else in this war, to take part in the patriotic deception plan, whereby Syoomeans must feign despair in order to fool the enemy. And what more logical way to show that they had given up, than to withdraw their objection to his wooing of Ralath Noom?

So they had no choice but to take the hint he had given them. The Signet of Discretion glinted at them from his palm as he hefted it idly. Even without the sight of it, they got the point all right; in fact Omwa had got it even before she had finished her own four points, which was no doubt why she had spoken with increasing acerbity. She must have struggled with her own private despair. Jovald could feel a contemptuous pity for her. She and the others were sincere enough, and genuinely feared the rebirth of Liucgr Ell. As to whether he, Jovald, could forgive the Society for the hundreds of lonely wasted days it had forced him to endure, that was another question.

"I see," rasped Omwa, her face sour with defeat. "The war has certainly changed things, so much so that, in these conditions of defeat, we should not take up one further moment of your time." Pushing their chairs back, she and her colleagues stood up, looking as though they were about to spit on the table, but they had to swallow their spit instead.

For a few moments Jovald drank in his triumph as he watched them go. Then, shyness and diffidence invaded him anew, as he turned to look at Ralath.

She returned his gaze levelly. "That was clever, Jovald."

"Provided it wasn't all for nothing. Provided..."

He did not quite know how to go on. *Provided I still have a chance with you*, was the blunt thing he needed to say.

"Yes," she broke in, misunderstanding him or pretending to – you could never tell with Ralath. "Your victory may be temporary, depending as it does on 'these conditions of defeat', as the woman said." But something in the curl of her smile gave him a surge of hope and courage.

"I am not going to ask you if you love me," he muttered. "I'm prepared to run the risk," and he lowered his voice further to a whisper, "that you will marry me merely as part of the deception to save Syoom."

"Risk?" she inquired, eyes dancing. Her hand slid across the table to his. "It's always a risk." A vast joy soothed him, convinced him that the hollow days were over.

6: The Wedding Deception

Jovald's courting of Ralath continued to be a public affair right up to the date fixed for the wedding – Day 42 of the young Strontium Era; fourteen days after the meeting at the Embers.

The publicity was a guarantee of protection for them. It also, however, made such protection doubly necessary. Plenty of ordinary folk in Vlamanor, though not members of the Clean Lines Society, were nevertheless influenced by CLS attitudes and therefore worried about who a child of this marriage might turn out to be. Superstitiously, some feared that even if it were not Liucgr Ell himself, it might be someone just as bad. Debates became fierce. Some people sprang to the couple's defence, arguing that even if Liucgr himself *were* reborn he need not follow the same evil path in his second life. For though the soul be the same, the character might have changed...

Over and above all this was the paramount and silent influence of the Sunnoad's plan. The open secret, the hidden hope and the feigned despair, meant that when it came to the point of action, nobody dared forcibly oppose the wedding of Jovald Veon and Ralath Noom.

To make doubly sure, Jovald let it be known to the Clean Lines Society that he and Ralath had both left documents, to be opened in the event of their deaths, which "told all". The hint, he trusted, would be enough. Deriving enormous satisfaction from thus forcing the CLS to work in his favour, he next proceeded to take his fiancée to public places of entertainment, flaunting their romance in the face of society, relishing the fact that there was nothing society could do about it since it was now doing the Sunnoad's bidding by giving the enemy supposed proof of the hopelessness of Syoom... and sure enough the occupying forces looked kindly on, while Jovald broadcast invitations to the wedding.

It was to be a lavish affair. Jovald hired the Yarpan, the great hall high near the airship docks, with its superb view over the city and its surrounding fields. Finally the big day came, and in his best cloak he stood in the foyer, welcoming his guests, while some yards away Ralath stood welcoming hers. Some truly were welcome: friends and well-wishers from near and far, private travel still being possible despite the war. Many others, he could tell, were present merely in order to take part in what to them was a charade, with the open secret's strategic aim, that the enemy might believe that Syoomeans no longer cared about their future. Besides, the food and drink were excellent... Jovald cynically greeted them all.

Somewhere inside him, like a secret cabinet drawer, lurked a compartment of disbelief. It contained a compressed fear: all this might turn out too good to be true. Did Ralath love him or was that, too, a part of the charade? *The trouble is, what with so much grand strategy, my personal judgement is a bit off.* Unavoidable... but then couldn't *she* have made it a bit clearer what her feelings were? Instead of giving him so many of those little stilted smiles! Those shy, clipped sentences! There she was now, rationing her greetings to a queue that shuffled past her. Suddenly it came to Jovald that there was another explanation to her manner: it was not that she was discontented, nor resentful of him. Instead, the reality was: she was terrified. And with cause.

Under the crust of my accomplishment, I also feel the quake. As if on cue, a hum became audible. The sound intensified, beating down from the domed ceiling. The guests murmured. They tilted their heads, to gaze up at the quivering chandelier.

Jovald, sensing the need for a split-second decision, sought assurance from Ralath: their eyes met. He nodded, and stepped aside to murmur an instruction to the master of ceremonies, who had been picked for solid reliability and who now obeyed immediately: he struck a gong.

That clang reigned supreme; nothing could compete with it to catch and hold the guests' attention. Following the bride and groom, they filed into the central hall. Meanwhile the outside humming slowly faded, while Jovald's thoughts remained in turmoil: what they had just heard, before the gong, was the departure of the garrison airship, and the most likely reason for *that* was that the Sunnoad's long-planned counter-attack had begun.

If all went well, within hours it would become conclusively apparent to the enemy that they had been fooled. Tricked. Trapped. Great news for Syoom –

But what about the marriage, no longer necessary for strategic reasons, no longer justifiable at all in the eyes of many?

Repeatedly he sought comfort and reassurance from the expression on Ralath's face. *Forgive me for bringing you into this.* It was not easy to say that with a wordless look. But she got themessage, raised her brows and somehow, thank goodness, contrived merriment to sparkle from her eyes. This ceremony, at any rate, was going ahead. Jovald turned his mind to what was appropriate for an occasion supposedly joyful, part of the immemorial custom which has made the act of standing in front of a full-length multi-planed mirror the common part of all marriage services on Ooranye. He took his bride's hand and ascended the platform which had been cleared for them. This was tradition; this was living history.

They stood there and kissed and their reflections and re-reflections symbolized the rebounding effects and criss-crossing supports of marriage and society.

After those key moments, they descended from the little platform, whereupon a cheer, loud enough to betoken sincerity, went up from the crowd of guests. Perhaps they were in a good mood because they, too, had realized the military significance of the garrison ship's departure and were sanguine about the prospects for Syoom.

On the other hand when they got round to thinking a bit more about it, they would most likely drift back to the Clean Lines stance, insisting that Ralath and Jovald ought to be kept apart…

A heavy man in a rich cloak strode towards the newlyweds. Jovald eyed him warily.

"I congratulate you both," Verzay Relk, City Co-ordinator, said coldly. "Your persistence, your… *ingenuity* has rewarded you."

"Like many men," agreed Jovald, "I had to win my bride against odds."

"Yes, you've been ruthless, all right. Nothing stands in your way, evidently."

Jovald matched the other's dry tone.

"But for hundreds of days I *did* allow you and your kind to stand in my way. To the detriment of my life."

"*Your* life – *your* life." Verzay's words now came with a definite sneer. He turned away, bowing ironically, barely preserving appearances.

Jovald ascertained, with a look towards his wife, that she and he happened fortunately to be standing a few paces apart from all the others. "Ralath," he murmured, "I do fervently hope that you don't regret what we've done…"

Stop, she gestured with a hand on his arm, and murmured back, "You fear, we've stored up too much hatred."

"No, not that. I can't believe that. Time will heal it if we're given enough – but that's the question: how are we going to live meanwhile? And the only answer –"

She forestalled him. Wonderful creature that she was, she said what needed saying. "We must get out. Out of Syoom."

He scrutinized her expression and saw no irony, no bitterness: she really did understand. It gave him the final reassurance he needed. Even if she was just making the best of a bad situation, the sufficient truth at this moment was that they had to get away; and if they did – if they gained a breathing-space – he would then have the opportunity to convince her that she had made a worthwhile choice of husband. "We have a few hours," he went on, "before battle explodes in earnest –"

She nodded, "That's my guess, too."

"So will you allow me to take you into Fyaym?" The sound of that last word unfurled in his mind like a banner of purple darkness. A bad moment for a bridegroom: though his intellect trusted hers, as a lover he cringed in advance at the scornful reply which any bride might be expected to make at such a mad suggestion.

She linked her arm to his, dispelling the nightmare: "Off we go, then. Honeymoon in Fyaym."

At every point in the conversation so far, he had been dreading that it would go sadly wrong, and only now could he admit that he needn't have worried. He had in every sense met his match. I've been slow, he thought. Slow to appreciate the full wonder of my prize.

Meanwhile he – like all Uranians – was in no danger of undervaluing the greatest, world-sized prize:

He knew, it being bred in the bone, that the giant planet Ooranye is an ideal world for those who wish to disappear.

7: To Get Lost

Context-awareness furnishes the natives of Ooranye with a powerful sense of their world's size and of the value of that size, especially for fugitives. Humanity is spread so thin, that what with the scarcity of patrols over areas so vast, you can always hope to slip away from a hostile regime if you can get access to a skimmer.

A so-called one-man skimmer can carry two if need be. The pilot can sit inside, like a canoeist, while the passenger sits behind and astride, nen's boots on the rests at the vehicle's sides, hands gripping the supplementary control lever.

Thus laden, the skimmer carrying Jovald and Ralath took three days to reach *sky-50*, the invisible safety-contour which marks the frontier between Syoom and Fyaym. They crossed it at a point about 6250 miles from Vlamanor and well inside the largely Fyayman region of Nyyn.

By that time they also knew that they were living in a new era. They had spent their wedding night wrapped in blankets next to their skimmer parked on the cold and endless plain. Discovering the warm, tender aliveness of each other was epochal in a merely personal sense, but when they also noticed a delay in the luminescence of the air next morning, an exterior truth dawned on them: the turning point in their own lives had coincided with a global diurnal shift, an *eomasp*. Though the atmosphere brightened as usual from pallyne to morningshine, it did so in two fluctuating stages, and the second pulse was about four hours late. The only force that could cause such bad time to be kept by the natural biological clockwork of Ooranye was a resonance with the mental excitement of millions of humans. That wave of emotion had sufficiently perturbed the mindless floating microscopic *throom* to put it off its thirty-hour stroke of brightening and darkening.

And what could have caused that burst of mental energy? It must be the Sunnoad's counter-attack. The product of so much secret planning, the bursting reward of all that self-restraint, this and only this could have caused the flutter in Nature's heartbeat. All over the world, therefore, people knew that the young Strontium Era had been cut short and that its Day 42 was being succeeded by Day 1 of the Yttrium Era.

"Really not such a coincidence after all," remarked Jovald, his smile full of pride and cheer.

"You mean, the world owed us a new era?"

"I just mean, that if we were ever going to get away, we had to have cover on this scale…"

"Well, isn't that lucky," Ralath replied, tartly.

Surprised at her tone, Jovald said: "Well, yes it is." Then, after a hesitant glance, he understood why her mouth had gone lopsided. To view the epic

196

transition from one era to the next as a background prop for their own needs did seem a trifle egotistic. "Anyhow, here we are, safe and sound," he concluded.

"I like you, Jovald. You're pleasant company, which is just as well, considering where you've brought me."

Fyaym, when one was in it, objectively could seem much like Syoom: an empty plain where the *gralm* extended as far as the eye could see, except where it was wrinkled by small ranges of hills, and dotted by groves of spiky *katora* bush or the blades of *narps*.

So, nothing special. Objectively, this was so. But from the start the additional colouring of expectation did tint the view. Gave it a difference…

Everyone grew up from childhood with the knowledge of how Fyaym in literal terms is statistically defined, as the land in which a lone skimmer-pilot has a less-than-fifty per cent chance of surviving a thousand-mile journey. Everyone brought nen's own imagination to bear on this idea and so draped it with some colour from nen's own personal store of hopes and fears. Anything might engulf an explorer in the wilderness where no city patrol would ever reach. For instance new weed-kingdoms might grow between one random voyage and the next. Isolated cultures, species might develop unseen. Oversights grown large, innumerable fates awaited the intruder.

How to better the odds of survival?

A couple of encouraging points:

The statistics agreed that two people were more likely to survive than one. Also: "less than fifty per cent" need not mean *much* less. The "continental shelf" of Syoom, where it existed, meant that, for some distance into Fyaym, hardened wayfarers could risk a long journey.

"Besides," argued Ralath, "maybe we have journeyed all we need. We're nicely lost. Can't be necessary to travel deeper from where we already are. From the authorities' viewpoint we must surely have disappeared already." Taking the silence of her husband for consent she went on, "So what with the situation back there, with Syoom and her enemies tearing at each other, no one will have time to spare to look for two runaways who've annoyed the Clean Lines Society." She folded her arms, satisfied with her own conclusion.

"And," said Jovald, "what about when the battle is over?"

Ralath shrugged and said nothing.

"I get the feeling," Jovald mused, "that the Yttrium, like the Strontium, may turn out to be a short era."

"So?"

"We can't rely on our respite lasting for ever."

"Reliance? What's that? Never heard of it," said Ralath sarcastically.

"And perhaps," continued Jovald, "we're still too close to the border, despite what you think. We'd better press on."

Ralath wanted to know how they would live in deep Fyaym. "I'm not starting to get difficult, you understand. I just want to know."

"You *do* know," Jovald replied, "else you would not have trusted me this far."

He said it promisingly, with his arms clasped tight around her, yet even so he only just got away with it. She jarred him loose as she spoke with bite in her tone:

"You *are* going to give me an answer, aren't you?"

Is this going to be our first quarrel, he wondered. Oh well, so far, doing simple things, making love, speaking their moods, praising the sights they saw, they had given themselves an uncomplicated rest that wiped away former habits and civilized stresses, allowing something else to grow: the wild, imaginative instinct for survival.

"We *can* live in deep Fyaym," he replied, "if we find a fortunate oasis."

"You mean that literally?"

"Why not? Could take the form of a fertile swale, a crystal grove, even a town, yes, a town in a sheltered spot; such mini-Syooms have been recorded now and then. We should have time, exploring, to find what we need. And given the luck, you and I between us have the skills to survive, do we not? How about it? Are you with me or would you rather return to face Omwa Sisk and the CLS?"

"When you put it that way..." she replied sweetly, and they laughed together.

Luck was with them. Deeper into Fyaym they skimmed, day after day, yet they lived on without any close brush with the manifold varieties of disaster which could so easily expunge explorers from the record.

And finally Jovald was able to point ahead to his "swale". Past a gentle hill, beyond the visible slope, came an unseen, self-explanatory touch inside their heads: a beacon of thought which allowed no doubt. It was without meaning, just a constantly repeated name: *svalg, svalg, svalg...* Jovald and Ralath halted their skimmers.

"Shall we...?" began Jovald.

He saw the assent written on her face. Instinct proclaimed to both of them, "it's worth the risk". The continuious beat in their brains – *svalg, svalg,* –

pushed feebly yet convincingly: something definite waited for them as they skimmed forward again.

Something that was perhaps trying to repulse them. Feebly.

Topping the rise they came in sight of the swale, the shallow, wide, bowl-shaped hollow about a mile across. Filling it was a leafy town, no, a towny plant: a single organism whose broad green blades were interspersed with human dwellings. Dots – people – moved among the leaves. Jovald and Ralath eyed the scene, discerning the kind of deal that must have been struck. Some bits of folklore concerning Fyaym helped them to make the correct kind of guess.

The *svalg* was probably the one and only individual of its species; Fyaym harboured many such unique productions. Doubtless immortal, un-reproducible, from time to time it invited another species into partnership. Currently, it dealt with Man.

"They've noticed us," murmured Ralath.

One of the human dots down below had ceased to move, and another swerved to it as at a summons. Others gathered; a group formed; it began to move.

"Yes," agreed Jovald, "and here they come."

Simultaneously with a yielding "pop" inside their heads they felt the thought-beat of the *svalg* turn from pushing to pulling. From discouragement to welcome.

Epilogue

Many thousands of miles away, and a lifetime later, the crack reporter Jegand was brought by his hunting instinct to the Tnedon Estate near the city of Nuvium. It was Day 22,716 of the Zirconium Era.

Jegand was a quietly ruthless young man. With cold, patient eyes he noted every detail of the beautiful sward and fine buildings amid the Tnedon grounds. The cork-textured gralm was springy underfoot, except where luxuriant grass bordered the central block. Around this, bright red flame-bushes were interspersed around the greenhouses, famous for the growth of the Graol herbs which had healed so many injuries.

Their discoverer, Lek Graol, lay dying somewhere in the estate, and Jegand was determined to speak with him before it was too late.

"Yes, it seems he actually does want to see you," said the house-chief when the reporter applied at the reception window. "So I have to let you in. But if you ask the wrong kind of question you may hasten his death."

"I'm not here to torment the fellow," protested Jegand. "He asked to see me!"

"I'm not disputing that." The house-chief looked glum, and continued, "But he didn't say you could go in without being warned, so listen while I warn you: he really is what he's reputed to be, namely self-critical, perfectionist, jittery about his past – "

"Oh, come on, he's not that weak. His life has been a triumph. He has always known what he was doing. And he has heard of me, he knows my field."

Jegand expected to be let in there and then. To say that Lek Graol's life was a triumph: that should have clinched the matter. A bit of flattery, but also true. It should have gone down well enough... but the house-chief still seemed inclined to hesitate. Something about Jegand evidently worried him.

"Also," the man added, "I can choose *when* to let you in. It might not be today."

It might not be ever, realized Jegand. He abruptly changed his tactics. He risked a startlement – the shock of absolute honesty.

"Look, even if he *does* die a bit sooner from telling what he wants to tell, have *you* the right to deny him?"

This worked. Without another word the house-chief, beckoning the reporter to follow, led him to a room where a shrivelled man of over twenty-two thousand days was lying on a large bed, his face immobile, his hands clenching and unclenching.

Jegand could sniff, figuratively speaking, the presence of his quarry. The world in the reporter's estimation was a sort of global graveyard, a haunted area revisited by unquiet mysteries. Any journalist could make a living simply from netting the reappearances of issues which refused to lie down. He had done it time and again. Here once more he had tracked a sinister old story, tracked it down to the right place and time, where he guessed it was due for resurrection.

The old man on the bed was speaking, pointing: "Sit there. I need to talk to you, youngster. Can you answer me?"

"Yes," replied Jegand, "we reporters can answer as well as ask."

The voice from the bed rose higher – the last spurt of a dying flame. "You know what used to be said about my parents and about me?"

"I have heard stories, but it was all a long time ago, wasn't it? So, Lek Graol," continued Jegand cunningly, "what can be worrying you so much *now*, I wonder? You have led a good life, I hear. A life of self-sacrifice. You have devoted yourself to the good of mankind. You have saved thousands of lives, and in the future this foundation of yours will save thousands more."

The reaction to these words confirmed the reputation of Lek Graol as a man who could not bear to hear himself praised. Jegand watched in fascination as the admired benefactor of humanity began to squirm. The fellow's movements were necessarily weak, but the impression he gave was that had his strength allowed him he would be thrashing about, under a torture of guilt.

Words came, words which must have gone through many agonized rehearsals.

"Suppose my parents cheated? Suppose *they* named me? Yes, what if they *gave* me the name I bear? Suppose it's not the real one, the one I pronounced with my first sound? All my life I have tried not to think about it. Resisted all thought of accusing them. But their situation was uniquely hard... they might have done it... and so, might I in actual fact be... not Lek Graol but... Liucgr Ell?"

The swelling panic in the man's voice, the desperation in his face, at last roused some pity in the hard-bitten reporter.

"Come on," said Jegand to the sinking man, "you must know there is an easy way to settle a question like this. You really want to know if you're Liucgr? *If you're worried about it, then no, you can't be...*"

As he finished his sentence, he noted that the sufferer's breath had grown shorter.

Jegand peered forward.

The head rolled slightly on the pillow; the chest ceased its feeble motion.

Jegand added in a whisper, "...At least, not in any way that could matter now."

The Worm of Poleva

Prologue

When Nature reclaims a ruin, crumbling the artificial structure, reducing it to an uninhabitable mound, overgrowing it with weeds, we can say that she has brought the object back to being a natural feature of the landscape. Her weapon of erosion has won her a battle.

Occasionally, though, the engagement can be decided another way.

On the giant planet Ooranye there was one artificial structure so enormous that it could not be comprehended by any human economy. Though a construction, it became an *independent* landscape feature. That is to say, the culture that built it failed to assimilate it. It was the architectural equivalent of an uncontrolled explosion.

This was the Great Wall, older than recorded history, and never owned by any single power. Even its builders lost control long before the project was finished.

Once in a while, when funds allowed, and other matters did not compete too strongly for the attention of the government, the city of Contahl achieved a temporary ascendancy over part of the length of the Great Wall. Troops cleared its passages and rooms of Gedars, driving the savage submen from their nests out into the Fyayman plains beyond the Wall. During such operations, airships floated overhead, firing down to sweep these and other less humanoid foes from the Wall's wide summit.

During most of Contahl's history its citizens have regarded the Great Wall not as an artefact but as something in the nature of a wild mountain range, no less perilous than the ocean of night which lies beyond it. But during the occasional expansions of their control, their attitude to the awesome structure has changed. It then begins to be seen as a possible defensive boundary. In a fit of memory, the government recalls that it has the right to occupy and garrison at lease some fraction of the ten-thousand-mile length of the Wall.

A circumstance of this sort occurred during the reign of Noad Govasswa

Hayt, in the middle of the Niobium Era, the forty-first era of civilization upon Ooranye.

We see through the eyes of Gengr Axtain, a young wayfarer who has volunteered for service on the Wall. Told that every place in the garrison has been filled, he nevertheless has come to look round.

Leaving his skimmer parked on the plain, he approached the nearest of the stairs set in the Wall's side. He could see no one and nothing except the huge vertical structure itself and the contrasting flatness over which he had travelled to get here. He could eke out this basic view with a few known facts.

The Wall runs straight: a slash of order cutting through the chaotic borderlands of Fyaym. On average six hundred yards high, and one hundred and sixty yards wide, it is porous with chambers, corridors and the ancient, pre-human luxury apartments adapted nowadays to comfort the modern exiles manning this rampart of civilization. Along the top runs a line of observation towers a little more than a mile apart. They seem, and are, incongruous; their small addition of height hardly affects the vantage provided by the wall itself. Indeed they are not part of the original structure but were added by humans, in the course of some ancient power-struggle upon the summit.

Gengr was not surprised that the scene appeared to be deserted. He knew that the attention of Contahl's garrison was likely to be fixed upon the Wall's further side. Confidently he began to climb.

He zigzagged upwards back and forth until he came to an open door at about fifty yards' altitude, where he first encountered some members of the garrison. One *sponndar* stood with laser drawn, and required Gengr to give an account of himself. The soldier then spoke into a transceiver, broadcasting Gengr's description, and waved him in.

Gengr was surprised at being accepted so easily. He was here uninvited, after all. "You're not worried that I might be a spy, an enemy?"

Before the soldier could reply another voice spoke from further in; Gengr had been overheard by an officer.

This man, seated writing at a desk, looked up and with a superior smile remarked, "Too much security is as dangerous as too little."

Gengr had approached, but now he stopped, uncertain.

"How so, sir?"

The officer waved an arm and said, "After all, what of the beings who built this thing? Where are they now? What good did 'security' do them?"

"Ah, you mean they relied on the Wall too much, sir. But then, perhaps they were insufficiently vigilant," suggested Gengr. It was a bit of a pointed remark, he realized when it had left his lips.

"Well," chuckled the officer, "*we're* vigilant enough. If you turn out to be an enemy, you're welcome – we'll thank you for the target practice."

Gengr laughed, "I'll have to disappoint you there, sir. I'm just a citizen, asking for a view from the top."

He resumed his ascent. It was like climbing a mountain. No elevator shafts had been inserted into the structure of the Wall. Presumably, the pre-human Builders had not minded this; it was one possible clue to their nature – they may have been winged beings, or, perhaps, controllers of gravity. Maybe, maybe, maybe... a dumb reminder of how little we know, thought Gengr. But then, we don't need to know. In fact there isn't such a thing, really, as knowing. *That* – surely – is the secret of the builders of the Wall.

Finally, after a restful interval spent in one of the garrison canteens, he attained the top floor and the last stair. From this he emerged at last onto the Wall's summit. He seemed to be standing on a cream-coloured road in the sky. Low battlemented parapets to either side were all that reminded him of the truth. This was one of the undamaged sections, smooth except for the hardly noticeable addition of the observation towers.

A few sponndarou were in sight but he avoided them, uninterested in meeting warriors at the moment. He wished to commune with the vista alone. He strode to the far side, to look out over the sinister Fyayman plains, those outer immensities lapping against civilization. The air in Fyaym might be bright during daytime, every bit as bright as it gets in Syoom, but night reigned in the soul – the darkness of the unknown. Gengr after a long stare wandered back to contemplate the country on his home side: recently pacified lands, glowing cultivated fields, well-tended roads which stretched back five hundred miles to Contahl itself.

Fyaym out there, Syoom over here. The Wall in between. It was a contrast which fired the nerves. And yet Gengr, though he almost staggered under the weight of awe, suddenly realized that he was no longer inspired by the prospect of service upon the Wall. No, it was not for him. Instead, he would stride far *beyond...*

That was the surprising lesson he had learned by coming here.

For the time being, this stretch of Wall has been won, he reminded himself. *And I know something of the expense; I have seen and heard official figures quoted. I can tell that Contahl has not the resources to keep up the garrison forever. As for mounting operations in the land beyond – to extend our empire deeper into Fyaym – that would be a futile project. Doomed to costly failure.*

He guessed that a few attempts would be made, and soon abandoned, defeated by the numbing infinity of the task. Meanwhile he, Gengr Axtain, would enhance the empire in another fashion…

Slowly he descended, enjoying his new sense of purpose. He left the ancient Wall, his boots once more crunching the gralm as he walked across the plain towards his skimmer. He mounted and sped away homewards.

He reached Contahl in two and a half hours, but it then took him as many days to obtain an audience with the Noad. In view of the many duties devolving upon her as Head of a State which had just expanded to its natural frontier, Govasswa Hayt was an extremely busy woman. Gengr knew this, yet he was simple-mindedly confident that soon *he* would become one of the matters she was busy with – and he was right in this; a simple man who had allowed an idea to get lodged in his head, he was too naïf to fail.

"Brrrmph… I like your idea, young man," said Govasswa Hayt, pacing the audience chamber, her grey cloak swirling about her stocky frame. Gengr noted that at each turn of her walk she looked at something – a screen, an indicator, a window. Multitasking, from moment to moment. "Not that I'm keen," she added sternly, "on the cost to the Treasury. But," she continued half to herself, "I can think of no excuse to turn you down…" She halted and swung round to face Gengr Axtain. Her sharp glance swept his pleasant face, as he stood patiently awaiting her inevitable verdict. She smiled faintly as she read his easy stance, the deportment of one whose ambition burns steady and serene as a main-sequence sun. She nodded with decision.

Noad in all three Syoomean tongues means *focus*. Govasswa Hayt was a middle-of-the-road Focus of her city. She avoided both extremes of political style: she had not *arelk* (the rigidity of a despot) and nor was she a *Fyffy*, that legendary buffoon who (if the story can be believed) actually went around soliciting for votes. She was a ruler of mature judgement with an instinctive focus upon the lines of political force, and as such she voted in her mind for Gengr.

She was old whereas he was young; she a wily Head of State, he an innocent adventurer; but the patriotic flame burned bright in both their souls.

"Return to the palace in five days," she commanded, "and, barring emergencies, you shall have your *krematar*." (Authorization, *immediatization*.)

No emergency intervened. These being heady days for the Contahlans, a mood of heroic generosity infected the people's hearts; their pride swelled at the vast expenditure proposed, as an old name returned to their tongues: "Poleva". *Yes, let us send comfort to long-lost Poleva, although we shall never get anything in return for the fare, except for the glory of the deed.* The

205

very letters of the word "Poleva" resounded with the glamour of past catastrophes. While Contahl was a frontier city, close to the boundary between the light of Syoomean civilization and the darkness of Fyayman chaos, Poleva was a different case, far *beyond* the frontier; a lost outpost in the deeps of Fyaym. Lost, that is, apart from one tenuous link – the matter-transmission Portal.

The Portals endured, though nowadays their use was almost unheard-of. Their physical fabric survived as one of the mighty works of the Phosphorus Era, the period when builders notoriously drew upon limitless supplies of energy looted from the Other Dimension, Chelth. No Uranian would dare try that game again, but modern man could still profit from his ancestors' robbery of Chelth, twenty-six eras later: after all, the great disc-on-stem cities of Ooranye had been constructed with the aid of the stolen power.

And just as the cities still lived, so, likewise, it was still possible to power the Portals. However, the price would now have to be fairly paid. Uranian resources must henceforth suffice, since access to Chelth had been discontinued forever.

If Contahl were willing to pay that price, it could flash a living body to Poleva, eighteen thousand miles distant, instantaneously attaining an objective which lies so deep in Fyaym that no one would try to reach it overland.

Gengr Axtain, and the officials whom he talked with, believed in the likelihood of finding people still alive at the other end. Records in the Contahlan vaults alleged that the Portal network had been used in the Phosphorus Era for quite significant movements of population. In fact, it had perhaps been a serious attempt to tame the vastness of Ooranye. They had thought to web the entire globe in a network of cities, finally to bring about the triumph of Syoom over Fyaym.

That attempt had of course been doomed. The plan could never have succeeded: first of all because Ooranye was too big and four-fifths of it was Fyaym; second, because the destruction of the Great Fleet in the global nightmare which ran down the curtain upon the Phosphorus Era left no one with any spare energy for aught but survival. Whole populations had thus found themselves stranded in the Fyayman wilds with no means of return. But the backwash of history did leave some achievement in its wake. Outposts such as Poleva, Olhoav, Nusun and Koar survived.

This was known in Syoom because on rare occasions the Portals had been reanimated to keep in touch with the outposts. Though no private individual was rich enough to activate the transmitters, governments – when flush with resources – might send news, supplies, or even an emissary.

206

The generous Contahlans approved their Noad's decision to transmit Gengr Axtain to Poleva.

1: Arrival

The instant the field switched on, the crowd of leave-takers became nothing more than a milky after-image on his retina. That sight, of their arms raised in farewell, would have to suffice for evermore.

One pressured moment of illusory speed and the squeezed-out pip of identity that was Gengr Axtain had jumped over the map from point to unrelated point. Next he was staggering on the disc at the receiving portal. An imaginary howl rang in his ears. It was a protest from the cheated fabric of space-time.

He was in the open, under a starry sky, a little way outside Poleva. He was seeing that city from about half a mile out. Out here the installers of the transmission network must have been more nervous about accidents than the builders at home – too nervous to site the receiver within the city boundary. Gengr did not condemn their caution. But neither was he happy at being deposited even a short distance outdoors in the far Fyayman wilderness; he dropped warily to the ground. Then, after a minute, he straightened, for he noticed he was, after all, safe within a kind of circuit – formed of glass ramparts that appeared to ring Poleva's fields of vheic. The plants themselves waved in the breeze, reassuringly familiar. Only the sky, with its strange stars, told him, "you are on the other side of the world".

Poleva itself, rising in the midst of its cultivated area, loomed like an oversized half-egg. Criss-crossed with struts and lines connecting its geodesic panes, its predominent glow was pale yellow, giving it a kind of paradoxical dim brightness against the black sky and the violet horizons. Gengr Axtain stared in resigned wonder at what must henceforth be his home. This was a city actually built on the ground, like his other home, ancient Contahl itself. That at least was one continuity: he would not need to get used to a disc-on-stem.

For the builders of the Phosphorus Era, mighty though they had been, had not been able to use their up-raised disc-on-stem design for their Fyayman outposts. While power was free in those days, the supply of *iedleis*, the ultimate metal, was not unlimited. What there was of it had had to go into the construction of the metropolitan cities of Syoom. Here, on the other hand, they'd had little choice but to squat their settlements down on the ground. Rash that might seem, out here in deep Fyaym, but what else could they have done? Gengr stepped thoughtfully down from the receiving platform.

With slow steps he walked along the road through the fields towards the gate. As he did so a hooting and clanging arose from that direction. Already, people were streaming out towards him.

They came on foot and on skimmers, and other skimmers swerved from elsewhere in the fields; no doubt his arrival must have registered upon every energy-detector in the city's vaults as well as on every human eye that happened to be turned in the receiver's direction. No citizen of this long-nighted land was going to miss the sight of the first visitor from Syoom for many an age.

Deafening him with greetings, the Polevans swarmed around him. They turned his entry through the gate into a triumphal procession in which he repeated his name scores of times on eager request. He was introduced to hundreds. His every reaction was scrutinized, devoured with avid stares. Each citizen seemed determined to share in the marvel and freshness of his experience, right up to his arrival at the globular palace which was hurriedly allotted to him. At its threshold he turned, with a trusting smile, and gazed back down the ramp at the buzzing cityscape while he waited for someone in authority.

A breathless laser-bearer no older than himself came forward to announce that the Noad of Poleva would certainly give him audience within the hour, immediately upon completion of that day's tour of the urban defences. The youth added, "I am Berr Ucht, the Noad's courier. I have been instructed to ask you what you would see in the meantime."

"I would see everything! I'd climb a tower, right now if possible, to get a view of your country."

"I heard that," said a commanding voice. Gengr turned to see an older, taller, heavyset man striding towards them round the curve of the building. The courier departed smartly. Gengr and the older man appraised each other.

"I am Nekkon Lalldorpl, the Noad's son. Because my father is not strong, I help him out with his social functions – such as welcoming a once-in-an-eon arrival from Syoom." The corners of the man's mouth turned down grimly. "Follow me: we have time to ascend the Rezram Tower." It was the weight of jowl, decided Gengr, that caused this fellow's statements to *thump*. They landed like a posted summons on the mat.

"Rezram? Ah, a hero of old Syoom," replied Gengr, and smiled regretfully when his comment went unanswered: apparently the reference meant nothing to Nekkon Lalldorpl. Perhaps anyhow it might be best not to refer to the culture which he, Gengr, would never see again.

As they strolled, the newcomer gazed down from the heights of the walkways, down through busy levels of the urban lattice, to the city floor. Poleva thrived, obviously. However, at each main intersection in the three-dimensional maze, checkpoints were staffed by watchful guards.

Nekkon observed Gengr's interest and said: "Spy-scare. Nusunian spy-scare rumour."

Gengr asked, "Isn't Nusun thousands of miles away?"

"I can see, you think it incredible that one Fyayman outpost should have any trouble from another. But our fear is, that if their city is failing, they may try to migrate here and seize ours. Unlikely but possible." Anger had appeared in Nekkon's tone. *Anger directed at me*, Gengr suddenly realized with a start of guilt. *He's highly intelligent, I must watch out. My expression must have told him what I was thinking: these stupid squabbling outposters, gurgling down the moral plug-hole of internecine conflict while Fyaym waits to engulf them...* Just then a burst of cheering made his guide pause to flash a smile at a group of arm-waving citizens who sped past them on a skimmway. "Well," continued Nekkon, "how does it feel to be a celebrity?"

Uneasy with the other's sardonic tone, Gengr tried to play up to it. "Not bad – if there's no catch."

"There's a catch for *you* all right," growled Nekkon. "The catch is, *no going back.*"

"Oh, I know that."

" – Unless," continued the other, "you wish to attempt the return journey overland, alone! You certainly won't find *us* stumping up the cash to operate the Portal from *this* end."

"I'm not grumbling in the slightest," replied Gengr, attempting to allay the other's grumpiness. "In fact I had no guarantee that I would find a surviving city at this end at all." He was not keen on what seemed to be implied by the other's words. To suggest that he, Gengr, might blench from the consequence of his own decision to come here - ! He was only human; he was bound to feel some homesickness. And furthermore, as he thought about the general welcome he had received, he had the strong impression that the Polevans themselves yearned to touch Syoom, even if only vicariously by feasting on the sight of a visitor.

By this time they had completed the spiral ascent of the Rezram Tower. They went to stand at the railing. Frome there they gazed down over Poleva, and to the belt of fields beyond, and the wilderness of Fyaym beyond that.

Fyaym – the antithesis of Syoom.

Fyaym – the land where a lone traveller had a less-than-fifty-per-cent probability of surviving a thousand-mile journey (and, in deep Fyaym, a *lot* less than fifty per cent).

Fyaym – defined thus statistically, for that was the way to label the problem, and to label the problem was the most you could do on this giant world of unpredictable threats, disasters, crises and foes which were apt to appear out of the dimness at any time. Fyaym was sixteen hundred million square miles of untamed twilit peril, out of which absolutely anything might emerge to harrow the civilization of mankind; and Poleva stood deep within this unknown four-fifths of Ooranye.

From the Rezram Tower's summit railing Gengr could see three terrain types. A canopy of dark green jungle stretched away towards one arc of horizon and, towards another, the contrasting wrinkles of a barren rocky area folded into ridges, one brown shade after another. In a third direction a bare plain extended to infinity.

He caught sight of a satisfied expression on the face of Nekkon Lalldorpl as this son-of-the-Noad asked, "Well now, man from Syoom, what do you think of all this?"

Gengr, for whom tact was not a strong point, had an impulse to pin down what was wrong in Poleva's location.

"An enemy army could be at the gates before you know it."

"Vigilance," shrugged Nekkon, "is the only answer. Unless…" he paused, now scrutinizing the Contahlan closely, "one were to get help from Syoom…"

"Which you won't. They could only just afford to send me – one lone body – through the Portal."

"So we both know the worst," smiled Nekkon. Then an odd, dramatic twitch overcame him. His eyes blazed, his jaw jutted. Theatrically, he seemed to grow as a laser appeared clenched in his fist. Cloak swirling, he brandished the weapon at the panorama of Fyaym. In that moment he symbolized for Gengr all the defiant heroism of the lost cities, the outposts, Poleva, Nusun, Olhoav and Koar, whose names echo like music in the mind.

What a renowned Noad this man could make – thought Gengr idly – at least as far as image was concerned! A pity it could never happen. The noadex – the office of Noad – was precisely the one post which the son of a Noad could not hold. Unless the taboo against hereditary monarchy had weakened out here in Fyaym…

"False hopes," rasped Nekkon Lalldorpl as he sheathed his laser. "Those head our list of enemies to kill."

They descended from Rezram Tower.

At its base, Ber Ucht waited to conduct Gengr to the Noad. Nekkon bowed curtly and took his leave.

Time, now, for the Syoomean emissary to meet the Polevan Head of State.

A cream-coloured wave, which rose from ground to thirty-yard crest, the Palace of the Noad shone modestly amid the crowded city centre. Exterior escalators fed in and out like veins to and from a heart. Gengr was told to go through one of these entrance tubes; he emerged from it inside a glittering suite with recording sensors sprinkled like diamond dust on every wall.

An elderly man sat writing at a desk. Reyeb Lalldorpl, Noad of Poleva. He looked up and his aged face beamed with the enthusiasm of a happy child. "I long to hear your story, Gengr," he said mildly, gesturing to the facing chair. "Never did I think to receive this good fortune in my lifetime. I suppose we are mythical to you, and you of Contahl are no less a myth to us."

Gengr sat. "I am relieved to find you and your people real," he confessed, swayed into a chuckle, for the other's obvious good nature made nervousness impossible.

"Oh, we're all too real – we and the things which keep us busy. Too busy. I regret I was not able to greet you on you arrival. Nekkon has been looking after you?"

"Most effectively, Noad R-L."

"You may think this strange, but it is precisely because he is my son, and cannot succeed me, that I feel free to load him with public duties. I can dump them onto him knowing that in so doing I am making no move to prejudice the succession... but enough of that. I am not so infirm that I need leave *all* the celebrations to Nekkon. Let us talk of Syoom, you and I."

They chatted for hours, at the end of which the Noad scribbled some introductions for him – "not that you'll need them," he added – and wished him happiness in his new life as a Polevan.

2: The Roil

A woman sat at a desk inside a dome, which itself fitted inside a cylindrical enclosure near the edge of the city. Inside and out, the complex was well lit, with an expenditure of energy that had caused some complaint – but, so far, the warden had been left to run her prison as she saw fit.

No longer in her youth, she remained attractive in a brittle kind of way, her

211

features retaining the tense beauty of a glass flower. Gengr Axtain walking into her office did not doubt for one second that he had entered the presence of the Daon of Poleva.

He had been warned by the Noad. "My successor, Polange Nsef," old Reyeb Lalldorpl had confided, "has what one might call a *hungry* charm, which serves her determination to persist with unpopular schemes…"

Obviously this Polange Nsef woman was convinced of her own destiny. She must feel that she had some special vocation which set her apart. Else why should a Daon of Poleva – heir to the noadex – choose the unappealing post of prison warden? She must certainly be endowed with an original mind to want *that* job.

"Gengr Axtain? Glad to meet you at last," she greeted him, warmly enough. "Like everybody else, I have been eager to meet The Syoomean! I expect you've been kept busy these past few days."

"Yes, I've turned into a sort of city mascot, it seems. People are making the most of me, knowing that they won't get another such specimen for an eon or so. But I assure you, Daon P-N, it wasn't on purpose that I left my visit to you until last."

"I know – I've been busy too – but now that you're here, you will no doubt wish to investigate my crazy idea of keeping prisoners alive."

Warily he objected, "I never said it was crazy."

"Ah, but others do, and you must have heard them."

"I know you are bound to have your reasons. But I can't guess what they are."

"You have no prison in Contahl?"

The ex-Contahlan grimaced. "We do have a prison, but only for malefactors awaiting judgement, or prisoners of war awaiting exchange. We do not have prison *sentences* as such. We have the death penalty, and the penalty of banishment. That is all."

"Here," remarked the Daon, "banishment would *be* a death penalty."

"I see that."

"But the main point is," she went on, "what is the use of capital punishment as a deterrent, when so few people are afraid of death? Most of us, at this early stage in the Great Cycle, are in our first life; we know we have our second life to come, and perhaps even a third after that. Why should anyone be afraid to die?"

Gengr mulled this over. Why indeed. Death was merely an escape to another time. There were plenty of phenomena which could inspire fear, but they all pertained to life, not death; phenomena such as injury, shame, responsibility for failure, or the many intrinsic horrors which needed no reason to be scary as they encroached from the borders of the unknown. Life, not death, was the terrifier. "Yes," he mused out loud, "I see that our death 'penalty' is really just our means of clearing nuisances out of the way."

"And their souls get recycled, and this is known, so people do not, as a rule, fear the process."

"So," deduced Gengr, "you want to do something worse to them instead."

"Loss of liberty," nodded Polange Nsef, "is more frightening than death, is it not?"

Gengr thought about prolonged incarceration, and shuddered. "I'm with you there."

"Besides, we cannot afford to kill able-bodied evildoers. Our population is small enough as it is."

"You use them?"

"It's not ideal but at a pinch, yes, they can be released and deployed as troops for defence. You must realize that Poleva is a beleaguered garrison with Fyaym the constant enemy, and every one of us may at short notice be needed to man the walls."

"I get the picture; but are prisoners really any help?"

"Oh yes, if they only stay employed a short time."

"And can they be given their freedom if they fight well?"

"Those who have undergone a change of heart, yes."

Gengr did not say out loud, *How can you tell?* He simply raised his eyebrows. For some reason it came to him at this particular moment, that he would not for all the world do anything to hurt or offend this woman. An amazing thing, which he had seen make fools of many of his friends, had just happened inside him for the first time. His whole outlook wheeled like an engine on a turntable, to face a new ideal. Polange Nsef was now his ideal. The first result of this incredible change was that he became protective, absurdly so. He knew it and could do nothing about it.

He noticed that her head was cocked to one side. Background noises had diminished. Ordinary, workaday sounds, which usually came in through the windows and doors, had faded into hush. Gengr held his breath – and then almost choked as a scream tore the air. YEE YEE YEE. The scream of a siren. Polange rushed to the window, opened it and tilted her head upwards.

Gengr followed her. He, too, looked out. His uncomprehending eyes swept the cityscape while other windows in the building sprouted their share of heads and hands – many of the hands holding binoculars.

"Get your heads back in!" shouted the Daon to her staff. She pulled Gengr back; his heart thrilled equally to her touch and to the crisis. Then the siren stopped, and now a new noise could be heard.

It was an eerie vast rumble, somewhere up in the sky, drifting closer. He heard Polange breathe a word which he did not recognize. She looked back at him, and he desperately gathered his wits as she spoke to him. "You and I, Gengr, can only hope and watch. I am not on the defence rota for today. Anyhow it will all be over in a few minutes, one way or another."

Still he did not understand.

The din grew in volume and it was becoming harder to ask questions and he decided he must use his eyes and shut his mouth. A roiling brown border of a cloud-mass hove into view above the prison wall. High above the city it prowled, but perhaps not high enough: an amoeboid shape, seeming to battle with itself as it churned and bubbled. To the tense faces below, it gloated its power, terrifyingly poised to smite downwards, and Gengr froze as his capacity for belief laboured to catch up with the demands of reality.

Scores of Polevans on defence duty had meanwhile scrambled to their posts. Searchlights flashed on in the upper city. The Daon, seeing the look on Gengr's face, explained to him that in each fortified emplacement the defenders were ready to produce salvos of laser bolts, plus pressor beams to repel, force-blades to chisel, force-planes to shield. But though the bristling cloak of armament began to hum, the order to fire was not given. Well might the Noad hesitate, Gengr imagined. For were not all these measures mere pin-pricks, irritants which could further enrage the already frenzied cloud?

He tried to express this. Polange shouted back, "It's not one, it's several clouds. Watch them fight each other."

By this time their mile-wide bodies were in full view, entwined as they gulped and howled, emitting fusillades of blinding white bolts and broader lava-like spurts, much of which spilled down onto Poleva. Gengr shook his dazed head; he had never heard of any sentient cloud that possessed this level of ferocity. At any moment he expected a full-scale exchange of fire between ground and sky, with ground overwhelmed.

That this did not happen, he realized after a couple more minutes, was due to the unintentional nature of the threat. The clouds were not interested, or not primarily interested, in attacking a human city. All that Poleva needed to do was to shield itself against the spillage of their fury. For this, the force-places produced by the defence-generators proved sufficient, though for several more minutes, after the echoes died away, Gengr marvelled that he was still alive.

"All clear," said the Daon with a twinkle in her eye as if to say, now you see what kind of life we lead in this part of the world. "Excitement over."

Gengr left the window and returned to his chair, hoping that his skin had not blanched overmuch. He was reasonably sure of the coolness of his outward behaviour. But – more urgently than ever – he knew he must find some definite role in Polevan life, to do his bit to thicken civilization's thin front line in this remote land. Thus he'd show the people that he was more than just their mascot from Syoom.

Polange plumped down into her chair. "Where were we?"

Gengr rapidly faced the truth: *this is the last of my introductions and, when it's over, all the receptions will be over and I shall be on my own, a foreigner with no native skills, no particular excuse to see her again.* The seconds were ticking away and his mouth felt dry. He wasn't used to coping with the sense that the person he was talking to was of infinite importance. He had never met anyone of infinite importance before. It magnified the dread of every act. Now, on his part, nothing less than perfection would suffice. Awkward, that. His choice of words would have to be faultless. And he must at all costs do the right thing, whatever that was. Strange, how impossible life had become. It had always seemed quite easy before...

A buzzer sounded upon the Daon's desk. "Excuse me a moment," she said, flipping a switch with one finger. "Yes, what is it – I am interviewing the Contahlan –" An urgent voice gabbled from the communicator and Polange Nsef slumped in her chair. A look of misery appeared on her face. She snapped back at the voice, "Very well, wait for my orders – I take full responsibility –" She clicked off and stared through Gengr.

He leaned towards her, searching her shocked face. "Please – what happened?"

She signed, "There has been an escape. Under cover of this storm. The first successful breakout in my tenure as Warden. This could finish me."

"Finish – ?"

"I can see (now that it is too late) how it must have been done... I must organize a search party, but –"

"I shall get them back for you," interrupted Gengr. "Dead or alive."

"You? Why you?" She seemed poised to laugh. "Are you raving, Contahlan?"

"Why me? Er... adventurer's luck – an outsider's viewpoint – I don't know – but here I am, for you to use." He *willed* her to believe.

She raised her eyes and shoulders, "I'll do it. I'll commission you."

"Thank you, Daon P-N." How grateful he was for the magic of the name of Syoom! That alone could account for his persuasion. "I'll not fail you."

"You'll need to know –"

Hustling, anxious to be underway before she recovered her senses, he broke in: "Brief me on the way to the departure point. The trail will be cold soon."

3: "This is Fyaym"

The escapers (it was soon discovered) had made for the forest whose near edge grew a few hundred yards from the outer vitreous ramparts of Poleva.

Into the dark green maze plunged Gengr Axtain, newly raised to the rank of *zamur*, followed by his *nyr* of eleven *sponndarou* (laser-bearers).

The lasers had to be put to use immediately in order to burn a path through the foliage; Gengr and his followers wielded their shimmering blades with a hacking rhythm, so that within minutes some of the *sponnds* had to be recharged. The fact that the pursuers were following a trail previously hewn by their quarry was of some help. However, mere minutes after its creation the path had become fuzzed by new growth. Unnervingly this vegetation grew not at a steady rate but in quanta: the crack! crack! of fresh branchings buffeted the men as they struggled onward. Adding to these discomforts were other unpleasant aspects of the forest – the noisome breezes set off by blower-plants, the pools of goo dropped by the sucker-plants, and the globular insectoids lurking as fake fruit inside hammock-sized leaves. It was a solace to Gengr, that for a while he was able to maintain contact with Polange Nsef by transceiver.

This was also a practical necessity, as otherwise he would have hardly been briefed at all – since he had insisted upon setting out straightaway. (Strange how he was being allowed to insist upon things.) But before long her voice faded, suffocated by bestial transmissions from the radio-emitting denizens of the forest. By that time, however, Gengr had learned enough to be able to inform the men under his command: "We're tracking nine convicts. To have made this trail, a good number of them must be armed. We have reason to believe, in fact," he spoke over his shoulder between swipes of the sponnd-blade, "that they *all* are. They impersonated Stormguard personnel and got their hands on Stormguard weapons – that's how they got out. Must have been long planned." He spoke on, giving more circumstantial details of the business, in the vague hope that this would enhance his status with his dubious followers.

"Well, zamur G-A," drawled his second-in-command, Lanok Ryr, lifting his sponnd-arm for another swipe at the vegetation, "if we're ambushed" (he huffed, blowed, swiped) "it could get interesting." His long, mournful face ran with sweat.

The exhausting struggle through the forest continued through another fifty yards of snapping, burning density. "Stop," Gengr ordered at last. He turned to check that he had been obeyed along the line. "I see bodies."

Lanok pushed forward to stare, alongside Gengr, at the light of a clearing. "So it's happened." The selfish thought occurred to all: *To them, not to us, this lesson applies. One of the infinite ways for luck to run out in Fyaym –*

"What do we do now, zamur G-A – bring them back?" asked one of the men.

"Maybe. *After* we've taken our look at what they saw. Is this *nyr* fully equipped?" asked Gengr loudly, turning to face his group.

Lanok Ryr curtly assured him, "It is."

As he led them into the grim clearing, Gengr noted that it was bare of vegetation because it was bare of soil; floored with slippery rock, it possibly comprised the ice-polished peak of a mountain whose base lay miles deep in Ooranye's frozen mantle.

Scattered over this bleak surface were the torn bodies of nine men, whose escape from prison had won them so brief an hour of liberty.

In silence the twelve men of the *nyr* gazed at the pathetic sight.

Gengr could guess what the men were thinking with regard to himself. *This, O foreigner, is Fyaym. Here, O Syoomean, death comes from nowhere. It comes in utter mystery, and how can you expect to deal with this kind of fate? How can you expect us to trust and follow you? Go back and seek some safe employment in the city. Your status as a mascot makes you popular there.*

He had seen insubordination coming. During the toilsome march through the forest he had seen it develop in the expression of Lanok Ryr, more wooden with every yard of progress. *Far be it from me,* it seemed to be saying, *to criticise my commander, even though, if he were not my commander, I should.* And now a flare of intuition illuminated to Gengr the full extent of the danger he was in – yet still he wasn't too worried. Admittedly, if his men did not trust him, he was likely to be in peril from them – precisely because no legal means existed to depose an incompetent commander. If, in other words, they thought he must go, then something unrecorded would have to happen. And nobody would ask too many questions afterwards, if the unrecorded thing was done "in a Fyayman situation".

Fortunately there was a way out.

He could be competent.

For a start, the shrewdest move he could make would be to take upon himself the frightful task which was next on the list of jobs to be done.

"Time to read one of those brains," he announced, pointing at a corpse which had an undamaged head. "Looks un-minced, that one. Now, who's been lugging the gear? You, Hyv Slarr? Set it up before the meat grows cold." His ghoulish bluntness went down well. It was certainly appropriate for the business he must now undertake – that of recording into one's own mind the last thoughts of a person who had died by violence.

One might see, hear or feel almost anything. The less sentiment, the better.

While most of the *nyr* kept watch, Gengr squatted beside the selected cadaver. Then the atrocious procedure was set in train. Hyv Slarr wired the crystals of the psych-scanner between the corpse's head and that of his commander. The last thing Gengr saw, before his vision blurred, was Lanok Ryr's expression – now fluid with unease.

Then came the shifting blur and the moments of double vision during which Gengr's mental reflexes tried to resist the influx of another's memory. After that short struggle, something within him surrendered. His own sight and hearing had gone. It was as if he had entered another's dream. He *was* this other person. In that role he was startled, he was glancing up to see things that looked like – what?

Like living rags launching themselves from the treetops. From their exaggerated mouths dribbled a blubbery screech, a deformed sound. Membranes, extending between their four outstretched limbs, and heads which were all gaping mouth stuffed with needle-fangs amid spiky tufts of fur, and taut corners like those of a kite, adorned with grasping claws – it all amounted, fortunately, to a very short dream. Gengr barely had time to forestall its end – to rip the crystals from his forehead before the vision collapsed in final darkness.

He had cut it fine. Even by proxy it would not do to experience that ultimate full stop. Otherwise his own heart and brain might well have shut down in sympathy.

Lanok Ryr stood over him, his long face anxious, as he repeated, "Zamur G-A, what did you see? Answer me. What did you see?"

"What? Yes, it's *my* memory now. Ah yes, um, what did I see? These men were killed by tree-dwellers."

"How," began Lanok, with a reflexive glance at the green canopy above.

"Kite-shaped things. Glided down, ripped the men to death. Claws, teeth."

"Intelligent creatures?"

"How should I know?" Gengr scrambled to his feet. "Let's hope not." Like the others he could not help repeatedly craning his neck at the opaque green cover which towered around the edges of the clearing. "Might make little difference." Nobody commented. He sensed, however, some approval of his words.

Under the circumstances there was no question of bringing the bodies back or of taking the time to bury them. Gengr ordered holographs to be taken of the scene, recording the wounds on the corpses. Then he rallied the *nyr*: "We have done all we can do here. Our duty now is to get back alive with what we know. Such as it is."

Lanok Ryr shrugged, "This is Fyaym. We have done well enough."

Gengr eyed him with some appreciation of those fatalistic words: *This is Fyaym*. The phrase could be echoed in every Uranian culture and period. Everywhere it was a condition of survival *not* to expect too much. The untameable lands punished the arrogance of those who thought they might seek to understand. Uranians born tens of thousands of miles and millions of days apart shared the shrugging reflex, *This is Fyaym*.

Through the swaying stems, the giant dangling leaves and the pummelling branches, they began to push back along the trail. The return journey was not going to be much easier than the journey out. The trail was fast disappearing, overgrown minute by minute.

Gengr panted, "At least we now have plenty of cover."

"Yes," replied Lanok, "we're certainly safe from the upper canopy. But if they're intelligent, zamur G-A, they may have other methods of attack."

"You think so? That they are intelligent, I mean."

"They didn't eat the men."

"Proves nothing. Dumb brutes can kill for other reasons than food. Defending territory, maybe."

"Doesn't matter, as you yourself suggested. Reckon the Worm's behind it, any way you look."

Those words caused Gengr to be close-mouthed for the rest of the journey back. *Worm?* It was the tone in which it was said: as though everybody was supposed to know of the thing. Gengr had a hunch that he would do best to guard his tongue for the moment.

An hour later, after they had won through safely to the city's perimeter, officials met them at the gate. "Well?" asked one.

Gengr tried an experiment. "The Worm," he said levelly.

Peculiar... it seemed to be enough! He and his company were let by without further questioning.

219

Shortly after that, he was in conference with old Noad Reyeb Lalldorpl and Daon Polange Nsef in a chamber in the Palace of the Noad. While Lalldorpl reviewed the recorded evidence, Gengr sat back in eerie comfort, ironically glancing at the magnificent potted plants which decorated various stands. Dizzy transitions from the perils of outside to the haven of a city were a commonplace of life, so why should he be feeling that in a sense he had not left the jungle?

The Noad was speaking to his designated heir, "The original breakout shows, of course, that the Worm can inspire and incite the inmates of your prison even through its walls."

The Daon formally replied, "It would seem so, Noad R-L."

"A serious development, do you not agree?"

"Undoubtedly," she agreed in a bleak voice. Having uttered this admission, Polange Nsef was left in silence for some seconds, and Gengr guessed that she was being "left to stew", but her next words sounded un-embarrassed. She merely mused, "And maybe, it is coiling at us from another direction also."

The Noad growled, "Go on, Daon P-N."

"Those kite-creatures that killed our people: it is the first report we have had of hostilities from that particular species. So we have to ask, is the Worm training new species in the forest, or –"

"Or," the Noad finished for her, "is the Worm bringing new species *to* the forest?"

Then both of them turned to Gengr, perhaps because they had sensed him stirring in his armchair. "Give us your opinion, zamur G-A," the Noad invited.

How in the name of all the skies can I possibly give an opinion? "As a foreigner, recently arrived," he evaded, "I have no idea what strategy this city ought to pursue."

"Come now, Gengr," said Polange with a kindly smile, so that the mere fact of being addressed by her in company was felt by him to be a special promotion, "you have one successful expedition under your belt – enough to make you one of us."

Much happened to Gengr in that instant. Polange Nsef had figuratively set him on his feet. Basking in her warmth without being intoxicated by it, Gengr could now reflect that his jaunt to the forest had at any rate gained him one undoubted benefit: it had allowed his sanity to be restored as far as his attitude to *her* was concerned, because, in gaining a bit of proper status of his own, he now found it possible to throw off the illusion that any one person can be of all-engrossing importance – or that one's conversations with such a person need be perfect. As a result he actually felt warmer still towards her. Closer,

220

too. He was able to love her ordinarily instead of languishing in a state of helpless worship. Wonderful how this development cleared the head.

"I suppose," he remarked, "that your unfortunate escapers had every motive to take the risk they did. Far worse than death, far more to be feared, is loss of liberty. That alone is enough to explain their crazy dash out into the jungle."

It was his little offering, his attempt to make sense of recent events. But it fell flat. They did not believe it was enough. He could see this in their faces. The Worm, the Worm caused it all, the Worm's to blame. And the ignorant foreigner Gengr Axtain was then glad that he had refrained from expressing his doubts about this Worm – though he feared that with every minute that passed his admission of ignorance would become more awkward, more fraught with risk. Yes, the longer he left it, the more embarrassing the prospect of having to confess that he did not know what they were talking about.

Fortunately, however, the courteous old Noad sensed his predicament, and deigned to impart some illumination to the baffled Contahlan.

"Our scientists and philosophers," he explained, "tell us of an agglomeration of souls which seeks to draw others into itself – a four-dimensional Worm expanding through history."

I can't get drawn in any further to this crazy rubbish – Gengr suddenly decided – *without at least making some sort of stand.*

"With all due respect to your savants, can you be certain that it is real?" he asked as politely as he could.

"It is real. The question is not 'if' but 'when' it will slither forth to attack us again."

"Forgive me for insisting on clarifying this point – but you are talking, are you, about a real physically harmful attack by *souls*?"

The Noad said placidly, "All attackers have souls."

"I see," said Gengr. Perhaps it did not matter whether he believed the old man or not. Either the Worm, as inspirer, existed, or it did not – but the attacks ascribed to it *did* obviously exist, and, from that point of view, the towers of a city were just as likely as the boles of a forest to count as the jungle in which such a Worm might hide.

The Noad continued, "And you, Gengr Axtain, being stranded here, must throw in your lot with us."

Gengr almost shook his head at that, not because he was about to say "no" but because he already felt the clinging force of these people's ridiculous beliefs. Worm, indeed! Outpost folk, stranded out here for aeons, might understandably develop their own quaint notions, but when said notions threatened to climb into *his* head, it was hard not to go b-r-r-r — but he had better pull himself together and reply. You can't not reply when the Noad has just spoken about you throwing in your lot...

"Of course I understand that I must now be a true Polevan till the day I die, Noad R-L."

"Thank you, zamur G-A. And your citizenship is off to a good start. The news that you have led a successful foray has already done some good to my people's morale."

4: War on the Worm

Gengr found the men of his *nyr* still waiting for him as he emerged from the palace into the street. They greeted him respectfully — they were in favour of him now — but he had no immediate use for the group. So he dismissed them with thanks, promising to call on them when he needed them. As they dispersed, he became aware of a figure leaning on a pillar close by. The figure then strode out from where he had been waiting, and Gengr recognized the tall, heavy presence of Nekkon Lalldorpl.

Sharp shadows are rare on Ooranye, where most of the daylight is diffused by the innate glow of the air itself; how then did this son of the Noad seem to cloak himself in an impression of almost clean cut shadow? It must stem from the fellow's character or mood. Gengr was surprised by his feeling of revulsion.

Nekkon demanded, "Are you ready to fight the Worm, zamur G-A?"

"I am ready to do what Noad Reyeb expects of me."

"Yes, but the *Worm* —"

"I am ready," repeated Gengr, rendered snappish.

"Hrrmm, that's more than any of *us* can say."

That made it definite to Gengr: he was being needled. Sure of this point, he felt in better humour. This encounter was quite ordinary, Nekkon's resentment quite understandable: mere natural jealousy, caused by the popularity of a foreign mascot. The Noad's son was no doubt already frustrated enough, barred as he was by iron-hard custom from the succession to the noadex. Well, it would do no harm to offer some modest concession to the fellow's pride. "What I am ready for," Gengr drily explained, "is not so much to succeed, as to look good trying."

"Ah," said Nekkon in a tone that laid a silken fuse, "so you do not believe that you will do us any real good?"

"Probably not."

Nekkon gazed into the Contahlan's face, and as he gazed, another of his domineering twitches took him over and he announced in a voice that rang:

"For as long as people are not disturbed in their resistance to the Worm by the scepticism of an outsider, an interloper who lacks their knowledge in his blood – for just so long will you, Gengr Axtain, enjoy a full life here in Poleva." And he stalked away.

This threw Gengr back into indignation. He reflexively sought to square his shoulders but then found himself enfeebled by perplexity. What, actually, was that alarming man worried about? Surely, in this strange city, maintenance of belief in the Worm could hardly be a problem. Both government and people claimed to see its influence just about everywhere. Scepticism was non-existent, apparently. So why had Nekkon lost his cool?

During the next few days Gengr kept his ears well open and simply confirmed his opinion that this Worm belief was unstoppable – certainly it was in no danger of losing credence through any remark of his. He began to see how the idea perpetuated itself. Any problem which could be related to any other problem, any elongation of a tale of woe, was counted as a wriggle of the Worm. For example he learned that the forest glade, where the Kites had attacked the fleeing convicts, had previously been the scene of a different attack, a few lifetimes ago, by an entirely different species upon another party of explorers. Coincidence? Never! It was the Worm stretching its coils across time and across many a situational divide.

Nonsensical, yes, but who am I, Gengr Axtain, to argue about what could or could not happen here?

He signed, shrugged and went along with it all. No doubt by the end of his life he would have learned wholeheartedly to share in the beliefs of the Polevans. By contrast, if by some miracle he could return to Syoom, it would not take long for him to despise the memory of such superstition. But then you couldn't reasonably expect Fyayman outposters to think like Syoomeans. It was hardly surprising that in their yearning for order the Polevans should prefer to blame one unified Worm for their plight, rather than an infinity of perils; and ultimately what difference did it make *what* you called things?

All in all, life was being good to Gengr. He had been given a home in a city he liked, inhabited by a people he liked and who liked him. The prospect of action enticed him, and if his next adventure had to originate in some bizarre fixation with a hypothetical four-dimensional Worm, so be it.

If anything disturbed him these days, it was the off-putting post of prison warden held by the woman he loved. What a saddening twist of fate: the gentle Polange as a denier of liberty. Someone had to do it, of course, but why did it have to be she? But – here a bit of useful sadness – his distaste for her occupation was going to make it easier for him to ration his time with her. He would limit his visits to her, lessening the danger that she might get tired of him before he could win a proper position for himself.

For ten days Gengr wandered the Polevan walkways, rambled around the city and lounged in the parks, listening, observing, learning; trying to identify those facts which a native finds familiar but which may take an immigrant a painfully long time to absorb. In order to be useful he must become attuned to the cultural environment while at the same time retaining his own Syoomean heritage – the one thing that made him special here, the perspective which he had brought along with him as a gift to his new home.

It was the mid-day hour; he was striding confidently down a ramp into the vaults of Poleva. His view of the cityscape steadily shrank as he descended into the subway which led to that much-thronged basement world of corridors, repositories, archives and maintenance machines called, generically, "the vaults" of a Uranian city. In the cavernous volume around him, no lamps were necessary; the airglow itself allowed him to read expressions on the crowded ramp when the sudden electrifying announcement blared over loudspeaker:

"Polevans! This is Nekkon Lalldorpl, speaking for the Noad, to tell you that our wayfarers have detected the approach of a hostile expeditionary force from Nusun. The Noad has given the order for our forces to mobilize in response. He has given me the field command: my rank is now omzyr of all Polevan armed forces. Citizens, this is our opportunity to hit back at the Worm! This time it has blundered – has donned a disguise too cumbersome to escape our vengeance! And so the Noad has authorised me to proclaim a *zemmg* against this Nusunian army, an unstoppable *zemmg* which will end only when our aim is accomplished. *Death to the Worm!* Officers will report to me by noon tomorrow."

The loudspeakers fell silent.

People were shouting, cheering the *zemmg*, and congregating to discuss the news. And what crazy news it was, thought Gengr. How could one Fyayman outpost invade another, and why should it try to do so? On the other hand – how great to have lived to hear a *zemmg* proclaimed, not just an ordinary war-effort but a real *zemmg*, a collective exaltation, such as even now he saw taking hold in the faces around him that were lit up with zeal as if already promoting those souls who would soon be lost in battle. Try to keep calm, Gengr told himself. Remember a *zemmg* is hedged about with traditional restrictions. It must not be proclaimed frequently lest the notion be devalued, and one must always check, always make sure: *was the occasion serious enough?* Apparently this time it was, to judge not only from the enthusiasm but also the hard-headed talk around him. "This invasion – is it a mass-migration?" "Could be." "The only way to cross Fyaym is to do it in force." "Wonder why it was announced by Nekkon and not by the Noad himself?" "The Noad must be unwell." "Sudden, isn't it?" Gengr meanwhile, regaining his original purpose, pressed on down into the vaults. He must not lose sight of *his* quarry.

He continued along an underground thoroughfare until he entered a series of side-corridors, each smaller than the last, which brought him at last to a lonely room with a desk and lamp. The desk had a transparent top, like a display case. Under it was a sheet of lettering, lit to reveal one of the historical records of Poleva.

That moment when eyes and text faced one another was the true call to arms for Gengr Axtain. In particular what kindled the fire in his brain was a message latent in the innocent list of regnal data:

2259th *Noad: Brenbl Lalldorpl: 3,622,710 Nb – 3,628,786 Nb*
2260th *Noad: Kren Yound: 3,628,786 Nb – 3,629,225 Nb*
2261st *Noad: Norpay Lalldorpl: 3,629,225 Nb – 3,640,576 Nb*
2262nd *Noad: Operlwa Pyon: 3,640,576 Nb – 3,640,800 Nb*
2263rd *Noad: Reyeb Lalldorpl: 3,640,800 Nb –*

Could other see what he saw in these names and dates?

The facts in this Noad-list were hardly a secret! And no-one else had yet drawn any dire conclusion from it, so it must certainly be too soon for a recent immigrant like himself to issue a public warning.

He must gather firmer evidence. Besides, he was in a state of some confusion himself. He suspected an enormous crime but could as yet imagine no motive for it.

At this rate he'd soon be a firm believer in the Worm…

Be that as it may, his adopted city was at war and invasion was imminent. The *zemmg* throbbed in his mind, telling him, don't play the detective today… He had a *nyr* to lead; fighting must come first.

…The encampment outside Poleva, which Gengr and the eleven men of his nyr joined the next day, was awash with the din of a mustering force of fifteen to sixteen thousand *sponndarou*, each laser-armed warrior crackling with eagerness to get at the enemy. Subliminally the *zemmg* was in full blast, the summons to enthusiasm thrumming along the nerves and chanting in the mind's ear so that one was forced to believe in victory. Gengr Axtain, as he made his way among billowing cloaks towards the Noad's command-post, experienced a sensation of wading, almost as if he could see, rippling around him, a shallow sea in the midst of which his destination rose as an island: the pyramidal platform from which the Noad and the omzyr and their staff could survey all the formations and sub-formations of the swirling encampment. Gengr reached the foot of the command-post. He began to mount the ramp.

Increasingly visible, in one direction, the forest twinkled, while in a different direction the serrated Badlands stretched to the horizon in a succession of naked brown ridges moderately smeared with dark blue ice. Surrounding all of this the loamland *gralm* – the great world plain – must widen and widen far beyond the horizon's curve, into the eternal solid ocean of Ooranye.

"Gengr the Syoomean, here to contribute his counsel."

It was the welcoming voice of Noad Reyeb Lalldorpl himself. He and his son, the omzyr, stood in a cluster of the principal zynzyrs. Next to this group was a canopy supported by four white poles. Underneath that, resting on a table, lay the city's most treasured possession. A priceless *banessyen* – a moving-map.

Meanwhile figuratively a carpet of welcome rolled out for Gengr Axtain, as hands beckoned and smiles drew him forward. As an officer, he had already reported for ordinary military duty to omzyr Nekkon, but this was different. Playing the part which he now understood, the role of an exotic Syoomean banner waving brightly over their campaign, Gengr spoke some suitable words to the Noad and his advisers and chief officers. The top-ranking *zynzyrs* listened respectfully to such statements of the obvious as, "If the enemy has any sense, he'll approach through the badlands." Would they also listen to something more urgent?

The old Noad was speaking to him again.

"Something still bothers you, zamur G-A."

The group of advisers was dissolving, each zynzyr leaving to take his place in the final formation. They were due to set out within minutes; the banessyen was lifted off its stand, for a moving-map must be borne away in the midst of the departing host... Gengr meanwhile, to his relief, was being given a chance to exchange a few private words with the Noad, whose son, the omzyr, had now departed from the platform.

From close up, Reyeb Lalldorpl looked drained. Small wonder that the actual field command had been given to a younger man. Even as matters stood it was the most that the Noad could do to bear up under the relentless cheerfulness and pride of the *zemmg*. It gouged through them all as a fast river gouges a hill, and all flesh must eventually yield under such strain.

"I was, er, concerned about our numbers," Gengr began.

"Fifteen thousand," waved the Noad. "Out of a total population of a mere one hundred thousand, and at short notice – we have done well, I think."

"Too well, perhaps." Gengr's voice of realism struggled to be overheard against the continual thrum of confidence in both their minds. "The city is being left depleted…"

"Tell me more –" Reyeb Lalldorpl flung out his arms – "or ask me more – ask me where in all that wasteland Nekkon things he will aim our force, and why we are not simply waiting here for the enemy's attack. He wants to carry the battle to them, so out we go."

"A risk," nodded Gengr.

"To be fair," shrugged Reyeb, "so is the alternative. And my son is more of a fighter than I am." The Noad smiled tiredly and his arms flopped to his sides. All of a sudden he and Gengr stood in a bubble of relative calm for the thrum of the *zemmg* became muted on the deserted platform, as the army began to recede from the pyramid's base.

Now, thought Gengr, was his oppoprtunity to confess his real unease to the Noad. Unease concerning the man's own family –

Impolitic or no, I must take the plunge. He explained, quickly, what he had noticed in the Archives.

"Ah," smiled Reyeb, "so you looked at the Noad-list. The Lalldorpl-list, as one might call it, ha-ha! Yes, I don't mind admitting, some of us were tyrants in the past. Poleva has had its fits of *arelk*, and may have them again one day… but rest assured, I have kept good watch for signs of it in my time."

Arelk – the political "hardening of the arteries" – was, in truth, absent at the moment from Poleva. Gengr would have sniffed it ere now if it had been present. Since it was not, his condemnation would have to wait. And in any case where could he find the audacity to voice criticisms in front of this charming old ruler whose good-humoured sincerity was so transparent? The civilized honest voice, quite prepared to admit past wrongs, was so much more effective at silencing Gengr's opposition than a peremptory command to cease discussion would have been. So the immigrant from Syoom did not have the impertinence to push his luck any further.

He took his leave of the Noad, looking back just once. Reyeb Lalldorpl was leaning on the empty map-stand, gazing at the departing host of his people, his worn-out face wearing that serene smile which says "it is all out of my hands now". Gengr descended to ground level and went back to his nyr.

His duty now was not to think deep thoughts but to stride about and issue orders, to manoeuvre his unit into correct position within its nyzyr. During minutes of local standstill, while other units changed places around them, he

227

made sure that his men checked their gear thoroughly, as they were carrying much more than usual on an expedition. The pockets of their cloaks did not suffice; they had to wear packs as well.

"Polevans!" came another blare from the loudspeakers. The men looked up to see the tall, heavy figure of their leader who stood on a wheeled platform well away from the command post which the Noad had used. "Warriors! Invicible-souled zemmgars! I call you forth to fight the Worm at last! That same Worm which, after so many blows struck against us, has finally poured itself into the form of a Nusunian army which – thank the skies – we can *hit*. This physical enemy has been winding towards us for the past few days through yonder ridged terrain, and we can trap it *there!* We all know, do we not, that the Worm never abandons its form until the next blow has been struck: so we need not fear any shift of identity before we crush it. Fate has gifted us an opportunity which may never recur. This is why I judge it worth the risk to lead you all on foot into country which is impassable by skimmers; into a barren land where we must carry all our provisions, but where the enemy must suffer the same disadvantages as we. An enemy of flesh and blood, whom we can beat. So, forward, Polevans, to your best-ever chance of victory over the entrapped Worm!"

Other, similar exhortations were given out at intervals of a few hours.

The units poured over the edge of the near canyon and soon the men's boots were crunching along a rubble-strewn path between inhospitable slopes. That evening, they bivouacked on a plateau between two gorges, still in sight of their now-distant city. Poleva had dwindled to a toy-sized coloured egg. The next evening, they could no longer see it at all. However, they could never be lost, so long as they retained the banessyen. The moving-map was guarded personally by omzyr Nekkon Lalldorpl.

Gengr was summoned by the omzyr for consultation in the evenings. In his own opinion he contributed little of substance to the discussion. Yet (so he was repeatedly told) the mere fact of his participation had a helpful effect upon the morale of the troops, who were bound to be impressed at the thought of a real Syoomean presence at the councils of war. It was the same old story, rather sad in a way: being valued for what one symbolized, rather than as an individual.

But it was also good luck, for he got to see the banessyen.

The very thought of this priceless object being taken outside the city's defences might have sown deep anxiety among the people, were it not for the continual thrum of the *zemmg*, the steady exaltation keeping the army more confident than it would otherwise have been, that the risk was

228

worthwhile. A banessyen was viewed almost as a guarantee of victory, at any rate of defensive victory. According to legend, backed up by archeology, one thousand three hundred and thirty-one of them had originally been made. By now there were only a few score in existence, rare enough for most cities (and a few airships) to possess only one, if any. They came in various designs, the most common being that of a hand-held lenticular object. The 'sheet' varieties, which could be unrolled and laid out like ordinary still maps, were the rarest of the rare. The Polevan banessyen was of this special sort. This meant that Gengr could actually stand and pore over it as he would a normal map.

He felt stupendously privileged to be accorded this sight. Even though nothing big was moving on it at the moment, it thrilled him merely to be able to see, on its dark purple background, the stationary fuzz which was the Polevan army encamped, some inches away from the similar-sized fuzz, also stationary, of the Nusunian army, likewise encamped. Tempting to puzzle out how the map's dots knew! Futile, to speculate on why those imprisoned dots – supposedly a microscopic race, tamed long ages ago by Phosphorus Era savants – should continue to serve as faithfully as ever. Perhaps they had been willingly enthralled. (Or more likely the legends were wrong and the thing was just a clever machine. Legends about the Phosphorus Era never ceased to grow in the telling.) Whatever the case, it was hard to take one's eyes off the object. Conversely, it also took some courage to look at it. The symbols adapted themselves to the user's emotions – an approaching peril, for example, depicted as a line with white teeth, might suddenly writhe into an unclassifiable shape which communicated terror direct, like a form seen in nightmare. To study a banessyen and to know that its symbols were somehow *true* was like having one's fortune told in blobs and moving lines with no choice but to believe it.

"What do you notice this time?"

The grate of the voice startled Gengr. What had invited the question? His focused gaze – that's what. He had just eyed a particular patch on the surface of the banessyen, a patch where the Polevan fuzziness showed a split. Meaning? Nekkon had ordered forth a vanguard, yes, that was it. To probe for enemy emplacements. The emplacements themselves might be too small to show up on the moving-map, but the fuzz that denoted the main Nusunian force was clearly visible.

"Well? What do you think?" insisted Nekkon.

It was as though a Syoomean opinion really *had* become important this evening, here at the fourth camp since the march began.

"Well, the Nusunians…" faltered Gengr, "er, they have started to veer."

229

"So?"

"And they're slowing their march."

"And?"

"We have slowed too. I suppose we're both going to dance around each other for a bit. And then we'll close in. I guess they have a banessyen too. Either that or their scouts are superb."

It must have been the right kind of thing to say, for he was allowed to go.

That night as he lay wrapped in his cloak, gradually sinking into sleep with the sense that he had escaped something narrowly, the piquant thought came: *if the Worm existed, would it not show up on the banessyen? Would I not see a live portrayal of it there, symbolically squirming?* Gengr snickered. He had seen no such shape, no trace at all. So much for the Polevan Worm-obsession.

The next day's march ceased shortly before noon. The zynzyrs had received a halt order from the omzyr. The army had got close to the summit of a windy, gravelly pass. The men removed their packs and sat on them.

As they rested and looked around at the stark horizons, rumours buzzed through the ranks: the omzyr had chosen this place for a stand; the Nusunian army had come into contact with the Polevan vanguard and fighting had begun; the omzyr was taking precautions against a flank attack... Gengr said as little as possible. Quite a few sponndarou asked him what was going on, but all he could think of to reply was, "We shall know soon enough," – for the first time wondering whether perhaps his own symbolic role might turn out to be more trouble than it was worth, to the authorities. *I know I've been some use for morale, but I could cause bad trouble for Nekkon, especially if I wanted to.*

An officer approached, summoning him to the omzyr. Bystanders nodded to one another meaningly. Gengr felt the eyes of the troops upon him as he rose and walked to the command tent, which was now guarded on either side of the entrance flap by men with lasers drawn.

He stepped in, had time for one glance at the surface of the banessyen –

"I have news for you, Gengr Axtain," said the omzyr, who was seated with his face turned three-quarters away from the tent entrance, while a noisy wind thumped at the tent walls, punching them inwards. Nekkon Lalldorpl continued quietly, "News flash relayed from Poleva: my father, Noad Reyeb Lalldorpl, died this morning."

So that was that. One kindly, beneficent ruler was no more. A city was bereft in its hour of need. "Sad news indeed, omzyr N-L," said Gengr, watching the other's face.

Nekkon sighed, "I have decided to call off the campaign. The new Noad is going to need the support of all the city's forces around her. I cannot leave her by herself at this crucial time." And while he spoke these incredible words, Gengr did nothing but sit and nod at every sentence.

On one level it was astonishing enough: he kept asking himself, what had become of the unstoppable *zemmg*, the drive to victory, the rousing pledge to go out and fight the enemy? But on another level came a spreading certainty like blood from a deep wound. He must stretch his mind and hide his feelings. At least till he got back to the city. Whereupon he must have his accusation ready. Which meant he must stay alive till then.

"I understand, omzyr N-L," he said. "You have my full co-operation."

5: The Worm unmasked

He understood only too well.

As the army pulled back towards Poleva he marched with a burden he could not share, though like a man with an ill-fitting pack he kept trying to rearrange it. Unfortunately the burden of knowledge and the weight of decision could not amount to a comfortable fit.

In the confused state of the army, enthusiasm had decayed into mere tension, and the men did not know whether they were winning or losing the war. Gengr for his part no longer cared about the danger from the Nusunians. He was concerned only with the question, how much the extent of his knowledge might be suspected by Nekkon Lalldorpl. To play safe might entail going into hiding as soon as they reached the city. On the other hand that might be the worst move he could make. Perhaps he should at all costs stay public, surround himself with witnesses, sleep in the dormitory of a public hostel…

In the end he went to neither extreme. While the army filed back into the city and the air buzzed with cries of reunion, he simply went alone to his assigned dwelling. He would trust, for one night at least, that Nekkon was betting upon his continued usefulness.

Exhausted, he lay on his bed. One moment his cheek was on the pillow and his drooping eyes caught a last fading sight of the lush curtains covering the window, as his mind spiralled down into sleep – then he found himself suddenly vertical, flicking those curtains aside, and, due to the excellent travel facilities of dream, looking out upon a scene far, far from Poleva.

It was a scene that blasted him with such yearning that he almost doubled up with homesickness. Yet the place was one which he had only seen twice before in his entire life: the foamscape of Ammye, in central Syoom. Rising in the midst of the foam was the glorious double-tiered disc of Skyyon.

The sunward polar city stood tall and proud on its glittering wineglass stem; stately airships and swarming skimmers clouded its aerial hangars and docks; from the midst of the upper reaches rose the Zairm, the Sunnoad's Palace, like a solid waterspout or flame that whipped eternally towards the pointlike zenith Sun.

The sight, though awesome, was as familiar as if he had lived in that palace as a child. Dreaming, he accepted this familiarity without question. Indeed there was no need to puzzle over it, for here was the centre of Syoom and it was Syoom that he wanted and needed... He moved forward. He drifted through the palace walls. Like a thirsty ghost he sipped at that sense of belonging, he truly believed that he was really there... even if it were but a dream; for did not the act of thinking about a place mean that one's mind was there? Anyhow the place itself did really exist, and his soul belonged in it, here at the sunward pole of Ooranye. Next his mind fluttered specifically towards the Sunnoad's throne. More real than real life, the dream's lemon-gold became the colour of *knowing*. This was the key awareness, awareness of the *worth* of what one saw. No force of gravity could pull so hard.

The palace, he knew, was built of smollk, the foamed ore of Ammye; the pumicelike segments had accumulated age by age, till the Zairm was the size of a small mountain, rising from the upper platform of a still vaster city. Gengr viewed all of it simultaneously, being, in dream fashion, somehow both inside and outside the great structure. The crust of memory was thick. It reached across a geological age in the throne-room, Zdinth Hall. Admittedly the succession of Sunnoads had sometimes been interrupted, but the traditions of the office had never been forgotten.

Traditions – their weight and power – were what he was going to need after he had awoken.

And that thought reminded him, alas, that this marvellous place was in actual fact not really around him; it was unattainably distant because THIS WAS ONLY A DREAM. He snatched at it as it began to fade. Snatch at a glow? Pathetically he zoomed around, trying to "drink" Zdinth Hall as though it were nectar, to grab what could not be grabbed. But suddenly, in reprieve from the gathering goodbye, the scene brightened one last time, as a hero strode into the hall.

The hero was a tall erect wayfarer who advanced between lines of notables towards the throne. Gengr lost no time in merging his own viewpoint with this man so that now *he* was the tough and successful character; none other, in fact, than the famous Rezram Pamek, who brought vital information for the Sunnoad during the Vrar Crisis of sixty or so lifetimes ago: Pamek, *bringing knowledge of the whereabouts of the enemy's lair…*

The viewpoint changed again.

The dream's atmosphere turned grumbly, became curtained with dissatisfaction as reverence fell away from the hero and the dream-ego reverted to a separate, critical Gengr Axtain who spoke out: *it was all right for him. But how am I to do that sort of thing here?*

The dream snapped and curled away like cut tape.

He awoke, feeling desolate.

The inspiring historical memory of Rezram Pamek merely irritated him now. The possibility of heroism seemed remote, impractical. Besides, in that famous old crisis, Rezram Pamek's task had simply been to uncover and explain the unexpected whereabouts of an enemy base where the *vrars*, those strange childlike pirates, were concealed. In doing this Pamek also succeeded in explaining why the base had not been located before. Easy when one knew. It had been none other than Yr, City of Mists, the invisible, mobile city of legend; in solid fact, a giant fortress floating through the air of Ooranye at the head of a trail of depredations. A problem, but no great puzzle. Simply a giant hovering metropolis on the move. Nothing much compared with what he, Gengr Axtain, must soon announce.

With a grunting laugh he swung out of bed. He reached for his cloak.

Time to go imitate a hero…

The sight of the streets, emptier than usual, encouraged the fancy that life itself was a kind of dream: but he knew the reason for the emptiness. Many people had gone where he must go.

The public was packed in a throng around the four sides of the audience chamber in the Palace of the Noad of Poleva, when the Syoomean hero, Gengr Axtain, came striding in. He took in the situation at a glance. It was a council of war, held in full sight of the public, out of respect for the people's involvement in the outcome, but, for security reasons, not in public *hearing*. The Noad and her commanders and advisors, down on the central floor, were boxed in by a shimmering sound-proof field which also sufficiently blurred their features to prevent lip-reading from outside the zone. Provision also existed for the government to make public announcements: just outside the luminous enclosure stood a guard with hand on switch, ready to drop the sound-proofing and allow the Noad's words to reach the waiting throng.

To survey his line of attack, the hero considered each obstacle in turn. *The spectators:* he could probably get past them without much trouble. *The guard at the mid-way switch:* there was the key point, that was where he must take the drastic step. Lastly *the officials surrounding the Noad, and the Noad herself:* they, for a little while – if he got that far – ought to listen to a few words at least. They could not risk not listening.

Keeping his empty hands in view Gengr pushed inwards through the crowded perimeter till he reached the rope that kept the crowd back from the force-field. Here he leaned forward, bending over the rope.

The guards saw no threat in his action; they recognized him, but only saw him as a curious onlooker. They did not foresee – as he took a deep breath – that when he released his breath it would defeat the power of their lasers.

Gengr Axtain bellowed, *"Syoom is here!"*

All conversation ceased; movement around him froze.

"Wherever we are, is Syoom!"

Having announced this truth, Gengr ducked under the rope and entered the narrow space next to the force-field. The guard at the switch raised his laser. Gengr nonetheless walked towards that guard. He counted on the crowd of witnesses, and sure enough the guard did not fire but stared back at him during the doubtful moment, unable to bring himself to fire at… Syoom.

Gengr pointed to the switch.

"Turn that off and let me speak to the Noad. Her life is in danger at this moment. Or if you think I am lying, shoot me."

Click – flicker – the field was off and the guard preceded Gengr, announcing, "Noad P-N, the Syoomean says your life is in immediate danger –" while the notables of Poleva turned whitely amazed faces towards the intruder.

Not wasting a moment Gengr cried out to Polange, "Danger not from the enemy, Noad P-N, but from one of your own."

"What?" "Who?" shouted many voices while the Noad's lips formed the word, "You!" – she looked aghast but Gengr gave no heed to emotion, he barely had time to put his case. Ideally he should begin with the personal accusation but if he did he would put the culprit on his guard, and then the fellow had many tactics he might use to throw doubt upon the incredible truth... *The audience would then turn against me, definitively. Their minds must first be prepared. I must give them some evidence. Hope that they'll then head part way towards the conclusion themselves...*

"Ask yourselves!" he cried, "you must have been wondering – why did we go out to look for the army of Nusun? We'd be much stronger meeting it here!"

Indeed, they had often wondered. It was touch and go, but they listened.

He bellowed on:

"The mental fumes of the *zemmg*, the zemmg *you* declared, Nekkon Lalldorpl, stopped us from thinking." *I've named a name. Haven't yet named a crime.* "Oh, I know it was Reyeb Lalldorpl who authorised it; it was he who had to sign the proclamation – but you took the lead, Nekkon, yours was the voice that propelled us all that way."

The late Noad's son took a step forward, hesitated and glanced around. His dark mind conceded that the others were, for the moment, prepared to listen to this Syoomean meddler, and so he, too, must humour Gengr Axtain.

Nekkon therefore made a gesture of acquiescence but Gengr was not fooled; he knew the man would never surrender and never forgive. So there was nothing for it but to go for total victory.

Gengr continued, "I see you are wearing the blue cloak now, Nekkon. Congratulations on your appointment as Daon of Poleva. Nothing wrong with that *now*, is there? Now that the current Noad is not your father, you *can* legally be next in line. And you know, it's funny, there's nothing new in that! Plenty of next-but-one, alternating Lalldorpls in the history of Poleva – it's the obvious way of getting round the rule against dynastic succession."

A murmur of puzzled anger told Gengr that he was approaching the most dangerous ground of all. He must tread carefully around the reputation of old Reyeb Lalldorpl.

"While his father was alive, Nekkon's only hope of ever becoming Noad lay in this alternation dodge. So he aimed to create an emergency that would allow custom to be circumvented in this way. And the only way to do *that* was to commit treason."

Gengr stopped, for he saw that his beloved, Noad Polange Nsef, was wearing a terrible smile. But there was nothing for it but to plunge on, though that expression on the new Noad's face might well encourage Nekkon Lalldorpl.

"A deliberately-courted military disaster," Gengr continued, "combined with the moral confusion of a failed zemmg, would, Nekkon hoped, throw the city into enough confusion. Then – quite unexpectedly – his father died and Daon Polange Nsef succeeded automatically and legally to the noadex. With Polange as Noad, the picture changed completely! No further need for the regrettable scheme of sacrificing a section of his army – a non-Lalldorpl Noad was now in office and a Lalldorpl Daon was now legally a possibility – and not only legal but likely, if the omzyr hurried home. So," added Gengr, turning to face Nekkon, "hurry home you did." He turned again, swinging round to face the whole crowd. "You credulous fools!" Now, shock tactics were his one remaining hope. "And I – I am almost as stupid as you! Though I would have spotted the truth a lot sooner, were it not for the accident that Reyeb Lalldorpl was a good man."

The hall was in an uproar, he was surrounded by armed enemies and the only reason he had been allowed to speak as long as he had was that Noad Polange Nsef had held up her hand. But now Nekkon likewise was demanding to be heard. His moment had plainly come. Polange moved her hand, silencing Gengr, allowing the new Daon his turn.

Nekkon did not bother to face Gengr.

With one contemptuous look askance the Daon then inquired of the assembled listeners: "Please, somebody, explain - what was in it for me? That's what I can't help wondering. What could have been my motive, what could be the motive of any person sane enough to have been appointed omzyr of an army – what possible reason could anyone have to wish to become Noad on the terms which our foreign friend so fancifully describes? *Dynastic* succession???" His voice rose towards a laugh. This was the moment of doom for Gengr.

For he, Gengr, could not answer this crucial question either. He had not, for the life of him, been able to work out "what was in it" for Nekkon. The man was, after all, obviously intelligent; why then should any intelligent man voluntarily seek the humiliation of becoming part of a ruling dynasty? The strength of the taboo against hereditary monarchy was rooted in the ruler's pride: any ruler must want to believe that nen held nen's position through nen's own merits rather than through the accident of birth. It was human nature. Anyone capable of the noadex must have a sufficiently robust ego to be determined to avoid the slur, the confession of failure, that dynasticism implied.

Gengr felt the surrounding pressure of anger bulging towards him. Like a bursting membrane shoved in his face, it squirted despair into him. The notables of Poleva and the gasping crowd beyond all leaned at him, demanding an answer and he had no answer, no defence, except a blind snatch at where the answer must be.

He cried it out with full lungs:

"You wanna know – what daft idea of self – could make Nekkon feel – that to *inherit* is a sign of worth? You wanna know what crawling thing could wriggle that far? Well, figure this: the Worm's not of Fyaym – the Worm's in your city – you can track it through your records – the dynastic Worm – *the Worm of Poleva!*"

Enough of them heard. Many of those who heard, and understood, flung out their arms. A wild protective gesture, in favour now of Gengr. "Makes

236

sense! Makes sense!" they shouted. Tempers subsided in awe; tempers flamed anew, at other targets. Friendly blunderers fell against Gengr and luckily blocked the aim of those who might still have fired. Noad Polange Nsef tried to make herself heard. As the crowd invaded the centre of the hall, she gave up the idea of re-energising the force-field. Instead, she drew some of the guards aside and gave each of them individual orders. The man who needed protection now was not Gengr Axtain; it was Daon (or rather, ex-Daon) Nekkon Lalldorpl.

Epilogue

All big defences are costly…

Gengr was standing in the lounge, where he had been told that the Noad would see him. It was a pleasant, peaceful room, one of the many informal spaces in her palace, and it tempted him into a flood of memories. He dwelt upon his old life in Contahl, and the particular house and street where he had been born; thence his thought flowed to the Great Wall about five hundred miles from Contahl… All big defences are costly, he reflected. And if they are big enough, they don't work in the way they are supposed to. They do work, but in an unimagined way… Yes, that Great Wall, porous and un-garrisoned though most of it was throughout most of history, by its mere dumb existence focused the efforts of the cities along its length, structuring a political will.

And if that is was a Wall can do, how about a Worm…

He would not worry about what was "real". If it worked, it was real. What else could one safely say, out here? Had it not been for their theory of the Worm, the Polevans might long since have succumbed to dazzle and bewilderment from the endlessly flaring mysteries of Fyaym. He smiled to himself and suddenly thought: I wish there were an equally effective defence against the "little" things, like my inconvenient love for an ex-prison-warden, now Head of State.

At that moment she glided into the room. "Sorry I kept you waiting," she said with one of her brisk smiles. "You know, I thought they were merely going to execute Nekkon. But they have been pressing for the ultimate penalty… How are you, Gengr?"

He couldn't tell her – or could he? "I feel strange, hearing you, a Noad, apologize to me."

She gave a snort of amusement. "Just wait till I really get under way in this job. I shall be apologizing right and left."

"That's what I should like to know, Noad P-N: what jobs do you have? Are you still prison warden as well as Noad?"

"Certainly. I wouldn't trust anybody else with the warden's task – though I'll have to delegate more of the admin from now on."

"But if you give up the admin, what does that leave you with?" (I'm cross-examining the Noad, he thought incredulously.)

"That's easily answered: I am the one who must decide when a prisoner has had a change of heart, and can be released. I'll decide it for Nekkon."

"How can you tell? Can you read minds?"

"Not minds," she said as she lifted her hands caressingly to his face, and in his wonderment he guessed that this Noad's reign was going to be long.

The Forgetters

1: Escape

He was sunny in temper and placid in manner, like a good-natured, overgrown boy; she, by contrast, was not "sunny" at all but a live wire that hummed with passion and impatience. Both were young, handsome, rich... Taldis Norkoten and his wife Athness Keprella lived in an expensive quarter of Vyanth, the largest, most splendid city of Syoom. Vyanth could boast nigh on a thousand palaces during the Osmium Era, and the home of Taldis and Athness was one of these opulent mansions: a pedestalled globe linked by walkways to other costly structures above, below and to the sides.

Taldis Norkoten employed a considerable staff to maintain his home, and usually one or more of them was in view, discreetly busy at tasks of cleaning, polishing, repairing, catering... but right now all the servants had made themselves scarce. Not one of them dared to begin to clear the table at the end of this particular mid-day meal, as Athness unleashed her fury on Taldis.

"I am sick and tired of your excuses," the black-silked goddess flashed at him (and he squeezed his eyes shut for a moment as he usually did when his senses had been blasted by her scornful beauty). Acidly she continued, "It's not as though we even needed your wretched salary to get along. Yet you insist on spending half your time risking your life for THEM. Even when we could be comfortably off without them. And to cap all of *that*," she almost choked, "you refuse to do your share of the house-admin this afternoon because you have a meeting – a SIC meeting!"

"But wait," he said, helplessly, "you *already knew*, you've known for a long time, that I'm an S.I.C...."

"Spy."

"A field operative for the Syoomean Intelligence Corps."

"Im-pressive," she intoned. "How lucky can a girl get!"

"And therefore," he persisted, "I take it as I should. Loyalty is loyalty. The interruptions are part of the job."

Athness now squeezed *her* eyes shut. "Oh you goody-good being," she sighed, realizing, not for the first time, that this was the root of the trouble between them: there *was* something too-good-to-be-true about Taldis. Despite having the sordid job of "spy", he was morally untouched by the cynicism which pervaded the SIC. Rather, he acted like some character dreamed up by simple-minded thriller-writers who routinely portrayed Intelligence Corps agents as heroes forever foiling Quonian agents' dastardly plots to subvert civilization. And though all this was far too much to swallow, you could not touch Taldis about it at all – he was not even priggish; you couldn't fault him in that or in any other way. So, detached as it was from the seamy side of real life, his stance was impossible to believe in but also impossible to smash – he was *impenetrably* good. Something, no doubt, was going on inside that curly head; but what?

"Go on," Ashness shrugged tiredly, "go to your meeting."

"So I shall," Taldis said. He rose from his chair. She was silently waving him away.

Knowing that he might well be gazing upon her for the last time, he spoke against his better judgement:

"Why didn't you tell me, Athness, before we were married, that you weren't in sympathy with my work?"

"Why didn't you tell *me*," she retorted, "that you didn't know what the word 'marriage' means?"

"I know what it means," he said quietly, turning to go.

"Then you should know it means putting me first."

"Ah, but perhaps I am."

She grinned at that. "You mean, by saving Syoom from the evil Quonians? Sparing me their nefarious attentions? Thanks for the rescue," she said sweetly. Seeing that he did not turn round or rise to the bait in any way – he was just walking off – she let out one final hiss of exasperation. She called after him the insult which no decent Syoomean every used in public. "You're such a *foregrounder*, Taldis!"

That word – he must not hear it, must not react to it. He ignored it. No matter that *foregrounder* hurt like a wallop in the guts. There was nothing he could do – except wonder what had happened to the lovely woman he had married twelve hundred days ago.

To admit that things might be partly his own fault would merely invite another blast, on the lines of, "Why don't you do something about it, then?" And he did not wish her to know that this afternoon he *was* going to do something about it.

So he merely shook his head as if to dislodge the nightmare of mutual incomprehension which his marriage had become. He could not afford to have it preying on his mind during his meeting with Director Woth.

The oval outer door swished open at the touch of a button. On the instant that he emerged from the mansion, the cityscape of Vyanth gripped his attention. It gave him the needed tonic to his morale. Taldis' inner strength came largely from his capacity never to take anything for granted; this is the general virtue of his species – the Nenns, Uranian humanity, are masters of context-awareness. He, however, had it to an exceptional degree. Though he had gazed upon the cityscape thousands of times, he was still as freshly struck by the wonder of it all, as if he had just arrived from another planet. The irregular lattice of globular palaces and walkways, like a model of some complex organic molecule, lanced and inter-threaded by the helical towers and pierced by the polyhedra which housed the economic and record-keeping functions of any great Uranian city – all were vibrant with colour and movement, as skimmers raced along the ways, and laden hover-rafts floated up and down. But there was more to it. The 3-D effect drew Taldis forth from himself; made his consciousness expand…

Spurning the use of skimmers, rafts or escalators, Taldis Norkoten tramped along a pedestrian walkway which sloped upwards into the sparser, loftier regions of the geometric urban forest.

SIC headquarters appeared as a discreet thickening of the branches of this "forest". The thickening in that region was caused by a larger than usual number of jutting or dangling rooms. They gleamed with new paint: the relocation of Headquarters from Skyyon to Vyanth had been quite recent.

After crossing the lobby, where a brief identifier ray tingled against his flesh, Taldis took the lift to the fourth floor where a pretty receptionist (trained to kill if necessary) waved him through the door beyond her desk.

It was not a good sign that there was so little paperwork on the much larger desk which he now faced. Director Woth was known for clearing the polished top before inviting someone in to be fired. On the other hand, it wasn't quite empty: there was *one* file lying on it.

Deep-set eyes brooded under the slope of Woth's gleaming forehead as Taldis advanced. "You haven't been doing too well, T-N," remarked the Director, giving the lone file a shove. "Is that why you drew up this proposal?"

"It is, sir." *In more ways than one.* He saw no reason to detail all his motives. The mission plan was valid in its own terms, or so he hoped.

"Sit down, T-N."

To be seated opposite that bony lean head, that face with its jutting sickle of a nose, was to feel pinned by the Director's will, even if the man's glance was pointed elsewhere. And when the glance became direct... then, even the toughest agents were apt to become subservient or, worse, self-justifyingly garrulous. Taldis, however, possessed a kind of somnambulistic calm. He had escaped from his miserable home; he had entered the consoling zone of work.

"This is the very first time," Woth was saying, fixing Taldis with his most ruthless glare, "that one of my agents has suggested hiring the services of the Vemorth Stazel."

The Society of Forgetters. The way he said it, it sounded ridiculous.

Woth continued after a ringing pause, "You realize, don't you, that the Forgetters are used nowadays merely by clients with business or engineering problems, who require nothing more than a dose of partial amnesia to get a fresh, unbiased look at a particular problem?"

"Or," said Taldis, "to protect their secrets by locking then away in the subconscious for a period."

Woth waved the comment aside. "That point is immaterial. You realize that the kind of 'global forgetting' you're suggesting is a much more rarely-used technique?"

"I know, sir, but the Stazel themselves have admitted to me that the, uh, global option is still available to one who cares to use it."

"Hmmph."

And from the tone of that snort, Taldis knew that he had won his point.

Woth crooked a smirk, "It's typical of your rather quaint approach that you present a plan which, as far as I can see, involves no spillage of enemy blood. No assassinations, no frame-ups. I rather like it. I must be getting soft, like you."

"Somehow I doubt that, sir." Taldis risked a smile of incredulity. After all, Woth was always telling him that a civilization engaged in a perpetual cold war with a ruthless adversary will inevitably descend to the moral level of its foes, at least as far as secret operations were concerned, and that nothing could be done about it.

"Well," proceeded the Director, "though your idea lacks *kick*, it's certainly sly enough. I dare say that if we don't try it, some day the Quonians will. You know it has always bothered me, the way we persistently underestimate them. Your idea amounts to a neat little move which we can make to forestall them in a minor way, at no risk to our organization, while at the same time giving you, T-N, an opportunity to restore some of your credit with us. None too soon, either. During the past couple of hundred days you have been allowing your personal problems to interfere with your professional competence. Fair comment?"

Athness would not agree. She would say it's the other way round.

"Fair comment, yes, sir."

Woth smiled the cold smile which was the highest temperature he allowed himself. "You're an unusual agent, T-N. I hope you continue to be as unpredictable to the enemy as you are to your own side. Be off with you now. I've sent on your authorisation ahead of you; you'll find it when you report to the Vemorth Stazel."

The Society of Forgetters will remember me.

Taldis said, "Thank you, sir," and meant it. *Not bad*, he thought elatedly as he strode out of the building. It was no common achievement to get away from old chisel-face with the feeling that one had got what one wanted.

The next step was to deposit a farewell cube in a transmission booth... He did not reproach himself for this seeming callousness. Just leaving a message might seem cruel, but he was in the right. To maximise his chances of survival, he must preserve his effectiveness and that meant, for a start, avoiding another reproachful good-bye. Ordeals like that were worse for the nerves than any mission into enemy territory. After all, Athness' complaint was that he kept risking his life, Well, then, he'd look after himself! Click – in the message went. Now he was free.

2: To Skyyon

One of his skimmers, ready-packed, would be his home for the day it took to fly at top speed to the sunward polar city.

He owned several of the craft, scattered in various banks throughout the city so that it was never far to walk to the nearest one, wherever he happened to be. He preferred to walk as far as he could, but when a skimmer was necessary it became a joy to him as he slid it from its storage bay. Affectionately he ran his palm along the hull of recycled metal, imagining contact with previous incarnations of that metal – probably other skimmers ridden by other adventurers, into the ubiquitous pool of adventure. He would not lose sight of his own particular mission and its current importance, or the fact that he was acting under orders, yet he mounted the saddle with the satisfied sureness of one who has leisure and freedom to wander where he wills, for it was easy to pretend, now, that he was his own boss.

And life could allow pretence to veer towards fact.

He switched on the motor, opened the throttle, gripped the steerstick, floated forth from the bank and swept into a glide – the perspectives of the city shifting around him like the boughs and fronds of a polyhedral jungle – down the skimway to disc level. Having reached this floor he wove his way till he struck a radial avenue. This led him directly to the rim: the clear *oalm* free of buildings, smooth as a ring around a gas-giant planet. He had hardly a moment to admire its Saturnian beauty before the tug of the *ayash* current gripped his vehicle and lifted it high, over and out of the city and down onto the plain.

The ayash airstream dropped him and he was on his own, now no longer carried by the air but tearing through it, as he skimmed just six yards above the plain. He put up the cowl before gunning the motor and increasing speed to the craft's limit of two hundred miles per hour. Only once did he glance back at the receding splendour of Vyanth. Sustenance for the soul: the giant tray piled high with lights and held aloft by a stem, the stem dropping away towards the rear horizon. What nobler work could there be, than to defend *that*? Spy though he was, he need feel no shame: his job was the most worthwhile expenditure of a man's life – helping to preserve the accumulated cultural riches of seventy-six eras. The sordid word "spy" meant, in his case, maintaining brilliance, guarding what brought warmth to the cold of a giant world. So he *was* free, for he was doing what he chose to do.

Thus the city of Vyanth, disappearing from sight like a fond parent who wisely allows freedom to nen's children (a city ought to be 'nen', not 'it', nen had personality), received love and loyalty in return. *I have survived unconquered,* said its metropolitan voice, *through ten thousand human lifetimes. I am always there for you, citizen Taldis Norkoten. I stand constant, wherever you are.*

In fact for the first twenty minutes or so Taldis had not yet left the ambit of Vyanth. The light from glowing fields of *vheic* provided an outer halo to the city's brilliance. But after that, as he bulleted past the last farms he experienced a new, firmer grip of infinity. The giant world had him in its hand, drew him out of the pull of his home city. The strong fingers of that global hand were the liver-coloured plain, the vault of sky and the remote, encircling horizon, and as always happened round about this point, Taldis adopted a suitably nomadic mood. There was a kind of hand-over. The mothering warmth of the city gave way to the "coolth" of the plains.

A skimmer's top stable altitude is six yards. Storm-riding techniques can make it go higher, but here there was no storm. So – six yards. Yet in this emptiness, as far as appearance was concerned it was impossible for Taldis to make out whether he was travelling at two hundred miles per hour six yards above the ground, or two thousand miles per hour sixty yards above ground, or maybe just twenty miles per hour at only 0.6 yards' altitude. This absence of scale and his steady speed nudged him into a dreamy state of mind.

On average once every ten minutes or so, scale returned to him at the sight of objects such as a lone hive-tree, a hill, a grove, a farming settlement or a flapping bird. They helped to keep him awake, but as they streamed past they accentuated the loneliness and the vastness. He knew that if this sensation ever became too much for him his mind might suffer the condition known as *nebulation*, wherein one's consciousness roves like a cloud and can no longer attend to human-sized concerns. A nebulated man can even forget his own name.

He wasn't worried that it would happen to him. Confident in his experience as a wayfarer, he was an old hand at checking his mental wanderings if they showed signs of an ominous tug. Anyhow, this particular stretch of wilderness was unusually friendly to Man. No hour went by without sight of a silver ovoid floating on patrol in the upper air. That frequent presence of airships was the basis of the Great Triangle, the special area bounded by the cities of Ao, Skyyon and Vyanth, each about six thousand miles from the other two. Each trusted the others to contribute resources for patrol of the area between them, in close alliance. Originally aimed at deterring piracy, the arrangement had evolved over lifetimes into a 'weeding' service whereby, in these fifteen million square miles, all kinds of trouble were prevented from taking deep root. And if the word "Syoom" ("Civilization") is used in its literal sense to mean "the area in which a lone wayfarer can travel a thousand miles with a fifty-or-greater per cent chance of survival", the Great Triangle provided its inhabitants with a super-Syoom where the value was better than ninety-nine per cent. The fact that Taldis' journey to Skyyon was turning out so uneventful was yet one more tribute to the everyday success of that alliance.

Six thousand miles at two thousand miles per hour: that made thirty hours, exactly one Uranian day, of journey time. When evenshine dimmed to anyne, he set the autopilot alarm to warn him of obstacles or topographic change; then he unfolded the deck-couch, erected the side-guard to prevent him from rolling off in his sleep, and lay enjoying *refelc*, the brief evening treat of a sight of the stars. Only during the atmosphere's transparent stage, between night and day, could the stars shine through it to share the sky with their polar chief, the faint and distant sun.

The air darkened further, towards the opaque blackness of yyne, the blanket which hid not only the stars but also the sun. Presently, Taldis Norkoten slept. He woke in time to see the stars again: in *pmetn*, their appearance at the end of pallyne, before they were obliterated by the brightening air of morningshine. More hours passed. The light grew further, into ayshine, the brightest time, the middle five-hour section of day. Skyyon's topmost spire should be appearing any time now. There – a flicker?

The plains were bright.

The plains were dim.

Taldis rubbed his eyes. What exactly was this? A real flicker, or was it in his mind?

The plains, he understood, were *bright* due to eye-adaptation. Uranian humanity, native to this world, must be accustomed to viewing it in its own light and to seeing that light as adequate.

Yet simultaneously the plains were *dim*. In some real, objective sense they possessed that quality of faintness.

For one weird freezing moment Taldis endured the blink between bright and dim, bright and dim – then he relaxed as his imagination righted itself.

More clearly than ever before he knew that he had chosen the correct path; that he was a natural for the Vemorth Stazel, the Society of Forgetters.

At that very instant a swelling star appeared on the forward horizon, a star that was no star but his first glimpse of the flame-shaped Zairm, the Palace of the Noad of Skyyon, its tip now revealed at a distance of two hundred miles.

3: At Skyyon

From the journal of Taldis Norkoten:
11,544,672 Os:

I awoke with a smell like burnt toast teasing my nostrils. Opening my eyes, I saw that I lay in a high-ceilinged, narrow room. My bed was up against one wall. Along the other three walls ran a long table interrupted at one point by a door. On the wall above the foot of my bed hung a poster.

I focused my eyes on the message on that poster. It said – in big blue letters, in my own handwriting –

YOU HAVE LOST YOUR MEMORY

BUT THAT DOESN'T MEAN YOU HAVE LOST YOUR MIND

I swung my legs to sit up and, as if that had been a signal, the door opened, sphincter-like. A woman stepped through. She stood hands on hips, surveying me. She wore trousers and blouse. It – the blouse – would have provided good camouflage in a field of garish wild-flowers. Ah, so I did still know what flowers were. The woman, who was maybe twice my age, had red hair and grey skin which puckered as she smiled. She gloated a bit, I thought.

"Confused?" she asked.

"Haven't even got that far yet," I replied grumpily.

Indeed it was more a matter of stuff in my head wanting to rear up and make trouble. "Why are you looking at me like that?" I demanded. "Am I a difficult patient of yours, or what?" I was verging on being scared.

She nodded. "Good sign, showing spirit. I am Diren Ev, Director of the Vemorth Stazel. And you are a customer named Taldis Norkoten, of Vyanth."

"Customer?"

"Literally, yes. You asked for what you've got. And we gave it to you, oh yes. Our work is of a high standard."

Her voice had grown vibrant, celebrating her professional joy. I cut in, "I need a friend, or at least an informative enemy. I have plenty of ideas of what *might* exist around me, but what I *know* amounts to nothing much, so – give!"

Without taking her eyes off me the woman sat on the edge of the table. She stretched her left arm and switched on a viewer.

A rapid flow of clipped scenes showed me standing in a lobby being welcomed, shaking hands with Diren Ev and others, being guided into an office, getting sucked into a whirlpool of inductions and demonstrations: sign this consent form, take your cloak off, sit there, put your head back there… "Never," remarked Diren, "had I met such confidence in a client, such utter lack of hesitation." She switched off the screen, stood up and moved closer to me. In a voice that grated towards hoarseness, she said: "In fact you're quite a *foregrounder*, aren't you, Taldis?"

Her tone was suddenly transformed, hostility had surfaced, and the word *foregrounder* put me on my mettle. Which goes to show how one can suspect an insult without knowing a thing about the circumstances.

I replied, "If that's something bad, I take it *you* are a *backgrounder*."

I wanted her to realize that despite the wiping of my personal memory I could still recognize resentment when I heard it. For if I didn't stand up for myself I might never learn *where* I stood.

Diren's cheeks quivered as her voice softened into a mush of resignation. "Ha, yes, I suppose I deserved that; *'backgrounder'*, yes, that's me, I'm off the spot-lit track all right, just one of life's extras, a bit-part at most... If *I* were to go off into the blue, the way *you* plan to, I'd pay. Heavily."

Something in her eyes made me decide I didn't wish to play whatever the game was. I back-pedalled: "Let's not have any further mention of *foregrounder* and *backgrounder*, please. I get the feeling they aren't polite terms. In fact, I suspect they're tabu."

Her face cleared. In a sunnier tone, she declared:

"Good, your social residue is intact!"

"I'm sorry, I don't understand."

She was all briskness now. "That was my little test. Regrettably, I had to use bad language."

"Test." I dumbly repeated the word.

"Naturally you don't understand – you're not meant to; just take it from me at this stage."

"Take what?"

"That the most efficient way to check that our delicate operations are successful, is to administer a little shock to the patient's sense of propriety."

"And so the social thing –"

"Social *residue*. What you can't do without. What we had to make sure you retained. To remove personal memories, while preserving social aptitude, is not easy. Since you are our first fully-dosed client for quite a while, I am particularly relieved at this evidence of our success. In short, my lad, you are house-trained. You can safely be let loose."

I thought about it and decided she was right. I felt blank, but not bewildered. In fact I had an oddly secure feeling within me, as though I had found the firmest path through life, wherever it might lead.

She handed me my cloak, my belt and my laser, plus a palm-sized electronic guide to the city (designed and written for children), and a notebook of instructions which I had apparently written to myself. In this last she drew my attention to the date and time and place of my next rendezvous. "Think of it! Off on a mission! How grand to be a spy, working for Director Woth! Meanwhile, come back to me if you need any help before you leave Skyyon," she added, "though I don't suppose you will."

Risking a snub, I asked: "Shall I let you know how I get on?"

"The news will reach me, never fear."

I bid her enigmatic face goodbye, went out of the room and out of the building, and lounged by the porch.

The first thing I noticed as I gazed around was the absence of sharp shadows. Definite shadows had been thrown indoors, caused by lamps and ceiling lights, but it was different outdoors, in the hazy urban jungle. Under the bulge of some great pod-like structure the light might be somewhat dimmer than elsewhere, but the variation was gradual.

I felt my clothes, felt the lining of my cloak, and ran a finger over the clips to which telescope and pouch were attached. The texture of my material possessions was comforting. Exploring the contents of my pouch I touched triangular coins and as soon as I felt their rounded vertices I knew: this must be money. Right then I understood what money was. Part of my "social residue", as Diren would call it. Then there was the metal laser tube at my belt, and the leather of my boots; textures which made me immediately see whole aspects of life: fighting, stock-raising, the life of the plains under a city's protective power. My wrist transceiver was of less interest just then, for I could not think of anyone to call.

Next – my notebook. I leafed through it, gazed at the paragraphs and noted a lot of facts which meant little to me as yet, apart from the details of my next rendezvous and the password I must use. Doubtless the other stuff would come in useful later on. The main thing right then was that I felt self-sufficient. Simply through sight and touch I could sense that the culture I was in had evolved through thousands of lifetimes towards allowing a man to go his own way. In a pleasant mood I stuffed the notebook back into my pocket. I started forward, strolling over the metal city floor.

The dumpy building I had just left, which looked like a squashed bread roll, was soon obscured by intervening stems of raised structures and skimmways, and I judged it unimpressive compared to other agency buildings which I soon found myself walking past: Departments of Cloud-Talkers, Orographers, Naturalists, Gralmers, Historians... The city-guide which Diren had given me explained, "Skyyon is the nerve-centre of Syoom." In fact one *could* picture the escalators and skimmways as nerves; the suspended buildings which they linked, body-organs...

I overheard snatches of conversation from the people walking and skimming about me. I could distinguish three languages spoken, all of which I understood although only one of them was my native tongue. As the city-guide said, "Skyyon is the cosmopolitan centre of Syoom, the inevitable site for the Sunnoad's Palace..."

I button-paged through the guide to read about the Sunnoad.

"...the Noad of Noads, the focus of foci. Ever since the remote past, the Sunnoad has led the allied cities of Syoom whenever danger threatens from Fyaym. The Sunnoad has to be the most lremd person in the world..."

More button-pressing to check I knew what LREMD meant – but in vain.

Nowhere was the word explained. Apparently, everyone, even every child, is supposed to know – so perhaps I must know, too.

Same for the dirty words *foregrounder* and *backgrounder*. I must already know them without yet knowing how to access the knowledge within me.

But as I write these words their meaning hits me at last: the two terms denote the two kinds of people: those who serve as main characters in a real-life story, and those who only form part of the supporting cast.

No wonder the words are offensive when spoken. Were such a distinction to become explicit, it must risk an explosion of envy. So the terms must remain secret, dirty, suppressed. The rule is, don't even hint of them out loud, lest the issue blow society apart. Diren Ev did dare to offload her resentment, but only in the presence of newly blanked old me.

In fact maybe I had better rip out this page of my diary.

No – on second thoughts I had better not rip it out. A report is a report. My boss, Director Woth, can stand the obscenity if anyone can.

11,544,673 Os:

...I managed to find myself a hotel. It's a globular palace high above the lower floor of Skyyon and close to the "roof" of the upper floor. I didn't have any trouble checking in. It seems that I can talk to people safely enough, in an ordinary, business-like context. Apart from that, though, I have refrained from socialising. A friendly chat might easily lead me to giving away my status as a Forgetter, and I don't know what view people might take of a dis-minded person wandering around loose. Diren Ev knows I am harmless but others might not. I want to stay out of trouble till the rendezvous; and it isn't anyone else's business what I am, anyway.

Lunch in the restaurant – crusty meats and fruits, cereal loaves, and a tall glass of fiery viscous liquid – put me in good form for spending an afternoon exploring the city. The next day, I did more of the same. I indulged my curiosity to the full. Let me admit it for the record – I am enjoying myself.

Most of Skyyon is exuberantly jungle-like with mansions sprouting like fruits at the ends of tubular ways, but a few districts at floor level are different – restrained in style. These dignified areas are built of imported stone, forming pavements and staid terraces of houses which immediately overlie the metal floor. In my view (and I'm after all supposed to record my impressions, no matter how silly they may seem) these low-key stone terraces require explanation. A rival dream appears to have inserted itself into our architectural heritage. Full of this idea, I ventured into the Institute of Urban Design, gave Worth's name as a referee and asked the opinion of one of their experts. Nothing in our species' past, he agreed, can explain the style of the stone terraces. I then put it to him, that we may be under the prescient pull of some future trend. Then, having scattered this little seed of speculation, I left. I gather that this is the way I am supposed to behave. This is why I have had my memory erased by the Vemorth Stazel. I hope the result will be useful to somebody. Meanwhile, I confess it, I have been having fun.

I have continued to saunter around, looking into what pleases me while I await the rendezvous. My basic social orientation, my "residue", gives me a sense of security while my clean-slate mind makes all things fresh and new. Without (so far) being alarming. Like a holiday, in fact. I went to a bank and hired a skimmer, to examine it as much as to ride it, and was fascinated to learn (from an amused attendant) that the basic design of these vehicles has remained unchanged since they were developed way back in the Neon Era.

My condition makes me able to look at the two seats – the high rearward saddle and the lower hollowed-out seat "amidships" – as though I had never seen them before. Likewise objectively I studied the storage compartments, the fuel-phials compressed from phosphorescent vheic-plants, the motor, the buoyancy tanks... To anyone who saw me I must have seemed like an overgrown child, gawping, poking, fiddling... well, Woth, you asked for it. You told me to note everything. But don't worry, I understand that there's a bigger picture.

You hope that as a newly blanked outsider-mentality I shall spot some vital thing to give us an edge over the Quonians.

Well, I shan't get anywhere by trying too hard. No use straining...

It occurred to me, Woth, that you might want me to delve into the great library, so I went to have a look. I found myself able to use the film-records easily enough. This was time well spent insofar as it proved I was able to understand technical instructions for the use of systems, but I couldn't see the point of staying there long; my emptied brain is meant to "travel light"...

11,544,674 Os:

I have extended my range.

To reach Skyyon's upper floor, you first proceed to the outer rim of the lower floor. There, you find fountains of skimmers riding the airstreams in two directions: the main one, out of the city and down to the plain, and a lesser stream, upwards and inwards. That second one takes you to the top city tier, half the diameter of the first, and half a mile higher.

That's where I am now, writing this on a park bench in sight of the Zairm,

251

the Sunnoad's Palace. The crowds up here are sparser. The atmosphere is more sedate. Over this rarefied district hangs the smell of power.

Skyyon, so my pocket guide makes clear, does not *rule* the other cities. Each disk-on-stem metropolis is independent of the others. Yet Skyyon is in an important sense the capital of Syoom. The Sunnoad, the Noad of Noads, the focus of foci, has nen's residence here. Goodness knows what qualities one must possess to hold down *that* job.

Lremd, no doubt, whatever that is.

As for formal rights and privileges, I am told they are few. By immemorial consent, the Sunnoad takes command when general danger threatens Syoom from Fyaym. To rebel against this authority is almost unheard-of. To obey, or even to be noticed by the Noad of Noads, is such an honour that there is no need of compulsion. History comes alive, and you fully know what it is to live, when the Sunnoad speaks to you. That's what many witnesses say. I sometimes crane my neck towards the summit of the Zairm and wonder if *he* is looking out of one of the windows. What must it be like to be such a person, imprisoned in such fame, knowing that whatever action one performs will be judged in the full glare of history?

11,544,676 Os:

I saw more open sky, as I climbed further into the thinned regions and upper sectors of the city, eventually reaching the airship docks. This gave me a view of the navy suspended at its moorings like globular clusters in a galactic halo. Along an aerial walkway I went up close to one of the docks at a moment when one of the airships was coming in. The ovoid hull, fifty yards long, swelled in view as it slowly turned to reveal the name *Knorol* painted on its side. It decelerated till it nudged the landing platform with feather-light precision.

The door cycled open and the crew began to disembark. Scores of men strode jauntily towards the freedom of a few days' leave at the end of their patrol. Meanwhile in the other direction I saw the replacement crew. They had been standing further back than I, for their numbers would have got in the way of the disembarkation, but now they all pushed forward. I backed out of their way, against the walkway railing. It would have been a long fall from there, to the city floor a mile below!

"Interested in my ship?" sounded a voice to the left of me. I turned to see a burly man in a cerulean cloak, whose trim beard matched the colour of his loam-brown eyes.

Having planted himself in the midst of the walkway he was waiting for my reply while other personnel edged past him.

I asked, "You are Captain Choad?"

"Yes, and you are Taldis Reperzint."

It was as if a light-bulb had flicked on in my head, and I knew what to reply:

"Not today, sir. Today I am plain Taldis Norkoten."

"Just so." This rigmarole over, the captain gestured towards the entrance to *Knorol*. "Come aboard. Your Director has told me all about you."

I followed him inside, and in the company of some other officers we threaded the grey corridors. The glow of the ceiling-strips guided us like arrows to the carpeted cavern which was the control room. Here I was invited to take a seat, while the crew prepared for departure.

My rendezvous had been successful.

4: To Quonia

When the floor trembled under my boots I stood up, eager as a child, and full of gratitude as the captain beckoned to me with the words, "Come and watch." I hurried over to stare through the glass "port" (actually one of the rear viewscreens) at the view of Skyyon as we receded from the dock.

Choad joined me a couple of minutes later at the screen. "A perfect departure, right on schedule. Indirectly, you are to thank."

I turned to him in surprise.

He nodded, explaining:

"My group has been waiting to charter this ship for scores of days. It might easily have taken longer still, without prompts from your boss. Welcome to the Survey Service."

I had been mildly curious as to how the Survey had come to co-operate with Woth. "I suppose," I shrugged, "you and Intelligence are natural allies."

The captain glanced round the control room and said, "Time for a drink in my cabin, I reckon."

When we got there he gave me a tall glass full of orange liquor and said, "Take it slowly. It's Grardesh – strong stuff. If you know what *getting drunk* means…?"

His face wore a facetious look, and I suspected he was holding back some amusing conclusion. To play safe I remained literal: I took his question seriously and thought about it. Drunkenness… it did have a vague significance to me. "Something to do with a substance in fermented juice

253

imbibed to excess," I replied, and added, "I doubt whether I could ever talk about it from personal experience."

"No need to sound so prim." He sat back and twirled his own glass, definitely amused. "Do you know where you're going? What you're doing? What you're discovering? No? Never mind... A special providence looks out for drunks and *Forgetters*."

11,544,681 Os:

Choad's friendliness springs from the interest I hold for him as an experiment. He is a devotee of an obscure science called 'psychology'. This motivates him to study how my blank-state mind reacts to data; and I don't object, since it gives me the run of the ship.

Yes, it's lucky for me, the way things have turned out. The Survey Service has few ships of its own, so it needs to charter others. The pure-science philosophy of men like Choad is, I gather, out of step with today's priorities. So they take what they can get, in alliance with the military, and Choad doesn't seem to resent the link; instead he compliments me, tongue in cheek, on my "valuable objectivity". I think he thinks Woth's ideas are a huge laugh.

But maybe contrasts are misleading. To me, at any rate, the Survey Service doesn't seem to be noticeably less tough than the military. Though the crew of *Knorol* are scientists first and foremost, I get the strong impression that they could put up a fight if they had to. And the foamed ore of *Knorol*'s hull could take quite a few hits – I can judge for myself the strength of the ship as I roam around it, observing its cellular structure and all the redundancies built into it.

I applied to join the official observers' rota and they paired me up with a plains-watcher named Tarpik, a bulky fellow with a mournful face and sleepy eyes, who muttered a greeting and then turned back to his scanscope. We took turns with it for many hours, session after session, to monitor the ground flowing past beneath the ship's keel. The task can get monotonous, but it's dreamy and narcotic rather than boring. You stare and stare at the surface a mile below, and you jot down your subjective impressions which are believed to be of some use in addition to the records of the automatic cameras. Sometimes there's more. I remember one occasion, when, just as I was beginning to get lulled by the dazzling blur, a carpet of blue marching spikes began to cross my field of view. No need for me to give a full description of the sight; the Director of SIC can demand to view Survey Ship data any time he likes. My point is, it seemed that none of my shipmates seemed to know or even care what the spikes actually were. Not even when they began to fire upwards at our ship. I felt the floor lurch under me as we rose higher to avoid the projectiles. No other action was taken, no attempt made to alter course to follow the things after they had crossed our path. I was tempted to remark that I was not the only empty-brained person on board. How could the personnel of a research ship be so lacking in curiosity? But all I said to Tarpik was, "Why don't we at least see if we can find out where they live?"

"Got to keep to our sample-line," he replied. "Preserve comparability with the previous transect. Else the entire voyage is wasted."

I muttered, "Scientific method, eh?"

He said nothing; he went back to his work.

I have no real complaint. Maybe they're right.

[Later.] The captain has increased our altitude to two miles. In addition to my stints on the scanscope I make observations of my own through my cabin window and the screens in the control room, where I'm allowed so long as I keep quiet. As in some wavy dream the colours of the plains meander continuously beneath us, while occasional wrinkles, mounds and saw-edged ridges that have heaved up through the surface pass us by. More rarely, we fly over larger humps: these are said to be the tips of mascons convected through the ice-mantle of Ooranye. Such frozen disturbances are often accompanied by clefts, chasms, gorges. Meanwhile, patches of life dot the desolation: lonely hive-trees, spiky groves, splotches of grassland, even the odd zone of human settlement. But what predominates is always the plain. Endless, like space itself, it shares the view with the sky. That brings me to mention the… clouds, one calls them, flocks of them, which throng and squirm in increasing numbers, around the ship and sometimes below it.

More and more it is the clouds which provoke me most strikingly as I stare from my cabin port. The nebular phylum, so I am warned, becomes denser in the hinterlands of Syoom, and it dominates the skies of Fyaym. I see veils and ropes of cloud, hunting or fighting each other, even at times flinging themselves against our hull, so that we sense a thud through the floor plates.

To me, as a Forgetter, it is a fantastic panorama, and I find it hard to believe that any bits of knowledge we acquire will amount to anything more than a few scant scrawls in the corner of a blank sheet of paper the size of the world. Come to think of it, I suppose you don't have to be a Forgetter to feel this way.

From my cabin terminal I can access all the archival viewtapes of *Knorol*. When tired of the actual view outside I have settled in front of the little screen to watch historical reconstructions, artists' impressions of the surface of Ooranye in past ages, right back to the Hydrogen Era when the plains were mostly covered with forests of weeds. In the movie the waving pods seem so real, they menace my imagination with the hugeness of Time and all its extinct realms, alive with foes that war against each other, savage vegetation and insectoids which threaten with their crossfire the scurrying forms of primitive man.

There was a knock on my door and it turned out to be the captain in one of his dissecting moods. "Free association: just ramble on," he instructed. "Vowel change from O to U."

I got something this time: "Noun, *Ooranye*; adjective, *Uranian.*"

"Ah-hah," he nodded with enthusiasm.

"Have I said something interesting, captain?"

"Just a datum, just a touch of the big picture."

"Aren't we Uranians *always* fond of the big picture, Forgetter or no? I mean, don't we all have a tendency to enlarge our frame of..." I faltered.

"Ah-hah," he repeated, grinning delightedly. "Note the way you say *we Uranians*. You're tinged with context."

"I'm what?"

"You view our world as one among many although we have never known any other."

I stayed thoughtfully silent.

Choad went on, "We all do it. You're right in that respect. We are all remarkably good at *not* taking things for granted. I'm doing it at this very moment, not taking for granted how good we all are at not taking things for granted. Infinite regress... semantic clowning... but we suspect that it is in preparation for some far-distant day when we *will* be one people among those of many worlds."

"So as a Forgetter I'm nothing special."

"Studies have suggested," he said carefully, "that a blanked mind like yours is especially prone to suffer invasion from the future."

"The pull of destiny? That doesn't sound very scientific, captain. If I may say so."

"Well, I don't use that d-word, myself. I collect facts."

That is true enough. He loves to collect facts. Actually, that's all he wants to do with them – collect them. He will cite theories, but he never really wants to get anywhere.

He spread a chart on my cabin table. Our route had been ruled in black ink. I goggled at it: it was childishly simple – an absolutely straight great-circle line from Skyyon all the way to the Quonian border. 19,967 miles to be exact, from start to finish – the finish being the border checkpoint known as the Zark.

Six and a half days' flight at one hundred miles per hour, all in an exact straight line.

The Transect. Or, as I was tempted to call it, the Affront to the Intelligence.

He could tell I disapproved.

"But why are you so surprised, Taldis Norkoten?"

"I realize," I hedged, "that this is how you do things… but when I see the whole thing marked out like a blind slash through the night, I can only tell you, I feel it in my bones, that to be so determined to keep your straight line no matter what you meet, is tempting fate."

He shrugged, "We want an unbiased sampling route. Mathematically pure. Untainted by human choice."

I smiled, "Let's hope that not too many of your samples are hostile."

But nothing so far – apart from the marching spikes I mentioned – has offered fight during this voyage. And yet not even the most desperate battle could have made it more exciting than it already was, for me. Just quietly taking part in this flight into the unknown has been the greatest thrill, has given me what I needed to fill in my sense of the world, to re-fuel the empty tank of my imagination. Thus content to watch, I watched, as day succeeded day and *Knorol* soared over the transect route. First, the richest Syoomean lands, from Skyyon in the direction of Hoog. Then past the Konteng of Nuvium. Then into wilder regions, till on this sixth day we have actually crossed the *sfy-50* safety-contour which separates Syoom from its antithesis, Fyaym. I saw nothing specially visible as we crossed that line. Nevertheless it was a real boundary line; I felt the difference in my nerves and heart.

I ought to be able to say more than this, but it is like trying to pin down a ghost. Words being inadequate to convey the awe and mystery of Fyaym, one is apt to take refuge in numbers and statistics. The books and view-tapes tell me that Fyaym comprises four-fifths of our planet's surface, in order words, about sixteen hundred million square miles, quite beyond any man's capacity to know or grasp. With regard to our own journey, Captain Choad tells me that from the boundary of Fyaym there remain 6,655 miles to the Zark…

I don't think I am as scared as I ought to be, about what this ship is doing and what I must do when I leave it. Ignorance has its advantages. In fact isn't that the whole idea? I'm rambling… but you asked for it, Director.

11,544,682 Os:

It was under an opaque black sky, during the deepnight of yyne, that we sighted the Quonian border.

By this time the crew had been briefed regarding the role I must play at the checkpoint.

Tarpik came to my cabin door and said, "Your time has come, you poor *nebulated* man."

"You mean the captain has sent for me?"

"Yes. Says he wants to hear you arguing with yourself one last time."

I hurried to the bridge and was startled and amazed by what I saw on the main forward viewscreen: a ribbon of metallic light stretching across the ship's path from horizon to horizon.

The captain, uninterested in this grandiose view – which I myself ought to have expected – was focused upon a lower, tighter part of the picture. I heard him say, "That's the *Zeem* already in dock. The delegation have arrived on time." He then took note of my presence. "Your Director's plans are on track, Taldis," he said, motioning me to a seat in front of one of the small screens. "I have spoken to the Quonians and we are going straight down. Within minutes we must hand you over. As a last favour to me, please speak your impressions –" and he pointed to a microphone.

Grateful for the excellent treatment I had received on this voyage, I was happy to obey. While the captain directed the landing approach I muttered my final recording as subject of his psychological experiments:

"Er, well, here I am at last. The floor starts to drop under me and the ship begins its slanting descent towards the *polikanomv*, the Quonian frontier line. That's one word of Quonian that everyone seems to know. And from what I've heard of those people, it's no great surprise that their best-known term denotes what separates them from the rest of Ooranye.

"I was warned that there'd be no mistaking it. I can well believe that no other frontier defences are comparable to this. It's actually a row of giant trees, spaces a couple of miles from each other, each a quarter of a mile high and shedding light to merge with that of its neighbours. The blended light from these trees – they are known as *osror*, plural *osrorv*, and it is their metallic fruit which glow – the light, I say, spills down to gleam upon the moat in which they stand. Beyond the moat, the land of Quonia lies dark at this hour…"

Pausing for breath, I heard the captain say to the chief pilot, "Careful of wind-currents, Gengr."

"As ever, captain," replied Gengr Axxan.

"*Not* quite as ever, pilot," retorted Choad. "Remember, no foreigner is allowed to overfly Quonia by so much as an inch. In fact, better go for a vertical drop right now. Leave it to others to test the capabilities of the *osrorv*, will you." He sounded quite edgy, not like his usual self at all. It was the only time I ever knew our captain to interfere with the details of piloting.

Gengr Axxan immediately punched switches to follow the order he had been given and in a few seconds we had sunk almost to ground level. From this point Axxan nosed us forward towards the waiting dock, avoiding any risk of an accidental encounter with the organic missiles reputedly hidden in the *osrorv*.

I continued my narration:

"I've heard that the Quonians are technologically advanced. Surely they must possess a sky-navy and need not rely upon pellet-throwing trees! But then," I changed tack, "what with a twelve-thousand-mile border to guard, perhaps they *do* need them. Perhaps a defence system which grows and maintains itself is indispensable. Or perhaps," I rambled on, "the *polikanomv* was around long before Quonia, and Quonia merely made use of it. I've heard that the *osrorv*'s questing roots melt and re-freeze the ice to cause a gradual displacement of the moat, shifting the land of Quonia a few yards per human lifetime…"

I halted my speech, conscious that I was merely re-hashing ideas which must have been discussed thousands of times. However, there was Choad nodding at me, expression approval and encouragement. Apparently he wanted me to go on; he thought I was doing fine.

I then realized that my contribution must lie not in my views or speculations, which were hardly likely to be interesting in themselves, but in the weighting of the phrases. The *way* I said things was what counted, no doubt, to a psychologist.

Humbled at this thought, I rounded off my commentary:

"Whatever the truth about the roots of the trees, and the trees' weapons, the Quonians must also possess *conventional* weapons at this stretch along the *polikanomv*. For right here is a dim gap where no *osror* stands."

As I spoke, the ship finally slid into dock. I peered through my viewscreen into the murk. "Here stands the Zark itself," I ended, "and beside the checkpoint stands the town, somewhere before us."

5: Into Quonia

"*A-R A-R,*" broadcast the captain in shipboard command language. All the crew listened. "*Remember that as soon as the ship's hull is in contact with the ground, any words we speak may be overheard by the Quonians. Security mode, operation nebulee."*

I felt a gentle bump as the airship touched down.

Completion of the transect from Skyyon to Quonia meant that the ordinary business of *Knorol* was over, without any need for captain or crew to enter the land of Quonia itself. The next survey mission would proceed from here in a different direction. But the captain had an agreement with my boss, Director Woth of Syoomean Intelligence:

Captain Choad would accompany me to the checkpoint.

He and I passed swiftly through the corridors and elevators of the airship towards the lower hatch. Farewells remained unspoken by the crew standing by. No one could be sure what surveillance devices the Quonians might possess. It was essential that I behave in character as a *nebulee,* and a *nebulee* would certainly not say good-bye.

As a matter of fact I was glad I did not have to speak. I found myself shockingly close to tears. Regret had ambushed me. The voyage had been so pleasant, such a comfortable way of getting re-aquainted with the world: I could have spent the rest of my life on mindless transects with the Survey Service.

Yes, these few days of rest and wonder had played the part of childhood in my new life as Forgetter. And well I knew that the sense of repose was irretrievable. Now I would have to "grow up". Adolescence telescoped into the next few minutes…

The captain and I rode the exit platform from hatch down to ground. Then we trudged across a hundred yards of gralm to the lit entrance of the Zark. I felt the eyes of the crew on my back, projecting their sympathy through ports and scanners. The Quonians, I was glad to reflect, could not read our minds, could not know what the sympathy really was for.

As an agent pretending to be a victim of *nebulation* I was in double danger. I was entering their realm under false pretences, which any agent must do. But also I was taking mean advantage of our enemies' adherence to a universal code of hospitality towards nebulees, and for that reason it would go all the harder with me if the trick were found out.

Choad's reply, when I had put this to him a few hours earlier, had been typically whimsical.

"It's a distasteful trick, yes, but it must surely come under routine expenses in the moral budget. I mean, disguise for a spy is so traditional."

And the other side would do the same, given the idea and the opportunity.

The Zark loomed in the scanty light from its entrance. "Get used to this," muttered the captain. I grasped what he meant. The outside walk. I was going to have to get used to approaching structures from the ground. Not only checkpoints but whole cities: everything in Quonia was built on the ground. No disk-on-stem structures here. He whispered, "They call our lofty cities arrogant; we retort that their possessive hugging of the world's surface is a greater arrogance…"

Choad and I reached the half-buried polyhedral mass. We stopped before a door which was flanked by sentries in jointed ceremonial armour.

One of them spoke, first in Quonian and then, harshly but comprehensibly, in our own Nouuan tongue: "Your names and business?"

The captain gave his own name first and then explained, "My business is an errand of mercy on behalf of this man, Taldis Norkoten of Vyanth, who cannot speak for himself. He is a nebulee – whom I wish to leave with the Syoomean delegation that's just arrived."

The sentry muttered into his wrist transceiver, then nodded us past him. We entered a pillared hall where, despite the very late (or early) hour, an official reception was in progress. The hum of chatter filled the air; Syoomean ambassadors nibbled delicacies from a long table. Choad guided me forward by the elbow while I put on a dazed air that I suppose wasn't too far different from my habitual expression. Choad called out heartily:

"Ambassador Trond, what a lucky coincidence! Lucky, that is, for this poor fellow."

"Ah, Choad. Yes, our hosts have told me, you want to leave him with us." Trond was a wide, heavy-jowled man with a routine smile.

"It is urgent that we do leave him," Choad explained. "Our voyage continues further into Fyaym, no place for a nebulee. Whereas you will be entering a civilized city soon. A Quonian city to be sure, but they are a polite race, after all."

I noted that he said this with no apparent regard for the ears of those white-robed Quonian waiters who were padding around us. It was as though he wanted to be overheard, wanted to annoy the Quonians. This applied to the Ambassador as well.

Trond asked, "And could you not stay a while?"

"If only it were feasible," the captain declined. "Our next transect mission, starting from here, is subject to a time factor. Especially as we need to allow time to skirt the *polikanomv*. Of course if it weren't for Quonian paranoia," and he orated louder than ever, "we could have flown straight over their country, adding *it* to our transect, in which case, Taldis here might have been cured without leaving our vessel – if, as they say, the overfly of populated areas, the psychic effluent of millions of ordered lives, can restore the mind of a nebulee. Ah well," he concluded sagely, "paranoia is for small minds. The small can't help being small."

The waiters padded and padded, bearing their trays, and their expressions remained blank. I had a queasy feeling in my stomach. If only Choad and Tronnd did not get such fun out of baiting the Quonians…

"You know," replied Tronnd, "you do them an injustice. Narrow and retarded they are in some respects, but not *small*…"

So the captain and the ambassador continued to enjoy themselves, pretending not to know what they weren't supposed to know, which was that the waiters were irrelevant, and that by far more sophisticated means the Quonian authorities were able to monitor every word that was spoken in their country. Doubtless both men had suffered various irritations from the isolationist Quonians, and now they were getting their own back.

One tall Quonian stepped forward. "Sponndar Ambassador," he said smoothly, "observe your nebulee."

I had distanced myself, disliking the way things were going. I moved to interrupt the game. Noises welled up in my throat, as I tried to sound like one who is about to recover his capacity for speech. "Hey," said Tronnd, "listen to him; he's benefitting already from being on the ground."

I tottered towards the drinks stand. Everyone was watching me by now, but I acted like I didn't care. Accepting a glass from the haughtily handsome Quonian at the stand, I bleared vaguely at his stony face. Like others of his countrymen in the hall, he was robed and cloaked in white; his skin, a lighter grey than mine, gleamed with that scrubbed, muscular health I had seen in martial artists from many lands. His expression contained the merest hint of scornful amusement. Despite his role of barman, the word that came to mind was *aristocrat*.

I sipped, looking bored. Then, asserting my independence a trifle further, I walked to the nearest window. I looked out and to my surprise, saw stars. Could it be pmetn already? Then I remembered: yes, it could. This is Starside, the half of Ooranye that never sees the Sun. From this dark hemisphere the stars are seen for longer; pmetn and refelc begin earlier and end later, lasting many minutes longer than they do on Sunside.

Choad walked over and bade me farewell. I mumbled; he slapped me on the back. Then he walked out of the hall.

I felt lonely and miserable all of a sudden. What was I doing at this crazy espionage game?

After some more minutes a Quonian muttered to Tronnd. I paid scant attention, as I fought my depression. I tried to view myself as a contented pawn, or a minor character in a story, who must not expect too much.

A *backgrounder*, in fact.

The wave of misery passed. Presently the twelve Syoomean delegates plus myself were ushered up a ramp, round the hall's side, through the back of the building and onto a terrace, outside.

We were level with the top of an embankment of hard-packed gralm seven yards or so above the plain. Visibility had greatly improved. The morning was starting to glow. The fading stars of pmetn shone their last upon a metal rail that began at our feet and shot away to the horizon, promising to bear us into infinite adventure; a *vlep* hovered a few yards off to carry out the promise. Just a few minutes ago, *vlep* and *monorail* would have been mere words to me. Now, however, my eyes drank their fill and my imagination strained forward. This, I saw, was the regular morning train service from the Zark to the capital.

I saw Tronnd go to speak with the four Quonians who were waiting for us in front of the vlep. In my latest mood-swing, danger was just another colour in the landscape. Sure enough, the next thing I knew, Tronnd was waving the rest of us forward. The whimsical notion came to me, that old Diren Ev was right: I *am* a foregrounder, not a backgrounder at all. I am marked out by Fate to get away with things. A dangerous belief, of course. One risks becoming so arrogant as to be mentally ill. And yet – there is something to it.

It's not mere imagination, or any special gift of self-confidence; it is a real exterior current which is bearing me along. I dare say the world is full of such currents, such "winning streaks", and those who can step into them and ride are the "foregounders".

Those who remain pedestrian (metaphorically speaking) are the "backgrounders", such as, no doubt, the Quonian driver of the vlep, who had no idea he was conveying a spy into the heart of his realm, and my twelve ambassadorial companions whose role was mere cover for me.

Tronnd saw to it that I had a seat by the window, as though I were a favourite child being given a treat. The vlep jerked into motion and rapidly picked up speed. Air whined past the window glass; the plains blurred at a velocity apparently greater than anything I had experienced on the airship. The monorail ride was utterly smooth. *Better say something,* came the thought. For on this civilized, regular, grounded train, a nebulee should recover his voice.

"How fast are we going?" I croaked.

Conversation halted as all eyes turned to me. "Ah!" said Tronnd, "our nebulee's brain-fog is clearing already! The answer to your question, stranger, is – four hundred miles per hour." He nodded as my eyes widened. "Well, after all," he added, "a vlep is the fastest form of transport on Ooranye. And welcome to our talk-see mission."

"What is a talk-see mission?" I asked, playing my dumb part.

"A diplomatic junket with no specific objective," drawled Tronnd. "A kind of safety-valve. To put it another way, it's as if we and the Quonians are taking each other's pulse. Reduces the scope for nasty surprises."

"Thanks for taking me with you."

"You are welcome. All civilized peoples will help a nebulee. Relax, don't try to force your memories; just sit back and enjoy the journey."

Under the brightening air the landscape became steadily more visible. Occasionally some near object streaked by, too fast for me to guess its nature, but most of the stuff in the middle distance I could identify: trees, groves, farms with square fields, and the gantries of compressor-factories that distil the luminosity of the vheic plants into the fuel-phials which we all depend on. More rarely we saw great cones in the far distance; I guess they're cities. I built up a picture of a rational, predictable people. Dangerous enemies, no doubt, but strategic rather than random opposition. Yes, it ought to be possible to avoid nasty surprises in our relations with the Quonians.

I said, "I have another question or two."

"My patience is equal to that," smiled Tronnd.

"Where are we going and when do we get there?"

"Nullapz, the capital of Quonia, in about three hours."

Normal exchange of crisp question and answer. Vigour of mind and common sense. Encouraged by looks of approval, I went on:

"Do you happen to possess a map of Quonia, that I could look at?"

"No, sorry."

The atmosphere had changed. It was a sudden alteration. Only a slight "greying" of tone, but I was put out.

I shook off the unease and said: "Well, can anyone lend me a sheet of paper and a pen?"

One of the team did so. They all watched while I set the paper on the table in front of me and lifted the pen.

"Try," murmured Tronnd with a nod.

A situation which I could not accept, which smacked of magic, loomed in that vlep's cabin as my brain plodded muttering: "Well, if Quonia is roughly the shape and size I had gleaned from *Knorol*'s archives – that's to say, an oval area nine million square miles in extent – and if we are going straight in, Nullapz ought to lie approximately in the centre of the realm. Surely I can sketch that much for starters: just an oval and a dot in its middle: what could be simpler? So why is my right hand not moving?"

I sat there gripping the pen, at first merely feeling a bit foolish, then creepily disconcerted. The muscles of my arm and hand would not obey me. My former sense of being in a "current" of good fortune veered now into a suspicion that a much bigger "current" was helping the Quonians.

I made vain efforts to speak out. Tronnd observed my struggle.

"Best to say nothing," he nodded. "Sit back and enjoy the ride." He, too, was *not* saying something, and I could say it for him: *Don't try to draw any maps of Quonia – it really can't be done. Back off gracefully while you can.*

One can't even speak cartography here. Or complain aloud that one can't speak. Only in these pages can the topic be expressed – because, for some reason, my private journal is still allowed.

6: Nullapz

11,544,687 Os:

In the second half of the journey the landscape became more crowded, with a thicker scattering of objects on the plains, and the flat smoothness more often interrupted by mountainous humps of metallic grey, like upturned hulls, shouldering into view. Rows and columns of lights streaked the closer of these mountains.

Doubts grew fast in me about that word, "mountains". A new crop of questions sprang up in my mind. However, the way I've figured it, I'm not even really a spy, I'm just a spy *probe.* An automatic gatherer. So I ploughed those questions under. The meaning of what I gather will only become apparent to my controllers (if and when I get back to them), so really I might as well relax, be blank, be wholeheartedly a Forgetter.

In fact it perhaps might have been better if I had not done all that reading in the library on *Knorol.*

As for the journey – the last stage was dead quick: a blur of warm colour, whipping past the *vlep* window, my first close sight of the Quonian capital. Then a wall leapt near and the view darkened as we entered the more high-built areas of Nullapz. Deceleration was sharp; in seconds we had stopped.

We emerged, with me tagging along like a stumbling moron. The usual solemn white-robed officials met us on the platform, and conducted us out of the station building.

Staring around in bewilderment I saw domes of fuzz, which after some moments became comprehensible as hemispheres of light enclosing blocks of buildings. The blocks were surrounded by smooth circular patches of ground, and strips of identical smoothness connected one dome with another. I was looking at ground-roads. No skimmers around here, not a single one. In any ordinary Syoomean city you'd see them gliding to and fro. Here, instead, vehicles went about on *wheels*.

One such ground-car awaited us. I tried to remember our route as we wove our way in a stream of traffic to the embassy compound, but a half-dozen turns was enough to wipe out my sense of direction.

Finally we were led on foot into one of the light-hemispheres, then into the building at its core.

No one inside appeared to greet our arrival. It seems that the buildings are only intermittently occupied. There is no permanent Syoomean embassy currently resident in Quonia.

Our guides left us after handing Ambassador Tronnd the keys. When the outer door had closed behind them, it seemed we were left alone, but Tronnd raised one hand to command continuing silence. With his other hand he took a torch-like device from his case and waved it around, making stroking motions as if to spray-paint the walls and ceiling.

"We can talk freely," he concluded. He turned to me. "I do, of course, know who sent you here, Taldis Norkoten. But before I let you go your own way… Leran," he called, "see to Taldis, please."

A brisk young man of about my own age stepped forward: this was Leran Otmott, otherwise known as "Better Safe Than Sorry".

He led me into a small utility room, opened a safe and too out a small box. Inside it on a little cushion lay a pill-sized device. "Swallow that."

I stared at it dubiously.

He urged, "It's a life-hook. For your own protection." I decided not to argue. "Henceforth," he continued as I gulped the thing down, "so long as you are alive, its signal will blip on our life-meter. What's more, it will tell us fairly accurately where you are. The Quonians know we possess this capability, so it provides you will some protection – at least in peacetime."

"So now I can go where I like?"

"And say what you like, too," smiled Leran Otmott, "as far as we are concerned. Assume the worst – that you defected – what secrets could you blab? None, in your condition! No, you can't do us harm. And you just may do us good."

"Then I shall go out this moment," I said, and turned, as if walking on air, self-sufficient in my dreamy Forgetfulness. Leran's superior manner played its part in propelling me away, but other gusts of emotion drew me. Curiosity, plus a certain pull, what seemed like destiny, or the "shape" of purpose. Out of the building I walked, with the clothes I wore and the contents of my pockets and belt-pouch, and the life-hook transmitting inside me. After all, are not all parts of the world equally fresh and strange to a Forgetter?

The mounds of light, the buildings they covered and the pavements which connected them, extended before me to the limit of vision: I was in an enormous city. Yet I stood, not on any platform, but on the surface of the planet. This is an unfamiliar combination of experience for most Syoomeans. Even I, the Forgetter, for a moment felt I was a squashed speck in this ground-city; then I adjusted. Accepting the scene, I ventured along the pavement.

Among the tall, white-robed pedestrians and the drone of the ground-cars whizzing by, I got used to the Quonian speech which I could not understand, as my ear relaxed into the rhythm of its accents; similarly I soaked in the unfamiliar sights of Nullapz with unquestioning eyes, despite lacking the knowledge to give them meaning.

After some hours of this I became hungry. My pockets contained some Syoomean coins and it seemed reasonable to hope, this close to the embassy and the monorail terminal, that the local eating-places would accept my money. I followed a mauve glow-sign into a dining area, was shown to a table and handed a menu. What would I do, I wondered, if the waiter spoke no word of Nouuan, Jommdan or Lrissj? The only two words of Quonian I knew were *osror* and *polikanomv*! But the bustle of life around me was reassuring. Queuing at counters and seated at tables, the Quonians seemed messier and more human here, their robes less tidy, their chatter and their wriggly restless children all stamping my ticket to ordinary life. "Please," I said when the waiter returned, "get me a snack and a drink, whatever your customers like most," and it worked. Not that *he* understood. But that didn't matter for I heard a female voice say in Nouuan, "Don't worry, I'll help you order."

A tall lady in a satin gown was slipping into a chair at the table next to mine. Her male escort, of smart military bearing, smiled tolerantly at her intervention.

After the lady had translated my request to the waiter I was soon brought a plate of meat slices, fruit and bread, plus a tall glass of sparkling fluid. "By the way," my benefactress said, "I am Miqua, and this is Anquit."

"Delighted, but –" I added with my most thankful nod and smile, "it's more than 'by the way', I'm sure."

She uttered a tinkling laugh. "Quite right, we have been keeping an eye on you, I admit."

"For my own good?"

The man, Anquit, spoke. "Yes, *nebulee*."

Miqua added: "Granted that city life is supposed to be good for those in your condition – you probably realize, don't you, that you'd reached your limit."

Anquit put in, "The limit of what you can fathom *unaided*."

"I'm in your hands," I replied to them both. Either I was sunk, or I wasn't. "Taldis Norkoten, at your service." As far as I could tell, I was taking only a small calculated risk. Woth had given me no alias. Therefore he must have had good reason to believe that nobody hereabouts knew me from previous missions. Anyhow, if this reasoning was wrong, and they *did* know me of old, it would not be any good trying to fool them by giving a false name at this late stage. Whereas being honest with my real name might salvage my mission if I could make real friends.

Besides, it is true, that without my former memories I am *not* the person I used to be.

"We have some free time," said Miqua, enticingly.

"All help, friendship, advice are welcome," I assured. "Already I've made strides, just by being in the crowd, but of course the more I get to understand, the more I can recover my former self."

"We'll recover it, don't you worry," she smiled.

7: The Blank Slate

Sophisticated Quonian society has received me with open arms. I have smiled my way through a whole round of parties where Miqua and Anquit took me as their guest. I'm grateful for their friendship and appreciative of the artistic wonders I have been shown, though I don't tell them what I think of their vaunted flower gardens, which, though full of warm colours and shapes, nevertheless don't fend off the dark roof of the Starside sky or the encircling presence of Fyaym.

Occasionally I glimpse the Syoomean cloaks of Tronnd and his delegation, swimming in and out of view in the blurred light. A couple of times they have approached me, for a brief, pointless exchange of banalities, monitored by Quonian listening devices. And now and then I return to the embassy, to write entries in my report for Director Woth.

Otmott, who gave me the "life-hook" to swallow, periodically checks its health by pointing a device at my stomach. He's had little to say, but he once asked, "Have they tried to write their own views on your blank slate yet?"

"I haven't encountered anything very political so far," I replied.

"They will try."

11,544,692 Os:

A messenger sent by Miqua drove me to one of the palaces and ushered me into a circular dance hall. By some trick the music seemed not to come from the central players but from banner-like streamers twirling in the air without visible means of support. Miqua threated her way towards me, then drew me to a couch-crescent, saying, "I'll speak to you later if I may. Meanwhile, Taldis, this is Deldli, who has been longing to meet you." I stooped to bow at a lounging, low-cut gown bursting with woman.

Deldli made a face at Miqua's retreating back, burbling:

"I didn't need *her* to tell me, you're Taldis Norkoten, you're the nebulated man from Syoom!"

"You make it sound decadent," I grimaced.

"The Quonant says so," she nodded. "He says, it's always one's own fault. No strong character ever succumbs to nebulation."

"I see. A message from on high." My own tone warned me to make the rest of my response mild: "I'm weak and lazy, I admit. In fact I haven't done a stroke of work for quite a few days now."

"Oh," she said, sounding disappointed. "But allowing you to stay loose like this, I wonder... I mean, if your mind has been stripped of its civilized veneer..."

I had no idea what Miqua's purpose could have been, off-loading me onto this character. But they were welcome to whatever they could learn from my emptied mind. Meanwhile I could keep trying to learn from them... "Well, what do you do with *your* nebulees?" I asked.

"They get sent to a place..."

"A sort of institution?"

"I believe so," she nodded vaguely.

"We don't bother to do that," I told her. "Syoomean policy is to leave folk like me alone. There's no risk at all in letting my sort run free. Nebulation only blanks our memories, not our inhibitions – *those* remain intact! So don't worry about me casting off all social restraint!" But at that point my inner alarm bell did ring. It warned me that nebulation might not really be the subject of our conversation at all. And if, at this gathering, somebody were to

269

mention the Forgetters by name, and if the room had face-readers or lie-detectors, I'd be caught.

I caught sight of Tronnd, excused myself and went over to him. He had just finished a dance, his glamorous partner still dangled on his arm and I guess he was none too pleased to be accosted by me. "Lost your way, Taldis?"

"Socially, yes," I admitted. "I'm making friends so fast, I'm at risk of *losing my head*."

He disengaged himself from his lady friend, saying, "Excuse me for a moment, Atalsa, my confused young compatriot here needs a bit of guidance." To me he growled, "What do you want to know?"

"How much can I tell them?"

"About what?"

"My impressions of Syoom…"

He made a swift pronouncement. "*You* can say what you like to them. No need for *you* to feign ignorance. Muddy their waters as much as you like." His advice was shoved at me like a pole. I faced the fact that I was on my own.

A hand fell on my shoulder and I looked up into a twisted smile. Anquit, Miqua's young man, said affably, "How's our classic case doing?"

"Fine, thank you." (Meanwhile, Tronnd took the opportunity to drift off.)

"I was just asking myself," said the Quonian, "why isn't the Ambassador more worried about our social investigation of your blank-state mind? Does he have some special confidence in you? Is he aware of some power in you? Or come to think of it, is he beginning to worry after all? I notice his face has gone rather glum."

"You amaze me," I said, speaking like an innocent nebulee. "What I need, in my condition, is clarity, not mystification. Keep things *simple*, please."

Next thing I knew, Miqua had arrived at my other side. She squeezed my arm as she drew me away from Anquit, and over her shoulder she rebuked him: "You don't have time for annoying games with our guest; you need to get back to your post."

Anquit departed, wearing the thunderous look he was wont to assume at her reproaches, while Miqua, as she thrilled me by the touch of her arm on mine, made Time stretch for me as it does for a child. "So what are you doing, Taldis?" she asked. "Listening to music that's playing inside your head?"

"Distract me from it," I suggested.

She laughed, "How? Pull you away from your embassy? Detach you from your allegiance?"

"You might give that a try." And in a way I meant it. "A nebulee is like a rogue asteroid, looking for some star to orbit."

"All right, I'll be your star this evening. I have more gravitation than Tronnd has."

Her words had re-set my vision: it was as if I saw her for the very first time. Taller than I am by an inch, she showered me with the kindness that shone from her trust-commanding face, while the rest of her person was an emitter, her gown crackling three-dimensional femininity at every move she made so that the total effect was so wonderful, it defeated itself because it couldn't be true: nothing could make me believe that I could matter to someone in that league.

The evening went on being huge. She led me out of the palace and into the night air, where a flyer was waiting. By this time I knew that only those in the richest stratum of Quonian society owned flyers. It figured. They'd send the best... The two-seater, powered (I suppose) by a null-grav chip of the kind used in airships – to judge from our noiseless vertical take-off – zoomed up to show me the city of Nullapz from a height which displayed its surrounding ring of hull-shaped mounds, which I had glimpsed individually from the train: the ring-range of artificial mountains, scored with lines of window-lights.

"The *drenndv*," Miqua said, seeing the direction of my awed look.

"But what..."

"Each is a city from the inside, a mountain from the outside. Our working class, and some of our military class, live inside them."

"Class?"

"You *are* a Forgetter, aren't you!" she chuckled.

Well, I had skimmed some history since my Forgetting, and understood – academically – what the word "class" was supposed to mean. A sinister concept. Of course in Syoom also there are servants and unskilled workers, but they are defined as such only temporarily; I must have performed such roles myself, during my work-trances. But we have no servant or worker *class*. Down that road one comes in the end to slavery, as we found to our cost in the Vanadium Era.

"Care to take a look inside?" Taking my consent for granted she touched the controls. The flyer surged forward through the night, to seal my allotted destiny; rather than try to escape, all I had to do was accept the current.

I asked, "Inside? Which one?"

"As it happens I said I'd meet Anquit this evening close to the summit of Drennd Forty-Six."

"Anything special about Forty-Six?"

"He's stationed there, that's all. You were getting bored with partying anyway, weren't you, Taldis?"

"Not this evening," I said dryly. "Though if I were trapped inside an economic class…"

She didn't answer that; meanwhile a kind of nausea at the hulking size of the artificial mountain, *because* it was artificial, caused me to blench from the thought of what its volume might contain, as our flier – like an insect buzzing into its colony – finally entered by a hole among a myriad other holes part way up the slope. Somewhere in a cavernous hall patchily lit by fluorescent globes, we came to rest amid smudged echoes and dim crowds.

An attendant walked over to us, and handed Miqua a receipt for her flyer before he rolled it away.

Miqua took me by the arm again, and led me to a moving road which whirled us on a tour of the enclosed universe of Drennd Forty-Six. From cavern to cavern we advanced and ascended. At times we travelled horizontally on fast strips which had kiosks and small shops built onto them; other times we went upwards on ramps. I saw outlines of what Miqua said were factories and dormitories, shops and schools, hospitals and offices. At one point she stepped over to a near part of the moving way, in order to greet a middle-aged mother who was escorting two small children. Then, while Miqua went to buy something from a kiosk, I remembered what I was in Quonia for. I said to the woman with the children, "How are things with you?" Inane though this remark was, it started a conversation. I learned that her husband worked in a metal parts factory. "And I help out when I can," she said, looking wan in the scanty light, "because I know that if we all work hard, we may surpass our production target this centemeron!" I looked at her in sick pity, though I also noted that the children seemed quite happy as they dodged each other round the kiosks. They knew no other life.

Miqua returned to my side. Amused at my perplexed expression, she remarked: "Lots more to see! You can have a look at the night shift, if you like."

I hoped she wasn't serious, but on a smaller branch of the moving road we came to a stop outside a closed arch which opened at her touch, and here I made the discovery which answered my expectation, as a nightmare will appal without surprise. Inside the factory complex I saw nothing wrong at first. The workers and administrators in their open-plan sections seemed to be performing their tasks in a way you'd expect of any large organization: quiet, adequate efficiency. Looking at it with the fresh eyes of a Forgetter, I saw no fundamental difference – except when the horror hit me. It happened when I was looking at some of the slower workers. You expect some to be more relaxed, their rhythms more leisurely, because such doings can't carry on for hours on end without variations in speed. But then I noticed that in one of these "slowed" sections the employees had ceased to work altogether. Some of them sat with mugs of steaming drink. Some perched on others' desks, chatting. Others read magazines. While my mind assembled these impressions, piece by ominious piece, one of the staff looked at his watch, sighed, and put his magazine back in a drawer. As he reached for a file – and the others likewise began to resume their tasks – I at last understood *that the section had taken a break.* And that, simultaneously, meant that a host of other indications which had crawled into my mind now chorused the truth: *work, in Quonia, is CONSCIOUS.* Daily repetitive economic tasks in Quonia are carried out by fully conscious people. They have to do their clerical jobs, their manufacturing jobs, all their routine unskilled or semi-skilled tasks, without the anaesthetic mercy of the work-trance. Hours of their days are taken up in the standard practice of dullness, completely without the benefit of that instinct which has enabled Syoomean economies to run themselves unconsciously for countless ages.

My thoughts leaped this way and that, darting at implications, gasping for explanations. No wonder there's a working class in this terrible country. Millions of human beings have to work and know what they're doing! Yet surely Quonia – which was as ancient as Syoom if not more so – must have had long enough for the unconscious reflexes of the work-trance to evolve, to allow a citizen to switch off during nen's stint. But something in the conditions here must have prevented it. Has isolation, for some reason, kept Quonia socially primitive though technologically advanced? I reel at the thought of the penalty this culture has paid: trillions of man-hours condemned to that mind-withering thing, *routine.* Syoom, you'd better watch out. No telling what such a warped people may attempt upon the more fortunate rest of the world.

Next, I wondered: had I alone observed this macabre disability of the Quonians? Or did other Syoomeans know about it? I was in no position to check. I *might* be in sole possession of this fact. I hoped I had hidden my dismay from Miqua. My "life-hook" really did not give me much protection – the bleeper I'd swallowed might prevent them from putting me away in some dungeon, but was no disincentive to getting rid of me by a plausible "accident". The important thing now was to get out, get away from Quonia, get back home.

I breathed easier when we were out of the factory and onto a moving road once more, sliding through a shopping mall. The city-mountain never slept; throngs were exploring the wares on view.

I asked, "Are *these* people working class?"

"Most of them," Miqua nodded.

"Do they live here always, in the Drennd?"

"Certainly."

"But they can leave if they want to?"

"They don't want to." Seeing the look on my face, she added firmly: "The core dwellers have never seen the sky and don't wish to. The rest sometimes visit other Drennds. My, you do look upset."

We entered a steep escalator tube. Up through the roofs of the last caverns we approached the summit of Drennd Forty-Six. I noticed greater numbers of men and women wearing red-and-black military dress. More forcibly than before I felt the emotional speed which precedes an event-crash, and my mind produced warnings in the form of proverbs: what goes up must come down, the harder the hit the harder the bounce, et cetera. Well, if I could retire with my winnings, I'd be happy ever after. Just for having got out of this place alive, I'd never stop being thankful. And to this end I would keep my mouth shut when Anquit joined our party. I reckoned without Miqua, however.

We were approaching a slab-sided, truncated pyramid about fifty feet tall with heavy, slid-apart doors. Not far above it was, I guessed, the final roof of the Drennd. We were closely under a cavern ceiling which sloped to a scarp summit.

"Anquit," said Miqua suddenly, "is a Semp."

"A what?"

"It's his family name: Semp."

"Oh?" I said politely.

"The clan is ancient and renowned, which is why he's stationed up here. Wouldn't settle for anything lower, you see."

"And *your* clan, Miqua?"

"I am a Veliv," she said with a quiet assurance, prouder than arrogance.

"I wonder," I said and my voice was a trifle tetchy, "if you realize how much the very idea of caste is anathema to Syoomeans."

"I know it. To be fair, you won't find anyone here being given promotion on hereditary grounds alone – the well-born must strive to live up to –"

"There you go," I protested; "even I, who have Forgotten so much, feel sick at that phrase 'well-born'."

"I see. Hatred of heredity is in your blood," she mocked.

"No contradiction in that! Soul-connections, not blood-loyalties, form the cement of our lives!" Why was I so argumentative all of a sudden? What did I hope to gain? Could it be – I goggled at the thought – an outburst of *jealousy*

274

on my part? Miqua had turned her gaze in the direction of Anquit, who now emerged from the pyramid. Extra straight and proud, he no longer looked like the moody young man whom I had first seen as her escort.

He strolled to us and said crisply, "You two have been scolding each other, I see."

Miqua replied, "Taldis was rebuking us Quonians for the evils of our class system."

Anquit stared down at me – he is immensely tall – his eyes glinting like wire-points. "And what about *your* privilege?"

I knew what he meant, and it was all I could do to stop myself hanging my head. Must think. Yes, I asked myself, what about the winning streaks? The life-lines which bear some and not others on their fortunate courses? A fair hit – but how had he known? How could he know what it was like in Syoom?

He's an agent, that's how. I saw the thin, triumphant smile grow on his face.

"The gulf," he continued, "separating *foregrounders* from *backgrounders* in your society – what could be less fair, or more privileged, than that? Before you condemn our aristocracy of blood and rank, remember your aristocracy of fate."

"I'm not used to speaking of it," I admitted. "It's not regarded as a fit subject for polite conversation, where I come from."

"I bet it isn't." He smiled crookedly. "But you're not in Syoom now. This is the summit of Drennd Forty-Six in the land where fate lets you down."

"You're pushing him too far," rebuked Miqua. She turned to me. "What he means is that in our isolated position, in the depths of Fyaym, we would have no chance of survival if we adopted your Syoomean ethos, of trusting that fortune favours the bold. We need…"

"We need authority," said Anquit.

I said: "Well, you've obviously got it." Subservience wasn't going to save me from burial in this Drennd. "Quonia is a despotism, as everyone knows."

Anquit's reply did nothing to refute the point. "Follow me, Taldis. See you later, Miqua."

The amount of light in these upper reaches is parcelled out, in blobs and planes of illumination which slice through the dim air, emphasizing the wider darkness. I might have eluded Anquit if I had wished to break away – but he was my only guide and I could not do without him.

As we strode, he began, in an implacable tone, to confront me with all the old accusations against Syoom.

"None of you like to talk about it, but – your cities can be classed as intelligent organisms. They run your economies for you. Or at least, you run

275

them in symbiosis. Here, we have nothing of that. We build honestly. And we didn't rob a universe for power to build disc-on-stem cities of ultimate metal…"

"You're alluding to something that happened a quarter of a billion days ago."

"Does that excuse it?"

"It excuses me."

He glanced at my face, and as if a guess had been confirmed, he nodded:

"Interesting, that you seem to find it easier than most of your people, to repudiate the guilt that has haunted your culture for so long. I rather like your style, Taldis."

He pushed against the outline of a door, which swung open to reveal a blaze of light and colour. Perspectives had fooled me. I suddenly blinked in a palace-sized volume, before a sumptuously dressed crowd. The sight lifted my mood; gone was the heavy, military atmosphere of the rest of the Drennd's summit. Perhaps the current of fate had deposited me on a brighter shoal.

Anquit continued his verbal fencing with me but now I enjoyed it. In the bright, friendly light of this gathering, as he continued to question me about Syoom, I felt as though we were two students arguing, making a game of political debate. During an interval in this battle of wits I rested against a pillar, wondering where he had suddenly gone. I looked around and glimpsed a spare, green-suited man in the background, talking to Anquit, whose head was bowed. The two of them stood in an alcove, and other folk nearby, in their stances and motions, seemed *careful*, somehow. From their subdued demeanour the truth tore into my mind. I ought to have known it sooner, but a man cannot be the same as his representation on a giant poster. Anquit's interlocutor was none other than Quarin the Hundred and Fourth, Quonant of Quonia.

Anquit's shoulders at that moment slumped, as the ruler looked in my direction and gave a nod.

Hands, round the pillar against which I had been leaning, clasped me on each arm. My laser was drawn from its sheath and I felt the jab of a needle. Then, as my sight darkened and my consciousness faded, I was walking, I knew not where.

8: The Time-Pit

I never learned for sure, what methods they used to determine that my nebulation was "put on". But one may guess.

I can recall movie sequences flashing before my eyes; recordings of historical episodes that were sure to register upon the emotional index of anyone possessing the social residue, the basics of Syoomean culture. Forgetters have it; nebulees don't. My mind must have betrayed me by its positive response.

Anyhow, all that mattered to me was the outcome.

If the results of the test had been otherwise, might they have let me go free? I think it possible. Despite all I had seen and heard inside the Drennd, I would pose no threat if I lacked the background to make sense of what I had learned. Nor – if I really had been a nebulee – could my Syoomean controllers have trusted me as a rational witness.

But a Forgetter is still a functioning citizen. In some ways all the more dangerous due to the freshness of his vision.

I kept turning and staring – round and round my unbelievable prison.

It was without walls, open to the sky. Tall, slowly waving stems, giant grasses and other supple vegetation, grew in clumps or groves from two to four yards high. Their boundaries curved like jigsaw pieces. And as though the pieces had been spread out in preparation for being fitted together, the outward curve of one grove faced the inward curve of another, across gaps carpeted with shorter grass. Numbed, my mental fires damped, I knew that what I faced was no ordinary death.

Time was not on my side.

On the contrary there was too much of it. I had oceans of time in which to contemplate the spacing of the groves. Their repulsion from one another, their buffer zones, offered me the truth that I kept trying to beat down as it reared over the parapet of my conscious mind. Likewise, all the time in the world was allowed me, to recognize the stems that were tipped with white tubes…

The closest analogy to my situation was the penalty which some cities inflict upon their malefactors: that of being marooned. A condemned criminal is taken into the midst of the plains, thousands of miles from anywhere, and there left to walk until nen drops, or meets some swifter end. But even this analogy is weak. *My* enemies' purpose would not be served by that kind of abandonment. If one has swallowed a "life-hook", one must be dumped with greater finality, dumped into the undetectable, and the unreachable.

Of course, "travel into the past" is a self-contradictory notion: the past is the past because it can't be regained. Yet here was I, in a scene from Era One. Even as I watched, one of the white-tube stems began to quest and arch… causing commotion in the facing plant-colony. Out peeped the yellow/black insectoid face of a *revestru*, to be immediately zapped by a laser bolt from the stem of the *wonarr*… All of this could have come from one of the documentaries I had watched on board *Knorol*, except that it was all around me and I smelled the burning when the bolt struck. My reflexes made me dive to the ground. I cowered, taking what grass cover I could, just as my remote ancestors must have done. Whatever protest my intellect might make, my body knew where I was. Henceforth I must inhabit this most distant of human eras, in which new-born Man, recently emerged from the pre-biotic lake of Dmara, was spreading gingerly through the still-forested plains amid deadly crossfire from the wars of more powerful creatures.

Yet something in me continued to wail, *I don't, can't, will not believe this.* And sure enough, after hours of dodging and crawling and aimless circling, I sensed a ripple around me like that of a curtain that's stirred in a breeze, the scene around me wavered, and as it began to fade, a rival scene appeared, becoming more solid, eclipsing the other.

The sky above me shrank to a restricted circle, which told me that I was not, after all, on the surface of the world, but rather at the bottom of a gigantic pit.

It was a stone pit, perhaps a hundred yards across, a hundred and fifty yards deep. I suppose there is no way to prove that the stone wall encircling me was that of a pit and not a tower, but I was certain, nonetheless. The dankness of the walls, the coldness of the floor, the fact that there were no doors, a sense of depth voiced by all my faculties, told me that the place had been dug rather than built.

Well, anyhow, I thought, now I could forget the nonsense about time travel. The plain dreary fact was that the Quonians had decided to keep me incarcerated in some drastic way which blocked the "life-hook" signal… or maybe they had simply made up their minds to defy Syoom.

But then, why the Era One illusion? And why had it now gone away? Perhaps I ought to take comfort from the fact that they were playing games with me. Better than abandonment in the oblivion of a vanished epoch…

Or was it? As I wandered around the granite walls in vain search for a way out, I began to regret the departure of the Era One scene. After all, if that had been real, I would be free to roam, perhaps find a few folk of my own kind alive in that long-lost age. Whereas in this pit I was doomed. The stone walls could not even be scratched.

More hours passed. I imagined hunger and thirst worsening steadily, though as yet I felt neither. I lay down and put my hands behind my head. If need be, I would die gazing at the sky. Death, here, I reminded myself, would only be the end of my first life. Still more hours passed with me in this resigned position, daydreaming, reviewing my life, wondering how I might have done better. The drift of thoughts came to an end when at last I saw something move.

Pale, fluttering, the object appeared against the sky and swayed downward like a falling leaf. Movement, change, life! I sprang up, supple and energized as though I had not been lying down for hours. One new thing had made all the difference. It landed close. A sheet of paper. A missive! I seized it and read:

Anquit Semp to Taldis Norkoten, greetings.

I regret what has been done to you. This, I dare say, will surprise you; but as a master of my craft, I recognize a kindred spirit.

In fact I went so far as to petition the Quonant for clemency in your case – alas, in vain. He was not impressed with my argument, which was that I, determined as I am to rise to the top in my profession, would benefit from the existence of an opponent worthy of my skills, and that this enhancement of my capability would be of benefit to Quonia. A cogent point, I should have thought, but His Luminosity dismissed my petition as "arrogant", so that is the end of the matter. The most he would concede, was that I might send this message after you. Other than that – well, one does not argue with the Quonant. And yet, when I think of the training I could have had – that we both might have had, pitted against each other – I sincerely regret your loss.

Miqua, by the way, had nothing to do with unmasking you. It was I who researched the link with the Vemorth Stazel. Once you were subjected to our tests, the verdict was inevitable.

One thing I can do, to ease your last hours. I can accord you the respect due to one who has the courage to face the truth... I can do this by telling you that truth.

You will have notice the shift in scene around you, between reality and illusion. What has been done to you is of such a nature that the human brain cannot accept it for long without rebelling, concocting alternative, imaginary sense-data.

These imaginary data retain a figurative link with reality. In other words, what your brain does is to build up an allegorical picture of how things are. A refuge in the form of metaphor, where your mind can shy from the literal truth.

For instance you may well be under the impression, at this moment, that you are in a deep stone-lined pit. As a matter of fact you aren't, in any literal sense. But, metaphorically, you can be said to be at the "bottom of a pit" of Time.

Literally, you have been sent back in Time to Era One.
You probably can't believe this –

Indeed, my mind gave another heave of rejection as I did my best to regurgitate the whole idea of this monstrous exile. A few minutes before, I had preferred it, theoretically, as the better alternative, but now the contradiction, the factual impossibility of time travel, together with a suspicion that it was true, combined to create an offence against reality that made my soul sick. Head swimming, I lurched towards the stone wall that seemed to encircle me. I tottered against it and felt its hardness, as real as could be, hard and real and yet I had seen it come and I knew I might equally see it go, dissolve, vanish. Suspended in my mental darkness, I read on:

Travel into the past, ordinarily, is of course impossible. It would mean denial of cause and effect.

However it has been discovered that a few "holes" or "pits" of isolation exist, or have existed, in which the chains of cause and effect are self-contained, possessing no links to the rest of the plenum. You can travel back into those pockets without making ripples of change beyond them. I suppose these exceptions are reasonable, given the laws of chance.

To be honest, we Quonians probably could not have discovered such "pockets" for ourselves, or the means to access them; we had help from the records of previous races. That is by the way. We deserve credit for the way we took advantage of the information which came to us.

To sum up: you are in Era One, but chance will decree – has decreed – that your presence there will not affect subsequent history. Any waves you may make will remain confined within the limitations of causality – the real "walls" of the metaphorical "pit" in which you must live out the rest of your days.

Even as I read those words, the paper I held was no longer a paper, it was an engraved foil, and I let it drop from my fingers as the scene around me likewise metamorphosed. The walls of stone ran like sloshings of wet paint and collapsed into a different identity: I was back among the waving groves, the giant stems, of the infinite Era One grasslands. In my left hand I held a pod from a water-bearing plant, from which, I now realized, I had been sipping on and off, for hours. That was why I had not felt the slightest twinge of thirst. Here was the truth, here was where I had been all the time. I really had been abandoned in Era One, and not only that – I was in a special dead-end "pocket" of Era One. No matter how long I survived here, no matter what I did here, I would not affect the future at all.

This strongly suggested that I was doomed not to find any companionship of my own species.

Futility enclosed me, overwhelmed me. I stooped and picked up the foil I had dropped. The last words on the note were my last link with humanity:

Though you yourself cannot be part of history any more, look at it this way: your defeat has become part of my history. I shall not forget.
Respectfully yours,
Anquit Semp
Intelligence Control, Nullapz HQ

Rather than give way to rage at the grandiloquence of the Quonian, I tried to take his words at their face value. Some day he would drop a hint to my own people, about what had become of me; and so I could live on in their memory. That was something to be thankful for.

Besides, it would be no use, it would be worse than useless, for me to mutter "pompous hypocrite" when I thought of Anquit Semp. The letter I held in my hand was my infinitely precious sole remaining link with my home time. I must clutch at whatever good there was in it. So in my mind I saluted the writer, as an honourable enemy. Arguably, he was that. I reserved more anger for Tronnd Sast, Syoomean Ambassador to Quonia. That stuffed cloak had been happy to let me wander as an expendable probe... with the result that I must moulder here.

Did I believe it, though? Was I really doomed? Granted that I was in Era One, must it follow that I had to be in some extra-causal 'Pit', in solitary confinement, out of the running as regards cause and effect? What could stop me wandering, searching, finding other people and thus joining in with the primitive human society of the Hydrogen Era? Why should I not acquire a family and become an ancestor of the future generations of Man?

The answer surrounded me: the sheer size of the forest, the immensity of the world, the inevitable paucity of human life. Any number of lethal fates might await me as I wandered, and soon one or another of them would put paid to any search for company, and the Time-Pit's wall in the form of death would knock against me.

Even as I thought this, my brain re-constructed the metaphor –

The grassy groves disappeared once more and my eyes once more told me that I languished within the circular wall of the Pit. I muttered, "The dungeon again." I let out a bitter laugh. The place might as well wear this guise. It was the most appropriate. I seemed to rest, lying on the stone floor once again, though doubtless – since I continued to feel nourished – in reality I went about in the grasslands and forests drinking and nibbling now and then. No matter what my eyes told me, no matter what I seemed to touch, I was still really in the open wilderness.

As for what might happen if a dangerous creature appeared while I slumped in metaphor-vision mode, I hoped I could switch back quickly enough to deal with it, but after all, did it matter much, one way or the other? My usual instinct for survival was now sapped by futility. Listlessly, I endured the sight of the pit – that scene which my brain had constructed as a picture of the truth. Further dead hours passed.

Change came with unexpected violence.

It announced itself with a grating, thrumming noise. The ground shook and cracks began to appear on the wall a yard or so up from the floor of the pit. Flakes of stone fell; the crumbling accelerated; the din increased. I retreated, holding my breath as pulverized rock billowed towards me; I held up my forearms in front of my face as I backed against the wall that was opposite from the disturbance.

The din subsided to a growl, whereupon I risked a look. The dust was settling, to reveal the bulky snout of a tunnelling machine. Its corkscrew *iedleis* drill was slowing to a stop. In the cabin to its rear a door opened.

Ambassador Tronnd leaned out and beckoned. "Get in here, fast!" I darted forward and scrambled into the seat behind Tronnd. All this might be illusion – the appearance of a rescuer could well denote my brain's welcome of death itself, the ultimate rescue, the prelude to my next life. On the other hand, Tronnd would be an odd symbol for this... increasingly I suspected that the rescue was real. But its apparatus, of course, could not be what it seemed to be.

"What," I asked, "are we actually doing?"

"Squandering the resouorces of our section," snapped Tronnd morosely, "to get your out of here. All covers blown," he added as he jabbed a switch to reverse the motor. He raised his voice as the tunneller's roar increased. "Techniques revealed, that cannot be used again," he fumed as the machine backed out the way it had come.

In my overflowing gratitude, I did not mind that he liked me less than ever; I was prepared to view him as the most wonderful Ambassador in all of history. "Put your mind at rest – I'm worth it," I grinned at him.

"Your boss seems to think so anyway," he grumbled on. We were both bent forward as though we were retching over a bowl as the tunneller reversed at almost forty-five degrees. I could laugh at the discomfort, especially as I didn't believe in any of it – that's to say, I was sure that my sensations weren't 'literal'. Some inter-dimensional thing, I assumed, is sucking us back to the future, and this is how we are forced to picture it. I said as much to Tronnd, adding, "As to how it's *really* being done –"

"Restrain your curiosity," he advised.

I ebulliently went on, "Two adjacent Time-Pits, maybe, and some kind of energy transfer between them to weaken both, so as to 'lift' us back to our home 'present'…"

Trondd twisted round in his seat. His face glared up into mine. I realized I was in for a telling-off and I didn't mind. Let him spout, I thought. Whatever he might say – in resentment of the sacrifices he'd had to make to get me out – I was still so grateful for being freed, that nothing could throw a shadow over this occasion. Here goes, I thought as his mouth gleamed open, but the words he bit out were not at all of the sort I expected to hear.

"In my youth, I, also, was a Forgetter."

"Ah – oh?" I said.

"Astonished?" His bare-toothed smile was grim.

"I confess it, if you like: yes, I'm astonished."

"Not that I was ever a client of the Vemorth Stazel. No volunteer, I. *My* amnesia came naturally – as a result of an accident."

I nodded, listening sympathetically. He continued:

"The amnesia took a chunk out of my life, so as you may imagine, it irks me to see anybody *voluntarily* undergo that horrid waste of life. Sick, I call it. Must be something very wrong with anyone who allows that to be done to him."

"Let's hope," I soothed, "that two wrongs make a right."

[Here ends the extract from the Journal of Taldis Norkoten.]

9: Home

The sheer delight of being alive and free to go home is by far the greatest reward for an agent upon the successful completion of an assignment. And next to that in importance, Taldis reflected, comes the glow of professional satisfaction.

Around these two main blessings cluster a host of minor warmths.

Such as the chance to sit back and relax in what, at other times, was a very uneasy chair...

"Looking back," mused Taldis, swivelling idly in front of Director Woth, "I see that Forgetting is a more dangerous pastime than even I realised. Agents shouldn't need to be rescued."

"No," agreed Woth with pungent emphasis. "And those who do need it, certainly can't claim the credit for pulling through."

Taldis continued in his innocent tone, "I don't think the procedure should be repeated in the foreseeable future."

"You can rest assured on that score. The Quonians are now wise to the Vemorth Stazel. Question is: was it worth it?"

"Sir, *you* should tell *me*."

"But I'm asking you what you think. Your discovery of the enemy's weakness – their lack of a work-trance –"

"Yes, on this occasion, the results were worth it." Taldis chose his words carefully, appreciating the luxury of being allowed to voice them. Give Woth his due, he always allowed his agents to supplement their reports with a personal interview. "I'm including some of those aspects which, in retrospect, I like least."

"Such as?" Woth's eyes flicked momentarily to the recording device which was noting Taldis' every word and voice-printing his tone for later analysis.

"My delusions of destiny, of invulnerability even. Part of the time I truly felt borne upon some actual physical current. This 'winning streak' you might say is sustained by a field of force which in principle could be verified scientifically."

He shot a meaningful look at the Director. In his presence one did not quite dare to use the dirty word *foregrounder*.

Woth smiled, "I am not so worried about *that*, especially as I know of a more mundane reason for your survival. I had a communication from my opposite number, Anquit Semp."

Taldis stared. Then, slowly, he began to laugh.

"Don't tell me – he claims to have tipped off Tronnd as to where I was."

"Precisely."

"The humbug!" said Taldis in admiration. "All that stuff in his letter about how he had no choice but to let me lie in the Pit forever..."

"...Was for the benefit of his boss, the Quonant. To make sure that although the Quonian government may guess that *someone* on their side leaked your location, Anquit will be the last person they suspect."

"And yet, when you come to think of it, the move could have been justified on their terms."

"Of course it could – for look at the result! Anquit lets Tronnd know where you are, whereupon we have to rescue you, using up all the resources and exhausting all the tricks of our embassy in Nullapz. The embassy itself departs in ignominy as we smuggle you away... Not a bad bargain, from their point of view! In fact I shouldn't be at all surprised if, some time after the commotion attending your escape has died down, Anquit drops the word to his own side that it was his idea – it might boost his standing, even though it cost them two secrets: their lack of a work-trance, and the existence of the Time-Pits."

"May I ask, about the Time-Pits…"

"No, you may not."

Taldis changed tack. "The 'life-hook' I swallowed: I want it taken out, please."

"Already done. In your sleep. You might as well not have had it, for all the use it was."

So that was that. Stretched in his chair, Taldis enjoyed freedom to the full. "I have one more insight to report, sir; though I doubt if you will believe me."

"Go on," said Woth impassively.

"Simply this: *our culture really is superior to that of the Quonians.* I can say this with all the objectivity of a Forgetter: our freedom is better, stronger, than their despotism – and therefore we can afford to fight clean. Leave the dirty tricks to them – that's my official recommendation." He knew his speech would be of no use but he was glad to have uttered it anyway.

"Forgetter," said Woth and stood up from his desk, "it is time you went home and started remembering."

Taldis stood up likewise. "The world spirit agrees," he insisted, "that we are stronger than Quonia."

"What *are* you talking about?"

"Try drawing a map of Quonia sometime, sir. You won't be able to, it's too shifty. The World Spirit is on their side – protecting their secrets –"

"Oh, and the reason being?" Woth raised his brows in amusement, as he ushered his agent towards the door.

"Because it's always on the weaker side. Lest we crawling humans combine and become too strong. So we never will. Pest control, you see. The world doesn't like its biosphere to get too uppity…"

He didn't finish because Woth burst into laughter. "I get it, you want a rise in salary for having bested the World Spirit! Good ploy, Taldis. Now be off, I have work to do."

The debrief over, Taldis trod the walkways of Vyanth, heading for home. He had not yet called in person, he had just left a message to say he was coming back; now the real return could not be put off any longer.

Better not think too much: just do it.

The sounds around him, the traffic's moderate hum, the warning beeps of hover-drays and skimmers, faded from his mind, and by the time he stepped up to his own front door he experienced an absolute white silence, a parching of all thought-streams. He went in and sought the lounge. There she was.

Silence? No. The singing in his ears as he approached her took precedence over all other thoughts, including the unhelpful one that he was still her husband. Marriage, his brain gabbled, is memory. He had allowed their life together to be wiped out. Really he had no business here.

But he kept walking forward.

Athness said stiffly, "Hello." She sounded puzzled.

The way she was looking at him, it was as if she, not he, had lost all memory.

Constraint ruled. Formality enclosed them like a dull cloud, but some defiant side of him went on singing in the cloud, and compelled him to place his hands on her shoulders.

Her eyes widened as he bent forward to kiss her. She did not resist, but neither did she respond. She stood like a statue.

For him, then, the inner singing stopped. He concluded that the right thing to do was to give up and walk away. But as he was about to turn, he heard her say in a tone of stupid wonder:

"Taldis! What has happened to you?"

"You know perfectly well..."

But she was still looking at him in dumbfoundment. Yet the Director had assured him, she had been told. She must know about the Forgetting.

"I am the same man," he asserted, his heart thumping. "You know that all they did to me was..."

"Clear out the rubbish," she said, breaking into a smile. "I often wanted to do that myself. It seems the Vemorth Stazel saved me the effort."

"Uh? Look, I'm sorry that I..."

"Shush, I believe you," she whispered, putting her arms around his neck at last. "Forget it."

Actinium Era:

Greenery

1: The Welcome

Over the cork-textured plain, the crawler *Uxtal* was advancing at five miles per hour, with its hold full of cargo and its nomadic family crew.

It wobbled, inevitably, as the vehicle's fortified superstructure, ten yards above the ground, swayed in the winds which blow eternally across the expanses of the giant planet Ooranye.

The three figures standing on the top deck kept their balance with unconscious skill. The powerful gusts frequently changed direction, as if deliberately seeking to dislodge the riders. Father and son, however, had been born on the plains, and the third figure, the new daughter-in-law, was likewise an experienced wayfarer. In their own eyes the Monray family were a component of the landscape.

Miokk Monray was in the prime of life, about 12,300 Uranian days old, while his son Gyan and Gyan's wife Hevad were half his age. The black-bearded Miokk had the greyer skin, the more confident jaw, the slower, more decisive speech; Gyan, clean-shaven, had more the look of a poet or philosopher, combined with spurts of excited speech whenever his pent-up ideas gushed forth. He had the kind of courage which his father would never need: that of the lone revolutionary, perhaps the martyr.

Heedless of this ideological time-bomb Miokk overflowed with pride as he contemplated how well the youngsters had followed in his footsteps; or say, in Hevad's case, the footsteps of tradition, which requires all young Uranians, whatever their station in life, to become adept at wilderness survival. At first he had feared that the girl might not fit into her new family's mode of life. She came from Linnt, and the big cities bred some stay-at-home types. Nevertheless he had trusted that every Uranian, even the most urban, must sometime in nen's life feel duty bound to become a Wayfarer, risking nen's life to feed data into the statistical maws of the cartographers of Syoom. In the case of Hevad, his trust had turned out well-founded.

Out of the corner of his eye Miokk assessed her for the twentieth time. The family could feel safely proud at the addition of a regal beauty with pale gold hair and gentle manner, a little reserved yet friendly to all; calm, capable, without the creative demons of discontent and personal ambition. Miokk repressed a sigh, which sprang from no particular cause, a vague reaction to life's inherent melancholy, because the world was so large and people so small… He brought back his attention to what he was saying to his son:

"Just as well you didn't seek my opinion prior to that exploit, Gyan. I would have told you that you'd never do it. Yet here you are. Seems we have a navigational genius in the family."

The younger man, delighted at having won such praise from his father, could not repress a grin, though he managed a modest reply, "I had to justify the time I'd spent studying the subject."

"Well, you're undeniably pleased with yourself – with reason, I admit."

The facts were creditable. Gyan and Hevad had set out during *pmetn*, the starry morning twilight. After skimming for over two thousand miles, they had sighted *Uxtal* almost on the stroke of ayshine, that is, when the air, at its brightest, conveniently revealed the Crawler from many miles away. Indeed, a remarkable feat of navigation and timing. All that Gyan had had to help him fix the position and direction of *Uxtal* was information ten days old, relayed from a passing merchant convoy. (The Crawler emitted no homing signal, lest it attract foe as well as friend. For similar reasons, ordinary radio was used sparingly out on the plains.)

In other words without any up-to-date communications link Gyan had achieved rendezvous with a moving target after a ten-hour journey by skimmer. Impressed by this, Miokk felt encouraged to involve his son more closely in the family business henceforth.

So he began to discuss the current state of his affairs, confident that this was a strategic move in life's endless contest of gain versus loss. He summarised the items of cargo currently in *Uxtal*'s hold (dried meats, seeds and nuts, some rare weeds and some Tungsten Era glass books), and listed the towns and cities to which they were destined.

Finally he got round to a more immediate topic:

"I'm particularly glad to have you back on board, Gyan, not only because of the splendid recruit you have brought us" (with a bow to Hevad), "but also due to *that*," and he jerked his head at the forward-left horizon.

A thin line stretched across that hazy limit. It was, they knew, a structure, towards which *Uxtal* was crawling; an embankment without visible end, receding in both directions till it vanished into apparent infinity.

Without any doubt it had to be part of the ancient monoline network of Syoom. "Must be the Vlamanor-Yoon," remarked Hevad. No one disagreed.

Seemingly immune to the ravages of time, the mighty Zinc Era network had left Syoom criss-crossed with embankments on which the empty rails still ran. Every few thousand miles, wayfarers were bound to cross one of these artificial ridges. On well-frequented routes this did not matter at all; however, grim experience had taught that any stretch of embankment which had not been visited for a thousand days or so must be approached gingerly. Preferably, a dray-master, raft-pilot or Crawler captain should send scouts ahead to peer cautiously over the rim, before any attempt to get over with the main vehicle. And the more lasers on one's side the better.

"Yes," decided Miokk, "it must be the Vlamanor-Yoon. But I see no ramp." No ramp, therefore no crossing. There was no way in which *Uxtal* could scale a sixty-degree slope. Again he took a telescope from his cloak-pouch. "Still don't see it... We'll scout this evening. After supper we can choose whether to go left or right."

Hevad then performed an inexplicable, astonishing act. With the index finger of her right hand she pointed straight up into the air and said, "Maybe his girlfriend," and she tossed her head at Gyan, "will tell us which way to go."

Miokk blinked. Had he heard right? Bafflement snuffed any immediate response; he postponed the question.

Dinner that evening was held in *Uxtal*'s "stateroom", a grandiloquent term for the family's little haven of luxury, six yards by eight, lined with wood and metal banding, and lit by spherical corner lamps. It was a snug cave of comfort within a structure forever on the move. The shutters had been thrown back from the windows. The vehicle's side-mirrors, moreover, had been extended so that the view ahead, including the approaching embankment, remained constantly visible to the diners.

Miokk Monray did not seriously consider any option other than to accept the challenge of the crossing. Uranian culture and etiquette demanded the meeting of challenges; the good of Syoom, the very definition of civilization required that those on the spot should venture forward. You had to dare to become a statistic, just one more in the eternal compilation of losses and gains, of deaths and survivals, without which the cartographers of Syoom could not do their work. The experience of hundreds of millions of days had shown that no other outlook was viable in the perpetual haze of distance and mystery on the enormous world, home not only to Man but to rival intelligences equally formidable. In this open-ended environment none but the mindless, statistical approach – percentages of safe arrivals, draughted onto maps as safety contours – might give quantity and shape to the unknowable, allowing humanity a chance.

Miokk knew enough history to realize that, from time to time, a different way had been tried. This other way was the attempt to *understand* the world. Useless foolishness. Failure was almost certain, and success, even if attained, was too dearly bought. A man who understood Ooranye was made vulnerable by his understanding. As the old saying went: if you get wise to the world, the world will get wise to you.

So, untroubled by the danger they must face at close of day, the Monray family chatted happily over their bowls. Zamena, the wife and mother, presided while the two younger children, Plenndwa and Traru, who had helped set out the banquet with artistic care, now sat listening to their elders' plans. The children had decided to adore Hevad; they were delighted with her willingness to share their nomadic life – she was a treat which enlarged their universe.

"Of course," Miokk had said to the newlyweds, "you will wish to purchase your own vehicle as soon as you can, but meanwhile there's room for you on *Uxtal.*"

"Certainly," Gyan had replied, "we'll be happy to stay on *Uxtal* until we get rich or until Hevad yearns for city life again –"

She demanded, "What makes you think I might do that?"

"It's in your blood. And maybe a bit of it in my head, too, by now. I've talked to Father this way before. He's heard me say, often enough, that some day I shall take service under Ierax's Noad. Or maybe, Linnt's Noad."

"Or how about," ventured Miokk Monray, "the Noad of Noads?"

It was said almost slyly. Gyan studied his father's face to gauge the seriousness of this remark.

"Yes, in fact I did go to Skyyon some few hundred days ago. To tell the truth, I felt so small there –" He chuckled, deprecatingly.

The older man remarked to Hevad, "Your husband is not usually as humble as this. I hope he is not in need of medical attention."

"Don't worry," said the girl, "I am sure he's simply waiting for the chance to make the Skyyonians sit up and listen."

The silent Zamena was relieved at the general laugh which followed. She doubted the wisdom of the way Miokk teased their boy. One day Gyan might really shoot off to measure himself against the world in some drastic manner – unless Hevad's common sense could curb his restlessness. Thank goodness the girl seemed pleased with her new home.

Hevad was saying, "I like this slow, comfortable crawl... here you've got

290

all the advantages of a gradual change of scene, plus those of a solid home. Five miles per hour is just right for me. And the engine's so powerful, you could add rooms to the vehicle, enlarge it plenty and it would still go... in fact you could attach more engines until you ended up with a moving city..."

"Don't talk about living in cities – even moving ones – to Father," advised Gyan.

"No, let her speculate," Miokk intervened. "She's the cement we need."

"Cement!" marvelled Gyan. "Pile on the flattery!"

"The *myxe* has flowed too freely," reproved Zamena. Actually, though, the bottle was still three-quarters full. They were being careful. All of them remembered the crossing which loomed mere hours ahead...

"'Cement' is maybe a lucky nickname," Hevad reassured them, "since we are about to attack a wall."

Nobody responded. Hevad looked around. "Do I hear silence?"

Miokk Monray said quietly, "Don't worry. We approve your attitude. We were simply uncertain as to how much you understood."

"City-dwellers know how to share risks, quite as well as you do, I can promise that."

"Good." Miokk slapped the table and formally ended the meal with a welcoming speech for the new family member. Then he remembered he had meant to ask her the meaning of her cryptic allusion to Gyan's up-in-the-sky "girl-friend". When he could, he would put the question privately.

2: Battle at the Crossing

Uxtal lumbered on hour after hour. The Crawler left no trail; its brief "wake" – the impress of its tracks in the corky, granular *gralm* which carpeted the plains – sprang back elastically to level within a couple of minutes.

The loneliness and the emptiness of the Uranian plains is indeed oceanic, but just as a sea has islands, so does one meet with interruptions in the wilderness of Ooranye. It was the middle of the eighteenth hour of the thirty-hour day and the monorail embankment was now a mere furlong distant.

Habitually during the eighteenth hour the family would gather on deck, taking the air at the beginning of evenshine. But not this day.

Everyone on *Uxtal* had retreated inside the vehicle. The windows were shuttered. Through forward slits, Miokk and Gyan scrutinised the ridge ahead.

The shape and dimensions of the embankment were standard. Height, seven yards; slope, sixty degrees; summit width, four yards. As for the length, they knew it to be about five thousand miles. What they did not know for sure, was whether they were due to strike it to the right or to the left of the ramp by which they must seek to cross.

The decision was left to Miokk, as he stood on the tiny command platform. He spun the helm clockwise; *Uxtal*'s front tracks veered to the right. Presently the great machine was crawling parallel to the embankment and about a hundred yards from it.

"I think we can dispense with the shutters," he called out.

Gyan, who had been waiting in the doorway, was glad to obey. With clear windows once more, the crew peered forward into the beige evening light which shimmered upon the hard-pack surface of the ridge to their left. Up ahead a mile or so, lay what appeared to be a dark, woolly lump. Closer, it was revealed as a dense grove.

The thorny black *katora*, growing close to the embankment, reared its spikes to a twenty-foot height. Gyan stirred and said, "I reckon the ramp may be just beyond that grove."

"It's often the way."

"Shall I reconnoitre?"

"*We* shall. Remember our rule – always scout in pairs. Call Zamena to take the wheel. While she's about it, she can teach the controls to Hevad."

From racks on *Uxtal*'s sides, Gyan and his father unclipped the canoe-shaped fliers. Bestriding them, the two scouts skimmed ahead of the Crawler. There was no question of going at full speed or of rising to the six-yard "ceiling", the skimmer's maximum altitude. On the contrary they hugged the ground. A mere yard above the gralm, they approached the grove at one-eighth speed.

Katora, in their long senescence, are a harmless plant species, but other, more dangerous relatives of theirs might well inhabit the grove. The sides of an embankment were apt to become the resting place for spores blown thousands of miles… Miokk, not altogether happily, allowed his son to outdistance him, for he knew that Gyan was the botanical expert.

Relief came as he heard the boy yell: "Look – I was right!"

Miokk floated over to where Gyan hovered on the far side of the grove. There, a ramp jutted at right angles from the embankment. It led up to the summit by a thirty-degree slope – a gradient which *Uxtal* could manage.

Making botanical conversation, Miokk remarked: "Quite likely, this is why the katora took root where it did – the ramp must have stopped the drifting spore." A banal statement of the obvious, a polite attempt to show interest in a subject which enthused his son. And yet, surprisingly, the youngster objected:

"No! That's not it – can't be."

"What do you mean, 'can't'?"

"I recognize this place now. Didn't we go past it just over a thousand days ago? And the grove wasn't there then, at all. And..."

"And katora take millions of days to grow from spores. All right. But are you sure we took this ramp, last time? Are you sure we didn't take the next one along?"

Gyan shook his head. Meanwhile his father edged back from both embankment and ramp. Sighting the gradually approaching Crawler, he waved to indicate that he and his fellow scout were safe. Gyan continued grumbling, "Why ever build these monorails anyway? And if they had to be built, why trouble to raise them on these enormous embankments which must have taken man-eras to build? The rails could have been laid along the ground."

The truth flashed upon Miokk. He ought to have guessed it before.

It was more than just the old habit of youth, of criticising their culture as if from an outside point of view.

"You've been talking to the Terrans."

"Yes," admitted Gyan proudly.

"I'm sure it must be a fascinating experience," said Miokk.

Nettled by this polite irony, Gyan boasted on: "I have been accredited to talk with a Professor Linda Cummings, who has been doing her stint in orbit for the past fifty days. I feel I know her quite well."

Miokk felt relieved that matters were no worse.

It was, after all, supposed to be an honour to be chosen as informant by the mysterious orbiting beings from the Sunward planet. Ever since First Contact a few lifetimes ago, the enigmatic Terrans – from a world so close to the Sun's glare that it was hardly visible to Uranian astronomers – had given scope for endless speculation, but they aroused no significant resentments, and hardly any fears, while their eagerness for knowledge of Uranian history and life was taken by and large as a compliment. The situation, while puzzling, would continue to be acceptable so long as the visitors remained content to study Ooranye from orbit, refusing all invitations to land, and readily communicating in Ooranye's own languages. While contact with an alien point of view might disturb some young minds, Gyan (in his father's opinion) possessed a sufficiently robust intelligence to avoid being led astray.

He simply needed (like all chirpy youngsters) an occasional grounding in common sense.

"About the monorails, Gyan. Bear in mind that they were built in the Zinc Era. The people of that age *knew* they had thirty million days to play around in; they could afford such a project. And if it's affordable, it does make sense: the height of the embankments give the drivers of the *vleps* a good defensive vantage. So the hugeness of it all is a helpful, practical advantage. And besides, the builders also hankered after glory..." It went without saying, Miokk assumed, that glory was a practical thing.

Gyan, however, turned his face away when the word was pronounced.

Without deigning to reply he set his skimmer in motion and veered it round to the ramp's other side...

Miokk skimmed over to join him and they silently contemplated the few weeds which nestled there between embankment and ramp: far smaller plants, hardly noticeable compared to the giant katora of the near side.

"Ha!" Gyan pointed downwards, at a short post stuck in the gralm and bearing a notice:

Veann passed this way
11,151,596 Ac
No disturbance
Harlei Breal

Miokk, who found it only mildly interesting, sensed his son's far greater interest. One way to discover the reason was to bait the lad with an obtuse remark:

"Good old Harlei; this is the first I've heard of him since the last trade fair at Pjourth..."

"Now," interrupted Gyan through clenched teeth.

His father looked blank.

"'Now' what?"

"Now we can stop pussyfooting around. Er- sorry," snickered Gyan. "Earth slang."

"Well, tell me what it means."

"Messing about, I suppose. Now, though, we shall be able to cross without hesitation." Jerking his skimmer into motion once more, Gyan flew onto the ramp itself.

A crowd of insights passed through Miokk's mind as his son raced towards the summit of the ridge.

Harlei Breal, according to the notice, had passed this way a mere 390 days ago. Gyan was influenced by Terran ideas and had probably picked up the quaint Terran belief that Nature was law-abiding, hence would not believe that any weed could grow dangerous in 390 days.

Never in his life had Miokk moved so swiftly. His normal unhurried manner dropped away like a discarded cloak. He yanked his own skimmer into an angle of ascent which allowed him to cut into the ramp from the side. This was the only way to narrow Gyan's lead. To fill one's lungs and bellow a warning would do no good, Miokk knew; in fact it would steepen the odds against them, for it would use up energy better spent in drawing one's laser –

Almost they reached the top together; almost as one, they saw beyond. As the sweep of the further plain met their eyes, so also did the rising clawlike leaves of a colossal *narp*, the deadliest weed to be found on the plains – the giant that could wait for lifetimes to perform its strike. And its root system, during the past few hours, must have heard *Uxtal*'s approach.

Intelligently, during that wait, the thing had drooped its leaves, but now the time for concealment was over and its spear-like points and jewel-tipped stems stretched abruptly higher than the ridge's summit as the narp fired first at Gyan.

Miokk was never afterwards sure whether his own shot helped to deflect the vegetable laser's aim. Perhaps indeed he could take credit for that, or perhaps Gyan with residual common sense shied at the last moment so that the dazzling bolt merely singed him as it hummed past.

A second shot from the plant impacted the bow compartment of Miokk's skimmer and an instant later his half-blinded eye glimpsed an array of stems limbering up in what seemed like slow motion. He then understood, that what he and Gyan had experienced so far would be insignificant in comparison with the imminent volley.

The two men reacted in the only way that could save their lives. They each cut the power of their skimmers. It meant abandoning control, which in its way was a harder thing for a skilled rider to do than to face death. However, the alternative – to make a controlled evasive turn – required time which was not available. Their one chance was for man and vehicle to *fall* – to tumble helplessly back to safety on their own side of the sheltering ridge. Luck was with them and they escaped injury, sliding to the ridge's base. Gyan slumped in his skimmer; Miokk rolled out of his, and stretched on the loam. Tough, fit Uranian bodies meant no bones broken, but they had to wait for their eyesight to recover.

Their muscles relaxed but their thoughts continued to slosh about like liquid in a suddenly stilled container.

"You idiot," Miokk finally growled.

"'Idiot', no; just another statistic," gasped Gyan.

A long pause.

"The statistics of Syoom," grated Miokk wearily, "aren't based upon cloud-brained actions."

"Really?" said Gyan.

"I'd rather you weren't insolent, son."

"I'd rather you didn't call me a cloud-brain, Father," retorted Gyan with ego unbruised, sure of his ground. "Common sense told me that there should not have been a narp here. The thing had no business growing from spore to ten-yard monster within 390 days."

"Spare me your Terran logic," sighed Miokk. "Your Professor Cummings wouldn't last a day down here."

Gyan laughed shortly. "Well put, Father. But while you can growl in your beard all you like, *I* want something more. *I want to understand.*"

"But you also, I presume, want to live to be old?"

"Yes, if –"

"Then you'd better *understand* what the Terrans don't get – that Nature can cheat."

"Doesn't make sense, what you're saying." Gyan's exasperated tone became something of a wail.

"Doesn't have to make sense. All it has to do, is to happen." It was Miokk's turn to feel he had won his point. He waited for comment. None came. After a minute he added gently, "Our ancestors cheated too, remember."

"Uh?" said Gyan.

"Think," his father nudged. "Why does Syoom possess its twenty-five great cities, after all?"

No need to answer that one out loud. Everyone could dig into the guilty cultural memory of the Phosphorus Era. It was not possible to forget that the men of that time had looted another dimension of its power. Stolen power was what had enabled them to build the disc-on-stem platforms of ultimate metal which adorned Syoom; they could never have done it otherwise.

Miokk finished: "Come on, Gyan, save the revolution for another day. We meanwhile have to get *Uxtal* across the embankment and we won't do it without a fight."

The two men got back to their feet. They waved to Zamena, who by now was manoeuvring the Crawler around the katora grove. She must be guessing some of what had happened; the narp's laser bolts must have been visible for miles.

Some distance further on she brought the vehicle to a halt, and the hold doors opened. Miokk on his crippled skimmer, and Gyan on his undamaged one, floated in through the opening.

Zamena yelled over her shoulder, "Either of you hurt?"

"Not a bit!" shouted Miokk. "Vital knowledge gained at expense of one dent in skimmer bow plus one fatherly lecture on philosophy of survival."

The family gathered in the control cabin to discuss the next move.

Gyan spoke: "I wonder, do we *have* to fight our way over? Couldn't we detour? Find the next ramp along?"

Puzzled anew by the erractic workings of his son's mind – impetuous one moment, ultra-cautious the next – Miokk said evenly, "But that would just leave the narp as a problem for the next people to come this way."

"We could leave a warning sign."

"If everybody took that attitude, these routes would become impassable."

Gyan grunted, "Let 'em become impassable."

"That is an amazing thing to say."

"The cities are self-sufficient. We traders are icing on the cake."

"More Terran gibberish!" snapped Miokk. He softened his tone and smiled, "Get ready again to become a statistic, Gyan."

During the next couple of minutes *Uxtal* moved in an arc which brought it to the foot of the ramp, ready to attempt the ascent. Meanwhile their enemy, no longer bothered with concealment, had extended its tallest stems. They wagged nightmarishly just beyond the ridge, like tips of warning fingers.

The thing was holding its fire till the Crawler had come closer. It was intelligent – how intelligent? Answer: as much as it needed to be.

One duty remained. Out of the door in the vehicle's rear Miokk stepped one more time, bearing a post which he then hammered into the gralm. It carried a notice:

11,151,986 Ac
Uxtal
Narp beyond – full grown
Unless we win
Miokk Monray

He re-entered, took over the controls and the command of the projectile gun, and gave the word to advance. The Crawler's treads were set in motion and it began to lurch up the ramp. Each adult member of the Monray family took nen's place, laser-sponnd at the ready, at one of the forward embrasures.

The vehicle swayed forward as it topped the ridge, and bumped level.

Now it lay across the rail which ran along the summit.

At this height the enemy writhed in full view. A Terran might have described the narp as a Hydra-headed dandelion, magnified to tree size, with laser-projecting buds. These promptly spat their whickering, incandescent bolts at the Crawler's armoured front. With every thud of impact the temperature inside the vehicle went up, and Miokk had to decide whether to continue forward or to fight it out where they were; he decided to press on. *Uxtal* therefore again lurched forward, now downwards, to descend the far ramp into the barrage of laser fire.

Miokk pressed the stud of the projectile gun to send a ball ploughing into the loam among the plant's stems, breaking some, damaging several more; he got in one other, more effective shot, but that was the gun's last effort: with terrifying accuracy the narp replied with a laser bolt which *entered the muzzle of Uxtal's cannon* and fused it into a useless knob.

Henceforth all the fire from *Uxtal* must come from its crew's personal, hand-held lasers. These sponnds now had to be adjusted to fire staccato, in bolt mode.

One further weapon remained at Miokk's disposal: the body of the Crawler itself. Reaching ground level, he drove the vehicle straight at the narp, intending to crush it entirely.

The battle was reduced to a race against time. Seconds would decide whether the plant could cook its opponent before being flattened by its advance.

In this situation, every hit from the Crawler's sponnd-wielding crew must be made to count, by destroying a stem or deflecting its aim. Miokk's gaze was therefore riveted upon the streams of bolts from his own side, as he ground forward, but meanwhile he most feared the million-to-one enemy shot which might penetrate an embrasure. Victory seemed within his grasp as the narp tangled about him in its final throes; the outer leaves were already being crunched by the Crawler's treads. Then his heart missed a beat as he heard boots behind him clattering down the spiral stair from superstructure to control room, just when one of the streams of fire from his side had ceased. News of tragedy? No, he corrected. Two faces of the same event. The person who had stopped firing was still alive, was the same one who was coming down from the upper deck. Out of the corner of his eye he saw without surprise that it was Gyan who had deserted his post.

This was not the moment to demand an explanation. Miokk continued to steer *Uxtal* to its literally crushing victory.

Only when the impact of enemy bolts had ceased, and the contorting stems were reduced to the occasional feeble twitch as they lay broken on the gralm, did he halt the vehicle to allow it at last to cool.

Wiping sweat from his brow he went into the stateroom, to question his son.

"Well?"

"You won, Father. You didn't need my contribution any more."

If I keep my tone mild, Miokk told himself, *I shall learn more.* "I ought to have been the judge of that –" he began.

He was interrupted by the others charging into the room. He did what was expected of him, hugging and congratulating them all, and in turn receiving their compliments and congratulations. Gyan partook of the mood insofar as he did not sulk, but as soon as the fervour had died down he said: "We need not have destroyed it. We could have gone the other way."

Rather than intervene, thought Miokk, *perhaps I'll first let the others say what needs to be said.*

He eyed young Trarv, who, sensing that he was being invited to comment, turned – nothing loath – to his elder brother with a "Why?"

And his sister Plendwa echoed him, adding, "We did well to clear it away, Gyan. It was a hazard."

Gyan retorted, "Primly spoken, Plendwa! But meanwhile we have destroyed something unique. Never seen a specimen like that one."

Judging his moment, Miokk nodded, "I dare say the narp *was* unique, but so are we, and so is each trade-lane across Syoom. Trade-lanes should not be allowed to die."

"Father," said Gyan, "I'm crushed flat by your logic. You win the debate as you won the battle."

3: Surprise in the Night

Weary after their triumph, the family achieved only a few miles of further progress in the dimming air of late evenshine, and then stopped for an early night.

It was not always their practice to maintain a night watch. However, in consideration of the release of energies in the battle with the narp, they agreed that it was advisable to take the precaution, in case their laser emissions had been detected by anything within range.

Zamena took the first watch. After four hours she woke Gyan and went to bed.

Yyne is the darkest time of the Uranian night, when the aerial *bneen* have not only ceased to glow but have become opaque and pitch-black, blotting out the Sun and the stars. The lights were off in *Uxtal* too. This was a security requirement when out in the wilderness. Hevad, carrying a torch, came to wake Miokk and Zamena.

"Gyan has disappeared," she told them. "He should have woken me for my watch, but I woke anyway, and found him gone." Her voice was steady – toneless – desolate. Miokk felt the pit of his stomach slump, though on the surface of his mind he was merely angry.

To abandon a watch was unforgiveable. But then, suppose Gyan had fallen prey to *nebulation*? That mental disorder can happen to anyone, out on the plains. Even in the midst of company it can strike – though the soul is more likely to be overwhelmed when the person is alone. Gyan had been behaving peculiarly of late…

"Has he taken his skimmer?"

"I don't know – I came straight to you."

Miokk said kindly, "Let's check that out first. Perhaps he hasn't gone far." But when they stood outside on the darkened gralm, a sweep with the torch showed them the empty rack on *Uxtal*'s side.

Miokk and Zamena hugged the quietly shivering Hevad and offered infinite sympathy, though they were in need of comfort themselves. Miokk remarked, "Admittedly, it's going to be more difficult to find him since he's taken his skimmer, but on the other hand I don't fear for his mind as I would if he had wandered off on foot."

Hevad said in a weary voice, "I know where he must have gone."

"Tell us – and tell us why," said Miokk, peering in vain through the dark at her unreadable face.

"Our destruction of the narp," said Hevad, "filled him with remorse. He has listened to his Terran mentor Cummings about the need to preserve rare creatures. It's a big idea on Earth, which I suppose you know is a small planet, its environments always fragile for some reason or other…"

"Earth influence," muttered Miokk. "I knew it."

"And," continued the girl, "he mumbled something about going some day to the Sunnoad to appeal for help to protect endangered species –"

"If it's not one thing it's another," snorted Miokk. "You just have to let them grow out of it. Got to wait for it to wear off." This firm dismissiveness was his attempt to reassure the women.

Besides, the fact that his son had left them in the middle of the night, risking life and sanity, did not invalidate the brusque judgement, "nonsense is nonsense", or so Miokk hoped.

4: Mission

A lone wayfarer may brave the wilderness for any one of countless reasons. Some skimmer-pilots bear messages across gaps in the radio relay system. Others sign up for data-gathering for a boss-cartographer. Some are merely curious about what may lie beyond a horizon; others are overcome by a restless urge or a craving for change for its own sake. Whatever the motive, once you start the journey, the experience can blur your consciousness, smudging, twisting your purpose. Especially at night.

The man on the skimmer, speeding polewards towards Skyoon over the everlasting windswept plain, found that the night encouraged him to forget his name and, almost, to forget his separate existence altogether and to become one with the darkness and the breeze. The darkness grew imperfect: flecks in the gralm raced below the keel as the air took on the slight and gradual visibility of pallyne, the prelude to morningshine.

He wondered what other voyagers had crossed this way; what invisible tracks, if any, history might have laid across this section of wilderness. Age, immensity, nuzzled him all around. The so-called "emptiness" thronged with possibilities. The air swished at him with the hem of its robe of mystery. Above his head, low cloud-groups bumped into each other with little coughs of thunder. No space travel was necessary for the planet-bound denizens of Ooranye to meet the challenge of the void. They did not need to travel upwards to encounter ultimate loneliness. It stooped at them already. It pawed the surface of the sighing, mind-stretching plains. The giant world was soaked in space, girdled with engulfment, inviting the bravado of some wayfarers, the liberating awareness of others. Either way, nature won. Either way, your sense of identity dwindled at last, and personal insignificance slid you into the happy daze of anonymity.

Besides dilution of the self, mature wayfarers can also experience an expansion of wisdom. It's a sort of roaming objectivity that dandles the world, hefts it and says: hmm, although this giant planet is the only world I know, I shall always pay it the respect of not being too familiar; I shall do it the honour of lifting my eyebrows in surprise.

301

This characteristic Uranian refusal to take things for granted can bring valuable insights, but on the other hand, the self being too small to have much effect, it gets to be *too* carefree, it acquires an irresponsibility… a detachment from life itself…

An experienced voyager must be on the alert for the delusions of *nebulation.*

Guard against this, the pilot warned himself. Focus on your gear. The reliable physical things which you have with you. Your skimmer and your compass. Torch, provisions, telescope, fuel-phials, maps: all stored in the bow-compartment. And of course your personal laser sponnd, engraved with your honorific initials. Furnished with these items, you're a gritty, roaming fleck of your culture. Small and light as a wind-blown dust particle, you are nevertheless in touch with practical reality, so long as you keep hold of your kit…

Thus the wayfarer used the texture of material things to keep himself in touch with his own personal reality. Inevitably, the result was to remind him of the home and family he had left. Consequently, a cry of conscience tore through the cave of his brain.

Did I do right, to leave Uxtal? Is my mission a good one?

Perhaps it was trivial, perhaps it would turn out to be a waste of the Sunnoad's time. In which case, he had distressed his family for no reason. If so, he did not deserve the luck which he needed to see him through. Don't think about luck. Those horizons encircling him now: were they frowning, would the frown become a glare, and something condense out of it, and come at him, and make him into a statistic: just another wayfarer who set out for Skyyon and never made it? He shrugged, the hours went by, the air grew brighter, and he risked an increase in speed. Dangerous at night, two hundred miles per hour without lights is feasible during the day. He sped on, and his mood gained a kind of exalted balance, steady as the velocity of the skimmer.

After seventeen hours of flight he sighted the first beads of tell-tale brilliance on the horizon ahead. The glowing fields of *vheic* in the cultivated region of Ammye caused a change in the wayfarer's consciousness. It brought down his distended, god-like self, which had ridden high above his body, and it furled the sails of his imagination, so that his awareness now descended towards the scurrying, anxious, limited physical self which bestrode the vehicle. Mind and body resumed their normal merger. The pilot took proper note of who he was.

And so Miokk Monray, following some hours behind his son, entered Skyyon's realm.

5: The Thuzolyrs

On the last lap of the journey Miokk understood that he had come close to nebulation, but that the danger of this was now over. The likely end of the trip would bring him a new and different set of worries.

Speeding past roads and farms, he gazed ahead impatiently now, in expectation of the city's topmost towers. Repeated reconsiderations made his head throb, but he could see no other course than the one he had chosen. Even if he turned out to be wrong, it seemed best to get it over and done with, since he had come this far.

Dots at long last appeared on the horizon ahead, rising as he approached. He knew they were airships moored above the docking platforms of Skyyon. Next he was able to see the platforms themselves, and then the summits of the highest towers slid up into view. Meanwhile in other directions other skimmers could now be seen, many of them headed in the same direction as he. The scale of the city became apparent as the upper disc-tier rose into complete view, then the stem below it, then the lower disc-tier and finally the sturdy base-stem.

By this time Skyyon towered above him and he was one with a stream of incoming traffic. The line of skimmers funnelled itself into a narrowing lane to converge upon the invisible elevator, the ayash current, which, some way ahead, already grasped the foremost city-bound travellers and fountained them up from the plain. Miokk and his neighbours in the line soon began rising too, as their vehicles in turn were gripped.

Though a nomad at heart, he never failed to thrill at the soaring entrance to a city, especially when momentarily poised at the highest point of the aerial fountain, from which he could gaze down into the geometric glow of Skyyon's heaped palaces and threaded walkways in all their mounded splendour. But then he must concentrate. The drop began, towards the oalm or landing-plain on the lower disc's rim. He kept his eyes down and his hand on the throttle, determined to make a good landing on the Polar City.

It *was* a good enough landing, with no last-moment wobble at touchdown. He stepped out, watching other arrivals to see where they stored their vehicles. Skimmer-banks were stacked to one side of the oalm, and he slid the canoe-shaped object into one of the available lockers, pocketing the key. (Absently he noted a small mirror-like shield, which hung at an angle from one end of the line of lockers. Something he should know about. He brushed the thought away. He was busy.) He walked a few yards to a rental where he hired a smaller skimmer more suitable for travel within a city. Here also he noticed one of the mirror-shield things. (Might be a scanning device, he thought. Doubtless placed there for security reasons. Again, he brushed the thought aside.)

His next step, he decided, must be to find some place to stay. He had no hope of getting an audience with the Sunnoad before quite a few days had passed. In fact, the more he thought about his mission the more he doubted his chances of obtaining a hearing at all. Out on the plains, in command of *Uxtal,* he was boss of all he surveyed, but here amid the teeming millions of the capital city of the Noad of Noads he was amazed at his own presumption...

He made a start: he skimmed a few hundred yards down one of the radial avenues. Then he decided to branch off into a side-street at random. Signs that promised visitors' accommodation looked to be more plentiful here... but as he turned, he saw something that put his mind on a different tack. It was yet *another* of the reflective shields, hanging at the street corner. This time education came to his aid. He knew what the thing he was seeing had to be.

He parked the skimmer and approached the *thuzolyr* on foot.

Other pedestrians likewise paused before passing on, so that there was a perpetually replenished knot of people standing close to the object, staring into its mirror surface. When his turn came to take a good look, his skin prickled at the glossy patterns which swirled on the thought-sensitive surface.

Such psionic tricks were not to his taste.

Oh for the simple life... he turned away. The sooner he was out of this place the better. Never mind the search for lodgings. He would make straight for the Sunnoad's Palace. At least he could get on the waiting list; and the fact that Gyan had preceded him was another reason to lose no more time...

Skyyon is two-tiered: its main stem supports not one but two discs – a structural feature unique among Uranian cities. The upper disc, smaller in radius, is reached by means of three interior ayash-airstreams rising from points spaced around the lower disc. So for the second time that day Miokk was fountained up and deposited upon a landing-plain – this time on the upper tier.

From the hub of this tier soared the flame-shaped, mountainous palace called the Zairm.

Miokk stood irresolute amidst the crowd of strolling sightseers in the Octagon which surrounded the Zairm. He felt futile. The multitude of thuzolyrs which hung from streetlamps and walkways irritated him. Why had the psionic mirrors been set out now? Were they simply in fashion? Wondering whom he might ask about the procedure for seeking audience with the Sunnoad, he peered at the entrances which radiated like tree-roots from the Zairm's base. The biggest crowd was waiting around the nearest one. It did not look like a queue, but maybe they had numbered tickets so that they did not have to wait in a line. Or perhaps they had gathered to read what was written on the door. He approached that door – and before he could examine it, it slid open.

Simultaneously he was aware of a flash from a thuzolyr hanging on the wall nearby.

He turned, to meet the stares of the waiting crowd.

"Go on in," said a man, a native Skyyonian from his accent. "What are you waiting for?"

With a clenching in his midriff, Miokk stepped into the Zairm.

At the end of the entrance corridor he saw another shield, flashing.

6: The Sunnoad

"Turn right," said a faceless voice. It seemed to come from behind the shield. He obeyed and walked on, towards the next wall-mounted thuzolyr.

"Turn left," said another hidden voice.

Again he obeyed – and after this he saw no further flashing shield to aim for. Instead, a door opened, into a well-lit room, and in the doorway stood a man wearing a garment which made all the difference to how one saw the rest of him.

The man's features would, perhaps, have been distinguished enough without it, but *with* it they were in a different class, for greatness was conferred, through inescapable suggestion, by the golden cloak around the fellow's shoulders. Miokk became still. He was seeing Zednas Tremol 80520 in person.

"You wanted to see me," said the Sunnoad.

"Yes…"

"Don't stand in the doorway."

Perspective came to Miokk's aid. He told himself that if you added together all the people who had been given audience by this person, and all those who had spoken with his 80,519 predecessors, it would come to so many millions, that there was no particular reason why the name Miokk Monray should not be added to their number. Yet it was strange that he had got in so quickly.

After all, he had expected to spend days on the waiting-list. Nevertheless, come to think of it, he *could* imagine one reason for the speed of events. Often enough, when he had amused himself with the idle game of thinking, "What would I do if I were Sunnoad?", he had pictured himself interviewing people summoned off the street at random... Some such fluky survey of public opinion might now be giving him his chance.

Beckoned in, he found himself standing on the floor of the Sunnoad's office which turned out to be a small lounge with ordinary armchairs, low table and book-lined walls. Zednas Tremol sat and motioned Miokk to a chair opposite.

The light of a globe-lamp fell on the Sunnoad's grizzled head. His moderately lined face, bidding farewell to middle age, possessed a heavy jaw, jutting chin and small twinkling eyes. The head was tilted as if keeping an eye on some message written on the ceiling... Miokk had to restrain himself from copying that tilt. Pull yourself together, he told himself.

Miokk said formally, "Thank you, Sunnoad Z-T, for seeing me. I wish to report, if I may, concerning the influence of the Terrans."

The Sunnoad simply said, "Proceed."

"I believe I have encountered," Miokk spoke the syllables with great care, "a case of ideological transplantation."

The Sunnoad gave a very slight, encouraging nod. His very quietness seemed to show he was interested. Encourged by this, Miokk told the story of the fight with the narp, and of Gyan's solicitude for the defeated weed.

"It looks to me," he concluded, "like a case of idea-contamination, from Earth to Ooranye. My son's words and actions, and his wife's explanation of them, are what lead me to suspect this."

"By "contamination" I take it you mean, inappropriate transplantation."

"Yes, Sunnoad Z-T. Of course, there's nothing wrong with Terran ideas in themselves – in Terran conditions."

"You mean you're not easy about this Terran idea of preserving endangered species, applied to our world."

"I sense it ought to concern us as part of a wider picture..."

"You are right about the wider picture," said the Sunnoad. "The Terrans call it *environmentalism*. Their world is small compared with ours, its ecosystem fragile, vulnerable to the actions of man... so they have to care for their environment as if it were a delicate old grandmother. Your son appears to have absorbed this idea and is mis-applying it to our own more robust world. It's a pity that he can't instead be grateful for the privilege of living on a planet that can look after itself."

"If Gyan is solely to blame, it is just a Monray family problem. But if the Terrans are playing some game –"

"No, I don't think they are disturbing us intentionally," opined the Sunnoad. "In fact I have reason to believe that this is unlikely."

The Sunnoad paused, and Miokk leaned forward in fascination, the hope strong within him, that the privilege of understanding was about to be shared. Zednas Tremol smiled at the nomad's keen expression, and explained:

"One of the main points about our world that attracts them, that causes them to study it so avidly, is that robustness I've alluded to. The fact that we, its human population, can pit ourselves against the challenges of our environment without fear that we might damage it, is balm to the poor Terrans. They must wish that *they* could live on as strong a world as we do. See what I'm getting at? So far from wishing 'environmentalism' onto us, they actually admire us for not needing it. The thought of Ooranye probably comforts them."

"So they're not trying to make trouble for us." *All that work to get here,* Miokk thought, *and it turns out I need not have bothered.*

The Sunnoad replied indirectly:

"Having said what I've said, I ought to add that it's doubtless true that their gut reactions to our scene remain inappropriate. Since they can't really grasp what it's like to live on a world where you can hunt, destroy, waste things and carelessly strive against Nature with the comfort of knowing that you will lose, they are likely to lead Gyan astray, and others like him, unintentionally."

"A minor problem, then," murmured Miokk. "Not some interplanetary plot after all."

"Indeed not so bad as that."

"I apologize for taking up your time, Sunnoad Z-T." Miokk was abruptly aware of how much worse the meeting might have gone. He had achieved this once-in-a-lifetime interview and certainly it had not been a disaster. It had even reassured him.

Zednas Tremol meanwhile tilted his head further in responce to a hiss from a slot in the wall. A message capsule had just appeared. The Sunnoad reached for it, unrolled it... "This confirms that your son arrived safely a few hours before you did."

"That's good to know; I suppose he applied –"

"The thuzolyrs," the Sunnoad interrupted. "They… speak to each other." He added: "I have had them programmed with some… discretion. I expect you wondered why you were let in here so quickly."

"I wondered," agreed Miokk – sudden apprehension smearing coldness all over his back.

The Sunnoad continued, "It was for the same reason that Gyan was *not* let in."

"I don't understand, Sunnoad Z-T."

"Oh, do you not? Then think. What use would I have for *him*? I leave *run-of-the-mill* revolutionaries and their stereotyped originality to be dealt with by my subordinates. Whereas…"

Miokk could not utter a word, such hoarseness clogged his throat. He could only listen as the kindly voice of the Noad of Noads thumped in his ears:

"…Whereas, *I* am on the look-out for the ultimate creativity…"

The words trampled on, flattening Miokk's resistance so that his attempts to misunderstand got nowhere; he could not fail to see where they led –

"…the ultimate creativity, which is exhibited by those who possess the will to make something great out of things *as they are*." He looked meaningly at Miokk, who still dared utter no word, not even a whisper. Zednas Tremol nodded to confirm, "I am telling you the real reason why you came here."

"No," he croaked.

"Yes," the Sunnoad insisted. "It was, that you had obtained a glimpse."

At last Miokk managed a more rational response.

"A glimpse… into what the Terrans are up to?"

Rational – yes. Plausible – no. Completely pointless, to pretend to misunderstand.

"Into what *you* shall be up to when I am gone," grinned the implacable Zednas Tremol.

Woe to the pinned insect that is I, thought Miokk in a feverish self-harming extravagance of imagery which amounted to his last silliness of denial; and it accomplished nothing and he had to listen on:

"You," the Sunnoad continued, "who, if I mistake not, shall be the next wearer of this cloak… Don't look so paralyzed; how do you think I felt when I learned I was next in line? Snap back, Miokk Monray; life and duty give us no choice. That fact should be a comfort. And don't think the thuzolyrs can be wrong –"

Miokk now accepted, deep down, that he was in for it. Yet he said inanely, "The thuzolyrs, or you, Sunnoad Z-T, must have made some idiotic mistake."

"Who are you to pronounce on that?"

"I am nobody, and that's the point."

"Who is nobody?" shrugged the Sunnoad. "I have never met 'nobody'."

"I mean, I have no desire to be a Noad, let alone a Noad of Noads."

"Another reason why you will make a good one."

"But –"

"No reason to believe me today, or even tomorrow," smiled Zednas Tremol. "Your hour will not come for a while yet – I hope!" He smiled, but the smile was wasted.

"What shall I do?" whispered Miokk.

"Take your son back with you to *Uxtal*. Live your life, and wait. Ah, you're smiling now – what's occurred to you?"

"I was just thinking, if I haven't dreamed all this, the day will come when my cheeky offspring *does* get his interview with the Sunnoad."

"Don't assume his cheekiness will end there. Even if it does, others will take up the task of correcting you." Zednas Tremol spoke wryly now. "Believe me, I know."

"Yes," the nomad mused, "I have heard of Correctors."

It did all seem like a dream: history come to life, *his* life. The great institutions of Syoom – thuzolyrs, Sunnoads, Correctors – converging upon his everyday thread.

His thoughts were echoed:

"So then, Miokk! You'll be target practice for those geniuses who think they know best – and as a father you're already part-beaded onto that thread, are you not? Now go back to your home for the time being. With luck, your next call here won't be for many a hundred days."

Miokk Monray strode to the door and then looked back, as if to check one more time that he had really spoken with the golden-cloaked man. Yes, he had; the sacred fabric was there, hunched about the sitting figure of Zednas Tremol. Miokk was nevertheless flooded with disbelief, sheer inability to credit the stupendous thing that had happened, and this denial held him fixed for a moment, blearing from the doorway.

The Sunnoad without difficulty read his expression, his repulsion at the sheer improbability of it all...

"Now then, when you saw the elective mirrors all over town, what ought you to have told yourself, Miokk?"

"I ought," he confessed, "to have said, aha..."

"That is a very good answer indeed, Miokk Monray. And what's more, you could have gone on to conclude: 'whomever it lights upon will be as surprised as I would be; and so it may light upon me.'"

"Yes, but…" he snickered desperately, "I could disappear."

"You could *try.*" The Sunnoad bent his head, went back to his work.

Uranopaedia

[note: in alphabetically sorted lists, Uranians are usually placed according to their first names]

Ahim Trarv 77062 the 77,062nd Sunnoad. He was murdered and then impersonated by **Nehal Fozdak**; this crime, and the other events associated with it, brought the Bismuth Era to an end.

Allv A city in the Starward Hemisphere. 2662 miles from the Starward Pole and 7853 miles from Poleva.

anyne the first five hours of the 15-hour Uranian night

Ao one of the greatest of the disc-on-stem cities of Syoom. In the Osmium Era it formed the alliance with Vyanth and Skyyon known as the Triangle, which patrolled the area between the three cities, giving an outstanding period of peace and security to a wide patch of Syoom. Over one hundred million days before that, in the Xenon Era, Ao was the most successful of hive minds, combining the freedom of the individual with the group consciousness of a city, in a way that has never been achieved before or since.

Ao is one of five cities which can trace its name, though not its physical identity, back to a settlement in the Hydrogen Era which existed close to the modern site.

Arclour the fabled starward polar region of Ooranye, antipodeal to Skyyon; the goal unattained by Fiarr Fosn's Great Fleet but finally attained in recent times by the Second Great Fleet. At the moment of the arrival of the Second Great Fleet, Arclour became the scene of the hinge event of Solar System history, the "write-over" or **Fostering**, whereby Ooranye's past was grafted onto the lifeless gas-giant planet Uranus, and validated retrospectively. This example of "reality engineering" remains unique.

arelk the political "hardening of the arteries" whereby the freedom of a **lremd noadex** ossifies into a rigidly authoritarian structure

ayshine the five hours around mid-day (two and a half hours of the end of morning, two and a half hours of the beginning of afternoon)

backgrounder minor character in a story; bit-player or "extra" in history. A term of abuse – a word regarded as obscene by Uranians.

banessyen "moving-map": a map showing existential threats by means of symbols which move as the threats move, around the user's symbol at centre

Bank of Light Phosphorus-era institution which enabled people to deposit and accumulate the results of contemplation; this hoarded awareness, released at a crucial moment in history, possibly saved Syoom in the aftermath of the loss of the Great Fleet

bneen see **throom**

Capfaym Duuv the psi-sensitive who communed with the world-spirit to obtain advice for humanity in the crisis at the end of the Thallium Era

Chelth the dimension, or universe, looted of much of its energy by the Uranians to fuel the greatness of the Phosphorus Era. This plundering of Chelth gave rise to the one major undercurrent of guilt in the otherwise self-confident Uranian mind-set.

Contahl a city in Oirr, the region in which the **Sun-Egg** was to be found, Contahl was the greatest city of Syoom during the Lithium Era and also during the Time of Troubles up to the beginning of the Phosphorus Era. It, and the other old cities of Oirr, declined in relative importance after the disc-on-stem cities were built with the power plundered from **Chelth**.

It was in Lithium-Era Contahl that the institutions of the **noadex** and the **dayonnad** had their origin.

Corrector the title given to someone who has taken it upon **nen**self to coerce a **Sunnoad**, and who has got away with it by getting the Sunnoad to see the error of nen's ways

Corruption Ray a weapon used in eras 7 and 84-85. It set up a mental field which attacked the sense of value. Its effect was to undermine moral fibre, by weakening attachment to cultural roots and causing civilizations to rot from within.

crystal groves small forests of crystalline plants, bristling with natural defences and almost immune from attack; the proprietors of the groves, who have spent generations in fostering trust with them, are the only humans who can enter them with impunity

Daon a Noad's heir. Strong taboos against hereditary government prevent any children of a Noad from being chosen as Daon. (See "The Worm of Poleva".)

dayonnad the rank or office of Daon

Deev a Starside city, 12,579 miles from Allv, 519 miles from Karth, and 12,166 miles from Olhoav. Deev is 13,484 miles from the Starward Pole, that is to say, from the centre of **Arclour**.

dlax (plural, **dlaxou**) Hemispheric forcefield atop a circular hover-raft. Invented early in the Phosphorus Era, when such energy-guzzling devices were most used.

Dmara the first human city. Previously, the prebiotic lake or **sivvan** from which the Liquid Men and then the Nenns themselves emerged.

Dynnt Eshnun explorer who captured an **eopc** during the Beryllium Era He took a blood-sample from the giant bird, and from tests made on this the **Rin-Stazel** discovered the existence of **Chelth**.

Dynnt Gilvar 48559 the 48,559th Sunnoad; reigned during the transition between the Lutetium and Hafnium Eras. It was he who made the crucial decision to follow Simulator advice and "appease" the Fyayman powers by putting an end to the prospecting for ell-light crystals. In his second incarnation, in the Actinium Era, Dynnt Gilvar was captain of a Nemyuran airship.

Dzolm colloquial nickname for the **Sun-Egg**

eomasp a disturbance in the normal rhythm of day and night due to the sensitivity of the **throom** to mass human emotions; indicative, therefore, of the waft of emotion accompanying some great event, eomasps mark the transition from one era to the next.

eopc giant bird, wingspan up to 70 yards; the largest known winged creature on Ooranye. It does not eat or drink, and the mystery of whence it obtained its energy led the researchers of the **Rin-Stazel** to discover the dimension called **Chelth**.

evenshine the last five hours of the 15-hour daylight

fdalm a wedge-shaped burrowing creature, creating ice-caverns under the plains. The accordion-like plasticity of the fdalm enables it to insert itself into cracks in the ice and split them further.

Fiarr Fosn 723 the 723rd Sunnoad. Commanded the Great Fleet which tried to conquer Fyaym at the end of the Phosphorus Era. He was killed in the disaster which overtook that fleet. His second incarnation is also recorded: he was a distinguished Noad of Jador during the latter part of the Vanadium era, showing none of that arrogance and hubris which had brought on the doom of Era 15. It is an example often cited, of how it is possible to learn from history.

flare of arrest the term given to the event which occupied and defined the Magnesium Era: a worldwide *frisson* – a psychic tap on the shoulder, thought to be caused by the action of a **Chelth**an entity who had become aware of the attempt by the Uranians to plunder nen's universe

foam Its advent was a stirring or a flare in the normally weak, faint life-force of the **gralm** – the granular material which covers the Uranian plains. Gralm is thought of as semi-alive, with a much fainter flicker of life than the lowliest organic entity, but, because of the vastness of the oceanic world-plain, its total life-force must be considerable. And in era 57, it suddenly and bizarrely expanded as though it were popcorn. Within days the plains around the cities of Syoom had humped and were threatening to bury the cities under a pumice-like covering, the "foam". (Note that the "foamed ore", called **smollk**, is a different substance.)

foregrounder one who rides a winning streak, or who fills an important rule in a story – the opposite of a **backgrounder**. The term is not used in polite conversation, and consensus has not been reached as to whether it refers to something real.

Fostering of Ooranye, the from the Terran point of view, the one successful example in history of "reality engineering"; the action taken, and the process which took place, on 10th July A.D. 3564, by which the gas giant planet **Uranus** became, and now *always has been*, more fully itself as the ice-giant planet **Ooranye**. By analogy the Fostering has been likened to the switching of points on a railway *after* a train has gone past: so that, if the train were to go into reverse, it would go back along a different track. In other words, a "new" past was grafted onto Uranus, and indeed some authorities suggest that the operation ought to be called the Grafting rather than the Fostering. On the other hand, "Fostering" better describes the relation between we Terrans and the resultant world: i.e. we did not create it, we encouraged it. Meanwhile the un-Fostered reality survives in one remaining clue: the "U" in the adjective 'Uranian'.

gedars submen rumoured to have originated from relics of the dying Dmaran *sivvan*. They came in a variety of builds and sizes, their faces misshapen like the products of an inexpert sculptor. The gedars became a general nuisance in the early Vanadium Era when, sensing the Nenns' weakness after the Great Winter, they swarmed over Syoom, looting and killing.

Ghepions machines that have evolved into sentience. To call them "artificial" intelligences is to beg the question, "where does sentience come from?" Ghepion-human relations have had a chequered history.

gralm the cork-textured substance covering most of the plains of Ooranye. Gralm is usually coloured brown, purple or grey.

Grard the most geographically isolated of the great disc-on-stem cities of Syoom. There have been times when it has lost contact with the rest of Syoom and become legendary. It was the native city of the nameless master-criminal known as the Grardesh Sponndar, the great opponent of the dective Restiprak Zentonan in the Tantalum Era. It is a mere 11,248 miles from Grard to Olhoav in the Starward Hemisphere. It was built somewhat later in the Phosphorus Era than the other disc-on-stem cities.

Great Cycle the period of 100,000 Uranian years (8.4 million Earth years) which is the largest unit of Uranian history. We are about one-seventh of the way through the current Great Cycle. Some artefacts and remains from previous Great Cycles exist, though they are few and puzzling. It is thought that in the next Great Cycle the **kalyars** will take over from the **Nenns** as the predominant human culture on Ooranye.

Great Triangle the Osmium Era alliance between Skyyon, Ao and Vyanth, to patrol the lands between them; the area thus patrolled

Gyan Ennye in his first incarnation, the Jaaxan officer who made the first 'dassan call. (See **kommassandassan**.) In his second incarnation, an eminent Lysyan officer of the Actinium Era.

gvo is semi-**kolv**; a compound of particulate and non-particulate matter, the latter component left over from the previous universe, and a source of enormous power. The **mascon** called the **Sun-Egg** was composed of glowing orange gvo.

Hevad Notoxt 69546 the 69,546th Sunnoad and probably the second most famous woman to hold that office (the first being Hyala Movoun 1). She was a psi, able not only to read minds but to operate on moods. Her great service to Syoom was the overthrow of the cyborgs, but she bears much responsibility for the subsequent persecution of the **Ghepions**.

Hoog disc-on-stem city, scene of a notoriously explicit hive-mind for a while during the latter part of the Phosphorus Era. Much later, some of the most memorable adventurers of the Vanadium Era came from Hoog. Along with Innb, Ao, Nuvium and Pjourth, Hoog can trace its name, though not its physical identity, back to a settlement in the Hydrogen Era that existed close to the modern site.

Hyala Movoun 1 the first Sunnoad, the most famous woman and arguably the most famous person in Uranian history. A teacher in Narar and Contahl in the late Nitrogen Era and in the Oxygen Era, she did much to cure civilization of the effects of the **Corruption Ray**. Her reign as Sunnoad comprised the Neon Era. She it was who made the final decision to plunder **Chelth**, and she paid for the act herself.

Idun-Sjalsk the **Sun-Egg**

iedleis (pronounced "eed-lice") the ultimate metal, the substance of which the disc-on-stems of Uranian cities are composed. Iedleis is believed to maintain its integrity invariant over an entire Great Cycle.

Ierax a disc-on-stem city of Syoom, Ierax was the scene of a great battle in which Sunnoad Miokk Monray 80521 met his death, and was succeeded by Unnd Dunaiv 80522.

Innb a disc-on-stem city of Syoom; one of the five which can trace their names back to the Hydrogen Era

Invun a disc-on-stem city of Syoom; it briefly fell to the Nemyurans under Pyoan Zour

Ipemenir Honnd the Jadorian who was energized by the "bank" of unconscious powers which had been accumulated by the **Other Syoom**. He saved that land from disaster during the Germanium Era.

Iyen Noom 80525 the 80,525th Sunnoad, currently reigning today at the beginning of Era 92, and one of the greatest of the great. A freakishly long-lived Nenn, he led the Second Great Fleet to **Arclour**, succeeding where **Fiarr Fosn 723** had failed, and still thrives as the focus of his world's destiny.

Jaax a disc-on-stem city of Syoom

Jad Darkal 35480 the 35,480th Sunnoad, whose resounding victory over invading forces saved Syoom after the fall of the Rubidium Fort. Usually regarded as the epitome of the "warrior Sunnoad".

Jador a disc-on-stem city of Syoom; often a rival of **Hoog**; but at times during the Vanadium Era Jador was a "lost city", isolated from the rest of civilization by a belt of difficult terrain and peculiar hazards

Jommdan the "high tongue" still spoken by about 21% of the Syoomean population; an elder cousin of **Nouuan**. Classical Jommdan in particular is many-layered, in such a way that the apparent length of a text adjusts itself according to the reader's background knowledge of the subject matter. The more you know, the more the words seem to run together, and the shorter it all seems. Unfortunately, the easier it is for the reader, the harder it is for the writer. Few have mastered Classical Jommdan.

Juxxt a disc-on-stem city of Syoom

Kalishan Voice telepathic broadcast accidentally triggered by an archaeologist investigating ruins in Oirr. The 57-minute broadcast - a warning against the **Quonians** - blanketed Syoom; it comprised the Nickel Era

kalyar "evolved man" - a vague, general term for a Uranian human being who belongs to one of the strains that, from the Tungsten Era onwards, have evolved away from the norm (the norm assumed to be that of the Nenns previous to that time)

Karth a city in the Starside Hemisphere. Founded along with **Deev**, according to tradition, by descendants of lost survivors of **Fiarr Fosn**'s Great Fleet. 519 miles from Deev; 13,045 miles from Allv; 12,246 miles from Olhoav. Distance to Yaz, in Syoom: 18,888 miles.

kolv the continuous, non-atomic substance, left over from the previous universe. Its part-atomic compound, semi-kolv or **gvo**, was the substance of the **Sun-Egg**.

kommassandassan one-word compression of a Nouuan sentence, colloquially translatable as "I am laying my life on the line". The speaker may use it in an emergency to interrupt anyone and gain a hearing. Penalty for failure to make one's case: death.

Lamiroth Eren 2 the Second Sunnoad

Lehal Thoal the first Corrector

Linnt a disc-on-stem city of Syoom. Only 819 miles from Nemyurur. 1557 miles from Invun.

Liquid Men the proto-humans or *Dmarnenn* who evolved in the *sivvan*. Instead of skin they possessed a form-field which needed frequent immersion to preserve its integrity; hence they could not travel far from the *sivvan* – until, late in their history, they developed an energized flexi-suit to increase their range, which enabled one of them to help **Tisswa Ardea** find the **Sun-Egg**.

Liucgr Ell arch-villain of Era 7; activator of the Corruption Ray. He may have atoned in his second life, if he can be identified as the benefactor Lek Graol. (See "The Open Secret".)

lotch a non-human species which looked human at medium range. Up close, you could recognize a Lotch by the jigsaw pattern of lines on nen's skin. These were the dividing lines between the components of a composite being. It is hoped that the lotch are now extinct. They took part in the great Fyayman invasion of the Strontium Era. A Lotch could split into dozens of flapping forms, recombining once their attack was over. It is suspected by some that they were planetary antibodies sent by the World Spirit to curb human expansion.

Lrar Verzak: the first **Nenn**. Thus, the Uranian "Adam". He emerged from the **sivvan** of Dmara on Day One of the Hydrogen Era.

lremd (adjective) See the noun **renl**. Someone who has renl is lremd.

Lrissj one of the three languages of Syoom. Spoken by 34% of the population, Lrissj is not at all closely related to Jommdan or Nouuan. It is spoken in four of the cities – Juxxt, Yoon, Narar and (surprisingly, since it is on the other side of Syoom) Grard. Apart from these centres it is the tongue of a large number of smaller settlements and farming communities scattered over the length and breadth of Syoom.

Lysyon a disc-on-stem city of Syoom, fairly close to the Fyayman border. Birthplace of **Unnd Dunaiv 80522**. Only 937 miles from Yaz. **Petraym Lairvdon** became Noad of Lysyon during the Nemyuran War.

mascon mass-concentration; a volume of greater-than-average density within the mantle of Ooranye. Very rarely convection within the mantle may bring one of them to break the surface. The **Sun-Egg** was one such emergent mascon. Much later, in the Bismuth Era, men found it possible to travel by means of the **tetrak** through the interior of Ooranye, to visit the embedded mascon worlds.

mawo A much larger relative of the **throom**, the mawo is an aerial corpuscle, wardrobe-size and shape – if you can imagine a wardrobe somewhat fuzzy at the corners and light enough to drift on the wind. (In the vegetable stage of its life-cycle it is called not a mawo but a **vrayn**.) Mawos avoid the presence of man, but nevertheless pose a danger, in that if left alone they will eventually block off huge areas of sky, crowding out the throom on which other living things depend for their light.

Melikon the village 90 miles from Skyyon where, ever since Era 88, stands the 'hut' which is the Sunnoad's official residence in lieu of the old Sunnoad's Palace in Skyyon itself

Miokk Monray 80521 the 80,521st Sunnoad (see the story "Greenery"). Miokk Monray perished in the Battle of Ierax during the Nemyuran War and was succeeded by **Unnd Dunaiv 80522**.

morningshine the first five hours of the 15-hour daylight

Mount Gnemek the highest peak on the planet Ooranye. Its summit reaches out into space. It was scaled by **Restiprak Zentonan**.

Nalre Zitpoidl 4854 the 4854th Sunnoad. The last Sunnoad of the Argon Era, he survived into the Vanadium Era. Some contend that he had been legally deposed by that time. Possibly the most controversial holder of the **sunnoadex**, he is notorious for the murder of the avian, Tjoren, whom he believed to be threatening Syoom with a misleading offer of help against the **White Sun**.

Narar a disc-on-stem city of Syoom. Narar has been notorious in more than one era for tyranny. In the Nitrogen Era, before modern Narar was built, its ground-based namesake was ruled by the autocratic Vroonwik Clarm (see "Basilisk"). Similar episodes abounded in the Vanadium Era. The most talked-about (perhaps because it is the most recent) example occurred as late as the Actinium Era, in the second reign of the dread Tyoar Ixx, a strange anomaly in the modern age.

narp a laser-tipped weed which can live for hundreds of human lifetimes on the plains of Ooranye, occasionally shooting down wayfarers and absorbing the wrecks of skimmers

Nehal Fozdak claimed by some (including himself) to be the greatest criminal in Uranian history, although he has rivals Liucgr Ell and Tyoar Ixx in the Hall of Infamy. Destroyer of Jersh, murderer of Sunnoad **Ahim Trarv 77062** and rediscoverer of the **Corruption Ray**, Fozdak was finally tracked down and killed by the lawmen of the Francium Era.

nemaeans generic term for all the Uranian insectoids - the large flying beings which swarm, particularly in Fyaym, often exhibiting a group intelligence of a malign character. The destruction of the **Great Fleet** was carried out by insectoid swarms, possibly under the control of higher entities.

Nemyurur a disc-on-stem city of Syoom. Headquarters of the irrational "Creed of the Destined Life-Force", the city challenged the rest of Syoom in the Nemyuran War, in which Sunnoad **Miokk Monray 80521** lost his life at the Battle of Ierax.

nen the unisex pronoun meaning "he or she" has been known to the Uranians ages before First Contact with the Terrans – a clear example of convergent cultural evolution

Nenn a Uranian human. Nenns are grey-skinned and have stronger metabolisms, but are otherwise identical to Terrans, though genetically unrelated – an example of convergent biological evolution, explicable only teleologically.

Nii a city and empire in the "**Other Syoom**". The city is 765 miles from the capital of its fellow-empire of **Yalar**. Other distances for reference: 16,133 miles from the Starward Pole. 21,431 miles from **Nusun**. 13,191 miles from **Oso**. 13,883 miles from **Toolv**.

Noad "focus", "co-ordinator"; the ruler of a city-state. No equivalent exists in Terrestrial history. Generally a Noad holds office for life, like a king, but is elected, like a president. A Noad of a healthy city will rule not through beaurocracy but through the quality of **renl**.

noadex the office of **Noad**

Nouuan the most widespread language of Syoom - currently spoken by 45% of the population

Nusun city in the Starward Hemisphere. Sometimes a rival of **Poleva**. Distances: Starward Pole, 9198 miles; Poleva, 2443 miles; Allv, 6815 miles; Grard, 15041 miles; Koar, 2769 miles; Nii, 21,431 miles; Olhoav, 9118 miles.

Nuvium a disc-on-stem city of Syoom. Nuvium can trace its name back to a Hydrogen Era settlement close to the present site. The area under its sway is called the Konteng of Nuvium.

Nyav Yuhlm 80438 the 80,438th Sunnoad. A rare example of a man who belongs to two planets. His soul possessed two bodies; his Earth self was Neville Yeadon of 1970's London. When that self was murdered, its consciousness was transferred to the body of Nyav Yuhlm and superimposed on the latter's mind. Nyav Yuhlm / Neville Yeadon used his unique two-world perspective to good effect during his epic rise to the sunnoadex, defeating Dempelath, tyrant of Olhoav, in one of the most astounding sagas of the Actinium Era.

nyr unit of 12 men: 11 plus the **zamur**

nyzyr unit of 133 men: 11 **nyr**s plus the **zyr**

Olhoav a city in the Starward Hemisphere. This was where **Nyav Yuhlm**, alias Neville Yeadon of Earth, first found himself on Ooranye. The city at that time was under the sway of the tyrant, Dempelath. Some distances: **Allv**, 13,244 miles; **Deev**, 12,166 miles; **Karth**, 12,246 miles; **Koar**, 6363 miles; **Nusun**, 9118 miles; **Poleva**, 6629 miles. Olhoav is a mere 11,248 miles from **Grard**, in Syoom. It is 20,339 miles from **Pjourth** and 18,302 miles from **Vyanth**.

omzyr general with 16,104 men under his command

Ooranye the planet Uranus in its "self-fulfilled" or Fostered aspect. Ooranye has "over-written" Uranus in retrospective history. Condensed to a diameter of 25,011 miles, Ooranye is slightly smaller than its un-Fostered retro-version, but is still a giant world with a surface area over ten times that of Earth.

Oso a disc-on-stem city of Syoom. The birthplace of **Nalre Zitpoidl 4854**. Much later, the "mad city" of the short Tin Era. Dire consequences followed its war against the rest of Syoom.

Other Syoom an area of civilization, comprising the empires of Yalar and Nii, surrounded by Fyaym and unsuspected by the rest of Syoom until the Gallium Era; it was the object of the Syoomean rescue expedition commanded by Sunnoad **Jad Darkal 35480**

pallyne the last five hours of the 15-hour Uranian night

Petraym Lairvdon famous Noad of Lysyon; a notable combination of intellectual and man-of-action, he succeeded to his city's noadex during the Nemyuran War and co-operated with **Unnd Dunaiv 80522**. Petraym is said to have come into contact with a renegade Earthman who broke the Terrans' self-imposed ban on landings upon Ooranye.

Pjourth disc-on-stem city of Syoom. Close to the Mountains of Flame. Pjourth can trace its name back to that of a nearby settlement during the Hydrogen Era.

pmetn "evening starsight" – a time when the upper air is transparent and the stars appear

Poleva Starside Hemisphere city, scene of the famous "Worm". Distances:

Allv, 7853 miles; **Koar**, 333 miles; **Nusun**, 2443 miles; **Olhoav**, 6629 miles. There is a matter-transmitter link between Poleva and **Contahl**.

Pyoan Tatham the last powerful director of the **Rin-Stazel**. He was responsible for the decision to solve the energy crisis by plundering **Chelth**. He was killed during the breakout of the captive **eopc**, during the disastrous day which became known as the Carbon Era.

Quonians a race of humans, physically only slightly different from the Nenns of Syoom, but considerably different culturally. They have discovered the secret of sending objects back in time, in certain limited cases where no paradoxes are thereby created. The Quonians arrived openly in Syoom during the Copper Era, though already in the last part of the Cobalt Era they had been surreptitiously planting "false pasts" in Syoomean archeological sites. Their cultural infiltration - amounting to an invasion - failed when their methods were exposed, partly due to the warning given by the **Kalishan Voice**. Discredited, they left Syoom at the end of the Copper Era. They were involved in another invasion which also failed, this time militarily, during eras 38-39. During the Osmium Era they fought a celebrated "Cold War" with Syoom, their most renowned opponent being **Taldis Norkoten**.

refelc "morning starsight" – a time when the upper air is transparent and the stars appear

Restiprak Zentonan 33337/45329 in his two incarnations, the 33,337th and the 45,329th Sunnoad respectively. The only person ever to become Sunnoad twice in two lives, RZ reigned, moreover, during two crises, transitions between eras. As 33337 he defeated the besiegers of the Other Syoom in the Gallium Era. In his second life he was the mountaineer who conquered Mt Gnemek, the highest point on the planet, the peak which reaches out into space. During that expedition he underwent the adventures which ended with him being elected the first Sunnoad of era 69.

It is possible that the Restiprak Zentonan who lived later, in the Tantalum Era - the great detective - was a third incarnation of the same person. Third incarnations are rare but not unknown, like third sets of teeth. However, in the somewhat decadent Tantalum Era it was fairly common for people to be named after other people. The uniqueness of names was not as jealously guarded then as it was in most eras; so it may not have been the same person.

renl the quality of being able to be at the right place at the right time; of juggling competing demands; of weaving one's way efficiently through complex situations without resort to rules, paperwork or beaurocratic structures. The strength of renl in the Uranian psyche must stem from adaptation to the giant world, whose immense mysteries would otherwise overwhelm humanity. Those Nenns who exhibit most renl are apt to become elected as Noads. The quality first became necessary and evident in the city of Contahl in the Lithium Era. The adjective **lremd** means "possessing renl".

revestru the insectoid species which warred with the Wonarr in the early Hydrogen Era

Rgiohafnarn Dzeld "Voluntary Contemplation Store" - proper name of the institution commonly called the **Bank of Light**

Rhenium Moment Era 75, which lasted five hours, during which the world-spirit communicated with the people of Syoom, and especially with the delegates to an international conference held in Zdinth Hall, Skyyon. Only gradually over the next era was the message of the Moment understood. It prevented a general inter-species war between Nenns and kalyars.

Rin-Stazel the scientific institution which grew out of the standing committee established by the Congress of Contahl at the end of the Lithium Era. During the Beryllium and Boron Eras the Rin-Stazel led research into ways of solving the looming energy crisis caused by the imminent depletion of the Sun-Egg. Under its last powerful director, **Pyoan Tatham**, the fateful decision was made, that steps must be taken to plunder the dimension of **Chelth**. The Rin-Stazel was disbanded during the troubles of the Nitrogen Era, but its aims were later carried out by **Hyala Movoun 1**.

Rubidium Fort fortress at the far point of the salient of Syoom which reached into Fyaym in the direction of the **Other Syoom**, during era 37. The fort fell at the end of that era.

sfy the safety-contours (or peril-contours) on Uranian maps

sfy-50 the boundary between Syoom and Fyaym. A safety-contour joining all those points on a map which represent places where the chance of surviving a lone journey of 1,000 miles is 50 per cent.

sivvan the pre-biotic lake from which Uranian humanity first emerged

skimmer the main personal vehicle used by Uranians. Designed as a one-man flier, it can carry two at a pinch. It is roughly canoe-shaped, five yards long and at the centre one yard wide. It cannot fly higher than six yards above ground, except during the risky manoeuvre known as "stormriding". Top speed: 200 miles per hour. Its lift is provided by one of the indestructible antigravity units produced in their billions in the Phosphorus Era; its propulsion comes from a related device fuelled by phials of ell-light extracted from the **vheic** plant.

skimmjard a word literally meaning "pilot of a skimmer"; sometimes used more generally to mean a traveller

Skyyon the Sunward Polar City – where the sun is always at the zenith. It is the "capital" disc-on-stem city of Syoom, or would be if Syoom were a state. In actual fact Skyyon, like all the other major cities of Ooranye, is politically independent of the others, and always has been, although until the fall of **Tu Rim 78860** in Era 88 it was the official residence of the Sunnoad, and it still tends to house the headquarters of most pan-Syoomean agencies.

The Palace at Skyyon is a flame-shaped building called the Zairm. Inside it is Zdinth Hall (now Norkoten Hall), scene of the **Rhenium Moment**.

Structurally, Skyyon is unique in that it has two discs on its stem. The lower disc has a diameter of about four miles; the upper, two miles. Altitude of the lower disc: a quarter of a mile. Altitude of the upper disc: three quarters of a mile. The tip of the Zairm reaches 1.6 miles above the plain.

Together with Ao and Vyanth, Skyyon forms the **Great Triangle**.

smollk the pumicelike ore of Ammye, related to, but distinct from, the foamed **gralm** which has played a huge part in the central dividing event of history. Smollk, unlike gralm, contains metal. The **Zairm** is constructed of smollk.

Solor also dubbed the Numinous Land. To some extent, the Uranian equivalent of Eden. Long assumed to be in Fyaym (if its existence was suspected at all), it was discovered to lie in Syoom after all, but it was hard to find, due to its space-stretching and psychic defences. The quest for Solor was mainly a preoccupation of the Gold Era. When at last its defences were breached (by an expedition secretly planned by the cyborgs), Solor seemed to disappear; later it was found still to exist occasionally, but with a new defence more powerful than before, a capacity to induce disbelief in its existence in the mind of any searcher who came too close. Solor finally, though gradually, faded from history during the Thallium Era.

Soolm an ancient city of Oirr, 981 miles from Vus. Other distances: **Ao**, 5697 miles; Arn, 1238 miles; **Contahl**, 2329 miles; **Jaax**, 5324 miles; **Skyyon**, 9038 miles; **Vyanth**, 4525 miles.

Spe Dalalt the officer who played the key part in the counter-deception which foiled the **Ghepion** plot to infiltrate the Sunnoad's Navy in the Platinum Era. Turning their own methods against them, he impersonated one of the Ghepions and discovered their headquarters. In so doing he also also discovered the reality behind the myth of **Solor**.

sponnd the personal weapon most commonly carried by Uranians. It is basically a laser, usable either in blade-mode or bolt-mode. It is often referred to with great respect, with the honorific initials of its owner.

sponndar in all three languages of the Nenns this word means, literally, "a person armed", or "warrior", and more loosely is used as a vague title of respect like our "Sir" or "Madam". It can also correspond to our use of the word "gentleman", mostly in its modern, imprecise sense, but also, at times during the Vanadium Era, in its old sense of a man who does not have to live by manual work or trade.

Sun-Egg an approximately globular **mascon** composed of semi-kolv or **gvo** , which surfaced due to crustal convection; its discovery marked the end of the Hydrogen Era and a quantum leap in the energy resources of Uranian mankind. At the time of its discovery the Sun-Egg was an ovoid mountain; by the Nitrogen Era it had all but disappeared; during the Sodium Era its last fragments were used up.

Sunnoad the Noad of Noads; holder of the highest and most revered office in Syoom. A Sunnoad is the only person entitled to wear the golden cloak of Skyyon, and to have a number after nen's name - the number denoting nen's place in the list of sunnoads. Nen's duties vary according to the period of history concerned. At the very least a Sunnoad has enormous prestige and advisory influence; usually nen has the customary right to command the military forces of Syoom in an international emergency; sometimes nen's powers are greater and more continuous, above all in the notorious case of **Tu Rim 78860**. However, it appears that a Sunnoad, unlike a Noad, is not a Head of State. Rather, nen is something less and more, for which no equivalent has ever existed on Earth.

sunnoadex the office of Sunnoad

Syoom literally the term applies to any area of the world in which a lone wayfarer has a more than 50% probability of surviving a thousand-mile journey. More loosely, and emotively, "Syoom" means "the area of civilization", "the civilized world". It is contrasted with **Fyaym**.

Taldis Norkoten 64702 the 64,702nd Sunnoad. Perhaps history's most popular hero, renowned as a secret agent before he acquired the golden cloak. He lived during the Osmium Era spy-craze, but as Sunnoad he tried to institute a permanent Syoomean Navy to calm international tensions. His efforts unravelled at his death, but were taken up much later: the Navy ideal triumphed in the Iridium Era. Zdinth Hall, Skyyon, scene of the Rhenium Moment, was renamed Norkoten Hall in his honour – an extremely rare instance of Uranian re-naming. Norkoten's second incarnation occurred at the end of the Radium Era, when he became the nemesis of **Tu Rim**.

Teleological Guilds, the organizations whose origins lie back in the Cobalt Era but which flourished only during the Zirconium and Niobium Eras. Their original purpose was to make discoveries about human destiny on Ooranye. By studying the racial and planetary consciousness, they hoped to uncover the broad outline of fate. This activity, on the borderline between science and superstition, never yielded much in the way of definite results. By the end of era 41 the Guilds were mere sociopolitical societies, promoting various mundane aims.

tetrak vehicle invented and used during the Bismuth Era. It was able to phase into vibrational modes which allowed it to slide through solid matter. It was used to explore the interior of Ooranye and visit the **mascon** worlds.

Thorium Whisper, the a hint received by the minds of Syoom, on the day of the departure of the Second Great Fleet for Arclour. Sunnoad **Iyen Noom 80525** has since admitted that the Whisper may have been triggered by his historic decision to risk the use of the **tetrak**'s method of transport for his ships. This bold move led to the success of the enterprise which the Fleet had undertaken, and led also, we believe, to a sharp separation between two alternate probability universes, the one in which he decided thus, and the one in which he did not. The latter continued with the Thorium Era; the former - ours - went straight on to the eight-day Protactinium Era, the triumph of the Fleet, the meeting of worlds, and the **Fostering of Ooranye**.

throom the aerial micro-organisms which by their 30-hour glow-cycle bring day and night to Ooranye. Primitive man believed the **throom** caused the brightness of day and the **bneen** caused the darkness of night; it is now known that one organism causes both effects, so the term **bneen** is redundant, except in folkloric phrases and proverbs

thuzolyr 'elective mirror': a thought-reading, personnel-selection device dating from the Phosphorus Era, sometimes used in elections to the sunnoadex, or to identify possible future Sunnoads. The thuzolyrs have been known to be self-directing. On such occasions they will switch themselves on and, in various modes, flash signs. This happened (in confidential mode) in the selection of Miokk Monray as successor to Zednas Tremol (see "Greenery"). On other occasions, such as the election of Unnd Dunaiv, the thuzolyrs were organized into a competition. The machines exist in their thousands, in communication with one another and, in a sense, all one.

Tisswa Ardea the human discoverer of the Sun-Egg (she may have had help from one of the Liquid Men)

Toolv a disc-on-stem city of Syoom. It has a Noad, as is normal, but otherwise its constitution is unique: there is no counterpart to the Four Hundred Lords anywhere else on Ooranye.

Tu Rim 78860 the 78,860th Sunnoad. Reigned at the end of the Radium Era (era 88). For most of the era, much of Syoom had been subjugated long-term by non-human races (the only era of history in which this was the case); Tu Rim was part of the movement to recover human control, but the methods he used - trying to convert the sunnoadex into an authoritarian empire - brought upheaval and chaos to Syoom. Tu Rim was overthrown by a movement headed by the second incarnation of **Taldis Norkoten**. As soon as he was victorious Taldis convened a conference to decide how a repetition of these events could be avoided for all time. The outcome was that the Sunnoads after Tu Rim were never allowed, or never allowed themselves, to dwell in Skyyon. Henceforth they always held it a point of honour to have their official dwelling in a "hut" in Melikon, a mere village outside Skyyon.

Tyoar Ixx tyrant-Noad of Narar twice: in his first life in the late Vanadium Era, and in his second in the Actinium. The second reign was considerably worse than the first.

umbna-jorraynt creature consisting of a plant part and an animal part joined by an organic cable. Energy can flow along this cable in either direction, depending on which end is contributing the most - the root system of the jorraynt, or the umbna's devouring of prey. The jorraynt maintains the function of both ends during ages of stasis; the umbna repays the favour during brief orgies of meat-eating. But the umbna may eventually snap the cable and live thereafter as an independent creature.

Unnd Dunaiv 80522 the $80,522^{nd}$ Sunnoad and the youngest person ever to hold the office. Unnd Dunaiv owed his elevation to his inborn strategic sense which may have been some sort of psi faculty. He mitigated the defeat at **Ierax** and led Syoom to subsequent victory against the Nemyurans, partly due to the exploits of his half-brother the wayfarer **Vyam Alorn**.

Uranus old Terran name for the seventh planet from the Sun, discovered by Terrans in A.D.1781, and known to its own people as **Ooranye**. Terrans now also call it Ooranye, but the former name survives in the adjective, "Uranian".

Valim Poand Noad of Vyanth at the end of the Vanadium Era who ended that era by freeing his city's slaves. This led to the upheaval of the pan-Syoomean slave revolt and the subsequent revolutions (eras 24-26).

velng (singular, **vellg**) ant-like race which builds artificial mountains on the plains, and which has been known, especially in the Vanadium Era, to hold humans captive

vheic a variety of glowing plant cultivated around the cities of Syoom. Its 'ell-light' in compressed phial-form provides fuel for vehicles and machinery, and backs the Syoomean currency. Before Era 7, vheic could only be used in its uncompressed form, as a relatively inefficient fuel, or for lighting.

Successful experiments in the use of compressed ell-light for power were first carried out in Era 7, the Nitrogen Era. The phials - a kind of standard fuel-cell - came into widespread use in Era 10, the Neon Era.

Vlamanor a disc-on-stem city of Syoom. Famous sights include: the Ezem, a perpetually circling avenue mid-way between city-circumference and hub; the Embers, a hotel and restaurant with a glowing centrepiece-fire of real coal, which tourists will come thousands of miles to see.

vlep monorail car

vrayk distant relatives of the Quonians, but far stupider than they, and used by them as 'cannon-fodder' during the invasion of era 37

vrayn the vegetable stage of the **mawo** life-cycle

Vus an ancient city of Oirr; 799 miles from Arn, 2208 miles from **Contahl**, 981 miles from **Soolm** and 9338 miles from **Skyyon**.

Vyam Alorn half-brother of **Unnd Dunaiv 80522**, Vyam Alorn was a great wayfarer of the later Actinium Era. He is reputed to have travelled off-world using the Nemyuran Portal.

Vyanth the largest of the disc-on-stem cities of Syoom, and the only one that has never once been conquered during all the eras since its construction. Diameter of disc: 5 miles. Height of disc above surrounding plain: 200 yards. Population of disc (in Actinium Era): 3 million. Its sights include: the Palace of Justice, Kioll Octagon and the Clears (see "The Shears of Night"), and the pedestalled globe which was the home of the great **Taldis Norkoten** (see "The Forgetters").

wayfarer member of the profession of voyagers who undertake to provide statistics for the safety-contours on Uranian maps. They provide these data by the mere fact of surviving or not surviving their journeys. Any additional information or understanding they achieve is pure bonus, beyond the call of duty.

White Sun the gleaming sphere which rose through the **gralm** during the reign of Sunnoad **Nalre Zitpoidl 4854**, and is believed to have caused the feeling of unfamiliarity with everyday objects which then began to plague Syoom

wonarr species of laser-tipped weed (ancestor of the **narp**) whose war with the **Revestru** made the environment dangerous to man during the early Hydrogen Era

world-spirit, the Ooranye's planetary id, and (later) planetary consciousness. The idea that the world is in some sense alive, or harbours a tutelary spirit or immanent Intelligence, has always been a part of popular Uranian folklore and the central tenet of what passes for Uranian religion. The existence of a planetary *unconscious* was first scientifically accepted during the Tin Era, during the war with **Ghepion**-controlled Oso. The *conscious* aspect of the world spirit spoke to humanity for the first time during the **Rhenium Moment**. Its existence was then understood as an emergent phenomenon, arising from the planet's variety and complexity. On one other famous occasion since then, during the Thallium Era, the world spirit was successfully consulted by the psi-sensitive **Capfaym Duuv**. It also seems that on several less-publicised occasions, individuals have at rare moments communed with the planetary mind, sometimes to their advantage, sometimes to their detriment.

Xaddanthye   Oorany's largest moon; it used to be named Titania by Terran astronomers

Xydur disc-on-stem city of Syoom, only 753 miles from **Vyanth**; 5724 miles from **Skyyon**.

Yalar a city and empire of the "**Other Syoom**". The city is 765 miles from the eponymous capital of its fellow-empire **Nii**. Other distances: **Deev**, 26,555 miles; **Yoon**, 18,236 miles.

Yaz the so-called "jokers' city". A disc-on-stem city of Syoom; a mere 375 miles from **Ierax**, it nevertheless escaped capture by the Nemyurans after the Battle of Ierax. Other distances: **Lysyon**, 937 miles; **Skyyon**, 8652 miles; **Karth**, 18,888 miles.

Yoad a disc-on-stem city of Syoom. A mere 413 miles from **Nuvium**. 2130 miles from **Pjourth**. 10,050 miles from **Skyyon**.

Yoon a disc-on-stem city of Syoom. Yoon lies in the region of Jersh, a land characterised by so-called "cold volcanoes". It is also one end of the famous Vlamanor-Yoon monorail.

Yr the 'City of Mists': a mobile, floating city launched during the Zirconium Era. It seems to have found some way of making itself invisible. Reports of its destruction are suspect; the consensus of opinion is that it still exists.

yyne the five hours around mindnight (two and a half hours the end of one day, two and a half hours the beginning of the next)

Zairm, the the flame-shaped Palace at Skyyon. Scene of the **Rhenium Moment**.

zamur officer with eleven men under his command

Zednas Tremol 80520 the 80,520[th] Sunnoad (see "Greenery")

zemmg an exalted war effort, analogous to a crusade (see "The Worm of Poleva")

zicena (singular, **zice**) Ooranye's lowest and hardest clouds, accreting crystals from the winds they summon. Zicena float at great speed exactly five yards above the ground, and pose a danger to transport on the plains.

zyr officer with 132 men under his command

Time Chart

Millions
of days

0

10   Hydrogen

———————————— *Syoom* and *Fyaym*

20   Lithium   Contahl

——————— Nitrogen Era; Neon Era – first Sunnoad and first Corrector

                  Great Patrols   Sunnoadex occasional

30   Phosphorus

                             Syoom's greatest extent and power

          Bank of Light   City hive minds - mostly innocent

40 ——————— Loss of Great Fleet

               Lone wayfarers   Sunnoadex continuous

                           Deev and Karth

     Argon

50

——————— Titanium Era "winter"; storms

     Vanadium

60   arelk

                          The hiveless era

70

Time Chart (cont.)

Millions
of days

70

80   **Vanadium**

                                            Gedars

90

                         slavery

100

————————— Iron Era. Revolution. Truth virus.

110   **Cobalt**   first teleologic investigations
                                      Quonians appear

120

                Construction
                         The   teleology
                of the
                         conscious   "on hold"
                monorail
130   **Zinc**   wait
                network

140

Time Chart (cont.)

Millions
of days

Millions of days		
140	Zinc	

150	Rubidium	Subtler teleologic missions
		Guild-style mysteries origin of Yr
	Zirconium	

160	Niobium	calmer culture
	Silver	spurt in machine evolution; Ghepions
		modus vivendi

| 170 | Cadmium | |
| | Xenon, Lanthanum ⟵ The Foam | |

| 180 | | orange glow; decreased wealth   The spotlit and the backgrounders |
| | Praesodymium | |

| 190 | | |

200		Prospectors
		Wealth recovers to pre-Foam levels
	Thulium	

| 210 | | |

Time Chart (cont.)

Millions
of days

210 _____ Black Smoke.   'dassan

Age of the Wise. Simulations.

220   Hafnium

230

Living on moral capital.

240   Tantalum

Easy age.   The Great Detective

250 _____

Fissiparous trends; evolutionary scatterings;
Fyayman colonies

260   Tungsten

270 ——————————Rhenium. Managed Transition

Varieties of species bring excitement and danger

Osmium   kalyars   vrars

280   The Great Triangle   Alliances, allegiances, loyalties.

Time Chart (cont.)

Millions
of days

280

Osmium

Quonians' Southern Empire.   Proof of the 92 eras.

290

————Iridium————————The Sunnoad's Navy   Platinum Era deception

Gold   Quest for Solor.   Philosophical Age

300

————————————mercury era: man-Ghepion hybrids rule briefly

310   Psi   Ruthless moves against Ghepions

Thallium

320

————————————————

Expeditions to mascon worlds in mantle

Bismuth

330

————————————polonium era: Sunnoad-impersonator   francium era lawmen

Radium   subjugation of most of Syoom

340   Tu Rim

Freeing of Syoom

Actinium

First Contact with Terrans

350   ————————————

Uranium   Beginning of the Final Era

Systems of Historical Dating in use upon Ooranye

The most commonly used of the three systems is the **era-day count**. To see how this works, let us take a famous date in Uranian history, the day of First Contact with Terrestrials, which on our calendar took place on 10th July, 3564 A.D. On Ooranye this was the 11,002,739th day of the Actinium Era and so is referred to simply as 11,002,739 Ac. [Needless to say, when translating into English we use our own English chemical symbol for the element for which the era is named; however, the Uranians' own abbreviations are similar in style to ours.]

The Uranians seem not to feel inconvenienced by the need to use and remember seven- or eight- or even nine-digit numbers. They don't mind long numbers any more than Germans mind long words. This is just as well since their basic unit is the day, and there are a lot of days in the major eras! As for why they use the day only and not the year: Ooranye's orbit round the sun takes 84 Earth years, roughly a lifetime, and so is far too long a period for most purposes of accurate dating.

However, the Uranian year does have a place in their culture - an astonishing place, to our way of thinking. The **U-year countdown** is a phenomenon which many Earth minds have found impossible to accept. It seems as ridiculous as a claim by an archaeologist to have found a Greek vase inscribed "500 B.C.". Yet the evidence is incontrovertible: from the very beginning, until the present era, Uranians had been counting the long years backwards!

During 91 eras they thus experienced a countdown towards the Last Era. The numbers in this system are prefaced in English translation with the letters UTU [Until the Ultimate or U-years Till the Ultimate]. Thus, for example, the event mentioned in the previous paragraph as occurring on day 11,002,739 of era 89 occurred also in UTU-8. A U-year later (remember, their years are 84 of ours) they were living in UTU-7. So - to emphasize the point once more - the fact is that right from the start of their history, way back in UTU-14,286 (1.2 million Earth years ago), their psychic inner clocks were telling them how many U-years lay ahead of them before the Last Era. Imagine a shadowy dial moving slowly towards the climax of a world's destiny; a remote but ever-present weight upon any reflective mind.

Lastly we must mention the most rarely used, and the simplest, Uranian dating system - the **absolute day count**. This is simply a count of the days from the very beginning, taking no notice of the division into eras. First Contact with Terrestrials according to this count took place 350,470,238 days after the first Uranian human being emerged from the pre-biotic *sivvan* at Dmara. The absolute count is relatively unimportant but it does have its uses. It can be convenient to refer to it when calculating time spans which straddle several eras.

Lightning Source UK Ltd.
Milton Keynes UK
UKOW02f0937210815

257310UK00002B/53/P